Please save
for Shen Nauima

On the Stroll

On the Stroll

ALIX
KATES
SHULMAN

Cassandra
Editions

Published in 1987 by

Academy Chicago Publishers
425 North Michigan Avenue
Chicago, Illinois 60611

Copyright © 1981 by Alix Kates Shulman

Printed and bound in the USA

Library of Congress Cataloging-in-Publication Data

Shulman, Alix Kates.
    On the stroll.
    Originally published: New York: Knopf, 1981.
    I. Title.
[PS3569.H7705 1987] 813'.54 86-32228
ISBN 0-89733-243-1 (pbk.)

For my children, Polly and Teddy, with love

Birds of a feather flock together,
And so will pigs and swine;
Rats and mice will have their choice,
And so will I have mine.

—OLD MOTHER GOOSE

One

The small circle of Midtown New York surrounding the Port Authority Bus Terminal for a radius of half a dozen blocks goes by many names. Tour guides call it the Crossroads of the World. The hookers who work it know it as the stroll. Pimps call it the fast track. Three-card monte players speak of Forty-Deuce. Maps show the neighborhood as Clinton. But to the stagestruck and starstruck it is still Broadway, to tourists it is Times Square, to the old people and derelicts who live off discards from the teeming Ninth Avenue food stalls of Paddy's Market it is more aptly Hell's Kitchen, and to the New York City Police, Vice Squad, and Mayor's Special Task Force on Crime it is simply the Midtown Enforcement Area.

What you see of this amazing neighborhood depends on the season, the hour, and your game. Are you a tourist after entertainment? A thrill-seeker? Are you an adolescent hunting freedom, a healer searching out the damned, an aged survivor seeking shelter and food for one more day? Whoever you are, you will probably see what interests you and turn away from the rest.

Here, for instance, on a weekend night, scores of theatergoers tip their waiters at ten to eight, tuck their credit cards into their wallets, and rush unseeing past the whores and hustlers lounging in the doorways of the stroll. By nine, as these innocents are applauding first-act chorus lines, second-shift diners are sipping espresso in the darkened interiors of Restaurant Row, preparing for the embarrassment of checking anonymously into a midtown hotel for half a night of illicit love with someone else's spouse. Though tied to the neighborhood by passion, these desperate adulterers conduct their affairs foolishly unaware that just down the street the Live Sex Acts are pulling in the marks, the dirty book parlors of 42d Street are doing a brisk business, and one block over behind the bus station the elderly homeless and alley cats slowly circle the vegetable stalls for handouts from grocers' assistants at closing time. Taxi drivers pull up before the emptying theaters and lock their doors until they find their fares, then speed quickly away. Their passengers dissect the show, oblivious of the gang of hoodlums across the street and of the men on the corner passing around a bottle of Midnight Special in a brown paper bag. For one moment, a speeding police car racing the wrong way up a one-way street, siren screaming, may startle pedestrians, cabbies, and passengers alike into wondering what terrible act they may be forced to witness. But soon the sound disappears and they resume their talk, unaware of the shopping-bag ladies and men who, expecting rain, either make their way to St. Agatha's to jockey for a bench on which to sleep or cautiously take a seat in the inadequate waiting room of the Port Authority Bus Terminal.

It was here in the bus station on a Friday night that the shopping-bag lady known to locals as Owl (and to the rookie cop patrolling the station as, simply, "one of your cleaner types") had her second mystical vision in twenty years. The first had come to her at the gate fifteen minutes before takeoff in Chicago's O'Hare Airport. The vision, she always believed, had been set in motion by a radio playing a Spanish-from-Spain version of "Siboney." She never discovered the source of the music (there were no radios at the gate, no airport Muzak in those days, and they were ready to board); yet the gypsy falsetto of that slightly Oriental song had brought into perfect harmony all the inhabitants of that exotic land: the mystic saints, the imperial guards, Ferdinand and Isabella, the Moors, the beautiful black-haired Iberian peasant women washing clothes on the riverbanks, the silent young men in the bars of Madrid, flamenco dancers, and, having herself once spent several months in Spain with an international refugee unit after the war, her own humble self, together with everyone she had ever known. Like mystics down through the ages, she had seen then in a flash the perfect unity of life. She would have traded her own to have the vision continue, but once it had ended, she was both sorry and glad: she had a plane to catch and a daughter to meet.

This time, however, she was only sorry. She had nowhere to go and no daughter. This second vision, coming some twenty years later, was far more timely, for her luck had long since run out. When during her worst times she'd touched bottom, her vision had drawn her back up. Maybe now that she was sinking again she was getting another lift from Beyond.

Here is what Owl saw that early evening as she sat among her shopping bags, resting her legs, in the main waiting room of the bus station.

Around her in the circle of molded plastic seats carefully designed to preclude a snooze sat the usual array of weary travelers, hustlers, and unknowns. In the center of the circle was a row of four pay-TV sets, their swivel bases bolted to chairs. In the tan plastic chairs facing the screens, eyes glazed, mouths slightly open, sat several large, unmoving teenaged males. Occupying the surrounding seats were families with crying babies, weary commuters, madmen, and innocents. Some of these no doubt waited for buses; others, like Owl herself, simply passed the time. All were shielded from too deep a scrutiny of each other (and themselves) by a thin curtain of complacency that concealed reality.

Now suddenly, without warning, Owl saw the curtain part. For perhaps ten seconds truth was revealed to her. She saw that all the people in the waiting room, together with everyone else alive in the universe at that particular instant, were in unique possession of a rare, infinitely precious and mysterious gift casually (so casually!) called life.

The light of this knowledge filled Owl with wonder and love. Before her enchanted eyes the ordinary differences among the living she had learned to recognize over more than half a century—differences in station and temperament, in awareness and privilege, in age, health, achievement, sorrow, fate—all disappeared and became as nothing beside that one miraculous singularity they shared. They had lived! They lived! Her feet hurt her, her welfare check was late, she had no one and no place, but she was infinitely blessed. If she had believed in God she might have called her vision religious, but she had always stood firmly with the atheists in matters of theology. Sister Theresa of the Shelter and Father Glendon who fought the pimps were the best citizens of the neighborhood, and the Church that backed them up was one of the few remaining places that embraced the homeless; but nothing they did could establish the truth of their beliefs. Truth was established otherwise. Truth was . . . not what you believed, not what you proclaimed, but what you saw.

And what Owl saw as she rested in the waiting room at seven o'clock on that otherwise uneventful Friday evening was that out of the infinity of inert souls past or possible, these and no others had been chosen to live, to partake of blessed life, and among them was herself. She peered hard at reality, searching for someone she knew. Her mother? Her lost boy? But like the cats and birds Owl fed each day, all absolutely equal in her eyes, everyone there in the room, bathed in life, looked equally precious. In that clear, vivid light, cats, birds, humans were all connected. One with her. Any waif she made a home for was her child. She saw that life was a gift, a precious gift, and she swelled with happiness.

Then, as suddenly as it had parted, the curtain closed, the veil descended, and she was once again seated among her shopping bags in the uncomfortable waiting room of the bus station, alone, disconnected, without hope, awaiting the inevitable tap on the shoulder from the man in blue.

Prince sipped at his coffee and looked nervously at his watch. Time to go; the bus from Boston was due in any minute. He knew he shouldn't be drinking coffee at all, but he hated this bus station crawling with cops, it made him nervous, and he had to do something for his nerves.

That wasn't all. The place was full of scum, smelly old hags, detectives, he-shes, perverts. . . . It was as bad as the sin hole of Hong Kong where he'd once spent three days' shore leave. But this was the best place to cop a girl. He'd heard there were lots of them coming through lately from Boston, and though waiting for a bus was a longshot, he had to get himself a girl, at least check it out.

Even when he spotted a likely prospect climbing off a bus and looking around, it was tricky to catch her. She might know someone already, she might be meeting her mother, she might slip away before he had a go at her, or run for a cop. Still, he had to take his chances. He was getting desperate. Today he had a pocketful of bills from last week's three-card monte game: enough to catch a bitch if his luck held out. Wasn't every chick a potential ho? And wasn't he a good-looking dude who could sweet-talk his way like the best of them? He knew how to be gentle, modest, loving; he could also be forceful, fierce, intense. He understood what women needed and what he needed. He money, they love: that winning combination.

Another time he might have blown his bucks in a day, as he and his buddies had done in each new port. He liked good clothes and good times. But in the navy with that paycheck growing all the time and nothing to spend it on at sea, life had been different. Now years had passed since he'd seen a paycheck.

He was overdue on his hotel bill, his wheels were in the shop, for a long time he'd sent nothing to his mother. Since Sissy had blown he needed money fast. So instead of partying, he'd got his copping clothes cleaned and pressed, had a manicure, a shave, and a shine, and prepared the rest for flashing. A fat roll of singles topped by three twenties in a gold money clip and a handful of silver dollars to give weight even to loose change were the oil that made his charm hum. Now all he needed was the chick to go for it. And soon. His stomach, which had kept him from signing up for another hitch at sea, was acting up all the time now. He used to be able to ignore it, but it seemed to be getting worse. Since he'd been alone it seemed to him he was always thinking about it—his stomach or his bad tooth or the way his hair had started coming out in his comb. Like his mother, he had fine, black, silky Filipino hair; but his fair-haired father, he'd been told, had been half bald at thirty. His luck, he'd probably gotten all his father's bad traits. Or else he was just getting old.

Old? He never thought he'd get old, not the Prince. But he had to do his pushups every morning now, he had to watch what he ate or his nerves would give out. If he'd jumped ship in Tahiti he might never have aged. It was the street that turned you old, keeping you hustling morning to night. In Tahiti, the women were for you, not against you. When you were hungry you picked a breadfruit off a tree or caught yourself a fish. But here, he felt thirty-five, not twenty-five. Who starts losing his hair at twenty-five? The place was turning into a sewer. The fags were everywhere and spreading. Crackos pulled knives in the street, winos sprawled in the gutters and pissed on the pavement as if they owned the place, perverts came right up to you, bag ladies, panhandlers, freaks roamed the streets like they were home. Even the cops had started dressing up like old women. They all belonged in Bellevue, but no one cared. If he hadn't wrecked his wheels he would have gone to Florida long ago, found out where Sissy was, and. . . .

But now, unless he pawned his ring, he couldn't spare the cash for bus fare. And who could he trust? No one.

For a brief moment he imagined the future in the sparkle of the diamond in his ring. A lady with that sparkle in her eyes and brains enough to understand his needs. But he was a practical man and knew how far he could get on dreams. For now, it was enough to hope the girl wasn't so dumb that she'd let herself get picked up by the Runaway Squad. He'd try to warn her. Some of the young ones from out of state were so dumb they wound up costing you more than they gave you, even if they had no mileage on them at all. Or so scared that they got themselves addicted. And some were so smart you couldn't hold on to them long enough to make them pay off. Better, then, to cop and blow—take what you could get and cut her loose. On the other hand, if he caught one with a little money it might be better to try to disappear until she spent it, and then move on in. He'd have to figure it out carefully and play it close. It wasn't an easy game. He bent down to the shiny reflecting surface of the cigarette machine to comb his hair. Not bad, he thought. He smoothed down his mustache and flashed a smile. Handsome son-of-a-bitch. Then, bouncing on the balls of his feet like his running partner, Sweet Rudy, he sauntered down to the gate to meet the Boston bus.

Robin Ward looked out over the steamy streets of Hell's Kitchen from the Greyhound window and wondered how she'd ever find Boots. The city was so vast. Buildings, stretching as far as she could see in all directions, pressed down on her like waves on the sea; as soon as you rolled past one block of them another was upon you and another after that. Where was the shore? She felt a momentary panic, the first since she'd boarded the bus in Maine eight hours before. She'd left home so abruptly she hadn't had time to be afraid. As soon as Billy had told her that their father was sitting in the principal's office with a cop and two men, she'd run home for her backpack and money and got ready to split. On the ferry from the island she'd been terrified her father would stop her; but once the bus had taken her out of the Portland station without him on board, every turn of the wheels had brought relief, and on the highway she'd been actually happy.

"But how do you know they called him in about you?" Billy had asked her, for Luke Ward had three kids in the school to answer for. She didn't know, but she had a good idea. She had watched Boots turn on her smile and relieve two men of several hundred dollars, then disappear. Besides, even if her father had been called in about one of the boys, chances were she'd still wind up getting the blame. With her father on the warpath, why wait and see? She was sorry to have put in most of the semester and not get credit, but if those two men were who she thought they were, running was safer than sticking around to see what developed. From the day she first ran away at eight to look for her mom to the time she'd been picked up with Boots on the highway for hitchhiking, running had always been easier. The only difference was this: the other times she'd run because she wanted to; this time she ran because she had to. This time she couldn't go back. Her past was finished, like sand pictures erased by the tide.

She pressed her nose against the window as if to squash the past. She needed a new name. She had pale skin that pinked in the sun and peeled, never tanning even in summer. Too delicate a skin for the Maine coast, said her mother. And indeed, she had a fragile look that kept her apart and made even the bullies ashamed when they teased her more than they teased others. She had a bump in her nose she hated, but otherwise she looked like an old poster for spring, with a small, delicate child's mouth that seemed smaller still when she was ready to cry and that opened into a bright disarming smile in those rare moments when she felt delight. Though her smile would now never grace the pages of any yearbook, it would carry her far, she hoped—farther than the school she had left abruptly in the middle of eleventh grade. With her mouth, her guileless hazel eyes, pale lashes, and the sweet voice that ranged from childlike innocence to haughty disdain, she hoped to pull off masterpieces of deceit. Already she had perfected a wide range of poses in her brief life and she considered herself an actress of no little talent. In a mere sixteen years she had accomplished painful and difficult deceptions. And still her full range had not begun to be tested and she had a whole life ahead of her. Once she got it together to have a portfolio made hinting at the variety of moods and ages she could do (for she could still pass for thirteen if she tried and with difficulty do twenty) she'd be on her way. Peter had suggested that New York was a little premature, that she ought to try herself out in Portland or Boston first, but she disagreed. The fare to New York was not all that much more than to Boston, and Boots, who had sent her a postcard with a New York number, had gone directly there and made it.

One thing was clear: she was not going back. In her yellow T-shirt that told the world she was "Born to Dance" (and incidentally that this kid would not be hampered by any bra!), carrying all she needed in her backpack, ready to move with benefit of smile, palm, and thumb for traveling, her terrible past was over. Now they would never find her, and she would never go back. Never.

The finality of that never was so fierce that it brought tears to her eyes, mourning tears. It was a never of dead gulls dashed on the rocks.

The driver pulled to a stop inside a tunnel and announced: "Port Authority."

Though the phrase was a mystery to Robin, she knew enough to heed it. You didn't argue with authority. She slung her pack onto her shoulder, hooked the tie of her bedroll over her wrist, and lined up in the aisle behind the other passengers.

2

As she entered the waiting area from Platform 83, someone handed Robin a leaflet. *Repent now. It's later than you think.*

Repent? That message carried everywhere by dedicated prophets of doom was lost on Robin. Repentance was a backward glance, and she looked only ahead; *later than you think*—what could that mean to her? With the century almost gone, it was late for everyone. The prophet of doom who alerted every new arrival had already begun the countdown, warning the world that there were fewer than seven hundred days left till Judgment Day. To Robin, seven hundred days was forever. If she could find Boots, she would call today not Number Seven Hundred counting down but Number One counting up.

Clutching the leaflet, she shifted the weight of her pack on her shoulder and moved onto the concourse. People glided along to a strange new rhythm. As she fell in step an old tune of fear began to play in her mind. A warning? It had the same wailing notes she'd heard the time her father got everyone but her into the boat and left her alone on the island. When she found they had all gone away, the music started pounding in her ears like surf. Was she six? Seven? Later her mother told her he'd planned all along to come back for her, he was only pretending to leave her there to scare her, to teach her a lesson. But for her, finding herself suddenly abandoned on an island with the tide coming in was a sentence of death. The sea was rising, she thought it would cover the entire nubble. She climbed to the highest rock and facing the sea she called and called. But the only answer that came back was the awesome music in her head.

This time it was she who had left them, putting a whole ocean between her and her father when she left the island. Yet the music was beating in her head, as if he might be waiting to catch her eye as she reached the end of the passage and close his hand around her elbow.

She deposited the leaflet in a back pocket of her jeans and stepped onto an escalator, hoping to leave the music behind. She could neither repent the past nor fear the future; her focus at that moment was narrow and sharp: how would she eat today and where would she sleep tonight? She was pretty sure she would manage. Boots had told her a hundred times, a girl could always find a man to buy her a meal and a bench to sleep on. She had brought her sleeping bag and thirty dollars for emergencies. If she couldn't get a job and worse came to worst, she could sell herself; and if that didn't work she could kill herself. But never never never would she go back.

Still, as the escalator rose to deposit her among the mob, it occurred to her for the first time that unless Boots answered the phone, she had no idea where she would go or what she would do.

Was that Milly Owl saw where the buses came in? Little yellow-haired, blue-eyed Milly? Should she trust her eyes?

No, no, it was a trick. This girl was a child and Milly would be grown by now. It was a dream. Visions could be true, but dreams deceived. Time often appeared to have stopped altogether, but it never did. Sometimes she could not believe that she had gotten old, that soldiers no longer loved her, that she'd been on welfare for years, that splendid new buildings had already been torn down, that Milly was grown and gone.

She shook her head to clear it of dreams. She had been abruptly wakened from a nap (for downstairs where the buses came in there were still a few long benches on which to sleep) by a prophet of doom. How many times had she heard before that the world would end, only to see it go reeling on without a glimmer of relief? (For this she woke from a dream of Milly!) These predictions were chronic, like the cough of the man in the room next to hers at the Hotel Venus. She had seen recessions and depressions, wars and revolutions, births, deaths, revivals, survivals, and yet it seemed to her that nothing much ever really changed. Men had gone to the moon and back, but what did it matter here? Her neighbor went on coughing. And if it were true that the world would end in a mere seven hundred days, if she could believe for a moment that the whole mess would soon disappear like whores from the street at election time, would she not shrivel with sadness for the loss? It was a terrible world, but there was no other.

Owl picked up her bags and snubbed the prophet as she moved toward the stairs. As for repentance, Owl could not repent. She had outlived regret. When Sister Theresa asked what prayers the women at the Shelter wanted said for them, Owl could think only of such vague requests as health, safety, and protection for all bag ladies—adding as an afterthought, freedom not to be moved to Long Island. (A dozen good families had responded to a TV appeal on behalf of homeless women by offering their extra rooms in the suburbs. Sooner would Owl repent than move to Long Island!)

She rode up the escalator and rested her bags on the stair. She would try her luck again in the waiting room.

She stood at the entrance for a moment and checked the clock before searching out the safest seat. The security shift was about to change; she hoped she would not be recognized.

Cautiously Owl lowered her weary bones into a molded chair near the clock side, placed her three bags on the floor beside her, sighed deeply, pulled her skirt demurely down over her knees, crossed her swollen ankles and closed her eyes. Today she had dressed carefully. Her skirt and sneakers were freshly laundered, her white hair was neatly bobbed, her sweater was dark enough to show no stains. She was certain she looked as respectable as most of the genuine travelers, and she caused half the nuisance. In they came with their retinue of satchels, crying kids, and radios, smelling of garlic, munching from bags full of food, scattering candy wrappers and potato chips in their wake. Yet just because they were transients with no intention of returning to this waiting room, just because they had money to purchase tickets and thought they had somewhere to go, their right to stay and mess the place was respected. The more baggage they carried the more respect they received. Whereas she, who never bothered anyone, who picked up after *them*, who had lived a decent life, buried her mother, defended her country, wept for soldiers, given plenty to the poor, and brought a beautiful daughter into this world—she, with her bad feet and her neat shopping bags, had at most twenty minutes to sit in peace before some heartless cop came along and made her leave. And to what purpose? She would be back again in half an hour or half a day; the cop knew it as well as she; she always came back.

Always, always. Where else could she go? Were they not all, every one of them, equally transients through this life? The difference between them and her was that some of them didn't know it yet, that was all. Well, they'd find out soon enough.

There was plenty of scum in this place for a cop to go after; why pick on her? She had only to open her eyes or step into the street to see the sick and spacey getting rolled, travelers being relieved of their wallets, pimps, hustlers, dope fiends, buyers and sellers of boys, women, "Live Sex". . . . Only an hour earlier, as she was passing through 43d Street on her way over, she saw one of the scum roll a crippled man—shoved him into a doorway with the victim's own crutch, reached into his pocket, and emptied it inside out. Brazenly the thief clutched the bills in his right hand while he stooped to collect the change he'd spilled on the ground with his left, as the victim stood cringing and helpless against the wall. Pray, where were the diligent officers then? Who were they off protecting then? Times had changed. She remembered receiving a summons for jaywalking and another for wearing shorts thirty years before; and now murderers got away. Instead of protecting the weak, the good police spent their tax-paid time collecting bribes or waking innocent citizens who were harming no one, who had perhaps even performed valuable services to society, who might be positive assets to the community!—while the muggers and thugs took over the streets.

Well, they wouldn't get her. With her bags surrounding her, they wouldn't dare come near. She knew how to be fierce. She took pleasure in the very thought that those treasures she carried with her everywhere were so feared and despised as to protect her from assault. There were items she carried of un- told value, including certain letters she would sell for a fortune when the time came, and checks she had not cashed. Together in their proper bags these treasures became amulets that pro- tected her from evil, thus greatly increasing their value. True, she carried a knife and a bit of food; but garbage? guns? vermin? disease? Let them go on thinking so! Let the scum despise her as a filthy bag lady—it would keep her safe. If she stank, she couldn't smell it. If she stank, they had themselves to thank. In the Hotel Venus, to which she turned over more than half her welfare money every month, she was afraid to use the shower room. It was a disgrace! Unclothed, alone, you were asking for it in the shower: there a woman had been murdered a month before. And if you left your bags and treasures in your room—you didn't want to get them wet— that was the time they robbed you. The fifty-cent showers in the bus terminal and the washrooms in the train stations had been closed down. The public baths that had once dotted the city, like ancient Rome, had disappeared. Now it was even forbidden to wash your hair in the ladies' room in the Port Authority.

Owl's legs were still okay. But for how long? The new molded chairs in this waiting room made it impossible to elevate your feet, much less stretch out. They wanted to make people lame! She, at least, had a bed to sleep in, so her legs were still okay, just a little swollen at the ankles. But she knew what happened to people who had to sleep sitting up and never had room to stretch out their legs. First the swelling, then the popped veins, then the ruptured skin and open sores and the pain. Once the veins went, that was it. Not even elastic bandages would help for long if you had to be on your feet. And if the cop made you move every time you took a little nap . . .

Owl's spine curled, her head slumped down on her breast, and she dreamed herself dancing at the GI club for enlisted men in Munich. She was holding a dimpled rookie against her breast, a mere boy! They rocked together under the blue lights. He was whispering something through her hair into her ear, something sad. . . . Goodbye? Was he leaving, then? To battle?

But the war was over! This was the Occupation. These were occupation forces. Where were they sending him?

Was it perhaps the Carnival? Or Oktoberfest? The music was getting faster, a German brass band, her head was reeling, she was confused.

Someone had given her absinthe. How kind. But . . . absinthe was forbidden; then this wasn't the GI club at all! This club was off limits! Dangerous. People sprawled over the tables in harlequin masks singing drinking songs and "O Tannenbaum." They were offering black market coffee, condoms, cigarettes, meat at staggering prices. Absinthe was said to make the heart go blind. Yes—if they played one more march she would scream! But how foolish to have come here. The place was well known to be off limits. Now she was in trouble. She could be court-martialed. And how would she ever get back to the base? Her long hair was curled and fluffed, she had little pads in the shoulders of her dark print dress, her stockings were real silk, she was young, beautiful. She was afraid for her stockings, they had cost her dear, she ought never to have gone dancing in them. She had to get them off! Before they played one more march!

Now it was the colonel she was dancing with. He looked shocked. "No," he said. "Don't take off those shoes."

"Why not?"

"Are you crazy? You know this club is off limits! You have to be ready to run. Do you want to lose your shoes? Besides, the smell of your feet will give you away. Who can bear the odor? Don't think that just because Munich is occupied, the war is over!"

"But it *is* over," she cried. "It *is* over!" And hearing the cop rapping his nightstick against the back of her chair, she jerked her head and forced herself awake.

3

Puzzled, Robin cocked her head at the phone as she lost her second dime. She had dialed Boots's number but there was no one there named Boots. Or so the man said. She had called twice to make sure; the second time the man cursed and hung up. There was nothing to do but get some food and try again later, disguising her voice.

Back in the busy station people moved like surf, sweeping her along; the shops along the sides of the concourse were like trees or cliffs, obscured by ceaseless flow; people appeared and disappeared lapped by the endless ebb and flow, like the creatures at water's edge when the tide was out. Robin thought of the broad rocks in the mud flats she liked to upend suddenly at low tide to expose the wriggling, swarming mass of life beneath. She would watch the surprised creatures from another world leap or plunge, then slither away—fat seaworms, clinging limpets, starfish changing shape in transit, scurrying crabs, tiny shrimp—until they had hidden themselves again in the ooze. And here, too—every sort of unimagined soul hurried away from her to some private, mysterious hiding place. More people moved through this terminal at this moment than she'd known in her entire life.

She spotted a familiar name, Walgreen's, and went in. She took a seat at the counter, placed her pack and roll behind her on the floor, and forgetting she was low on funds, ordered her heart's desire: club sandwich, french fries, and double shake. In summers, she and Boots had spare-changed tourists at the fancy beach towns for a lark; if she had to she'd do it again here.

She did not notice the man who sat down beside her until he brushed her straw to the floor and apologized. "I'm really sorry. Here, let me get you another one."

"That's okay. I don't need a straw."

"But I want you to have one," he said quickly, procuring two. Gallantly he tore the paper off one end of each and presented them to her with a little dip of his head, a flourish. "Straws for the lady."

"Thank you."

"Not at all, not at all." He smiled at her, a dazzling smile of white, even teeth beneath a neat black mustache. His voice was deep and low; his quick body was trim and muscular; his strange almond eyes sent charges of embarrassment through her when he looked at her.

"I hope you don't mind me sayin this," he said. "But I wouldn't leave my roll over there on the floor. It could go like that." He snapped his fingers with one hand and made a spoon disappear up his jacket sleeve with the other. She laughed. "This bus station is too fast a place for a trustin young lady like yourself." He moved her pack and roll between their feet. "This place is trouble for someone like you."

She knew she shouldn't take up with the first stranger to come along. But he was well dressed and polite; his shoes were polished, he spoke in respectful tones. First he had tried to amuse her, now he was looking out for her; ending the conversation abruptly might insult him, and for no reason. Worse, he would assume a reason, the wrong one, and she did not want to seem that kind of person. "What kind of trouble?" she asked.

"Someone young like you and all alone is practically askin to be picked up by the Runaway Squad. Ever hear of it?"

Robin shrugged. He wore an elaborate wristwatch with a gold face, no numbers, and baffling dials. And a large gold ring set with a small white stone. A diamond? His cuffs were clean, his nails manicured. The high cheekbones of his mysterious face made her think of the Penobscot Indians she'd once watched at a fair in Maine—beautiful and strange.

"They have plainclothes detectives cruisin this place just lookin to pick up anyone under eighteen. You don't have to be doin nothin. They've got to run in a certain number every day and they don't care who. Of course, it's none of my business, you might be here with your mother, you might be between buses and have a valid ticket to DC. You show that ticket, they'll let you go. Otherwise, like if you just came to have yourself a look around the town, if you're travelin on your own, they won't waste their time guessin. They'll call up your folks and send you home on the next bus out. Or else they'll throw you in Spofford. That's a fact. Ever hear of Spofford? What they call"—he bobbed his head, raised his eyebrows, closed his eyes, and smiled—"a secure facility."

Robin sipped her shake and said nothing. She and Boots had been picked up twice on the highway and sent home for doing nothing but being underage. The troopers were always stopping kids. She'd heard of the Runaway Squad.

"You mean they have detectives right here in the bus station? That's not fair."

"That's right. They move around in pairs, just like ordinary men and women, lookin for kids. They got a whole special office down there. Want me to show you?"

That was the last thing she wanted to see; she shook her head.

"Well, don't worry. As long as you appear to know your business you're okay. Anyone comes up and stops you, you just tell em you're with me."

There was an awkward silence. Then he said, "May I ask you your name? Mine's Prince—Prince among men."

"Robin Ward," she said, forgetting to change it.

"But the police, that's only one of your problems, Robin.

There's worse. Once you get outside into the street there's a whole lot of folks layin for you out there." He lowered his head earnestly and moved his face closer to hers. "They're just waitin for a pretty little lady like you to come along. Oh, they might treat you real nice at first, talk to you pretty, show you a good time, buy you pretty things, but before you know what's happenin they got you out on the bricks."

She was listening hard now, her eyes open wide.

"Just take a good hard look around," he said, moving his eyes even closer to hers. They were large, clear, almond-shaped eyes, beneath delicate, long-lashed lids. Their milk-blue whites and eggplant-colored irises bore deep into her. His olive skin stretched taut across handsome bones, and his velvet voice spun out dangers she could barely imagine. "They find young ladies like yourself from out of town—where'd you say you're from, Robin?"

"Portland."

"From Portland, say. They tell em what they want to hear, give em what they want to have, and then—*whammo!*" He leaned back and punched one hand with the other with a startling crack. "And then when they've got em, they put em to work. Unscrupulous."

Robin was staring now; her jaw had dropped, half in terror, half disbelief.

Prince smiled. "You don't believe me? Newcomers just don't believe what goes on here. The Apple is definitely not like Portland, Maine. This is the fast track. Do you have people here? A place to stay? Any definite plans while you're visiting the city?"

"No plans, really," she said. "I never make plans. I like to see what turns up. I have a friend here, but she's not home. Maybe I'll go to a hotel till I can reach her. Know any cheap hotels?"

"Sure. The Moon. It's not fancy but it's cheap, as cheap

as you can get, and they've got a ladies' floor, too. It could be all booked, but the desk clerk's a friend of mine. Want me to take you over there, see what he can do?"

"You wouldn't mind?"

"Mind?" He tossed his black hair out of his eyes and laughed. "Too bad I'm not gonna be in town, I'd try to help you find somethin a little nicer. But tomorrow night I got to go away for a few days about some business. Too bad," he repeated and slowly shook his head.

"Yes, it is too bad," said Robin. She could use a friend.

"Anyway," he said, patting her arm comfortingly, "that's not till late tomorrow. Now I'll take you over to the Moon, let you drop your stuff, then I'll show you around a bit. Would you like me to do that?"

She nodded. She liked the feel of his hand on her arm.

"Good. Then when I get back I'll see if we can't do better. I know a few folks. We'll go out and have some fun. I can see by your shirt that you like to dance. There are some fabulous places if you know where to go. Let me give you a phone number where you can reach me when I'm back in town." He took a silver pen from his pocket and wrote his number on the inside of a book of matches. "Call me when you want to." He handed her the matches.

She dropped them into her bag and started to take out some money.

"No," said Prince, putting his hand over hers, "this is on me." He took out a thick roll of bills, peeled off several singles, and left them on the counter. "Don't lose my number, now. And while I'm away be careful who you talk to. This is a fast place; don't trust anyone."

"You sound like my father," she said. "Don't worry. I'll manage. I always do." Ready to believe her own claims, she tossed her head. Without even trying, she'd already managed to get one free meal; if she couldn't find a job she had no doubt she could manage to get others. With summer coming she could live on the street. She'd be all right. But it pleased her anyway that he worried.

They stood up. Prince was tall, slim, muscular. As he leaned down for her pack, she saw the muscles of his back beneath his fitted green shirt as clearly as the gold chain and cross resting against his collarbone. He helped her on with her pack, and as he lifted her hair, his hand lingered a moment at her neck. A shiver ran through her, a moment's distrust, until she remembered that Prince was leaving town. She had his phone number in her bag to use whenever she wanted, but if she chose to disappear he'd never find her.

He picked up her bedroll. "Ready?" he said, taking her arm.

She noted the large hand, long fingers ringed and manicured, against her slender freckled arm, and thought, Oh, if Dad could see me now!

Owl proceeded from the waiting room by her regular route, circling slowly around the lockers, peeking into the coffee shop, and, on her way to Walgreen's, where she liked to check the trash, inspected the newsstand for headlines.

Not that anything that happened could surprise her. She'd seen too much. The most amazing events had long been forgotten. Still, she did like to know. Starting in her youth, she had saved the papers that carried the most sensational headlines: Lindbergh's flight, Pearl Harbor, FDR's fourth term, his death, V-J Day, peace, the astronauts, the assassinations, Jackie, the hijackings; then she'd thrown out the papers and saved only the front pages; then, slowly, she'd discarded most of them, headlines, pictures, and all, till she had only the contents of several manila envelopes left.

Ah, well, she thought, events seemed less and less startling.

The truly startling events were private and never made the papers. Nothing public was startling after you'd lived a while. And who would care about the past at all but those who had lived through it? Nowadays the only newspapers she carried were local papers from the towns that dispatched buses to the gates with the most comfortable benches, for sometimes they made her seem like a real commuter. For practical reasons she kept them open in her lap to fool a cop, but as for news, why bother? She'd read it all before. The same names kept appearing on the casualty lists; politicians kept resigning with the same excuses; youth was on the rampage, the old had no hope, the young became old. That was the great lesson she had learned through it all: the young become old. The past was always ready to play again. Like that child over there with that fancy man—wasn't that Milly?

Once, after standing on line at the post office so long she forgot what she had come for, she asked for a three-cent stamp to mail a letter to Milly. The clerk looked at her with understanding and said, "They're not three cents anymore, ma'am." "No?" Then she couldn't decide quite what she did want. "Ten cents for a postcard, ma'am," he said helpfully. But weren't postcards a penny? They'd always been a penny. She was confused. Ten cents sent an airmail letter not so long ago. And now? There was so much to keep track of. The rates had changed so often, yet the changes just kept coming. Candy bars, coffee—who could keep up? It was worse than the black market, these new prices. Besides, what did the prices mean, since the money kept changing like everything else? Even things that seemed unchangeable from one day or year to the next were not: the same garment worn by different people, or in different years, had entirely different values. Black, platforms, silver, berets. She had checks from past years that no one would cash. Some of the streets bore the same names they always had, but the inhabitants were unrecognizable. Others, she was sure, despite new names, were streets she had known for years. True, the street signs had all been switched one night, but she knew it was a trick.

Or was it? Which was true? That nothing lasted or that nothing changed? She had thought about that question more than any other, and through the years with increasing obsession. All the cells in your body were replaced by new ones every seven years, it was an established fact; were you then not the same person? Were you a different person if you lived on bread from the person you'd be if you lived on meat? If all the people in the city were replaced with new ones every fifty years, was it the same city? She thought briefly, lovingly, of the precious cells in her body, the more fragile they were the more precious; like the people in the city, miraculously, blessedly alive. How absolutely different from all the millions and billions who had perished by nature or catastrophe. Milly, whom she herself had created, had disappeared, and though the city tried its best to annihilate her too, yet here she was still; she was still here. Alive!

And yet Owl also knew there was something drastically missing from her life. Yes, she was alive, and rich in treasures besides; for the sake of survival she had spent the best part of her later years collecting, sorting, salvaging, and weeding every day until she had amassed a collection for which certain connoisseurs might one day offer a small fortune. She knew such judgments were fickle and highly subjective; nevertheless, she had faith that if she were circumspect and canny these treasures, over which she had taken endless trouble, might even in the end keep her out of the nursing homes. Should her circumstances change, they would be indispensable for her survival.

But if she were suddenly to die, what a waste it would all have been! All that rummaging through trash, saving pennies, hauling her heavy bags around with her wherever she went. Oh, then what a pity to have made her sacrifices and drastic compromises—to have lived as a pauper, to have let go certain very precious items because of their bulk, to have given over scarce space to the more compactly valuable or more widely appealing. The things she had kept and now lugged with her everywhere, up and down flights of stairs, outdoors in the morning, indoors in the rain—she could not bear to think of them capriciously dumped into the river or set aflame or flung carelessly under the West Side Highway without ever having been seen, admired, acknowledged.

There, there was half her problem. What should she do with this burdensome treasure, this monument to her life? For they were not to be dismissed with a shrug, as the foolish dismissed them, these precious bags of hers. For what had she stalled her death if she couldn't pass them on, share their meaning, see one face light up with understanding looking into her bags?

But—and there was the other half of her problem—she could not let anyone know what treasures she carried. Disguise was essential. If the robbers were alerted, if they even suspected that she carried with her items of immeasurable value, she would be forced to live in even greater confinement and under greater threat than she lived already. Her disguise, which rendered her vulnerable to every citizen or outlaw who despised a shopping-bag lady, was yet necessary for survival. Though it brought her dangerously near to assault, arrest, even wanton death, it also protected her. She kept to herself, avoided officials, do-gooders, deserted places, bus exhaust; nothing would get her near a hospital; she strictly limited her alcohol and even her cigarettes (well, she tried); nor would she beg, steal, complain, or preach. She was extremely prudent in her program to prolong her life. Terror kept her alert. In the Susan bag she kept smelling salts and Digitalis and, for that ultimate emergency, cash. True, she had not solved the problem of how to make them serve her while they were so perfectly hidden; but without them she hadn't a chance. A coded inventory of her most important possessions—one copy of which she kept hidden in her room and another, carefully disguised, on her person—was of no use when she alone knew the code.

And here again, flying like dust into her eyes, bringing the tears, was that too painful paradox: now, when she almost understood life's pattern and accepted it; when she wanted no diversion from its contemplation and pursuit; when all had finally become almost comprehensible and she had three bags full of irreplaceable testimony to her life's significance; when she had a right in her brief remaining time on earth to contemplate for its own sake the past, to remember the sizzle and smell of steam radiators in her Aunt Hilda's house, the silence of snow falling past the streetlight, the roller coasters of her youth, "The Hit Parade," the stir and whir of a ceiling fan; to handle knowingly her souvenirs; to play over in her head the fox-trots and waltzes forever; now to be forced to think still of the unknown and dwell in the murky, hopeless future— such knowledge sometimes pushed her toward despair. If only she had Milly! If only there were one person she could trust! She would never rest until she had found someone to hear her secrets, recognize her treasures, accept her gifts. If not Milly, then another would have to do. Otherwise, all that she hauled and hid and knew might be lost forever, like the doomed species that had already disappeared.

As she peered into Walgreen's she thought she saw Milly again, just getting up to leave with a man. Blond hair hanging loose, eyes alert, backpack slung over her shoulder like a modern kid. Could it be? She pressed her face against the door and squinted. Beautiful Milly, getting up from the counter in Walgreen's drugstore, lighting a cigarette?

No, no, it couldn't be. Owl wasn't ready for Milly yet. She still had to prepare her room, arrange her inventory, redo her will before she could embrace her daughter again. She wanted everything to be right. The last time she'd seen her, Milly had been ashamed. Owl had spent her last dollar to fix herself up— a new dress, shoes, a permanent wave—but still Milly had been ashamed. *Now see what you've done. Everyone's all upset. Why must you interfere?* she had said, and Owl had gone away again. The next time, she wanted Milly to be proud. She wanted to offer her more than the cheap bribes Bert had used to steal her away; the next time she saw her daughter she wanted to win her over completely, make her her heir. She needed time.

On the other hand, her life had been full of untimely surprises. She hadn't expected to lose her mother when she did, or to see the boy die, or to receive a divorce by registered mail. The package was tied gaily with red ribbons, it was hand delivered by the mailman—naturally she took it for a present. A gift certificate, maybe; or a prize. "We are pleased to announce that you are the lucky winner of—" But no. It had to be from Bert because no one else knew her address at that time. Opening it she'd been almost ready to forgive him, she wanted to forgive him.

It was written in Spanish. *Copia certificada de sentencia de divorcio.* Sentence of divorce. Even with her rusty Spanish she was able to read the grounds: *Incompatibilidad de carácteres.* Incompatibility of character.

Owl reached into the Barbara bag, felt among her papers, and retrieved the official document. Carefully she untied the ribbon and unrolled the scroll. *Signed and sealed by Judge, Secretary, and Official Clerk of the Second Civil Court of the Judicial District of Bravos, State of Chihuahua, Republic of Mexico.* (Bravos indeed!) *Witnessed by the Vice-Consul of the USA,* her own officer, duped by Bertram Fox, whom she had once trusted enough to marry. . . .

Abruptly she rolled up the scroll and put it away before her mind began to play tricks on her. Was that Milly? She wanted to see. But she knew if she walked into Walgreen's with her bags the cashier would make her leave at once and Milly would recoil in shame. And if she waited at the door, Milly would walk past her pretending not to see her at all.

Her pulse was throbbing now. It was too much. As Milly approached the exit, Owl turned her back to the door and squatted quietly between her shopping bags until she was invisible.

They walked into the lobby of the Moon past a cluster of winos drinking on the curb and a loudly laughing couple lounging on the steps. It was an ugly place, with dirty, peeling walls, a vase of garish plastic flowers decorating the only table, and a bent, whispering man in the single chair that adorned the lobby. Even the signs over the desk (POSITIVELY NO REFUNDS, NO CREDIT, NOT RESPONSIBLE FOR PERSONAL PROPERTY) were hostile.

"Wait right here," said Prince, putting her bedroll inside the door. She watched him walk to the desk with that special bounce of his. When the clerk greeted him with a big smile, she felt proud.

They had walked from the bus station up Eighth Avenue through dazzling crowds of lights and people. Dangerous? Maybe, but that was half the thrill. Porn shops and skin flicks nestled among the theaters and restaurants; the hookers in wigs and wild shoes whom Prince had pointed out to her (though anyone with half an eye could spot them), handsome black men in fancy suits and wide-brimmed hats whom Prince had contemptuously named "popcorn pimps"—all, all were part of the thrill. She was a stranger, a dreamer in a dream. All through the walk Prince had leaned protectively over her, whispering in her ear, naming the dangers, initiating her with the names; but with his arm around her shoulder she wasn't afraid.

A couple walked past Robin to the desk. The woman

twirled her bag by the chain and eyed Robin while the man waited behind Prince. The woman was elaborately made up and the man had long hair.

She was relieved when Prince returned to her, leaving the desk to the couple. "Here's the key. You're in five eighty-two. I'm gonna wait right here for you to drop off your things upstairs. You better not leave any money in your room. Or valuables. Why push your luck? Make sure the door has a tight lock and a metal strip over the crack so no one can jimmy it open. If you want me to, I'll hold on to your money for you till you need it."

"Ah," she said coyly, "but how do I know I'll get it back?"

He looked at her as if she had suddenly dashed her cold question over his head like a bucket of ice.

"I mean," she retreated, "how do I know I'll see you again?"

First dismay, then anger, then humiliation played over his face. He lowered his head, clasped his hands behind his back, and said slowly, softly, "Robin, Robin, you don't want to say that. That's all wrong. I wanted us to be friends. For a long time. Why would I walk out on you? What would I gain by lyin to you? I planned to be waitin for you right here on this very spot after you move into your room, and I planned to be right back here tomorrow morning when you get up, and many mornings. The way you been makin up to me and givin up rhythm, I thought sure we'd be spendin time together. I thought you wanted it like that. But if you feel the way you just said you feel, well then, I have to say goodbye to you right now. It was nice to know you, Robin, and now I'll be leavin you."

Robin grabbed his arms. "No! No! Don't go! I didn't mean anything. I didn't say I felt any way, I just asked a question. I'm sorry. I didn't mean anything. Please wait for me here, please, I'll just dump my stuff and be right down."

She pressed her hand frantically against the elevator call

button, but the elevator traveled at its own rate. When it finally arrived, she rushed in, then turned quickly to grin at Prince, to keep his face in focus, while the operator slowly cranked the gate closed. Slowly the elevator rose, slowly stopping at every floor, before dispatching her on five.

In her room she dropped her roll and pack on the ancient metal bed, barely taking notice of the cracked walls, the bare floor, the narrow room. Prudently, as Prince had advised, she removed her money from her pocket, placed it in the small pink satin case containing jewelry she had hidden deep inside her pack, and deposited it in her shoulder bag.

Again, the wait for the elevator seemed endless. Down the narrow hall an old wrinkled woman wrapped up in a sheet berated an invisible enemy. When the elevator came, Robin all but prayed during the descent. As the door opened, her eyes darted anxiously across the lobby, searching for Prince, afraid he had gone, until she saw him exactly where she had left him, leaning tall and supple against a plaster pillar, a man in control, a man to trust, sending a gleaming smile across to her.

She hurried across the lobby toward the now familiar face. Ashamed for having doubted him, she felt connected to him by more than a brief hour.

"How's the room?" he asked, as if she had never insulted him.

"Okay, I guess. I checked the lock. It works."

He took her hand and pulled her toward him. "Ready for a drink?" he asked. "I sure am."

Gratefully she looked up into his eyes.

4

"So tell me your story," said Prince when the bartender had placed their drinks before them—Johnny Walker Red for him, a pink lady for her.

Her story here? Everyone in the bar was dressed in fancy clothes, the black men in shiny fitted suits, the white men with chains around their necks, the women in tight dresses. She felt pitifully out of place. This was how she'd felt the time she ran away from home and pitched her tent with the Hillside Hippies, a group of older people whose men each wore one earring and whose women called themselves midwives, and who lived by selling kelp and pot to tourists. She'd heard they took in anyone (though Boots said you'd be just as free joining a convent as staying with those creepy hippies), and where else could she go? They took the ten dollars she'd arrived with, let her pitch her tent on their land, gave her a new name (Shawna, which they wrote up on the chore list), and let her skip the yoga because, as Larry, the head hippie, said, they "weren't into hassling people." But the first time she got stoned, Larry the head hippie crawled into her tent and fucked her, though she found him repulsive, his silly earring catching the little light there was as he moved up and down; and then when her father, having learned where she was, came charging in like a madman ready to kill her a week later, Larry turned her right over to him, muttering his line about their not wanting to hassle anyone. (Anyone except her!) That night after a terrible scene, her father actually wept because she had "gone with hippies."

"My story? You'd never believe it," said Robin, sipping the pink drink Prince had ordered. It was strange and sweet, like everything in the Casanova Bar: the long mirror behind the massive wooden bar with photos of boxers and showgirls taped to it, glasses hanging upside down from a ceiling rack, low music coming from the back.

"No? Try me."

But how could she tell him her story when she hardly knew it herself? First there was a happy time when she was small, before they moved to the island, before Billy was born. Then the fights: her father with blazing eyes shouting at her mother, who was guarding Adam, "He's my son, don't you dare try to interfere. If I decide to march that boy outside and pull his arm right out of its socket, you'll say nothing about it!" Later, the foster homes—the Douglas place, the Farm—unbearably lonely, ashamed.

Thinking over her life always upset her. Her mind gave up a jumble of images that made no sense, one moment rosy, the next moment grim. Dappled shadows on the kitchen table in the big old rented house in Portland. A wicker chair. Her baby brother Adam waving his arms on a red plaid blanket out in back. Fear of the bees. The dark attic with its treasures of musty cartons that belonged to the landlord, a trunkful of clothes she used to dress up in until her father, smelling the mothballs, locked the attic door. When had her mother started drinking? She couldn't say. Not until Robin was sent to the Farm at eight was she told that her mother was in a sanatorium "drying out." The red newts she had captured in the woods in spring and kept in a glass bowl had dried out and died. Her mother? When they told her, she ran away from the Farm, hitched to the ferry, and got all the way to the island by herself, hoping to find her mom. But her father met the ferry and took her straight back to the Farm, and not until years later did she discover what "drying out" really meant.

"The first time I ran away I was eight," she said proudly; "been doing it on and off ever since."

"That bad at home?" asked Prince.

"I think it just runs in the family. My dad takes off whenever he feels like it and my mom goes away to dry out. My dad—" She shook her head and sipped her drink. She couldn't explain. She remembered the puff sofa stuffed with goose down in the living room of the Portland house where she lay after her tonsils were removed, watching the shadows of the swaying elm against the window. Her father, finding a store of feathers she had pulled out of the pillow, had slapped her hand, making her cry. The pain in her throat was worse than the sting in her hand, but worst of all was the terrible humiliation, for she had not known she was pulling out the feathers or that doing so was wrong. She had betrayed him, she had angered him, she was so sorry, she wanted to die. When her mother had rushed to her side, crying, "Her throat!" he had turned against her mother too.

"My dad's a mean bastard," said Robin, seeing Prince's expectant look. "Thinks he's God on earth. Look at him cross-eyed and he's punching. Punches my mom for no reason. I always know when he's been at her by her long sleeves at breakfast. Bigshot. His idea of fun is to tickle my brothers to death. The more they beg him to stop the more he does it."

He was different with her. After she turned thirteen he stopped tickling her. Instead, he started watching her, criticizing her—the way she walked, talked, dressed, everything. Sometimes she thought he read her thoughts, the way he noticed her and checked up on her, as if she couldn't be trusted, calling her a sneak and a slut. With no reason; at thirteen she'd never even kissed a boy. While he—she'd seen him pinching the girl who worked at Smiley's Pizza and coming on to her French teacher, embarrassing her at school. And the way he acted with her best friend, Boots, like a hound dog on his belly, it sickened her; especially when he turned around and tried to forbid Robin to see Boots, saying she was "sinful" and "a bad influence."

"Nothing wrong with my dad two death pills wouldn't fix!" she said. Instantly she regretted the betrayal and rapped three times on the wooden bar to prevent her father's death. Wasn't her father the same man who had built their house on the island with his own two hands? Who fought the seas for lobster, battled fires in the Maine woods, logged up-country, trapped herring in nets with lonely crews, built additions to summer houses for the Boston and Portland rich?

"And your mom?" asked Prince.

Still less could Robin speak to him of her mother. Everyone said she was a drunk. Yet Robin remembered her from those first years in the Portland house as a gentle, graceful lady with the sweet high voice of a songbird. When she tried, Robin could still feel and smell her mother's silky robe and rose perfume, the warmth of her body as she held her in her lap and sang to her, the kindness of those blue, protective eyes. It had been ten years since they'd moved to the island, but Robin could still remember watching her mother dress up in the evenings in the Portland house.

"Do me a favor, baby? While I'm doing my face take the small things out of my shoulder bag and put them in here— I'm so late, Luke will be furious!" Then Robin would proudly lift out each of the precious objects—the lipstick in the golden case, the silver compact, the tortoiseshell comb, the perfumed handkerchief with the swirling letter, the wallet in which her mother carried pictures of her and Adam and their father, Luke, the cylindrical cigarette lighter, the cigarettes, the keys. One at a time she took them in her trusted hands and deposited them with care in the small plastic bag with the brass chain her mother held out to her. Only then, when her mother bent to kiss her a hurried goodbye would she realize she had traded away her bedtime songs and begin to cry. No matter how tenderly her mother kissed her, no matter how tightly the neighbor held her, she would sob as she watched her mother leave.

Of her father in those early days she had two memories

that kept returning like a tune she couldn't get out of her head. The first she called Lion. In it he is lathering his beard to a rich white froth before the bathroom mirror, with Robin watching him. His red lips move inside his white mane. She watches half terrified, half adoring, until that dread awaited moment when he zooms toward her, bringing his face close to hers with a roar like a wild animal, and she lets out an even wilder scream. It is the same delicious terror she feels when he throws her high in the air or tickles her suddenly or teases her with his special tease. She knows that inside the white roar hides her father; still, there is a doubt. . . . He always stood naked while he shaved. Until one day, he saw her staring at his thing, eye level. "What are you looking at?" he asked. "Nothing." After that, he wrapped himself in a towel when he shaved, and she was so ashamed to think he knew what she'd been looking at that she couldn't watch him anymore. After that, whenever her father threw her in the air, she didn't know if he would catch her or not.

The other memory she called Grace. In it her father sits at the head of the table, his two children on either side, saying grace. His head is bowed. Robin is frightened: if she can't see his face, she can't know his mood. (Once he spat a mouthful of chowder back into his bowl and stormed out of the house. Another time he forced Adam to eat a whole plateful of turnips because he had refused to taste them.) This time, in the middle of dinner he throws down his napkin, yanks up both children by the arms, races up the stairs with one of them under each arm, and flings them violently down on their beds. Robin sobs and sobs until she can't breathe, which somehow makes him madder. "Stop it!" he orders and shoves her to the mattress. "You stop it now!" She struggles to sit up in order to catch her breath, but he only pushes her back down again. She wants to explain that she just can't breathe, but every time she tries to sit up he pushes her back down, and speech requires breath. Finally, her mother rushes into the room; he stands up and she is able to breathe again. In and out she breathes, shuddering softly as the sobs gradually subside until at last, exhausted, she falls asleep.

But she couldn't speak of these things to Prince. Instead, she told him about the island off the coast where they'd moved when she was six, where they lived in a green tent that first summer while her father built their house with his two hands. She seemed to recall walking out one morning at low tide with Adam to play in the tidal islands and tidal pools that nestled between the great spray-pocked rocks, and returning a few hours later to see the bare frame of a house standing erect against the sky. That summer she fell asleep each night to the sound of her father's voice laying before her mother extravagant plans for more land, extra wings, sheds, guest cabins, studios, and awoke to the sound of the hammer. But by the time winter came, there was nothing to move into but one large, cluttered room with no plumbing, only a rain barrel, no heat except a Franklin stove, no light except Coleman lanterns, no power except manpower.

Was it then that all her memories changed and the lovely lady with the pale blue eyes and the delicate songbird's voice flew away to return as someone else with the baby Billy? Robin knew only part of the story. At first they'd stayed on the island all year round; but after Billy was born her mother refused to spend another winter without running water or heat. When the fishing season was over at the beginning of November, her father rented an apartment in Portland for the family and looked for work. He was sullen all winter, angry to be away from his land. Often he took his boat out to the island and stayed there by himself. When he got work in Lewiston or Bangor, he sometimes stayed away for weeks at a time, and in those dark, lonely winter nights her mother began to drink, often lying in bed for days letting everything slip by.

One February the children went to school so little that a

social worker was sent to investigate. Her mother was drunk when he came, and the case was officially opened. At first her father tried to manage things himself. But after a while he sent his wife away to dry out and arranged for the children to be placed in foster homes until spring, when they could all return to the island. And after that he always had his way.

Sometimes Robin wondered if she had only dreamed the beautiful lady in the Portland house, as the islanders, during the harsh winters when the wind howled for weeks, dreamed up endless yarns, insisting in spring and after that they were true. But whether they were dreams or real memories, they continued to visit her unexpectedly, like the rare blue heron she had three times seen in the cove or the occasional school of dolphin she watched at sea, leaving her moved and shaken and sad.

Robin emptied her drink and asked for another. When their drinks had been replaced Prince prodded her for more. "How many times you run away anyhow?"

"Depends how you're counting," said Robin, prepared to inflate the number. Actually, whenever she tried to count them up she came up with a different total. She took off when her father was really mad at her, or she at him, or whenever she couldn't stand it. Once, when her mother was away, her father kept Robin in the house for five weeks straight, cooking and cleaning and baby-sitting, till she was afraid she'd be left behind her class in school. Then she took her sleeping bag to school and hid in the basement behind the boiler room. Boots told her she was crazy to run away from home in April when it was so close to summer. She said if Robin would only wait until school let out in June they'd both run together, maybe to New York. But Robin couldn't stand to sit through one more of her father's sermons or cook him one more meal while he sat out on the front deck throwing his knife at the railing as if the house were a ship and he the captain. She stayed at the school until the assistant principal discovered her sleeping in the basement and offered to place her in another foster home; then she reluctantly went home. Another time she and Boots decided to hitchhike to Canada for the hell of it. It was summer and they had no plans. They might have kept going forever if they hadn't been picked up by troopers on the highway for hitchhiking and booked as juveniles. They were packed back home before they'd even been missed. "After that, I wasn't allowed to see Boots or even talk to her. Can you believe it? My best friend."

"You poor kid," said Prince.

Hearing him call her that made Robin want to cry. Suddenly she remembered her terror when Billy told her that he'd seen their father going into the principal's office with the island cop and two men. She was never sure who the men were, but with Boots already gone to New York, she knew everything would be pinned on her. Not that she and Boots had done anything so bad. The worst was to have removed the winter boards nailed over a side window of one of the nicer summer cottages on South Beach, broken one pane of glass, and taken over the place as their own until the owners returned for the summer. That was all. They'd gathered driftwood for the fireplace instead of using the owners' supply of logs; they'd slept on the floor before the fire in their own sleeping bags, smoking the pot Boots got from one of her boyfriends and drinking their own beer instead of using the beds and supplies of the owners. Each time they visited the place they left everything in perfect order, taking out their empties, cleaning the ashtrays, replacing the boards over the window. They were supercareful to leave behind no clues that could trip them up, because her father had threatened to turn her over to the state the next time she got in trouble. Her mother would protest if he tried it, but sometimes that only made it worse.

Or maybe the two men Billy saw with their father and the

principal had nothing to do with the cottage. Maybe they were the men Boots had talked into driving her down to New York. Robin had done nothing but sit with them in a bar while Boots did the talking. She didn't even know what had really happened or how much money Boots had taken them for; but it must have been a lot, because later Boots wrote from New York, "You should of come. They were loaded." To her father it was enough to know that Robin had been in a bar with a couple of men, money or no money; he'd beaten her for less. And if the police were involved, he'd be ready to kill her.

She hadn't even enjoyed herself. No more than the other times she'd gone along, protesting nothing, whenever Boots was asked to "bring along someone for a friend." Robin thought of those unpleasant encounters with strangers in waterfront bars and the backs of cars as virtuous sacrifices she made for the sake of friendship, hardly the orgies her father imagined. She never had anything to say to those men; she disliked the booze they drank and the way they sweated and moved while dancing; she hated missing the movies when they went to drive-in theaters; she dreaded the drunken joyrides on the highway Boots dared her men to take and the feel of the vinyl seat covers sticking to her skin. And after the men had finished doing with Robin what she'd been brought along to do (and Boots might still be doing in the front), they had nothing to say to her, either. Afterwards, they avoided looking her in the eye.

It was different for Boots. She loved the bars, and her men were the handsome ones. She enjoyed thinking up schemes that came to life. She danced when she felt like dancing, kissed whom she felt like kissing. When she wanted someone, she walked up to him, tossed her straight black hair over her shoulder, laughed, and took him. Robin's father called her sneaky, but really, she was broad-minded and open. That was why Robin liked her. Who else in the world could Robin have told about her strangest moments, the ones that made her feel

weird and proud? Like the time the boys who hated her came
snooping around her tent and she took down her jeans and
shook her ass at them? Or the other time when, hearing them
prowling around the tent, she took off all her clothes, raised her
knees, and just lay there naked, with her eyes closed and her
heart pounding, so they could look in and see everything she
had (which wasn't much)? Boots understood the triumph
Robin felt, knowing that though the boys thought they were
getting something from her, it was really she, Robin, who had
the laugh on them. Boots laughed and laughed and called
Robin crazy when she heard the stories. But Robin knew her
friend really admired her.

Prince shook his head slowly, as Robin bit her lip and
blinked back tears. "What kinda way is that to treat your little
girl?" he said, taking Robin's hands and locking her eyes. "Send
you away, try to run your life. That's no way to be." He pulled
her head to his shoulder and patted her back. "Poor little kid,"
he said, "poor scared little kid." From his jacket pocket he
took a large ironed silk handkerchief, shook it open, and
dabbed at her face. Then fixing her with his eyes, he let his
voice stroke her again.

"If I was your daddy I'd never hurt you. What kinda daddy
acts like that? If I was your daddy you'd never need to run away
from me. I'd take care of you so good you wouldn't want to
leave. If I was your daddy I'd treat you like a lady. It wouldn't
be no *do this, do that*, it wouldn't be no *you* or *I*, it would be
us, baby, *us*. I'd see to it you had your heart's desire, long as I
had the cake to buy it with. I'd do for you and you'd do for me,
that's the kind of daddy I'd be. My little lady wouldn't *want* to
run away, no way."

She was listening rapt, her mouth half open.

"That past is past. Now you're here in the Apple your
worries are over. I aim to protect you. The man raises a hand to

you, I don't care if he's your daddy or who he is, from now on that man's got to deal with *me*."

He peeled some bills off his roll and left them on the bar. "Now I'm gonna take you back to your room so you can get some sleep. You must be all tired out. But when you wake up tomorrow, fresh and rested, I'll be right downstairs waitin. I'll be waitin for you at eleven thirty. Then we're gonna get us some breakfast and see what we can do for you till I come back to town."

As he slipped his arm around Robin's shoulders to lead her out, he saw her watching them in the mirror behind the bar. A good-looking pair. One wiry kid in jeans with long yellow hair, and a tall, lean player in a custom-made shirt. Women had always gone for him. He paused to let her fill her eyes.

"Look nice?" he asked, raising his brows.

He watched her blush to see him see her. He did not let go of her hand until they were back inside the shabby hotel lobby. There he held her pale face between his large hands and kissed her chastely on top of her head, then pressed her room key into her hand and backed away.

"Wait, Prince," she called.

"Baby?"

"Hold on to this for me, okay?" She reached into her shoulder bag and offered him the satin case that held her money.

"Sure, baby, if you want me to." He took the case quickly and slipped it into his pocket. Handing over her money was the way a ho chose a pimp, though this little girl didn't know it yet. He'd make sure she found out when the time was right. He took her head between his hands again and looked into her eyes.

"I want you to," she said.

Again, he kissed the top of her head, then backed quickly out the door before she could change her mind.

. . .

All night long, Robin kept waking to strange noises. Voices shrieked, glass shattered, people ran through the halls. Once, something or someone thudded against her door, filling her with terror, and she did not sleep again. Instead, she lay awake watching the lights reflect off the wall and thought about Prince's mysterious eyes and undemanding kiss.

She had been wildly impulsive to hand her money over to a stranger. If he had tricked her, she would never see him again. But if he did show up in the morning . . .

Once before she'd felt the same terror. Boots called it being in love and said it was normal, but Robin disagreed. Maybe sex was normal, something you could take or leave, but being in love, that awful scary feeling, was sick. The one time it had happened to her she was fourteen. That summer her father had brought a man in to help him set his lobster traps and work on the house. Since her mother was "away" that month, her father had taken him straight to Robin and said, "This is Peter Delawney. He'll be living with us. I want you to see that he has whatever he needs. Why don't you start now by bringing us each a beer?"

He was a great bear of a man, about thirty, with brown grizzled beard and chest, the beginnings of a paunch, a rough manner, hands and feet like paws, deep-set eyes that matched the growling, beer-slurred voice that filled the house nightly as he traded stories with her father. She found him ugly and frightening, yet she lay on her bed just beyond the wall listening entranced to the strange low music of his voice, too excited to note the words. Whenever they were together she knew he watched her; she didn't have to see him to sense it, he didn't even have to be looking her way. When she found herself alone with him he had only to say her name to make her leap with fear or bristle with excitement. Not that he was indiscreet; he spoke to her as respectfully as any stranger. Nor could he hurt her; he moved too heavily to catch her if she ran. Yet she always knew he would be able to stop her with a word if he chose to. He had the sort of power over her that snakes were said to have over birds, and she wanted to be a bird. She wanted him to use his power, get it over with.

One day she and her brothers were helping the men work on the exterior of the new room. She was sawing lengths of batten, and her brothers were nailing them between the boards. Then her father ordered the boys into the boat to help him transport lumber from the mainland, and suddenly she knew she would be alone with Peter for the rest of the day.

As nothing had been acknowledged, she continued to saw, her knee against the board, her arm working furiously, while the motor of the boat faded away.

After a few minutes, Peter put down his own saw and approached her. "Want a tip?" he asked. He moved up behind her, pressed his body against hers, and with his left arm reached over her left arm to hold the wood, with his right arm reached over and covered her right hand. Then slowly, his hand upon hers, he moved the saw, working it slowly up and down, into the wood. "Go easy," he said. "Let the blade do the cutting. Keep the pressure steady and guide the saw, but let the blade do the work. Forget about speed."

She was practically faint with the sensation of his big body pressing against hers, his hard penis against her back. She saw the smooth bicep moving back and forth below her eye, guiding the saw in and out of the wood. Her breath came short, her pulse pounded in her ears, until she abandoned all pretense of sawing. She let her arm go limp under his, and finally as his own motion slowed to a stop she turned her body into his great enfolding embrace. The saw remained deep in the wood as they sank together to the deck. Beneath his hulking body she tugged at his neck, opening her mouth for his rough kiss, abandoning her will to it.

He took her hand and raised her, then led her down the

plank ramp to the soft sandy earth below the house. "Come here," he said.

She obeyed. She was thrilled and terrified, proud and ashamed, to be so powerful and powerless at once. She had had sex before but not desire. Now she was lost in desire.

He undid the belts and zippers of their jeans and lay on top of her. Feeling him big and hard against her she spread her legs wide. Once he was in her, instead of watching detached, she clutched him with her arms and legs to hold him inside her. To go on feeling his heavy, sweaty body sliding over hers was all she wanted in the world.

He grunted and moaned and was finished, while she lay tense and ashamed. After resting a while, Peter stood up, buckled his jeans, and said, "Luke'd kill me if he found out."

"You?" said Robin. "No, me; he'd kill *me*."

"He won't kill anybody, honey, cause he's not gonna know. There's nothing for him to know, right? What happened? Nothing happened."

And after that, Robin had never again felt desire, until just now.

5

These were the best of times for collecting, said newspapers and newscasters, with prices rising and money falling and nothing valuable but things themselves. Owl knew that forty-eight cents for a cup of coffee presaged fifty cents soon, and who knew after that? Her welfare checks drove home to her the value of things themselves.

A forager by profession, Owl preferred to finish her collections in the mornings before the competition was out on the streets. After securing a free breakfast from one of her few friends in the neighborhood, a waitress at Sallee's Coffee Shop named Grace who would often leave something for her in a paper bag behind the back door, she would rummage through the trash heaps set out for collection, look after her cats and birds, take a turn through the bus terminal to note the headlines and hear the news, and return to her room, where she would rest, rearrange the contents of her bags, and be free to spend her afternoons in the park behind the library or in the bus station, according to weather.

Afternoons, she tried to take a coffee break—on Mondays at the Shelter where the sisters offered coffee and donuts at four, other days wherever she could, preferably at a diner where the sugar, catsup, mustard, and salt were left in plastic packets on the tables for anyone to take—and still have time to check the food stands and vegetable stalls in Paddy's Market at closing time to procure something for her dinner. But her real collecting she liked to do early, before the streets were full. If she ignored the peep shows that opened at eleven to lure in local school-boys during their lunch period, the streets of the neighborhood, so dangerous at night, seemed unremarkable in the mornings. The commercial trash, piled up neatly for collection, had not yet been contaminated by the day's garbage or ruined by shattered empty pints.

Yet there were certain things from which she could not protect herself, no matter what the hour. Even now, having almost finished her rounds, there was something to fear: there in the gutter was another dead bird. It was so tiny most people would pass by without noticing. But one who spent her days searching the gutters soon came to recognize the dead things everywhere lining the streets. In spring the broken eggs with chicks inside; in summer fledglings fallen from the nests; in winter the full grown, frozen or starved. Everywhere, the dead birds: decomposing, flies buzzing around them; dashed against windshields on the highways; electrocuted on the trolley wires. In museums, too, their preserved carcasses were displayed in glass cases for anyone who cared to see. Tilted heads, wings folded, unbelievable colors mingling in their tails, concealing mysterious secrets in the beat of their wings, the speed of their flight. If you found them alive you would take them home, feed them, tend them—and then one day they were gone. Like your children who toddled up to you, threw their plump arms around your knees, then your thighs, then your waist, then, finally, your neck, where they hung while they grew strong. Then—a kiss goodbye, and gone. Sometimes not even a card at Christmas. She'd heard it so many times. Gone, gone. You might not even recognize them if you saw them again, your own children, nor would they recognize you.

Not so the birds. Even the tiny featherless fetus of the small wild bird had a shape she would always recognize in any state of disintegration. She stooped to get a better look. Larger than its flattened body, the tiny head was wider than long, an ellipse scored by the inverted V of the bill. Whether closed or open as in life, the silhouette of the bill, organ of sustenance, was the giveaway. The rest of the birdling, crushed or decomposing, might be nothing more than an indefinite shadow etched on the pavement by its fermenting juices, easily mistaken for a trampled water bug or one of the other local creatures; but the head with its beak was unmistakable to her practiced eye, ever since the first one Milly had found practically in front of the house.

"Come, Mommy. See what I found," she cried, pulling Owl back. "See?" She pointed her finger at something squirming on a square of slate. "What is it?"

It raised its head on its sinuous neck and lolled for an instant like a gyroscope, just before toppling, then dragged itself out of its shell.

"My god, I think it's a bird," said Owl.

"Can we take it home? Please? Can we keep it?"

It was so tiny she was afraid it would die. She searched for a way to say no. "What would we feed it?"

"We can feed it worms."

"How would it ever learn to fly?"

"*I'll* teach it," said Milly.

The whole of it was smaller than Owl's thumbnail. It was pink and featherless. There was no nest overhead, no mother in sight. How could she abandon it to the neighborhood cats or leave it for some other child? Finally, they carried it home on a leaf and made it a nest of cotton in a straw basket that had once held Easter eggs. It slept while Owl phoned the zoo, the ASPCA, the Audubon Society, to find out what to do.

Feed it hard-boiled egg yolk rolled into pellets. Boiled milk and cereal. Strained liver on the tip of a toothpick. Not on a toothpick, feed it from a match. Be careful not to scratch its throat.

Feed egg to a bird? It seemed unnatural. It was so small it could live off a single yolk for weeks. When it picked up its head to cheep it opened its bill so wide it all but disappeared behind it, and Owl pushed a bit of food into its throat.

Seeing its first swallow, Owl thought of the boy, her

firstborn, who lived for three days swallowing her milk, then flew away. Both unworldly creatures with tiny feet.

Between feedings the bird slept, pulsating on its cotton bed, then waking to feed every twenty minutes, a creature bent on survival.

When Bert came home that night Milly told him over and over how she'd found it. After she finally went to sleep, Bert sat with Owl at the window watching over the tiny bird lost in its basket. "Do you think it will live?" she asked; but he never answered.

In the morning it was still alive, though its cheep was weak. "Come on, Mommy, it's begging for food," prodded Milly. When Owl fed it, its nourishment seemed to go straight through it. She watched the pellet of food go down its throat through transparent tubes into its enlarged stomach, bloated like the stomachs of the starving she had seen in the camps at the end of the war. Then the bird passed yellow liquid onto its bed of cotton. After that, it would not swallow again. Its movements were feeble. Though Owl kept trying to feed it, the thin mixture seeped out onto its breast like the drool of sleepers. She rolled the bird over to wipe it by raising one side of the basket and then the other; it weighed so little and its stomach was so bloated that it rolled like a marble. But it was too weak to right itself, remaining beak down in the cotton, and it never ate or cheeped again.

"The bird is dead," said Bert, angel of death, coming into the kitchen that night. Owl ran to look. In the brief time it took her to cook dinner, the bird had already begun to decompose. It had turned from pink to yellow and the cotton beneath it was wet with yellow. So fragile was its life that the dampness spread like a shadow. Owl covered it with Kleenex and returned to the kitchen. The next time she looked in the basket the bird and all its cotton were gone. At the time, Owl thought Bert must have flushed it down the toilet to spare her the job, but she was never sure. Now, remembering how Bert had taken everything from her, she thought how easy it would be to slip quietly out of the world like the dead bird disintegrating at her feet. But she was unwilling to give him that satisfaction.

At the near corner of her block, she probed for fortune in a wire-mesh trash can with an umbrella shaft. Each day held the prospect of sudden wealth. Already, trash cans of this neighborhood had yielded astonishing finds. A woman from the Shelter named Red Mary had once found a wallet stuffed with money, probably abandoned by a thief. Another acquaintance had found a new pair of leather boots he had sold for cash. Stories circulated in the park of stashes of narcotics, sterling silver candlesticks, murdered newborns; and Owl herself had once discovered a damaged but glorious leatherbound book in which s's looked like f's and the thick pages were tipped in gold. Indeed, for someone with Owl's keen eye, the problem was not to find but to reject. Nothing raised her higher than giving new life and love to the forsaken; yet if she did not ruthlessly discriminate, she was in danger of being buried in the glut. With two full bags of acquisitions on her arm, she considered and rejected a broken lamp, a dirty pink comb, a rusty ice-cream scoop, and moved on to the next station on her route, pleased with her frugality. Not so long ago she had gone to Sunday church sales at the hour when the ladies gave the stuff away: all you could carry for the price of the bus fare. But now she tried to be selective, knowing that once she adopted a discard, redeeming it through love, it became dangerously part of her. Every loss was like a little death. She remembered the priceless treasures she had lost already—the beautiful Balinese painting of a hundred dancing figures with golden peaked helmets and serene faces that a soldier had brought back to her from the war. She had placed it carefully, in its cardboard sleeve, behind a chest of drawers; but when she packed to move it was gone—

thrown out, she assumed; found by someone else, she hoped. A mosaic butterfly pin from Florence, Italy, fallen from her clothes. An old book of fables she had let fall as she dozed, with the picture of the black fox ever reaching for the grapes. Gone, all gone, some lost for fifty years; gone as if to the bottom of the sea where lost treasures go.

Her last stop was the alley to feed her cats. This time as Owl arrived at the fence, not all her cats leaped to welcome her. Ignoring their daily ration of dry cat food which Owl purchased each fortnight out of her welfare check, the largest tom in the colony, a ragged calico missing part of an ear, and several other long-term residents raced around in a frenzy of excitement over some large object of prey they batted back and forth among them, pounced upon, and shook rapidly in their jaws like wild animals.

At first Owl thought they must have killed a rat. She had often seen rats in the area: dead in the hotel courtyard, alive in the park, once running boldly across a side street in the middle of the night and now and then in an underground passage. But as the big tom, racing forward with the prey in his mouth, skidded past her chased by the others, she recognized a wing hanging down from a bloody body.

Two dead birds in a day: a bad omen. "For shame!" she cried, forgetting nature; then, switching tactics, she tried to believe the bird had been dead when the cats found it, for there were corpses everywhere.

But she knew there were also wounded birds and sick ones in the streets, perfect prey for alley cats. She had seen them in the park, wings immobile, hiding in bushes and under benches, or dragging themselves like old people into the shadowed doorways of the side streets where they puffed up their feathers and waited alone to heal. Once she had found an injured pigeon, left for dead in a trash can or tossed there to die. She had carried it to the park and hidden it, surrounded by bread, in a hedge. The next day it was gone. She chose to believe it had flown away, but even so, she tried not to think about that bird, vulnerable to every carnivore.

She knew the cats were driven, like everyone, by more than hunger; still, she tried to divert them from their bloody pursuits by pushing morsels of food under the fence until all she had was gone. As best she could, she watched the kittens eat, ignoring the tom still tearing at the bird. There was a reason to all this, she assured herself; there was a reason for everything. But as she left the alley for the Hotel Venus she could not remember what it was.

Prince ambled into the lobby of the Moon a half hour before his date to meet Robin. The place revolted him. Broken chairs and fixtures, wrappers on the floor, peeling paint, and in the air the sickly sweet smell of disinfectant, the same smell that filled the peep shows where as a porter he had scrubbed down the viewing booths several times a night to get the jism off the walls.

In contrast, Prince was showered, shaved, perfumed, shined. It didn't take much to make yourself presentable. Growing up in Washington, he remembered garbage in the halls and even rats in the basements of all the houses he had lived in; yet his mother had managed to keep their own apartments spotless. Instead of English, she spoke cleanliness. After working eleven hours in a shop, she came home to clean. (For the day his father returned, she said—though he hadn't been seen since his unit left Manila when she was five months pregnant with Prince.) He could barely remember a kitchen floor without a newspaper covering to protect the newly applied wax. Not even the swabbed decks of the training ship after he'd joined the navy gleamed like his mother's kitchen floor.

Prince lit a cigarette and checked his watch. So far, everything had gone according to plan, but certain problems would have to be dealt with. The friend Boots was one: if she turned up, he'd have to catch her too. The runaway habit was worse: he'd have to turn that around if he wanted to lock the bitch. At least she wasn't a junkie. But there was still plenty about her he didn't know. Some players skimped when they took an application from a ho, but Prince knew the importance of a complete record. According to the pimping code, every little fact had to be put to use. Otherwise, you might catch your girl but fail to lock her, or lock her up but train her wrong. The rules were all there for a reason. With so few chicks coming through anymore, you couldn't leave anything to chance.

Back in the old days, when he was in the service with that check coming every month, he'd had plenty of women. They swarmed around him, ogling the uniform, admiring the tattoos, fingering the cash. He'd had enough for everything then, even a wife and son. But when he got out he blew them all: checks, women, wife, son. Back on the street with no job and no money, he couldn't even buy a woman a drink. When his wife took him to court for alimony, he left Washington for New York and changed his name to Prince. At twenty-two, unable to use his real name, the only square jobs he could land were porter in a peep show or straight messenger boy. What did he care? He was young and good-looking. He hung out on the street and in the sailors' bars, admiring the players' craft, eager to be a runner, a hustler for anyone with cash. But pimping never crossed his mind.

He met a man named Clem who told him he had a money-making talent if he'd only use it: his way with women. Prince had merely laughed. He was so broke, he said, that if he took a woman for a beer he wouldn't be able to pay. "Pay?" said Clem. "Tricks pay. Pimps get paid. Which one you want to be?"

Then one night an ex-dancer named Alma put him in a pimping position, and by the following week he had to admit

Clem was right. He did have something of a talent. Shaky from his battles with his wife, he'd been slow to respond to Alma. She was a slender, delicate woman, much older than he, with maple-brown skin, soft heavy-lidded eyes, a pretty face marred by a mysterious scar, firm small breasts, and a slight limp, but one of the best-loved hookers on the stroll. For some reason he didn't understand, she attached herself to him, sitting in a booth at the back of a bar buying him drinks and talking. He found her touching but felt awkward without money. She stirred him by painting pitiful scenes of her life: a hip injury that had finished her for dancing, a man who beat her, another who left her, a baby abandoned, a second child sick. . . . Listening to Alma talk, Prince was unaware that she was submitting her application to be his ho. Not even when she pressed into his hands a small purse containing a thousand dollars and a promise of that much more each week if he would be her man, did he know what she was offering. At twenty-two, fresh from the service, he lacked imagination. He thought Alma had simply been scared someone would rob her. He'd never heard of "choosing money," much less a thousand dollars of it. He didn't even know that a ho chooses her man, not a man his ho. He certainly didn't dream that she was choosing him. And when, half out of pity, he took Alma back to his run-down room to make love to her later, he had no idea he had taken the job of pimp.

But as Alma continued to present him each week with more money than he'd ever made, he began to appreciate his talent. Alma might be trouble and getting old; but how could you beat two hundred dollars a night just to be there listening and now and then give up a little dick? It was as if he had been handed a treasure map in a difficult code, and then a key to the code. All he had to do was read the map, dig, and pick up the gold. He started learning the names of things all over again. Bad meant good.

Alma in love was eager to front off her young Prince. When

she learned he was part Filipino, she bought him a purple silk kimono ("to go with your eyes"). She dressed him in elegant clothes, gave him a diamond ring, and introduced him to everyone she thought might help guide him into the life. Sweet Rudy, a friend of Alma's, undertook to school him, even though Prince wasn't black. "I'll do what I can," he told Alma, appraising Prince. "Maybe he'll get the style down, but he ain't got the blood." Nevertheless, he taught Prince three-card monte and the murphy game, where a shill who looked like Prince could be a real asset, and gave him his own copy of Iceberg Slim's famous memoirs to read. He talked game with him at every chance, lectured him on the pimping code, instilled contempt for the small-time popcorns and respect for the real boss players, those beautiful, legendary black men known all over the east for their furs and suedes and eye-turning women and long custom cars whose names (Eldorado Eddie, Mark V) they took for themselves.

At last Robin emerged from the elevator. Prince jumped to his feet and donned his Mr. Reliable smile. Fifteen minutes early: could she have been planning to sneak off before he arrived? He doubted it. She looked too scared. She probably just didn't know the time. First thing he'd buy her was a watch.

Her face lit up as she spotted him.

"Mornin, Robin," he said, walking over and taking her arm like a longtime friend.

"You're here."

"Well, sure I'm here. Didn't I say I'd be?"

She was holding on to his arm like someone up a tall, shaky tree holding on to the trunk. The way she was giving up rhythm, he figured he could probably have her right there and then, but he was going to play this one carefully. She needed reassurance more than dick.

He held her hand up close against his ribs and steered her toward a diner, allowing no space for doubts. "How'd you like

to call up your friend and ask her to meet us for breakfast?"
he asked. If she said yes, he'd be able to see who he was up
against, maybe take on both of them. If she said no, then
either there was no friend, or Robin preferred him to her at
the moment. Either way, he'd score a point of confidence,
showing her he had nothing to hide.

"No, that's okay, I'll try her again tonight. She may be
sleeping."

Her answer was cool, but Prince could see his suggestion
upset her. He filed the fact away for the day he might need it
and ordered them donuts and coffee.

"So tell me, pretty lady, how'd you sleep?"

She shrugged. "It was noisy. Kinda scared me. I have to
get used to the city, I guess."

He took her hands while she told him of her terrors, and
leaning close to her, he said at last, "You know, baby, you don't
have to stay at the Moon. You can stay with me if you choose
to."

She inhaled sharply, as if she had been caught out at
something. He waited patiently for her reply, holding her in
an eyelock, hoping to disarm her with directness.

"Aren't you going away tonight, though?" she stalled.

"Not till tomorrow. Tomorrow I got to leave you alone.
So you better hang on to this till I get back." He slid the satin
treasure bag across the table, watching her closely.

Good timing, he thought, feeling her relax. Timing was
everything. It felt like the moment in three-card monte when
the bets go down. First your partner's bet and then the mark's.
Returning the satin bag was the partner's bet. And now he
waited for the mark's.

She picked up the case and tucked it into her shoulder
bag.

"But how come you'll let me stay with you?" she asked,
stalling or fishing, he wasn't sure which.

"Where else you gonna stay?"

"But how come?"

"How come? You got to ask me how come? Not enough I feel for you, I want to see you on your feet, I got to have a special reason besides?" He withdrew his hands from hers and let his mouth form a pout, then waited to see the regret in her eyes before he finally gave her what she wanted. "Maybe I just like you. That's how come."

Her pleasure spread over her face. He was sure she would take the bet. (When she was his, he'd have to teach her how to hide her feelings, he thought, jumping ahead.) He paid for their breakfasts and said nothing more about where she'd sleep, allowing her to think the decision was hers. But when he set out to show her the town, tucking her hand back under his arm, he could tell by the way she leaned on him that the first round belonged to him.

6

Even before she opened her eyes, the whines of small children, a radio through the wall, the smell of coffee let Robin know it was day. No birds or peepers, no surf; still, day: city day.

She had been dreaming about the island. About Bruce Stockton from outside Newton, Mass., whose family had rented a beach house on the island for the month of August of the summer between her eighth and ninth grades and to whom she'd lost her virginity. It was just before high school, after she'd started to get breasts. They'd been good friends that summer, so naturally they spent the night before he left lying around on the beach, drinking Cokes, listening to the local rock station on his portable radio, looking up at the stars and the Northern Lights, and it had just "happened." It was the last thing she'd expected, for she was not like the others, the popular crowd, she never ran after boys, she was a tomboy type, despite her uninvited breasts; why, she'd never seriously even kissed a boy before. But people talked about it so much, her father thought of nothing else, all the songs were about it, so that when it did happen it seemed natural, and she didn't understand why people made so much fuss about it.

She opened her eyes cautiously, but the dream disappeared. Here she lay, stretched out in a well-used bed, still wearing the bikini underpants and the yellow T-shirt that said "Born to Dance." It was the bed Prince had tucked her into after buying her drinks in two more spots and taking her for a big dinner of Chinese food, food she'd never eaten before.

Across the room lay yesterday's clothes in a heap beside her backpack. Where was Prince? They'd slept in the same bed—

she remembered the strange tattoos on his chest and arms, a moon over a palm tree—but without touching. She'd certainly been willing after all his kindness—she'd done it with others for less—but he'd gone out before she woke up.

She sat up and looked around. Dusty light and steady traffic sounds seeped past a shaded window into the pleasant white room. A leopard fur rug and gay print pillows gave an air of decoration to the otherwise plain room. But even the drab beige sofa, chest of drawers, several shiny lamps, and simple chairs seemed elegant after the awful Moon. Slowly the night came back to her: the doors on her left led to a bathroom and a closet, and a short corridor across the room led to a tiny compact kitchen where Prince had mixed them their last drinks and toasted her, looking deep into her eyes.

She reached over and fiddled with the clock-radio dial till she found her own music. The clock read 12:42; she'd already slept away half the day! Quickly she scrambled out of bed, stopping for clean clothes and shampoo from her pack, then headed straight for the shower.

The water, responding to her every whim, came bubbling forth, hot or cold, in a soft steady stream. It filled up an entire little room lined in patterns of pink tile, and there was a soap dish shaped like a shell. Not like the hand-held showers on the island. (Prince said Manhattan was an island too, but she didn't believe it.) When she was clean and dry, she put on a fresh T-shirt and a clean pair of jeans, brushed her long wet hair and her teeth, and then, pulling a chair over to the window where she could dry her hair in the sun, snapped up the shade on the strange city.

There was a great bustle of activity in the street below, like the chattering and feeding of a thousand birds. Pedestrians rushed by, horns bellowed without letup, in the alley across the street cats cried like gulls. Her father would have cursed them if he were sober, pelted them if he were drunk. But instead, they were being offered scraps of food from a ragged shopping bag by an old woman dressed like a witch. Robin smiled as she realized her father was hundreds of miles away and would never be able to find her.

A new kitten had entered the colony—a frail gray-striped creature too small for its pelt with ungainly white paws, a white muzzle, and large bewildered eyes, lost in the world. No native, Owl was sure. Without visible connection in the alley, it had probably been newly exiled from some human family— another tossaway. It had not rushed to greet Owl like the others when she arrived with their food but had hung back bewildered. Neither did it eat when the others ate. Remembering the kittens she had ignored, the starving cats of Europe she had failed to notice in her wild youth, all the creatures she had once in her ignorance passed callously by, Owl sucked air through her missing tooth at this cowering kitten and held out her hand, her heart.

It did not move.

But noting that it did not flee either, Owl allowed herself the luxury of pity that felt like love. Her bosom swelled, her heart lifted, and, like that impulsive girl she once had been who knew how to give herself to a man in an unguarded moment without sacrificing a drop of integrity, she pulled the kitten under the fence and lifted it to her cheek.

The first kitten she'd loved she'd got for Milly because Bert, who hated cats, had left them. For months after he'd gone Milly would climb into Owl's big half-empty bed each morning and cry.

"Where's Daddy?"

"He's in California."

"When's he coming home?"

"I don't know, darling."

"I want him to come home now."

"I know, I know," soothed Owl, stroking her child's fine yellow hair. She tried to be strong, though she was grief-stricken; when Milly cried Owl had to console her. Still, she didn't know what to say. Should she tell Milly the truth about her father? Or should she cover for him to spare Milly pain? For a while she wanted to keep everything as it was before Bert left, on the chance that he might come back.

But then Bert failed to call Milly for Christmas. Instead, he sent a large plastic present, some kind of game too old for her. Placing it with her own presents to Milly beneath the small tree she had decorated (what a bleak ceremony, opening presents for two), Owl resolved not to wait anymore.

When, later that day, one of the neighbor children showed Milly the kitten she'd gotten for Christmas, Milly begged for one of her own, knowing there were still four more in the litter.

Owl had never much liked cats; she had thought attachments to pets sentimental. She had once let her fish die out of laziness and agreed with Bert that the smell of cats was distasteful. But now on an impulse she decided to take one of the kittens. For Bert, the cat hater. Now that he was gone they didn't have to cater to his objections. They were free to do whatever they wanted.

The kitten they took was a tiny black and white tiger—a miracle, all head, paws, and fur. Never had Owl imagined what a joy it might be to have a kitten. The first day they had him at home she and Milly did nothing but follow him around in astonishment, observing his movements, marveling over his odd feline ways. The way he licked himself all over, beginning with his head—first wetting a paw and rubbing it over his ears, face, muzzle, neck, then working his way with his tongue systematically down to the tip of his tail. The way he used the litter box from the start, neatly covering every sign of soil. The way he invariably curled up on any small, flat, discrete object—

the page of the book Milly was reading on the floor, an envelope, a napkin. For one full day the spectacle of instinct distracted them from their pain. But that night, after they had gone to bed, the kitten whimpered continually, and Owl could not sleep. At the very first whimper Owl woke with a start, as she had when Milly was a baby. (If you didn't respond to a baby's cry, it might not stay alive!) Then, once she was fully awake, painfully sensitive to the kitten's pain, she began to think about Bert and how he had gone off to California and left them, and their wasted past—and when dawn came she was still awake.

The next night when the kitten cried she woke again, and again she couldn't get back to sleep. And the next night again, and the next. Soon she was one of those people who wake every morning at four to stalk a specter in the corner of the room. Instead of sleeping, she would lie in bed in the dark trying to sleep and rail against Bert the betrayer, giving him all her reasons, going over and over in her mind every minute detail of the quarrel between them, all their recriminations. And even after the kitten learned to be silent through the night, even after Owl understood what a privilege it was to be able to live in such intimacy with a creature of another species (as, later, after Milly had gone, she would know what a gift it had been to be made guardian to another human soul), Owl remained an early-morning waker, someone who found sleep an ordeal and faced the nights with dread.

Now, feeling this new kitten against her cheek, helpless, soft, needy, she knew she would take it home. Let the manager use it against her, she had no choice: if it didn't eat, it would die.

She stroked the small animal absently until she had fully accepted her new responsibility. It meant trouble, but so did everything she did. This was an emergency. Carefully she rearranged the contents of her shopping bags, moving a few things from the fragile Ellen to the heavier Barbara, until she had cleared enough room. She lifted the kitten by the loose pelt at its neck and lowered it in (it belonged, like her, to a species fond of shopping bags) and covered it gently with a large scrap of chenille, the old-fashioned tufted kind used widely for bedspreads, that she kept on hand for just such purposes.

Her rounds finished, Owl proceeded home, hoping to make it to her room before the thugs and thieves were stirring. But as soon as she entered the Hotel Venus and saw a girl bound past her, gazellelike, pursued by a hunter's murderous cries, she knew she was already too late. Cowering inside the narrow doorway with her shopping bags, Owl saw the hunter leap down the stairs advancing toward her. She tried desperately to flatten herself and her bags against the open door and let him pass, but she was no longer of a shape to flatten. On the contrary, her fate was now, perhaps forever, to stick out like a tumor, protrude like a wen. As for her bags, they had been created for no other purpose than to expand when filled and were at that moment stuffed to overflowing with the morning's haul.

"Outa my way!" screamed the man, plowing into Owl as the girl flew by. "Witch! I'll kill you!"

Recognizing the rage, Owl hid her head in the crook of her arm before the blows began. She remembered the Peruvian painter she'd picked up in Rome who'd drawn her portrait in chalk on walls all over the student quarter. He had called her bewitching, a beautiful witch, and as she saw herself flat against the walls of Rome so charmingly drawn, she had agreed. But the following day while they made love in his room, the rains washed all the pictures away. Nothing remained. And soon she had had to leave the city—or was it he who left?

She heard a thud against her head as from a great distance and stoically steeled herself. When her glasses were dangling from one ear, the other earpiece gone, her attacker turned his wrath to her property, going at her shopping bags with alternate feet.

The kitten! She knew it would end like this. It was her bags they hated most!

She spat out a deep and righteous curse composed of a long string of epithets in five languages and the complete range of human inflection. While her enemy the manager cackled in appreciation (but wouldn't stoop to help her!), her astonished assailant sheathed his fists in his pockets and swaggered off, leaving Owl to try to re-collect her things.

She would salvage what she could. She wanted to examine the kitten, to see if it was still alive. (Had it escaped in the melee? Why no sound?) But the manager and several residents were watching her. Smart kitten, to make no sound, she thought, moving toward the stairs with her bags. Either smart or dead.

When her hair was dry and brushed, Robin pocketed the key Prince had thoughtfully left for her on the table, popped a stick of gum into her mouth, and walked down the stairs to the lobby of the Royal Arms.

A cluster of men stood gossiping at the desk and did not notice her. She slipped past them into the noisy street, where pedestrians rushed by like crabs in the mud flats, spilling over the curb.

She looked around for a phone booth. The first one she spotted was occupied by a man shaving before a mirror hung over the dial. Sheepishly she entered the adjacent booth and dialed Boots's number, but when the same gruff voice answered she hung up.

Walking downtown, she was overwhelmed by the fierce wheeled traffic: kids on skateboards, men on roller skates, women with shopping carts, only inches from death; cars and buses attacking traffic; enormous trucks backing up blind; three-wheeled delivery carts pedaled by men. Sometimes when the traffic lights turned red, motorists stepped into the streets, leaving their motors running, and shook their voices and fists at one another, then returned to their cars on green and tore away.

Wide-eyed, she watched it all—the whores and hags, the sex peddlers with their wares, the noisy, brash pedestrians. Risky, exciting; yet whatever the dangers, she knew she was among survivors. As she pressed down Eighth Avenue, she wondered why she had waited so long to come to this place, why anyone would stay in Maine when the city was only a day's ride away, and why her mother, who had once had her feet underneath her, hadn't just packed up her children and run away.

She didn't know which had been more terrible, to see her mother slip silently into drunkenness where she would sit or lie beyond reach, or to hear her rail loudly against the pain of her bitter life. Like the time one of the summer people, enchanted by their simple hand-built house, had crossed the beach and climbed the stairs to borrow a cup of sugar.

Sugar! It was funny. Hadn't anyone warned her? She had even brought her small child with her.

"Well, of course you may," her mother said, inviting them in. It was early in the day—early enough for her still to be acting normal.

"What a charming house, what a magnificent spot," said the visitor, while the child tentatively explored the house.

"Oh, yes," said her mother, with her cynical smile, "it's very pretty here," and poured sugar into the woman's cup. She handed it to her with a strained smile, and they all walked out together to the porch.

While the two women drew out their goodbyes, the child

strayed unobserved to the very edge of the porch. No one noticed until Robin's mother suddenly cried, "Watch him!" and leaped to snatch the boy back. The house, built high over thorny brush, was encircled by a railing of a single board about three feet off the porch floor—well designed to enhance the view but far too high to protect anyone under eight years of age. As she pulled the startled child back from under the railing to safety and he began to scream, she let out a long wail of despair and spewed forth her own pent-up bitterness.

"There, now! You see what I've had to live with? Three children and I begged him to enclose this porch. At least put up another rail. And still—still!—it's like this! All the years of watching them, waiting for them to fall, worrying over them, while *he*...."

She beat her fists against the railing. "See why I hate this place? Hate it! I know, I know. Everyone who comes out here loves it. The magnificent view, the workmanship. How lucky you are, they say to me. Lucky? Sure. But no one ever thinks what it means to raise three children with no railing, no water, no separate rooms, no heat. Or what it's like just getting a meal. Sure, the pioneers did it, sure the country's being ruined, big business, TV, welfare. But I'm not a pioneer! Luke—there's the pioneer. Luke sacrifices, Luke provides. Now he's going to build us a new wing, he says. But where's my rail? Now he'll build a wind generator, solar heating, a sauna. And my rail? And does he bring us what we need? He doesn't even *know* what we need! And when his own family aren't labor enough, he brings home his lackey, his whores. To *live*, when there's hardly space for us to live!"

By the time she had finished, tears were streaming down her cheeks, and her words were incoherent. "Please, Mom, please," whimpered Robin, mortified. But her mother didn't hear. The visitor, embarrassed, took her child and the sugar and tiptoed down the stairs. Even when they were halfway across the beach, Robin's mother was still standing alone on the deck, addressing herself to the sky, shaking her fist at the sun.

"Heeey," said Prince, long and low, when Robin walked in. "Pretty girl. Like I said—a shower, a night's sleep, a decent meal . . ."

"Prince! You're back!"

"Yeah. My trip's been put off. But I brought you some presents. A couple a new outfits to try on, they'll give you a whole new personality—you can be anyone you want to be now, you know?"

"For me?"

He looked around. "No one else here they're gonna fit." He held out the packages and winked. "Well, aren't you gonna help me with this stuff?"

She stood watching him. No one had ever brought her presents.

"Well?" he repeated, still holding out the packages, cocking his head to one side. "Don't I at least get a kiss?"

Her legs carried her across the room and her lips shaped themselves for a kiss.

Prince wrapped her in his arms and dropped the packages to the floor. Robin remembered her dream of Bruce Stockton lying on top of her, but as Prince began to kiss her, in her mind Bruce gave way to Peter, to a longing she couldn't control. One moment she barely acknowledged the feeling, and the next moment it was filling her up, the way the tide sometimes filled the cove so suddenly that you'd drown if you couldn't swim.

Prince pulled away with a friendly pat on her behind. "C'mon," he said, piling the packages on the table. "Style em for me."

While Prince withdrew to the bed to watch, Robin opened the boxes, one by one. Delight lit her face. A black skirt, two pretty sleeveless tops, one red, one striped, and a pair of sheer black pantyhose, all with labels intact.

As she took the skirt out of its box and began to open the zipper, she realized that to try it on she would have to remove her jeans, and for the tops she would have to take off her shirt. Overcome by embarrassment, for one agonizing moment she hesitated; then, taking courage from the memory of having once defiantly stripped naked in her tent, she changed into the skirt and pulled the T-shirt quickly over her head, exposing her breasts.

"Very nice, I like it," said Prince, absorbed in the clothes. "Turn around."

She turned.

"Now try the other one."

Again, she removed the top and stood exposed until the new top was on.

"You look very good in an outfit like that," he said without emotion. "You're a natural. You don't have to go around like a high-school dropout, you know, askin for it."

She put her own clothes back on, refolded the new ones neatly, then sat beside him on the bed, grateful and relieved that the ordeal was over.

They talked till it was quite late. Finally Prince looked at his watch, yawned, and began to take off his clothes. Robin wanted to trace his strange tattoos with her fingers and ask him what they meant. But Prince had said he was done talking. He stripped down to his underpants; Robin did the same. When they were both under the sheet, he kissed her chastely on top of the head, ruffled her hair, turned off the light, and put his arm limply around her shoulders. She moved close to him in the dark, half wishing to go on talking, half wishing something more. In her mind she kept repeating the single word "please," without knowing exactly what it was she wanted, until she fell asleep.

In the morning when she opened her eyes the word was still on her lips. She felt it like a call.

"What do you say?" said Prince, greeting her cheerfully. Music was playing softly, and she smelled the strong smell of the city.

"Please," she said, "please."

He looked at her with his dark-lashed languid eyes until she "pleased" again. "If you want me to, baby," he said. He covered her raw loneliness with a long and ardent kiss. She breathed him into her.

He removed their underclothes until he was lying naked beside her. With no fear of her father or of anyone, she lay in his bed, and soon he was covering her with kisses and caresses, even there between her legs. After a while a feeling she had never felt rose up in her. It began to assail her like a sudden storm, filling her with fear. She could almost hear the thunder, rumbling its distant threat, getting closer and closer. She lay very still, waiting, listening, barely able to breathe. She wanted to run for shelter before it broke, but Prince wouldn't let her go. He kept on with his caresses, steady, insistent, until suddenly the storm was bursting upon her, it was everywhere, pounding in her ears, stopping her heart. She was drenched and shaken. On it came, wave after wave, and no escape. Soon he was inside her, moving with the music, pressing his lips to her lips and his hands to her hands, swaying inside her until the storm broke again.

She shuddered, she cried, she couldn't believe what had happened. This feeling, filling her, drenching her, sinking her down, down, down, had nothing to do with what she'd known of sex. It frightened, it terrified her. Lying beneath him, feeling his weight upon her, she squeezed his hands as if he were a raft and could save her from her own pounding pulse. And as she felt his penis wither inside her, she held his hands so he wouldn't leave.

"That what you wanted me to do, baby? That make you feel happy?"

"Yes," she whispered, afraid to hear her own voice speak the truth.

"That's good, baby. That's good. All I want to do is make you happy."

7

Owl had seen Milly twice now without speaking, both yesterday and the day before; the next time she must be ready to make contact. She must offer her treasures more precious than Bert's to win her over. She must offer her everything she had, from a kitten to a mother's love, before she disappeared again.

Seating herself on her bed, ignoring her neighbor's cough, Owl shooed away the new kitten and carefully arranged around her her five main bags (three that traveled with her and two that stayed home), preparing to take inventory for Milly's sake.

The first bag, a plain brown bag named Belle, contained the remnants of her childhood, the crumbling contents of her cedar box: her mother's picture, her father's postcards from the West—those photos of snow-covered trolleys climbing steep hills that reminded her of home, pictures of milk wagons and beer wagons pulled by large drayhorses with flowers behind their ears. She could no longer tell if the old pictures reminded her of something real she could recall or if her memories were only of the pictures, they'd been with her so long. One picture she was sure of: a rare snapshot of their Buffalo house when her mother was alive, with Owl as the child Lilly on a kiddie car in the long shadow of her father the photographer. "Come on, Lilly," she could hear him call, "we're taking some pictures." She remembered leaving the others, racing up the hill to where Papa stood fiddling with the Brownie. Her mother was not in the picture, but Owl felt her presence in the scene. In this same bag she also kept, miraculously, the very pin she had made for her mother in school, out of copper and wood—her last gift to her before she had died. Holding it brought back everything—the last Christmas, her mother's smile, her own joy making the pin. So many steps to completion, so many pitfalls. Her own toys and jewelry were gone, but not this pin she had made for her mother. Here in this bag, named after her mother, she also kept new reminders of those days. Once she had found a discarded cache of old sheet music and had rescued those songs that belonged in the piano bench at her grandmother's house: "Bye, Bye Blackbird," "Button Up Your Overcoat," "Over There" (with a picture of Caruso on the cover). Winter evenings with her mother and all the aunts playing their best pieces and singing in harmony in the parlor with the gas fire lit. In summer they sang a cappella on the front porch, sliding the glider back and forth in time to the music. In this bag she put scraps of oilcloth and old wallpaper that reminded her of back then and would have put, if only she still had them, the shark's-tooth necklace from her papa, the rabbit's foot, the cocoons she'd tried to hatch, pressed flowers from the rock garden, the silver snake ring with the green glass eye from her Aunt Hilda she had lost along the way, and her autograph book. Gone. She'd found another autograph book like her own but not her own. The verses were familiar but the names were not, and she refused to keep it in the Belle.

The second bag, Ellen (Altman's to the unknowing), recorded her wild youth, her beauty, her stint as a WAC, her reckless love affairs all over Europe. This bag was full of lies. Pictures of Owl with many men, pictures of young men, of soldiers. Steamer stickers, cheap souvenirs of resorts, a travel notebook with addresses of friends and long defunct restaurants in Paris and Geneva with their bygone prices that made her laugh when she read them. Precious picture postcards of Venice and Rome, maps, coded lists of lovers and near-lovers, voluptuous poems never sent, deceitful and passionate letters written in dark blue ink on light blue mailgrams, every usable corner consumed, including copies of two love letters from a now famous poet, the originals of which she had sold to a collector some years back, proud letters home from around the world saved for her by her Aunt Hilda. Lies. Lies. And what had she left of those European years? She closed her eyes and counted. The taste of absinthe, the blue of ski slopes rushing past (on a forty-eight-hour pass), an endless train whistle, feel of featherbed, the warm body of Jay nestled against her, Voice of America. A headful of stories and no one to tell, a souvenir packet in her shopping bag. Here too she kept her honorable discharge, a yellowed letter from the colonel *To whom it may concern*, and her postwar passport.

The Barbara bag into which the kitten had climbed held the truth of her life. Sturdy plastic bag printed with ugly pink flowers. Owl removed the kitten by the scruff of his neck and peered inside. To look at the bag, who would guess it contained the essence of her marriage? Actually, her second marriage. Her first, her foolish marriage, didn't count. She remembered the name, the wedding, the clothes, the too-high voice of her husband; otherwise, that time was all but lost to her. Was there a honeymoon? She remembered their apartment over the Chinese restaurant. When she thought of her first husband she saw not his face but the bowl of his cherrywood pipe, carved like a head, on a curved amber neck. Otherwise, blank—though she remembered thinking him quite handsome when they met. He'd had a shrill accusing voice which kept her guilty and a forced laugh she came to dread. Now he's going to make that laugh, she'd predict, and he would. Their life? Her days of wedlock were spent in the same office she'd worked in before him and again after him. She remembered the office better than she remembered him. The liaisons, the politics, her dark oak desk, certain conversations at coffee break—Mary B. the Marxist saying she would never invest in the stock market and support the system and Norman suggesting that if she felt that strongly about it then she could always sell short; the would-be actresses in the typing pool. But of their homelife she remembered chiefly the apartment, the kitchenette, the menus and the price of food: Monday pork chops (49¢ a lb.), Tuesday chicken (39¢), Wednesday beef (79¢), Thursday a casserole, Friday fish (39¢), weekends open. A few stories, a few jokes; otherwise, of her first, her childless, marriage, she remembered almost nothing. She'd heard from a neighbor in their building that her husband had remarried almost at once and that his new wife wore Owl's abandoned clothes. This knowledge somehow relieved her of guilt, as if he considered her and her successor interchangeable. After that, though she had worn his name for several years, she almost never thought of her first husband.

But her second husband, that one, she never stopped thinking about. She needed a truck, a warehouse, not a shopping bag. Fifteen years building a nest, making room in the closets, rocking in that rocking chair, cooking, making peace, squabbling, soothing, packing, unpacking. Even now, still, remembering him worried, aroused, servile, enraged could make her sick if she let it. An office romance! She should have known the signs; why hadn't she seen? Finding lipstick on the collar when she did the wash—couldn't he have spared her *that*? Who did he think did the wash? Fifteen years wasted. Sometimes she thought it was wrong to keep Milly's things in the same bag with his even separated by a box of their own (Milly's baby teeth, Milly's class pictures, Milly's Music Prize, Milly's valentines and drawings and poems). If only he hadn't married that bitch. Things were all right till he remarried. He'd left Owl once and come back; why not again? She'd told him he didn't have to marry the bitch, but he was worried about the scandal. Why did he go and marry and take Milly away? It was in this bag that Owl kept her wedding pictures, the footprint of the boy, the divorce decree from Mexico gaudily sealed with sealing wax and red satin ribbons (why hadn't she strangled him with those ribbons?), her precious instruments of revenge. Here she kept the lawyers' documents, the intercepted letters from *her* to Bert and from Bert to *her*, including one retrieved in pieces from the waste-basket and carefully pieced together (where Owl read the awful name the lovebirds called her), one stolen from his wallet along with a picture of them taken on a street where palm trees grew. And the lipstick (Devil Dance) she'd found in the car, and the calendar she'd kept that year she discovered them, on which she'd noted the exact time he came home each night. (And still, despite the evidence, she'd believed his story.) Besides the original evidence, she had newspaper accounts of similar cases, Supreme Court citations, stories and poems that nailed him, her own letters to Bert. She knew she had an airtight case against him. When she filed her suit he would have to answer for ten separate counts: alienation of affection, desertion, breach of promise, incarceration, lies and perjury, false witness, assault, kidnapping, fraud, and deceit! And the damages—how could she assess them? A million dollars at least. Not for herself; she could live on bitterness alone; she wanted them for Milly.

This time she would tell Milly all. No longer would she try to protect her from the knowledge of her father's cruelty. She was old enough now to know the truth. And when she won her suit for pain and damages she would have a million to leave to Milly, and not one penny for Bert. Sister Theresa had once said, "You're still pretty angry at him, aren't you, Owl?" But Sister Theresa had been wrong. "Angry?" Owl had replied. "No, I'm not angry. I loathe him. I hope he roasts in hell!"

The fourth bag (really, two bags, a sturdy brown paper one inside a water-proof plastic one, just in case), named Susan (Shopwell to passersby), commenced after the divorce. It held necessities, all the things she might suddenly need. Welfare forms, elastic bandages, spare bags large and small, flashlight, scissors and knife, paper and pens, a bankbook with a balance of

$236.57 plus interest, a bit of cash, medicine, tape, eating utensils, including her precious fish knife.

She held up the fish knife with pride and wondered again, for the hundredth time, whether it belonged here in the Susan among the other eating utensils or in the Ellen with her souvenirs. Heavy, broad, flat, blunt-bladed silver knife, beautifully shaped, ornately monogrammed with the initials of that unpronounceable inn where the colonel had taken her, it belonged in the Ellen. But if she was not to use it for fish, then it would be only a remnant of the past and like so much of the intricate knowledge she had acquired in her years, wasted. Waste of any kind distressed and saddened her, but particularly waste of experience. It was hopeless to sort her possessions once and for all. She turned over the fish knife and thought how much she wanted to give it to Milly, who had years ahead of eating fish, whereas she, Owl, with no place to cook, might never get to use it again.

I could get a fish from the market and broil it over a trash-can fire, but if I tried to use my fish knife it would be stolen as soon as I looked away. Maybe I should keep it in the Ellen after all, with all the other things I have to thank the colonel for, because never again will I have a fish like that first one. Bless the colonel's appetite—otherwise we would never have stopped for lunch so early. A week with him was enough. Not that I wasn't happy to go with him to France, but when he wanted to stop at "a little inn I know on the Bodensee" on the way back to Stuttgart so soon after breakfast, I objected. Naturally, we stopped. I was along for his pleasure, not mine. We went around to the terrace where tables were set for lunch in the open air at the edge of the still, blue lake. After the base and the rubble of France it was enchanting there; I thought we must be in Switzerland. The waiter frightened me, portly and severe beside our table, waiting stiffly, linen napkin folded over his arm, as we read over the large handwritten menus with red tassels hanging down the centers as if there'd never been a war. "What will you order?" I whispered, afraid of being overheard by the intimidating waiter. "Order on the Bodensee? Naturally we'll order fish," cried the colonel.

Naturally.

As it was still morning, we were the only diners. I was glad not to have to consider the impression of my ignorance on anyone but the waiter. The colonel didn't count, he was used to it, he enjoyed teaching me things which made him feel all the more . . . bighearted, yes, that's how he wanted me to think of him. The sky and lake were a single, perfect blue, cloudless, clear; you could hear the plop and echo of each pebble the colonel flicked into the lake as we waited for our fish. We drank white wine while the waiter removed our dinner knives and replaced them with the blunt-bladed fish knives.

"What are these?" I whispered. The ignorant would have taken them for butter knives, but I knew better; they were far too big for butter knives, they were instruments of some importance.

"They're fish knives," said the colonel. "You know, no steel blade must ever touch a fish."

For all his self-importance, he did impress me, that colonel. I never knew that about fish. I wondered what steel did to a fish.

At last the steaming fish arrived at our table. I don't know anymore what kind it was; the names of fish were always strange. (Untranslatable, said the colonel. Rouget in Marseilles, sole in England, and the birds, too. He said since they lived only in their native habitats there were no translations.) But whatever its name, there it lay on its silver platter, a large fish with a flared tail of silver blue, and iridescent fins as green as a parrot, and a large white staring eye. One whole fish for each of us. Sprigs of parsley and slices of shallot were arranged around them—to make them appear more comfortable on land? But that fish was of the lake; the skin glistened like the sunlight on the surface of the water. I couldn't bear to break the moment (there were few enough magic moments when I was traveling with the colonel) by breaking the shiny skin or cutting off the head. Besides, I had no idea how to proceed.

The colonel shook open the large linen napkin, laid it across his lap, and tucked it into his belt. I did the same. Then, lifting his fork in one hand and the marvelous fish knife in the other, he flourished both and said, "Now watch." I watched, engrossed, as he proceeded to press the edge of the knife into his fish, opening it from gill to tail. "Go only as far as the bone," he said, "but not through the bone. Then slip the side of the knife under the flesh along the bone like this and flip back one side."

The fillet came up clean, whole, and boneless.

"Then do the same on the other side," he said, doing the same on the other side, "and there it is. See the skeleton?" The skeleton was laid bare. "It's ready to be lifted off with the head, and you're left with the other fillet on the bottom, clean as a whistle. That's all there is to it. Now you try it. Go on. Take your fish knife and try."

It was true, the flesh came away from the bones clean and whole, even on my first try. I, who avoided fish because of the bones, had filleted it perfectly. Of course I couldn't leave that enchanted knife behind at the inn. I was not even ashamed. People took ashtrays and towels without a thought; soldiers were going home with paintings from palaces and statuettes from churches, not to mention china, figurines, silver, you name it. I could have asked the colonel to buy me one, but it might not have been the same. I slipped the magic fish knife into my bag.

Reluctantly she put the fish knife back into the Susan, where it would remain as long as she had hope, and turned to the next bag.

The fifth bag, the Gloria, was named for the City Council

candidate whose name and picture appeared on its side. Also known as Miscellaneous (Misc. Gloria, she sometimes said or, nowadays, Ms. Gloria), it held her wig, her other shoes, soap, certain special items of clothing, and sheets of plastic for rain protection which she kept tucked over the top. Here too she kept the cat food and breadcrumbs for the birds, and here she carried the kitten when she went out.

But the bulk of her daily goods—towels, food, clothing for warmth and disguise, books, pots, newspapers and rags for insulation—were distributed throughout her room for temporary transfer to one bag or another. It didn't bother her to spread them about, knowing that, in the end, all things are connected with all other things, making her divisions ultimately arbitrary, like the arrangement of pictures on a wall or dishes on a shelf. Her supplementary possessions too were temporarily stored in an order that sometimes pleased but sometimes troubled her in piles, bags, and cartons around her room. Most of them were reserve supplies or inessentials which, however, gave her the sense of security, even comfort, that goes with being well supplied. You never knew when an emergency would arise. She had three basic wardrobes in case she grew fat or thin again. She kept a full complement of kitchen utensils in case she found a place with a kitchen. She had a line of beauty aids in case she fell in love one more time.

She hoped Milly would recognize the value of her things, but she wondered if they were enough. Money: that was how Bert had won her away. Should she close out her bank account and offer Milly cash?

Owl lay down on the bed in the corner of the room. She was tired, weary of striving. If she got Milly back she could rest. Through the window she saw the tower of a forgotten building, ornately shaped and decorated, whose beauty was now hidden to all but her. She drew the kitten inside the sleeping bag and hummed a lullaby.

8

On the one-week anniversary of Prince's rescue operation at the Port Authority, he did not show up all day or night.

He had drawn their baths and bathed her, he had brushed her hair, he had brought in their breakfast; then he had kissed her a reluctant goodbye, warning her as usual of the dangers of the street.

"Don't worry," she'd said, "I won't talk to anyone. Who would I talk to? I'll be right here waiting."

When dinnertime came and went without his return, Robin told herself he was planning a surprise because it was their anniversary, and she dressed up specially for his return. But the hours came and went without him until midnight ended their anniversary. She took off her clothes and got into bed alone.

For one whole week she had been happy, happier than she'd ever been, more than happy. She'd felt cared for, even cherished. The other men she'd known had only used her, and afterwards had avoided her eyes. But Prince searched her eyes. His interest in her was so keen that sometimes he reminded her of her father keeping tabs. He wanted to know everything, and instead of despising her life, as she did herself, he accepted it, claiming even to love her for it.

Love. She had not believed in it, and then, suddenly, there it was. She knew it by these signs: that he chose to be with her every day he was in town for seven days from the moment he'd met her until now; that he looked deep into her eyes when she spoke; that he wanted to know her feelings; that he brought her presents, watching her face light up; that he taught her how to avoid the police; that he bathed her, brushed her hair, and carried her to bed to make love to her.

Now, without Prince, she plunged into despair. She knew all about disappearing; it was her own best trick. Now, to be its victim, to be left alone like her mother . . . She could not get out of bed in the morning. She lay there all day as her mother used to do, betrayed, but willing him back.

When he finally returned late that evening, she was so glad that she didn't ask about his absence. Instead, she tried to make him believe she had just got into bed. He took off his clothes and lay beside her without a word. When she leaned over to kiss him, he kissed her back quickly, then turned away. "Not now, baby," he said wearily.

"Is something wrong, Prince?"

"I got a lot on my mind, baby," he said, silencing her with a look.

She said nothing more. From the beginning she had been outside his confidence. When they talked it was about her, not him. She knew only that he was of mixed parents, that he'd grown up in the toughest slums of DC, and that he'd served a stretch in the navy. The rest, even his work, was a mystery. She guessed it had something to do with gambling—he frequently telephoned from the bar and at night practiced dealing cards for three-card monte—but he never discussed it. Now she realized she had no idea what he did with his time away from her, what his life had been like before he met her.

The next day too he stayed out until very late. He spoke vaguely of "money trouble," and acted resentful, as though she were somehow to blame. When she tried to be comforting he snapped that she'd better start thinking about what she was going to do now, because he couldn't go on feeding them forever. "Maybe I can find Boots, then," she suggested unhappily. "Boots," he said with contempt; "Boots!"

She was afraid to dial Boots's number again, but the next

day when Prince had gone out she decided to look for her. Not since her first day in the city had she walked the streets alone. Either Prince had been with her, or she had stayed inside. He had filled her head with bleak tales of the fate awaiting runaways: of the sly questions the authorities would put to her, of their clever means of detection. "You can get picked up just for walkin down the street if you're underage," Prince had warned, advising her precisely what to say if she were caught— false name, false age, false origins and residence. "You look like a kid," he said, shaking his head, his voice filled with pity. "You're a setup. Me, I know em, I can take care of em, you're safe with me. But alone on the street? Not a chance." And when she proposed to work as a waitress or a checker as she'd briefly done in Maine, he'd merely snickered and said, "Yeah, can I see your workin papers, miss? Your Social Security card? Name? Address?" So protective had he been that he'd bought her clothes (a low-cut red dress, a sequined shirt, the newest high-heeled shoes) to make her look, he said, "older." But now she thought he no longer cared how she looked or what happened to her.

She walked among the streets vaguely looking for Boots, sinking into a state of lethargy. Instead of exciting her, now the streets depressed her, with their sordid store fronts and dirty windows, their screaming billboards and broken sidewalks, their trash-strewn gutters and grease-filled air. Everywhere she saw ugliness, squalor. Even the excitement of evening approaching, the sparkle of the women, the gaiety of the bars, seemed false as she made her way back toward Prince's place at the Royal Arms. Looking for comfort, she crossed over to peer down an alley at the neighborhood cats whose gull-like cries made her think of Maine. But they were city cats, lean, caged behind a fence, probably mean. A dozen or more moved about, scuffing, scrapping, watching, or crying their endless lament. The alley reminded her of the dark hollows among the rocks, the space under the eaves, the boiler room in the school basement, the ladies' room in the bus station, and all the hidden, unregarded spaces where she too had sought refuge from a cruel or indifferent humanity. "Here, kitty, kitty, kitty," she said, wriggling her fingers through the fence. But they ignored her.

All of a sudden cats came bounding from the back recesses of the alley to gather at the fence, as Robin had seen them do from the window, and she knew that the old woman with the shopping bags who fed the cats was somewhere near.

She stepped aside as the cat lady stooped before the fence. Her large skirt formed a tent around her feet as she reached out to pet and comfort her charges. Patiently the old woman extracted an assortment of newspaper-wrapped morsels from one of her shopping bags, unwrapped them, then pushed them through the fence. Not until the cats were busily lapping the food, and she stood up to steal a look at Robin, did Robin see her face straight on.

She was old and wrinkled. Her grayish skin was marked by several moles and unexpected dark hairs. Her cheeks hung like jowls around her sagging mouth, and her blue, wide-set eyes, now gleaming excitedly, were red-rimmed. Perhaps because they were almost devoid of lashes, or perhaps because the old woman was now staring fixedly at Robin, her eyes appeared extraordinarily round. Robin avoided her gaze, first raising her glance to the uneven fringe of white hair circling the old woman's face, then dropping her glance to the equally uneven hem of her large flowered skirt, which dragged along two torn, dirty sneakers, from each of which a toe protruded.

But feeling the beady stare, Robin could not long avoid the woman's eyes. Though she found her grotesque, Robin stood transfixed in her stare, until slowly the woman raised one knobby finger, took a step forward, and spread her lips into a smile that revealed two appalling things: first, a black hole where a tooth belonged, and second, an intention to speak to her.

The prospect of being suddenly spoken to by a witch so unnerved Robin that she tore herself free of the evil spell, turned abruptly, and fled across the street, not daring to stop till she had reached the Royal Arms. At the distant end of the block, she saw the sunset redden the luminous sky, silhouetting the warehouses against the rapidly descending evening, and she ached for the solace of the surf, for something familiar, for someone who cared about her.

The room was just as she'd left it, empty. She turned the radio on very loud, hoping to take her mind off the image of the toothless witch smiling down on her, now fixed in her eye. She showered, dressed, straightened up the room, dabbed perfume (that Prince had given her) behind each ear, determined to be cheerful when he came in.

But as soon as he walked through the door she felt her own resolution dissolve into his mood. She felt like her mother facing her father, all her will slipping away. If only he'd kissed her, maybe she could have pulled it off. But he avoided her eyes, and when she asked him what was the matter, a small muscle in his jaw began to jump—as if there were trapped words pressing to get out—but he said nothing.

"Please," said Robin, "please."

He looked at her, then clapped his hands. "Oh, what the hell?" he said, relenting, and carried Robin to the bed.

They made feverish love. She felt as if her world had disappeared and then come back. Afraid to ask him what was wrong, she pretended to be happy.

He told her to put on the red dress he had brought her, he was taking her out. He had taken her out before—to bars, for ribs, for Chinese meals; but she knew this was going to be different.

When he was dressed in a fancy suit of cream-colored silk, he opened a small packet of cocaine, which he carried to his nostrils on a tiny gold spoon; then he showed her how to use it.

"You look like a million," he said when she was ready. She had lipstick on her mouth and high-heeled sandals on her feet. She looked up into his beautiful face, his long almond-shaped eyes, and felt that whatever had been wrong was now over; he was no longer angry, he cared for her again, she was safe again.

They went to a small restaurant in what seemed like a private residence, for there was no sign outside, only the name "Continental" on a brass plate beside the entrance. A doorman opened the door, a slender woman in a snaky gown played piano softly and sang low torch songs from Broadway's past while men and women in elegant clothes mingled at the bar. Smoke rose slowly in the softly tinted light. As Prince led Robin by the elbow past the bar, several people greeted him by name and looked her over—admiringly, she thought. A waiter in black took them to a small table near the piano and, after pulling out a chair for her, suggested several entrees that were not listed on the menu. She was proud to be with Prince, pleased to be admired by his friends and served by his waiter, but bewildered by the new way people looked at her. Was it the high heels and the red dress? She felt that Prince must be proud of her, too—as if the dress and he had somehow turned her into a different person.

Prince ordered himself a Scotch and her a marguerita. While she sipped the salty, sweetened drink, he took her hand and told her with stoical regret that this dinner might be their last one together for a long time. "The honeymoon's over," he said, shaking his head.

She opened her eyes incredulously. She could feel the tears welling up.

"Well, what did you expect? That you could just go on living off me? Forever? That what you thought?"

She had no answer to give. She hadn't thought that, but she hadn't thought anything else either. She had simply lived day by day for the entire week they had been together with no idea what would happen to her. "I love you, Prince," she said simply. The tears began to slip down her cheeks.

"Chicks. Don't you know you don't get nothin for nothin?"

She seemed to be hearing a recording of Prince rather than Prince himself. She tried to concentrate on staying upright.

"I was happy to help you out as long as I had the cash. But now I don't have it. My deal didn't work out. Now it's your turn. Now you got to get us some cash."

"But how? You told me I can't get a job without papers. You told me . . ."

He shook his head. "There's plenty of work you could get if you wanted to. Beautiful little girl like you could make us a small fortune if you wanted to. One, two, three hundred a night, easy. There's lots of money around. It would be easy for you. Like *that!*"—he snapped his fingers in the air.

Robin felt her stomach drop. She didn't have to ask him to explain, for somewhere she had always known what he intended for her. Slowly she shook her head.

He shrugged. "You've done it plenty for free, baby, it never bothered you much. You did it for Boots, for strangers. Now you can do it for us. You can do the same thing and get paid."

"Please don't make me," she said, half to herself, shaking her head.

"Make you? No, baby, I would never 'make you.' You've got to want to. For us."

For them? But didn't he want her just for himself?

"Just your body, baby. You save your *feelings* for me."

She shook her head. "I couldn't. I couldn't."

Prince looked at her mockingly. Now she was moaning her "couldn'ts" like so many pleas. But each time she repeated it, it became less and less true, until finally she knew that for him, in fact, to keep him, she could. "I wouldn't know how to begin."

"Anything doesn't come natural you can leave to me."

Now she felt herself grappling to find an out, stalling for each extra moment. "But what if I can't?" she asked weakly.

"Can't? Did you ever have any trouble?"

Oh, she had always had trouble.

"Of course," said Prince, "you could always go home. You could always—"

"But," she interrupted in desperation, "I mean, what if"— her voice was now barely audible—"what if I just *can't?*"

He leaned forward toward her across the table. His eyes glistened. "Can't? How *can't?* You owe me this."

She could see he was beginning to lose patience.

"If you really *can't,* then you'll just have to pay me back what you owe me and find yourself another daddy. Cause this one can't carry you no more."

Prince flagged the waiter to bring them each another drink. As their glasses were removed Robin remembered that she was about to get her period. No one would want her, she rejoiced, while she had her period. When the waiter had gone, she looked up at Prince sitting poised and unruffled across the table and asked soberly, "Starting when, Prince? I'm getting the curse."

"Starting now, baby," he said softly. "Starting now."

Two

9

Although they spent their days in the same ten-block area and frequent nights on opposite sides of the same wall, Owl and Robin seldom encountered each other after Robin had been turned out on the street. To gather enough food Owl needed to search the gutters on the western side of the bus station where the markets were, while Robin was obliged to hustle on the eastern side. Owl's well-being demanded nights indoors and days on the street, whereas Robin had been directed by Prince to work the night shift. Thus, even though Robin took her tricks to the very Hotel Venus to which Owl handed over more than half her welfare money every month, neither one knew it.

The Hotel Venus had once been a minor monument of the area. Richly decorated with moldings and marble, it had been known for its six-story-tall central stairwell, with every stair carved of marble and the entire flight ringed to the top by a delicately turned mahogany banister. Though its graceful proportions were unchanged and its handsome facade was concealed by nothing more than several decades of grime, the hotel, like the neighborhood—indeed, like Owl herself—had fallen on hard times; now the world saw only squalor. A skylight at the top of that graceful stairwell lit up the shame of the once fashionable place, now a last resort for the desperate and destitute. The lower floors were reserved for prostitutes and their tricks while the upper floors had been converted through repeated subdivisions into Single Room Occupancy for the otherwise homeless. The mirror in the forlorn lobby was dirty and cracked. On each landing rotting trash overflowed the containers and spilled across the hall. Plaster fell in clumps from the walls. Faucets dripped ceaselessly, lights burned out and were forgotten, no piece of furniture was whole, the ancient rugs were no longer of discernible color. A glassed-in courtyard beside the stairs, once a source of air and light, was now piled up well beyond the second floor with broken furniture, trash, and the carcasses of several disintegrating pigeons and rats, trapped long before in the shaft—all on permanent display. The tiled shower rooms were dark and musty; the elevator was dangerous. Outside, the facade, with its elegantly carved statue of Venus, who lent her name to the hotel and still held up a graceful balcony adjacent to what had once been a lovers' suite, went unadmired.

Now, in fact, that balcony was fitted out with a formidable booby trap, rigged by Owl as an alarm to secure her room's only window against intruders. Of course the manager complained, seeing only another pile of junk; but given that for the previous year alone police records of the hotel reported three kidnapping-rapes, four dead-on-arrivals, one murder, and eighteen prostitution charges originating under the averted eye of Venus, he quieted down at check time when he got his rent. As for Owl, she felt completely justified. Danger was everywhere. Given such odds, she felt the fewer neighbors she encountered the better, and like most residents of the Hotel Venus she refused to answer a knock on her door.

She had not always been so prudent. In her youth, thinking herself immortal, she had chased after thrills as ardently as any of the young toughs and molls who now strutted through the streets of the neighborhood. She remembered as a child watching a fire destroy a neighbor's house, her first grand spectacle. While great, mysterious, yellow flames leaped crackling into the Buffalo sky, she watched rapturously and envious as firemen in black boots and red helmets trained their huge hoses on the flames and climbed tall ladders to the roof before an enthralled audience. It seemed to her that the worst misfortune of the dead man laid out on the lawn (Eric Ludlow's grand-father, who, it was later reported, had caused the blaze by smoking in bed) was his having to miss the wondrous event. The terrifying spectacle had lit in her a fascination with danger that eventually took her all over Europe. In her fifteenth summer she landed a job near the deadliest roller coaster on Lake Erie and befriended the concessionaire in order to establish for herself free of charge the world's record number of uninterrupted consecutive rides, no hands. For years she recklessly trusted strangers, running off on a whim with some, antagonizing others; she had joined the WACs, taken joyrides on deadly mountain roads, swum in shark-infested waters, made love without precautions, hitchhiked through occupied war-torn lands where people wondered at a young woman alone.

But as she gradually aged, her experience ground her down until she knew even more intimately how predictable were setbacks, how common reversals, how precarious survival, how inevitable disaster. Eric Ludlow's grandfather, jackknifed over the fireman's shoulder, replaced the flames in the center of that memory; after the birth of her child, roller coasters made her shudder. Death could happen in any unguarded moment.

That very morning, in fact, her next-door neighbor, the old man with the terrible cough who smelled up the hallway with whiskey, had left the hotel on a stretcher. Now, as she crossed the lobby toward the elevator, she heard the gossips still discussing him.

"Dead or alive?"

"They don't take corpses out through the lobby, stupid."

"Oh, don't they? Then why did they put him in a hearse?"

"It was an ambulance."

"Was his face covered? Did you see?"

"I didn't hear no sirens."

Hearing the talk of death, Owl decided to forgo the elevator for the safer stairs, despite the weight of her bags and the ache in her legs. Given the hazards, few precautions seemed too troublesome to consider. Like every decision, it required a trade-off: safety for comfort, or comfort for freedom, sometimes one way, sometimes another—nothing was clear-cut. If she were neat enough to escape police detection, the greater her chances of being robbed: the perfect victim was a small, clean, defenseless possessor of several very interesting shopping bags. If, on the other hand, she looked fierce enough to repel muggers, the lobbies of banks and public buildings would be barred to her.

As she was turning the key in the door of her room, she sensed something wrong. The feeling was often with her lately: several people on her floor had been attacked in their rooms in recent weeks while she had been spared. Could she have been saved for something worse? Was this Bert's doing? She put down her bags and, hesitating on the threshhold, peered in. But the single window adjoining the balcony was covered with a velvet cloth that kept out light, the switch was halfway down the wall, and Owl's flashlight had only one battery.

She felt in the Susan bag until she found her knife, but as she was afraid to have it wrenched from her hand and turned against her, she stealthily held it behind the folds of her skirt as she inched her way into the room.

Something hit her knee.

The kitten, leaping toward her skirts, mewing for food. With pounding heart she picked him up with her free hand and, holding him like an amulet, took several cautious steps toward the light switch.

She flicked it on. No one. Nothing. Yet she could not shake the feeling that her room had been invaded, contaminated. Nothing seemed disturbed; still, the danger she'd felt so often lately came through strong and clear. More than a feeling, it was a message, a warning from Beyond.

She knew to respect such messages. A couple of years earlier, a freak auto accident had sent her on a detour through the very intersection where the sisters of the Shelter were doing outreach to homeless women on the very day a fire in the Midway Hotel had left her homeless. The very intersection, the very day! Clearly a message. Or the time she had followed a sudden impulse to go to the dance hall by herself and wound up meeting the person who would introduce her to Jay. That must have been according to a plan. Or the time she decided for absolutely no good reason to demand her love letters back from Jay, the entire collection of them, his and hers, only to learn a week later that he'd been killed. An accident on the autobahn. He'd survived the war only to fall on a maneuver. She could still see the tall, awkward sergeant telling her, as he turned his hat nervously in his hands, how Jay had been thrown from the jeep clear off the road and a branch of a tree had gone through his trachea. "It's lucky he wasn't decapitated," the sergeant had said to her. She had been so shocked that more than thirty years later her throat still ached when she remembered; she would never really recover. A freak accident? If it hadn't been planned, why would she have taken back her letters just then? If she'd done it a week later, it would have been too late; the whole camp would have been able to read their most intimate declarations. So amazing did such "coincidences" seem that sometimes she believed she had powers not only to receive warnings but maybe to control events as well, nor did she rule out powers of life and death. Wasn't it true, for instance, that for several months wherever she went people fell down on the ground in epileptic fits? In the bus station, on the pavement, once two rows behind her in the balcony of the theater where she was watching the last performance of a closing play with Sister Theresa and some of the other Shelter women. She alone had heard that unearthly epileptic cry over the sounds of the orchestra and had gotten Sister Theresa to summon an usher. It had been terrible: they stopped the show, turned up the houselights, and sent someone out onto the stage to beg for a doctor to rush to the balcony. Who knew who else would fall down frothing in her path? And Milly's husband Harry almost died of a fit too when he heard of Owl's impending visit, or so he said.

Owl held the kitten and searched the corners of the room. Now she was convinced her scare was Bert's doing. He knew Owl had a sworn statement out against him and a suit for millions of dollars which, if she managed to find him, she would press and win. And whatever money she won would only be a fraction, a symbol, of what he owed her.

She put down the cat and took a packet of papers out of the Barbara bag.

First: he owed her for the house and all the furnishings he'd stolen—the car, the gardening tools, the rug she'd hooked by hand while she was pregnant with the boy, the picture of the Balinese dancers. . . . Everything but one trunkful of clothes and personals left behind in the attic. He'd driven her mad with betrayals, then packed her off to the looney bin and stolen everything. He'd planned it all—otherwise why had he come back to her after leaving the first time? After her discharge she'd gone back to her house ready to start again. She had walked up the drive and seen a strange car in the garage with Jersey plates (the garage door had foolishly been left open) and a green swing set in the backyard she'd never seen before and a new set of redwood lawn furniture. And the box hedge neatly trimmed. Bert had never trimmed the hedge unless she'd carried on about it. She remembered thinking, looking at that hedge, *Maybe he's really changed*, and she looked around for Milly.

And then she saw a strange woman in a print housedress with her hair in a bun coming through the screen door. *This can't be his new woman*, Owl had thought, *she's not his type, she's too old*.

What do you want? asked the woman in a cold, suspicious voice.

What do you mean asking me what I want. I ought to ask you what you want. This is my house.

Your house, she said, her hands on her hips. Your house. And then she reached up to her dark temples and smoothed back her hair and said, Oh, you must be Mrs. Fox, and now you've come back.

That's right.

Didn't you know this house was sold? Almost a year ago. Didn't they tell you?

Didn't who tell me? I asked. I didn't trust her.

Your husband.

Him. Of course, I thought, this has to be his doing. I looked at her hard. After everything else he'd done, there was nothing he could do that would surprise me. But why tell her? Finally I said, Do you really expect me to believe a thing like that? I knew my own house when I saw it, whatever the woman said; I'd lived there for eleven years. Hey, I said, angry as hell, what are those swings doing here? And where's my daughter, anyway?

She stepped back inside and talked through the screen door. Listen, she said, we moved in here nearly a year ago. They're my kids' swings, we put them up. I don't know where your kid is. The place was broom clean when we arrived, the only thing they left behind was one trunk in the attic. Do you want to take a look? Listen, they should have told you, this is terrible, I'm really sorry, you know?

I'm sorry, she said to me. I should have told her to get out of my house. But instead, like a fool, I asked, didn't they leave any letters for me?

Letters. Where were my letters from Jay? Did Bert steal them too?

Jay's letters weren't in the trunk, just my clothes and all the things I'd kept in the front hall—Milly's report cards and poems, my cedar box, old datebooks, but nothing of Jay.

And that's the second thing Bert owes me for, thought Owl. Jay's pictures. The only two pictures she'd ever had of him Bert made her destroy. Out of pure jealousy. And because she wanted to start out the marriage clean, she'd let him take Jay's pictures and burn a piece of her. Because everyone was trying to forget the war and start again. So many had died, so much had been destroyed, everyone wanted to bury the past and make life grow again. You don't need these anymore, Bert said as he put a match to Jay. I'm going to take care of you now. You don't need anyone but me now.

She believed him. With the war over, the whole country was pairing off, settling down, and moving into new houses like the one Bert bought on a GI loan the minute she got pregnant, a two-bedroom ranch with a front yard and a back-yard. This is okay for now, he said, but just wait till you see how I'm going to take care of you.

Lies: the third charge against him. Now he owed her hundreds of thousands of dollars for ten thousand lies. The Easter he said he was going fishing with two salesmen but he never went fishing. The season he said he was taking an extra line on the road that turned out to be a redhead. And after the boy died and Milly was born, he was never there when she needed him. That time Milly fell off the swing and needed seventeen stitches in her head, Bert couldn't be found at his office, at the customer's, anywhere. Three hours after he left for work, at eleven o'clock in the morning, he couldn't be found. Where was he? By the time she realized he couldn't be trusted she'd buried one baby and half raised another and had forgotten how to fix a light switch. By then she could barely remember she'd once traveled all over Europe, the indispensable right-hand gal of a colonel in the US Army, the fiancée of the handsomest soldier in France. In that township of brand-new houses, where everyone started out equal, nobody had a past. You had nicer parties or duller ones, better eggnog or worse, a larger car or smaller, smarter kids or dumber ones, more money or less money. But no one had a past. Since the war ended people admitted only to futures.

Plus damages, of course, unspecified amounts, for all he had made her suffer. She couldn't begin to name the damages. To every lawyer's consternation, the amount would have to remain unspecified, because the longer she lived the greater the damage, the deeper the debt. And when you counted inflation, time, cost of living, compound interest, the damage became incalculable. Even without adjustments, he could never repay her for the damage he'd done. The debt could only be wiped out by death—

And suddenly Owl knew what was wrong in her room. It was the missing sound and smell of her neighbor. The whiskey smell had been erased by the fumigators whom the city hired to follow two steps behind the corpses and scrub away the smell of death. The ceaseless cough Owl had gradually come to count on had abruptly ceased. In its place was only a silent threat: death on the way.

This was the warning, then, the message from Beyond: death on the way.

She put away her knife and stooped to mix milk for the kitten, sprinkling powder from a box into a saucer of water. She hoped it would forestall death (though milk from her own breasts had not saved the boy) and welcomed the scream coming from somewhere down the hall. Indeed, if one day the familiar scream failed to come, she would worry, she would wonder why, she would mourn, so precious were all the signs of life, even the questionable ones like the sound of sex coming through the floor and walls that most nights kept her awake.

The first night Robin took a trick into the Hotel Venus as Prince had instructed, she was so terrified that her trembling fingers could not undo her buttons. (Later they laughed about this, and she took the street name of Button.) On the street where Prince had left her with praises, reassurances, and a few brief instructions as to price and procedures, she had been merely numb. Standing alone, she had talked the project up as an adventure (thinking of Boots) and down as just another job, reminding herself how sex was nothing but a diddle and a squirt and how in the past she had been able to do it painlessly with strangers and how the worst that could happen was she'd lose her nerve and be back where she was when she'd arrived. Carefully she observed the way the other girls along the street posed and spoke their lines, until the first man approached her. It happened so quickly, she didn't have time to be afraid. She performed by rote, following her cues like an actress in a play, reciting lines she had memorized. He said his, she said hers, and she was proud of her performance.

But once she was alone with him in the second-floor room of the Hotel Venus, she began to sicken and shake. All alone on an island with the tide coming up and no boat to save her.

He was her father's age, of medium height but solidly built, even plump, with hardly any neck and a beer belly and small gray beady eyes that frightened her. The minute he closed the door behind him and leaned against it, his eyes, terrifyingly bright, bore right into her. She thought there was murder in his eyes. (She had seen that look before!)

Frantically she looked around for some escape. But the tiny room was barely large enough to hold the bed, one broken folding chair, and a small drawerless bureau. She remembered each detail of the room, that prison: Room 206. Graffiti on the wall in nail polish: Indio y Esmeralda, Feb. 7, 1978. Ancient, green-flowered wallpaper, ugly stains on the floor. The patched and repatched door frame, betraying many forced entries, offered no hope. The ceiling was pocked with bubbles of bulging plaster, the remnants of years of unattended leaks which now threatened to burst through like crashing surf. The wall behind the sagging bed was disfigured with gouges and holes where the ill-fitting headboard had been banged repeatedly (and she knew how!) against the wall. In the corner, a small marble basin, cracked and discolored, echoed a faucet's steady drip. The only light, a bare bulb screwed into a wall socket, left her in semidarkness. The single window was covered by a gaudy paper curtain tacked to the frame, disguising whether beyond it lay safety or death.

How had she managed to pull a madman for her first trick? She suddenly felt frail and tiny and young, a country person in a big city. She backed toward the window corner, afraid to anger him by screaming but ready if necessary to jump.

Instead of pursuing her, the man stopped at the bed, removed his pants, tossed them over the chair, and lay down. Once his pants were off and he was flat on his back, Robin felt a giddy surge of relief. She remembered the giant Ferris wheel in Birchville. Hanging in terror at the top, nothing below you but sheer drop, then a sudden lurch, a plunge—and just in time, as she felt her heart ready to burst from her and save itself, the reprieve from annihilation that returned her safely to the ground.

She began to giggle, then laugh, like someone suddenly saved. Laughing, her hands shaking, she fumbled with her buttons.

"What's so funny?" asked the trick. Now, he seemed not frightening but ridiculous.

"Nothing, really," she said, but went on laughing.

"Come on. What's the joke?" He raised himself on one elbow and peered past his belly.

"I'm just embarrassed," she said coyly.

"Aw," said the trick, "you want me not to look?"

Suddenly she couldn't wait to tell Prince. Suddenly she remembered everything he had told her to do—get the money up front, fill the basin, soap the washcloth. Now she was eager to do it right and get it over with, for she knew that this act, completed, would somehow bind Prince to her as nothing else could.

At last the buttons yielded. As she pulled her top over her head ("You want me not to look?" he said again) embarrassment flowered into contempt.

They were partners now, Prince had said. He had promised her a golden charm to wear around her neck to commemorate her first trick. He had given her a pep talk and advice, then had taken her by the hand down to the Hotel Venus where he'd introduced her personally to the night porter Vego and had shown her where to stand a few doors down on the stroll.

"I'm in your corner, baby; remember that," he had said, squeezing her hand. "Now you got to show me you're in mine." Then he had let go and moved away.

"Prince!" she called after him, afraid to let the next moment come. "Wait."

He turned and blinked his eyes. "Baby?"

"Tell me what I'm supposed to say."

He smiled and shook his head. "Nothin, baby. Trick's not buyin conversation." And as he continued walking away, leaving her to stay or run, she saw her choice.

The bed creaked as she worked her first trick with her hand, getting him ready. A cat was crying somewhere near. She hoped, as she remembered hoping before, that he would come quickly, that her hand might even be enough. The cat went on, like a crying gull at dusk swooping over the rocks (and the sky behind the distant pines streaked with red, and her mother on the deck with a cigarette in her red hand).

The trick put his hand on hers and gave her his rhythm. "A little faster now, sweetheart, like this. That's a good girl."

She listened for the wind in the pines and the surf pounding against the rocks. But she kept hearing the cat cry, and her heart went out to it.

Owl opened her eyes. Flash of red and green neon at the dark window behind the velvet cloth, harsh music through the thin walls; bass guitar, something rattling the glass, monotonous thud, thud, thud of sex.

Once Owl wouldn't have cared about the sounds of sex, or, if she had, would merely have turned up the music on the radio. But in recent years she had become a light sleeper, with fear or memories lurking behind every sound, and her radio had long since gone to thieves. The walls, thrown up quickly to make ever smaller and smaller rooms, were thin enough to be kicked through. This knowledge kept her alert. The moans and thuds of sex were indistinguishable from those of assault; the sounds of pleasure were like those of pain. Whereas once it would have taken a great disturbance to wake her, now all it took was that monotonous, steady thud.

She unzipped one side of her sleeping bag to check the kitten. She knew she shouldn't let him sleep with her, for how would he ever learn to survive in the alley? But somewhere she had lost her knack of discipline and lived by the kindness of the moment. She stroked the kitten, accepting her wakefulness, and, listening to the sounds, imagined lovers.

In Roma, in Munich, the walls had been thicker, the rooms made for love. Even the crumbling palazzos with their peeling paint were adorned with ornately framed mirrors on whose gilded moldings smiling cupids sometimes rode. Outside, rubble might still fill the streets, but inside lovers lay intertwined, fresh curtains hung at the windows. When the love sounds came through the walls up went the music out of modesty. Fox-trots and waltzes had played on the GI station, war songs, "The White Cliffs of Dover," gay songs of homecoming, and love songs about remaining lonely and faithful and true. Owl closed her eyes, moved her body rhythmically, and hummed a tune from the past. Sometimes, she recalled, if there was wine, we kicked off our shoes and danced in the rooms. And if he had a thirty-six-hour pass we called it love.

The rhythm from below stopped abruptly. Was it to be three tricks an hour, then, all night long? Twenty minutes a trick, cash in advance, plus ten dollars at the desk protection fee for transients. TOS's they were called: Tricks Off the Street. Pulling in fifty dollars a night and more. No wonder there were fewer and fewer rooms for rent to ordinary people. The manager did anything for money. He could forbid pets, true love, but TOS's with their moans and groans that kept the residents awake were perfectly acceptable. Money, money, money.

Owl remembered hotels in other times where people cared about other things. Not only the rich had nice hotels (though she remembered the Excelsior on the Via Veneto in Rome where the prostitutes were movie stars, and the thieves were some of the richest and shrewdest men in Europe and fat King Farouk of Egypt sipped aperitifs with his entourage). She also remembered the poor pensions on the Ramblas of Barcelona with their iron balconies and white-washed walls over-looking the fresh flower stalls, where, when you wanted to go home, no matter what the hour you clapped your hands and a gatekeeper appeared with a great ring of keys to unlock the door for you. She remembered the antiseptic Swiss pensions where, even in the hotels of the lowest class, your room was spotless, there were two fat pillows, and you were treated with respect. She remembered the cold rented rooms of London where bed and breakfast included tea with your landlady, who tucked a blanket over your legs at teatime to make you cozy and even covered the teapot with a fitted quilt on the frostier days and always heated your bed at night with a bedwarmer filled with hot coals. She remembered the funny room in Paris she had shared for a month with Jay before they sent him off to die: the ancient floor slanted steeply, the walls had layers of flowered papers going back centuries, the WC in the hall was often clogged or occupied, for that winter there was an epidemic of dysentery in the quarter; but the people made that one the nicest room of all. Almost immediately Fouchet the concierge began sending a fresh flower in on the breakfast tray, sometimes a carnation, sometimes a rose, to celebrate the presence of lovers. (How French! Jay had said.) Later, they discovered the flowers came from the trash can across the street next to a theater where Fouchet's young daughter played; but that only made the gesture nicer when you thought about it. And even in the poorest quarter of Naples, where it seemed everyone was forced to steal or sell themselves at the end of the war, Giuliano, the one-armed youth who sold his cousins to officers, shared his food with orphans.

But here! Now! How many times had she found herself swearing to leave, to sweep her belongings into a blanket, throw her whole life's remains into one of the laundry carts left standing unguarded in the halls while the maid was cleaning the transients' rooms, and depart?

But then it would begin to rain, or the sun would shine familiarly on the little cactus on the windowsill (if it was morning), or her sleeping bag would look too worn to make the move, and she would remember that people had grown cruel everywhere (for times had changed and she was an old woman now); and here at least she had only two flights of stairs to climb to her room.

Yes, she was lucky to have the room at all. Sometimes she wished she were the sort of person who could simply stay inside her room for days at a time. Some did. There were even groups of volunteers who regularly dropped in on the "housebound" to make sure they hadn't croaked. But for herself, she would have found such a life unhealthy; she would rather drop in on the volunteers. Indoors for too long one suffocated. If she were the sort who could stand being a prisoner even in her own room, then she'd have been better off submitting to a home, where at least her meals would be provided, or the grave, where they'd be unnecessary. But she was not yet ready for oblivion. Shut up inside she knew she would soon be forgotten. Whereas, on the street, around the corner a free breakfast awaited her, it was only two blocks to the bus station, the neighborhood cats and birds now counted on her, and soon she would invite Milly to stay with her. Better to live as she did than risk the unknown. The rent, though exorbitant, was manageable if she was careful about everything else; the neighborhood, though alarming, was familiar. And though she no longer had a radio, she could start music in her mind at will to drown out the sounds of sex, and use the past for entertainment.

The thumping had started again; someone was banging on the wall. So what? Her nights of easy sleep had long since vanished; it didn't matter what went on in the rooms below. Her window stuck, soot piled up on the sill, the neighborhood was finished, the whole world had gone to hell. Bombed-out buildings, dirty kids begging in the streets, selling black market cigarettes, coffee, older sisters, meat. Where had the time gone? What had happened to the years? She wanted to save one more memory from oblivion before it was too late. Tomorrow she would start. She would try to arrange her things in some inevitable, irreducible order, strip down, consolidate, and prepare her room for Milly.

Noisily Owl collected into one small compact mass the thin layer of nighttime phlegm that lined her throat, rolled it along her tongue, and with precision spat it into the litter box. A beginning. She rezipped her bag, buried her better ear, and selected . . . a tango.

10

As he waited in their room at the Royal Arms for Button to come back from work, Prince slapped the three cards between his fingers, shuffled them, and called to an imaginary mark:

> "You can win and your money wins too.
> Pick the red, forget about the black.
> Pick the Queen, forget about the Jack."

He liked the rhythm of the monte rap, the charm you had to use with it. Three-card monte was a cleaner game than poker, more challenging than craps, requiring speed, skill, psychology, and art. The player needed a magician's sleight of hand and an actor's presence. He'd been a shill and a lookout in other men's games, but now he wanted to move up into his own game. He was good, but not yet good enough. Even experienced players sometimes made mistakes that cost them ten to thirty days in the joint. He'd been in once; that was enough for him. He wanted to raise his game so high he'd never have to worry about the joint again. One day he hoped to join the top players in real estate, banking, government, gold, men who were rich enough to be jailproof. Work didn't scare him: every morning and every night he did an hour of pushups, deep knee bends, and one hundred shuffles, just for investment. A true player was on the job twenty-four hours a day, always ready to pursue an opportunity. Because if it was you against the world, you never knew when you might have to split; you always had to be ready to live some other way. You couldn't afford to have only one game or be dependent on only one person.

That was the mistake most people made, trusting others when folks were really out for themselves. He'd made the mistake himself once, getting married. Even his own mother had been a chump, putting all her faith in one disappearing man. Leaving her family in the barrio near Manila, leaving her home, traveling all the way to Washington with a baby inside her to search out a tall, fair-haired, balding man who had told her only lies. Finding instead? Work, work, and more work. For years she waited, praying in church, enlisting priest and neighbor to petition the government, finding nothing. She was so single-minded that not until Prince was twelve years old did he understand the truth: his father had never wanted them; his mother would never find him. No matter how much she prayed or slaved or preached right and wrong, Prince could see there was no one in the world to do right by her unless it was Prince himself. His father, on whom she pinned her hopes, was of no more use to her than he'd been to Prince. Prince's white blood meant nothing to the handful of neighborhood white kids, though it won Prince hostile looks when his black friends talked about whitey. Who was he? He didn't know. He only knew that he had been duped no less than his mother.

He learned many things that year he turned twelve and wised up. When his class moved up to junior high, an almost all-black school, the very whites who had excluded him because of his mother's eyes were themselves excluded from the newfound pleasures of the street. He was glad to see them put in their place, even by the girls whose kisses were prized and who preferred his looks to theirs. Neither black nor white but always the exception, he studied the ways of both. Hanging out on the street, he copied the walk of one friend, the smile of another, the jive of a third, learning how to move ahead. His mother, a saint, was also a fool, trying to hold him back. Though he wore a cross around his neck to please her, he knew that the dead life of the believer or the slavery of the trusting was not for him. That year he made a private vow: to outsmart every-one. He valued brains and cunning above all. Not school brains that studied books (which he mastered in the arms of girls who lent him their homework to copy and let him crib off their tests) but a man's brains that mastered life. He'd wanted all his options open.

And still did. Because you never knew what might happen. You could spend all your time on your main lady—making the necessary appearances on the stroll and in the bars, checking out the new arrivals, staying in shape, arranging your woman's ID, medical checks, comfort, bail, knowing the movements of the heat, giving up a little dick—and still she could go down to work one night and never come back. She could decide to blow (like Sissy), she could get herself busted, copped, even killed, and there wasn't much you could do about it. Like the poor suckers who got themselves killed in Nam, while he cheated death by joining the navy. But even on a ship, or even with two or three women working for you, it was an insecure life. One night they could all run off, and then? With most chicks it was cop and blow—cop one week and blow the next. And it was hard work copping, you couldn't hope to catch every day. You could run down your best shit six days a week and still draw a blank or lose out to the competition. So you had to do your pushups every morning and do your shuffles every night and keep your eyes open for every chance to lift your game.

Button came into the room, dropped her purse on the table, kicked off her shoes, and collapsed onto the bed.

Prince put down the cards. "How you feelin, baby?"

"Okay."

"Just okay?" He walked to the bed, knelt beside her, searched her face, and kissed her mouth. She looked troubled. "Somethin wrong, baby?"

She started to say something, then hesitated. "Just tired, I guess."

But there was something in her voice that bothered him. He'd have to figure it out fast; this might be the moment he'd either lock her or blow her. He tried every way he knew to ease her job, tuning her up with candy, jewelry, and smoke before she went out, tuning her down with baths, rubs, and understanding when she came home. But the pressures of the street were hard on a fresh young ho like Button, and it took skill to get her thinking like a ho.

"Anything happen you wanna tell me?" he asked, gently stroking her cheek with his knuckles.

She closed her fingers over the gold heart he had given her to wear around her neck and shook her head.

"Okay, then why don't you just lie there and rest yourself while I fix you a bath? Close your eyes and relax till I call you." He turned back his shirt sleeves, picked her purse up off the table, and walked back toward the bathroom.

Robin closed her eyes and waited on the bed while Prince ran her bath. Usually the thought of the bath awaiting her when she came off the street got her through her last few tricks, but tonight nothing would relax her. For the first time in the week since she'd been hooking she hadn't made her trap. She was afraid of what Prince would do. Since it was the first time, maybe he'd let her off; but she'd listened to the other hos enough to know that coming in short was serious. Lana wouldn't have dared go home short; her man would think she was stashing money for herself or taking time off the job. Robin wanted to explain to Prince that it wasn't her fault; it was simply a slow night, the tricks hadn't chosen her, maybe she just wasn't made for hooking.

When she could smell the lilac bath salts, she took off her clothes. Soon Prince came in from the bathroom, took her hand, and led her to the tub. He was big on washing. He'd bought her a douche bag, bubble baths, bath salts, mouthwash, and assorted lotions and scents. Just as he kept their shoes heeled and shined, their clothes laundered and pressed, he saw that their hands were manicured and their bodies clean. On the island she'd seldom taken baths. Her father's grand future plans for solar heating meant they had to heat their bath water on the wood stove. In summer when you could bathe in the ocean no one ever bothered and in winter the air was so cold that the water cooled down as soon as you got in. Until Prince took charge of her body, she hadn't known what pleasure a bath could be. Until Prince took care of her, she hadn't known what it was to be taken care of.

He splashed her gently with the warm scented suds, then took a bath sponge from the shelf and, starting with her toes, washed her all over, working slowly up her body, bathing away all the bad she'd felt that night.

Always before she had loathed her body—the knobby knees, the smells, the pubic hair. But knowing herself under Prince's care, she came to see her body as a thing of value and even, when he washed her, of loveliness. Besides insisting she use the douche bag twice a day, he made sure she took her pill each morning and her bath each night. He scheduled her for a monthly visit to the doctor—to check on her "little gold mine." Now he was patting her dry with clean towels, gently rubbing her thighs, placing a sweet kiss on her navel.

"Come to bed and I'll rub your back for you," said Prince, throwing the towels in a heap.

While he kneaded her shoulders, she closed her eyes and fell immediately into a half-sleep. She wanted to stop, sleep forever, never go back to the stroll; she wanted to ask Prince to let her quit, or at least to lower her trap. But she knew he would never agree. If she gave up hooking she'd have to give up Prince, and that she couldn't do. Only a couple of weeks, but he was part of her now; even in her dreams she was hooking.

. . .

He kneaded her shoulders and watched her doze. He had counted her money and found her short. So that was the problem. Now he had to decide how to handle it. Some pimps would discipline their bitches for being a penny short, but Prince liked to think he played a higher game. Of course, every bitch needed a certain amount of discipline and maybe an occasional scare to keep her in line. But if you felt you had to use threats of force all the time on your woman, then something was seriously wrong. Because as soon as she saw the opportunity, that woman was going to cut out. You couldn't just blindly follow the rules. You had to know your woman. With a kid like Button, affection was better than discipline, she was so grateful for every little bit. If you scared her she would probably run. You wanted her trusting, not afraid. Trust was her greatest need, and therefore her weakness.

Not that he wouldn't play on her fears if necessary, but they had to be fears of what would happen to her without him. Getting picked up, being sent back home—these were the fears she harbored all the time. It would be stupid to threaten to hurt her, like any dumb popcorn, when her own natural fears were working for you and a hint would probably be enough.

He watched her firm young flesh resist the pressure of his thumbs and wondered why she was short, what she was doing wrong. Young pussy ought to draw the best; that was why he risked the dangers of baby-pro. (If a kid dropped a dime on you, you could pull seven years.) He doubted she was holding out on him. In fact, if he trained her right and she didn't burn out or get hooked on junk, he believed she had the makings of a first-class ho. But like anyone in the life, she had to correct her mistakes and keep lifting her game. Maybe now was the time to teach her how.

.   .   .

She opened her eyes abruptly to Prince's voice. "You know, baby," he was saying, kneading the last trick's touch out of her hips, "I notice you're a little short tonight. That's not good. Now don't worry, I'm not gonna send you back out there tonight, though you know I have every right to. I just want to talk it over with you so you can learn some better ways to make your trap."

She was angry and grateful at once. "Thank you," she said, unable to voice the complaint that rose like a welt in her heart.

"Forget it, baby. If I had money comin in and it was you here countin on me, I expect you'd treat me just the same. You'd rub my back; you'd do the listenin. When I have money in my pocket, you can be sure my lady's gonna have money in hers. Right now, my lady's the one out there workin. Naturally, when she comes off the bricks after workin all night, I got to make her feel good. She's got to know that her work is appreciated. She's got to feel glad she had that opportunity; otherwise, why's she out there at all?"

It was true, she was out there for him, because he took care of her; that was the deal. And he did his part so well, how could she not do hers? He kept saying he only needed a little more time to tighten up his own game, and then he had big plans for them. He wanted her off the street and back in school, "taking care of the brains." She'd have liked to hear more about his plans, but she didn't want to press him. When she was suspicious, so was he; when she was trusting, he relaxed. He called her his lady, slipped spending money into her pocket, dressed her, fed her, bought her anything she wanted, took her hand when he walked beside her as if he was proud. He thought about her life, her future; since he'd paid off his bills and got back his wheels he was even putting money in a joint bank account for them. How could she ask for more? But she was glad she was lying on her stomach so he wouldn't see her face.

"How we ever gonna get ahead if you keep comin in short? A few nights like this and we'll be really hurtin. There's lots of things I want to see us doin, things you ought to have. Like a nice warm coat for winter made of some soft, pretty fur. And a diamond ring like mine. Hmm? I'd like to see you back in school, too. But all those things cost."

He was waiting for her comment, but all she could think of was how she wasn't really a whore at all, she was just an understudy who'd landed the part for two hundred dollars a night and ought to feel lucky to have the break.

"I'm real proud of the way you been workin, Button. You're a smart little girl; you learn fast. But now it's time for you to spread out, climb on up to the next step. You got to make your trap and save your body at the same time. For example, you could start doin a little creepin."

"What's that?" she asked. She was an actress and Prince was her director, her audience, her fan, waiting in the wings with a bouquet of flowers, ready to praise or criticize her performance.

"Basically, it's very simple. After the john takes his pants off, you make sure they're hangin over a chair right near the door. Then when you're workin him over, another ho—your partner, Jacki, say—will creep into the room, slip out the wallet, take out the cake, and put the empty wallet back. If you're doin your job, trick's too busy to notice a thing. You get on top, kinda cover his face, let your hair fall down on his eyes—that's all there is to it. You do the same thing for your partner, and you split the take, fifty-fifty. Now isn't that a ways up from just layin on your back all night?"

"But that's stealing," said Robin, alarmed.

Prince smiled. "Stealin? From a trick? I wouldn't call it that. I'd call it gamin. You got to remember, every trick is basically out to game off you. Now it's up to you to turn that game around. A trick'll rip you off every chance he gets. You don't believe me, just forget to ask for your money up front some time and see what happens."

It was true. They always tried to beat her down. "But what about later, when he finds out?"

"What about it? You're just as surprised as he is. You don't know a thing about it. He was with you the whole time, right?"

"But what if he sees?"

"What if he does? He sees someone else in his pants, not you. You don't know nothin about it. The way he's dressed at that moment, he's not gonna go chasin your partner, either. That's the beauty of it." Prince's voice purred with satisfaction. "And you can always run off before he's in his pants again."

Robin knew she could probably run faster than any trick, in pants or out. Running was her specialty. But if he went for the police? "What if he gets a cop?"

"Come on, Button, use your brains. What's he gonna tell a cop? 'I was fuckin with this ho, see, and someone rifled my wallet, officer. I don't know who she was, officer.' No, forget your what-ifs, baby. Creepin is just part of the game. It's a matter of skill like all the rest."

He turned her over onto her back and smiled down at her, while she studied his beautiful face. She hated everything about his plan, but she was too exhausted to protest. Even when she was fresh, he could sweet talk her into anything. Now all she wanted to do was sleep.

"I just want to see us get ahead, baby, that's all. If you're goin back to school, we only got the summer to work with. How you make the trap is up to you, you know that. But creepin, you can make it in half the time. Think about it. Smart little girl like you is gonna come up with the right answer, sooner or later, I guarantee."

11

Usually Owl tried to get back to her room by dark. But today was Saturday, and Saturdays she stayed out late to feed her cats. On Saturday a certain fish store threw out whatever fish wouldn't last the weekend. Then Owl took an extra plastic bag from her reserves, filled it with fish treats, and walked directly to the alley. The pleasure she took watching her cats gobble up the fish and lick the last morsels from their whiskers and mouths made up for the fact that her own meals lacked such luxuries.

Now, returning late to the Hotel Venus, her munificence was rewarded. For there across the street was Milly again, playing dress up, walking up and down the street on high glittery heels with the other whores.

Bert would never permit Milly to go hooking! Then, thought Owl, she must be on her own and Owl might have a chance to win her back. She got out her glasses for a better look.

How the time flies, she thought. The old-fashioned shoes are back again. The high spikes with ankle straps, glittering platforms, silver ornaments, open-toed sling-back pumps, and the round-toed ones called babydolls. Wait long enough and everything returns: long skirts, short skirts, long hair, short hair, low heels, high heels, even the wonderful hats—their day is coming too.

Now, thought Owl, I could wear a comfortable blouse from any year and sneakers that fit; but poor little whores refuse to be seen in last year's clothes. . . . Whores? Just little girls dangling cold butts from their lips, Lucky Strikes or Camels, cheap men's cigarettes, same as in the war. Hardly anyone actually smoked them, of course; they brought too good a price to smoke. Like the soldiers, the girls also knew how to trade them for better things. Owl wondered briefly if anyone ever smoked them, or if they just went round and round, tobacco money?

Owl feared she had nothing to offer Milly now. All the beautiful clothes, the spring hats and pastel toppers and little white gloves Milly had loved to wear, all were gone. In the Misc. Gloria bag she had nothing of value but a bit of old lace and a curly brown wig she had picked up at the Shelter. (Sister Theresa had insisted she take the wig, saying someone had donated two hundred shiny new wigs and what were they to do with them?) And some very beautiful old jet buttons. But nothing with which to buy Milly. For without a doubt she was up for sale. For rent, at least. Owl wasn't surprised. She'd seen it in the war: young girls in bombed-out cities and even in Paris, selling themselves for their next meal. The soldiers paid for a night or a week or even bought them up for life, taking them back to the States like black market treasures.

She had to admit she had sold herself too—down the river, into marriage. She should have known better. She'd seen the faithless officers, she knew what happened to wives. She'd been reluctant to become one a second time, but Bert had convinced her to trust him. Then he turned out exactly like the rest. His betrayals—so trite, so predictable. Lipstick on the collar, out-of-town trips, furtive phone calls, erratic hours, a sudden interest in new subjects, new music he'd never listened to before. Oh, she could tell. After so many years a wife could certainly recognize the signs.

When he'd finally confessed, it turned out he had not one woman but a string of them, all kinds of them, a private phone in his office, a room in town. He was no different from all the rest!

"But Lilly," he said, "they meant nothing to me."

"Get out! Get out! Get out! Get out!" she screamed, and went on screaming long after he had gone.

For herself, she thought she would not have cared, seeing how he was. But for Milly . . .

"Where's Daddy?"

"In California."

"Will he come back for my birthday?"

Seeing Milly weep, Owl wished needles sunk into the centers of Bert's cold brown eyes, she wished his hands scalded in boiling oil and worse.

"I can't talk to you when you're hysterical, Lil. Get hold of yourself. I'm going to count to five and if you haven't calmed down, then I'm going to hang up the phone."

Even now, when she read over the letters she had sent to him in California she would weep or scream again. Even now. After she left the hospital her bitterness, like the bitter poison deep inside the convoluted pit of the peach, continued to poison her, keeping her half-crazed. Her letters to him preserved the bitter taste, she still carried them in the Barbara bag, a strong bracing spice to flavor her hate that she could take in small or large doses whenever she chose. On doses of poison she grew strong, she grew fierce, her bitterness gave her strength and reason to live. Now she was very strong. She needed no one.

A man with a limp approached Milly and her friend. Owl knew what he wanted, what they all wanted. Owl wished she could spare the girls. None of those men had anything to offer but cash, whereas Owl was willing to share a lifetime of treasures, knowledge, priceless love. What a pity there were so many children sleeping in doorways, begging on corners, selling their favors, or she would take all of them home. She wanted to rush up to the two girls, hug them, whisk them off the street, give them something to eat—fruit, chocolate, something to delight them as the fish had delighted her cats, something to make Milly hers again. She wanted to fold her child into a shopping bag, take her to her room, and begin to show, tell, and explain. She would start with now, pour out her heart, explain the shape of her life, how she had come to this, then go back and back and back until the vise of the past came open and Milly finally understood.

The man with the limp had gone off with the other girl, leaving Milly alone. Now was Owl's chance to make her move. Oblivious of oncoming cars tooting their horns, she lifted her bags from the curb and moved into the street. Screeching wheels swerved close to her, puffing out her skirts. What did she care? Across the street she marched, lugging her bags, her eye on Milly, until the light turned yellow and a long van hurtled to a stop, cutting her off. "Dirty old bag!" shouted the driver, honking his horn. "Account of you I miss my light!" Now all the horns were honking as she stood her ground in the middle of the avenue, stranded behind the truck, unable to see through it to the far side of the street.

Let them honk, she didn't care. Old bag? She could not be dismissed so easily. If she'd waited for the light to change, she could have lost Milly. Let the cars wait instead. She pressed ahead, swinging her bags, weaving among the cars as the light changed again and the mad traffic resumed.

When she finally reached the other curb, she saw Milly running up the stairs of the Hotel Venus with the colonel close behind her. Owl could hardly believe her luck. After all those years of thinking Milly dead, to find her staying in her own hotel!

Quickly she would prepare her room for company and invite Milly in.

As soon as they got to the room, the trick moved close to Robin, explored her face, and in a voice barely over a whisper offered her an extra twenty if she would give him a golden shower.

"What is that exactly?" she asked.

He laughed gleefully at her innocence. "You just sit on me the way I show you and . . . urinate."

Her eyes opened wide as she stared at him. "You mean, pee on you?"

"You got it, honey. Do it and this is all yours." He held out five crisp tens. "Don't worry, I'll tell you exactly where to sit and what to say. It's easy. Think you can do it?"

Robin looked longingly at the bills. Almost as much as she'd get for two plain tricks. "I don't know. Maybe you should explain it first."

"Okay," he said. "Here's what I want you to do. You're a little kid, see, on your way home from school. You've gotta go real bad, you're practically peeing in your pants. When you get to the corner there's an empty field—right here." He patted the bed. "You know you just can't hold it anymore, so you go into the field and take off your pants and squat down. Meanwhile, you don't know it, but I'll be waiting right there in the bushes. I come up and—" He shrugged his shoulders. "That's it. I get under and then you pee. Okay?"

Robin wondered what Vego would have to say about her getting the bed wet and if the pee would come out at the moment she wanted it to. "I'll try," she said, taking the money and slipping it into her pocket.

Owl offered the kitten a fish treat and explained her plan to him. She would divide everything into three rough categories: those to be saved, those to be reconsidered, and those to be dumped, in preparation for Milly's return, for the room was a mess. Invoking her old rule of travel, she vowed to keep nothing she had not used in a year.

But as soon as she set herself the task, it became clearly impossible. That rule of her youth no longer applied. For one thing, it assumed a long future in which there'd be plenty of time to replace whatever might be hastily abandoned. But having long since turned that corner beyond which her future was a rapidly diminishing fraction of her past, whatever she dumped she would probably never recover. And how could she tell when her reserves, now piled to the ceiling around her room, might be required? For another thing, such a rule was mindless of the irreplaceable value of the old. That no one else wanted a thing was to her reason in itself to preserve it; the most precious creatures in the world were the nearly extinct. For these reasons she was afraid to part with anything. Even her books and magazines, seemingly dispensable, she was reluctant to give up, for those she'd read were now part of her, and as for the others, having once assessed them readable and lugged them to her room, how could she prematurely jettison them unread? If she had had access to a library, then she might, in the interest of order, have gritted her teeth and banished them all. But the library—that great, vast storehouse of the past, that enviable public monument to order, which she circled every day—was barred to her as long as she refused to check her bags. And recklessly check her bags in a public checkroom for any clerk to ransack was one thing she could never bring herself to do so long as she was free, not even for access to all the knowledge in the world. It would be like placing her soul in a 42d Street checkroom. If she could do that, she could use a public shelter (where they searched your bags), submit to a home (where they emptied them), consign herself to a hospital, a suburb, or a prison (where they confiscated them). No, she could as soon abandon a wounded bird as return a treasure to trash.

Her head was beginning to throb from the effort of fighting against herself. She could assign each object in her room a value on whatever scale she chose; she could class an item essential, important, of interest, possibly useful, worth considering, unimportant, unnecessary, probably useless, and so on, to as narrow a category as she liked, but she could not consign it to oblivion. Let there be a thousand classes, or a thousand thousand, to choose from; the lowest would remain empty. The only way she would ever be able to reduce her inventory was to stock a shop with her treasures and sell them off, or let it all go up in flames.

She sat down on her bed and lit a cigarette. The kitten leaped into her lap. The fact was, she had accomplished no more than to divide her possessions into new and subtle categories spread all over the floor and shift them from one spot to another around the room. To be "reconsidered" later—all of them. For to decide firmly one way or another what to keep and what to dump required an exact knowledge of the future, or a disregard for it, equally beyond her capacities. Of her own future, she knew only that she wanted it to end well. She could not afford to enter it ill-equipped. Whatever she had so far failed to acquire, she would probably never have; what she had failed to accomplish would remain undone. She was formed, fixed. She could not change herself even for Milly; Milly would have to adapt to her.

She decided she would be content if she could simply pile the piles higher to clear off the table and chairs for a place to serve Milly tea, and empty a spot on the floor for Milly's sleeping bag. The Fourth of July was approaching: celebration time. She would pick some flowers in the park to brighten up the place and hope for the best.

At the start of rush hour on Friday, to the signal of a cherry bomb prematurely exploded in Bryant Park, a flock of pigeons rose as one, soared over the park, circled the great New York Public Library, and with a whir of wings landed on a lintel above the side entrance, touching off the long weekend on 42d Street. Below them on the sidewalk a virtuoso combo, consisting of a youth on alto, another on tenor, and a seasoned old-timer on vibes, took up their instruments to blow holiday spirit into the hearts of office workers now heading for the subway and their long-awaited holiday weekend. The summer's first; the hustlers' best. Downstairs in the subway station, a pickpocket couple (he the jostler, she the snatcher) searched for the unlatched purse or the carelessly pocketed wallet as each customer left the token booth. Across the street the un-flappable three-card monte team, consisting of Sweet Rudy shuffling, Bluejay as shill, and Prince as slide, used more subtle means to separate the suckers from their cash.

> "You can win and your money wins too.
> Pick the red, forget about black.
> Pick the Queen, forget about the Jack.
> Pick the red, get your money back,"

sang out Sweet Rudy, dealing a red queen and two black jacks onto a hastily upturned cardboard box. Prince listened to the music of Sweet Rudy's rap while he watched for signs of police. He knew it by heart—the rhythm of the words, the feel of the cards slipping between the fingers, deliberate and devastating, like whispers slipped between lovers' lips. He practiced the shuffle every day, those movements fast as the flick of a tongue, the tips of the cards bent like winks, the lightning signal to the shill, the split-second timing, the teasing play of win and lose breeding confidence and greed. Soon, now, he would be ready to deal.

Of course, the slide was essential too. Without Prince to warn of danger, Sweet Rudy would not be able to concentrate all his skill on the cards and his attention on the mark. But anyone could serve as lookout, and what Prince had in mind for himself was not for anyone. He wanted to be on top, call-ing the plays himself. It wasn't just the flash of the game that made him want to deal, though he longed to show off those skillful fingers and seduce strangers with his tongue. It wasn't so hard to entice a sucker into thinking he could pick the one red card out of three and then prove he was wrong. Nor was three-card monte, which any dude could pick up quickly in the joint, particularly high game. Working in the open, you risked arrest, and splitting the take with at least two others, you couldn't get rich off it. But you could get smart. Unlike mugging or thieving, buying or selling, or working for chump change, monte was a mind game requiring discipline and nerve that could train you for life. It gave you capital for higher game, kept you careful, and best of all, gave you a quick win. It was the start of all Prince wanted: to impress, stay out of jail, and win.

Once he had been inside for fifteen days. A six-by-eight cell with iron bars, twenty watts of light, a dripping faucet, a clogged piss hole, and three cellmates, all losers. That was all, that was enough. Fifteen days to think, fifteen nights to feel bugs crawling through your bed, to breathe the stench of vomit and filth, to hear junkies sob, to see men humiliated like animals. Shortly before he was to leave, a young hustler named Black Oscar joined his cell, replacing one of the losers. Small and alert as a weasel, Black Oscar used jail like a training camp: starting the days with sit-ups and pushups in the cell, running in place on mess line, dressing in his prison garb as if he were going dancing in custom clothes, making contacts and conquests at every meal, befriending the guards, using his spare minutes to make plans, dealing imaginary cards in his bunk at night. Respectfully Prince watched him, amazed at the possibilities of life in a cell, regretting his own wasted days. On the day Prince was to leave, Black Oscar asked him to deliver a message for him when he got out; Prince accepted the mission as if it were a personal gift.

Later that day, just before he was released, Prince suffered a lecture on the future from the warden. "You're young. Your life is ahead of you. No one can decide how to live it for you. Except you. You can work for a living or you can wind up back in here. It's up to you to decide. We've got plenty here who haven't made up their minds. They're in and out, in and out, till one day they find out they're in for good. Ten years, fifteen, twenty-five, life—you name it. Now, you can go out and find yourself a job or you can go right back to the street. Be a winner or a loser. Think about that, young man. It's all up to you."

Prince had been thinking about just that, hard, for fifteen days. Long enough to play right past the warden and his jive. The only chump jobs he could ever get were just like being in the joint. Break your ass for a paycheck too small to let you live and wind up back inside anyway. No, he had decided; he would give himself a break. Walking out that prison gate into the sweet autumn air with Black Oscar's message and trust, he knew he could never again be a chump working for pennies and death if he could be a player working for riches and life.

At a signal from Sweet Rudy, Bluejay adjusted his black eye patch, donned his most earnest look, and put two tens down on a losing jack. Two marks in jackets and loosened ties groaned no in unison. "I know where it is. There's the red," said the towheaded mark, bending toward his friend. "Isn't that it?" asked the other politely, pointing.

Sweet Rudy spread his lips upward like the tips of his black mustache and thrust a twenty into the mark's hand. "The money's yours if you call it right. You want to bet? Put up your cash and I'll let you see it."

But both marks refused the money, taking a step backwards.

Down the street rolled the plain green Chevy Prince knew as the wheels of the pussy posse. As slide, his job was to spot the blue dangers—marked cars, uniformed men. Lately, plainclothesmen had been entering the game, changing the rules and the odds. Sometimes Prince wondered why the police even bothered with pussy and street gambling when the rest of the world did the same things for higher stakes. How did they draw their lines? Now, you never knew when a mark or a trick would flash a badge, when a bag lady would turn out to be a decoy or a bum stand up and make an arrest. It got harder and harder to tell who was gaming and who was for real, or if there was any difference at all, with plainclothesmen tricking players, players gaming off squares, hos off tricks, pimps off hos, the rich off everyone. The whole world was into it. Even the squarest square thought he'd outsmart the rest when he tried to pick the red. In the end, thought Prince, you could only tell the chumps from the players by who won and who lost. He let the green Chevy roll on past without sounding his alarm, knowing it was stalking female game, and wondered if Button was where she was supposed to be.

Sweet Rudy picked up Bluejay's bet and with a sympathetic grin turned up the losing black. "Almost," he said consolingly, falling back into the rhythm, "almost but not quite. You can win, all you got to do is play it right. Pick the red. Pick the red. Pick the red." Again he threw the three cards down on the box in quick succession, capturing the longings of the growing crowd. Under and over he dealt out the cards, face down, while all up and down the block, every fifty yards, wherever a game was set up, marks emboldened by shills reached for their wallets.

Some people, thought Prince, were dying to lose. But what did he care as long as his team didn't? One blast of his whistle, one shout from his lungs, and the team would kick over the box and disappear into the crowd as quickly as the cards flew under Sweet Rudy's fingers. Each would pivot on his heel, push his hands into his pockets and join the marks, leaving no trace of the game but a cardboard box. "Beautiful," said Sweet Rudy proudly each time they reconvened safely around the corner for another go.

That day they'd already played four different gigs. Between two and three the team had bagged three hundred plus from the paycheck-happy crowd emerging with stuffed pockets from the bank conveniently located at Fifth and 43d Street. "Like Willy Sutton said," observed Bluejay, "you got to go where the money is." Following the money, they snagged another two from afternoon shoppers several blocks up Fifth. Now the money was en route to the bus and train stations in the pockets of commuters on their way home, and when that supply diminished, they could work the visitors coming in. Bluejay had carefully plotted their movements to coincide with the movements of the marks. "Marketing," he called it.

Bluejay bet another twenty, this time on the bent card, the red. "I knew it!" repeated the towheaded one, as Sweet Rudy paid Bluejay off, two for one.

Three pretty teenaged girls sharing an ice-cream cone sauntered by, catching Prince's eye. "Hey, pretty baby, got a lick for me?" he called, flashing his best smile as they came abreast. They turned on him with a snarl. "Fuck off, jerk!" "Punk!" "Pig!"

If he hadn't been working he would have shown them who was a punk and who was a pig. "I'll get you later," he hissed menacingly, marking them as dykes or libbers from the way they screamed. It disturbed him deeply, the way the world had turned. People had revolted against nature. In Tahiti he had seen the way life ought to be, but here, it seemed, men were giving up control and everywhere women were taking over. Soon no one would even remember what nature meant. With their power slipping away every day, men became lax, weak; some even sold their manhood, their bodies, to other men, like low-down hos. No wonder women thought they could walk all over men. When men acted like women, women were free to act like men. And even the best of women, like his mother, who wanted nothing more than for her man to rule her, were forced to live unnaturally. He sent her money when he could, but not even money could make up for his father's failure. Every man who went against nature made it worse for all the rest. No longer was there any respect. Men who couldn't control their wives turned into tricks, forced to buy what nature gave to them by rights. He watched the three bitches swing on into the crowd as if he didn't exist. Sometimes, he thought, he'd like to let go and smash heads.

And then he saw them—two men in blue moving in fast from across the street. Had the chicks been decoys sent to distract him? No time to think—he had to sound the alarm. He shoved the whistle between his lips and blew two shorts and a long, loud and shrill. Too late? "Slide em up!" he yelled, wildly waving his arms. He leaped for the corner, his heart thumping, as the other players, transformed into pedestrians, disappeared before the approaching police.

Prince turned the corner to see someone who looked like Button with her arm linked in a man's cross the street. She could be cheating on him or working overtime, or the chick could be someone else. No time to check on her now. Behind him another whistle blew. More cops or another slide from another game? Four games in the block including a dice game called cilo had dissolved like raindrops in dust at the first sound of the whistle. In their place, clutching twenty-dollar bills, stood several bewildered marks, now doomed to live out their lives without knowing if they had been denied their just winnings or luckily saved from scam.

In that eternity between flight and safety, when anything could happen, Prince wondered if in the end you could ever really know who were the chumps and who the winners.

12

Owl woke to a sharp, hammerlike clap just outside her room. The kitten tore across the floor, from their mattress to the door and back again, where he cowered in a corner. Gradually Owl focused her eyes. A man was leaning against the door, just inside, staring down at her.

It was dark in the room; only a periodic flash from across the street relieved the darkness; yet the man's feverish eyes glowed bright, his long narrow teeth shone iridescent in a demented grin, his greasy blond hair glinted as it brushed against his shoulders, his narrow nose was like a blade, and his watch, buttons, and belt buckle flashed a harsh metallic flash.

Let it be a dream. A dream? Yes—for her failing senses were perfect again!

But everything was happening too fast to be a dream; too fast and too slow. The man grinned. Her heartbeat raced, her breath stopped, the pulses were pounding in her ears so that she couldn't hear, her hands were icy, her knees uncertain, all the tempos and temperatures of her body were madly out of whack. One minute she was dozing and the next she was staring up into an absolutely terrifying grin. How, without breath, would she continue to *live*?

Slowly the truth seeped in. A man. Half grin, half leer. She couldn't look away. She filled with disgust at having placed herself in this predicament. It was check time; she should have taken double precautions. That day she'd cashed her check and paid her rent and everyone in the lobby knew it. Paying her rent set her up for the jack rollers. She should have waited or gone to the sisters; she had *known* it was unsafe at the Hotel Venus.

And she had seen that face before, too. Once near the bus station in front of a grown-over lot where a burned-out building had stood (that was the first time). She was sure now that it was the same face, same man she had noticed standing alone, his hands thrust deep in the pockets of his long jeans, his shoulders hunched over to disguise his height, that demented leer on his face. Creep, she had thought, first seeing him, creep! creep!—and in the same moment had regretted the thought, knowing how people looked at her with loathing too. Still, she had crossed to the other side of the street (just as people often crossed away from her), but those bright feverish eyes and grin had stuck in her mind. She recognized it several times again after that, as she saw the man alone in a doorway smoking cigarettes on her own street, doors from the hotel. Yes, it was the same man; with her sudden super-vision she was quite certain, even in the dark, of the nicotine stains on his long fingers with the bitten stubs of nails—drifter's hands now tugging at the buckle of his belt.

Belt! Then it was not her money he was after, it was herself!

He took one step toward her, slowly, that mad look on his face. Her bags were out of reach. Terrified, she forced herself to her feet, bracing her body against a pile of cartons against the wall. Seconds more, she knew, and his belt would be open and then his pants—and once he had gone that far he would never retreat until he had her. If she had only been awake, if she had only grabbed the knife she kept in the Susan bag, she might have plunged it into his middle, or hit the bull's-eye of his Adam's apple on that too long stem of a neck. What loathing she felt; she tasted loathing on her tongue, felt it constricting her throat; each discrete instant of this passage was suffused with loathing that filled her mouth, making her fierce enough to kill. But her bags were out of reach, there was nothing but papers and old clothes in the cartons at hand, and she had no other weapon than her body, herself. Herself—all but useless against the hulking form leaning toward her with that hideous grin. Yet she had to act—now—before the hands were done, now! Instinctively she opened her mouth and let out a terrible rolling scream.

He could have silenced her forever with one well-directed blow; still, she had to scream. She had led several lives and known many men, some needy, some dangerous, some careless, some cruel; but until this moment she had never felt such rage. Enraged by her own terror, she could hardly meet her attacker without puffing out her feathers and fur, without arching her back, hissing, fluffing her tail, like the animals and birds she fed, letting loose her most ferocious cry. It was not a calculated scream, for she had not even known it was inside her; yet it was deep and necessary, a missile with which she pitted her will against her assailant. It filled the space they shared, it spilled into the hallway, invaded the corridors, rang like a siren through the empty street, shrill, resonating, desperate; she heard it rise and build, becoming an impenetrable wall of sound, a barricade against that monstrous leer. On it rang, one long, unflinching note, and far above it like dream music she heard her voice weave intricate flourishes of sound that carried her high and away.

Those feverish eyes were glazing over and she thought she saw the grin intensify into a look of pain. She increased the volume of her scream, higher, higher, as high as she could go. She wanted to deafen her assailant with her scream, stop him, turn him back, obliterate him. She would never have guessed such a scream lay waiting inside her.

His eyes wavered, feared; his hands fumbled on the belt; she saw him hesitate—and then very slowly they began gliding apart, he was growing smaller, less sharply focused, he was holding his pants together at the waist, backing out of the room. He turned and fled.

. . .

Robin had grown accustomed to the screams and cries in the Hotel Venus, as she had to the sirens and the sharp crack of trucks backfiring on the street. A moment's panic, then calm again. But this scream was such a long wailing cry, like the wailing note of the foghorn in Hewitt's Sound, that she forgot herself. "Jesus, what's that?" she said, breaking the rhythm of the trick on the bed; for fishermen could founder on the shoals in such a fog, boats could break, men could drown, wives would worry and get drunk.

"Don't worry, honey, please," said the trick, moving her hips with his hands. "You gotta keep going and I won't take too long."

The way he swallowed his words and glanced sideways at her from behind his glasses, she could tell he was half embarrassed, half ashamed. And when he came right out with apologies, pitying her for having to service him, she almost pitied him for needing her. For however unpleasant this flabby, defeated flesh (turkey throat, drooping breasts, Buddha belly attached to the little pink penis), she favored it over the proud and dangerous kind. She looked down on his face, thrashing back and forth as she moved her hips in small circles, and felt her pity drown in contempt. Tricking was like Indian wrestling —seeing whose contempt was stronger: his toward her for selling it, hers toward him for buying it. For there was power in being able to buy your way, but there was also power in being desired. She'd learned that from Jacki, whom Prince had entrusted with her instruction. Now, hearing the trick grunt (and the scream still coming through the wall), seeing the sweat on his brow, Robin knew she had learned the lesson well.

Jacki was a large, impressive woman: fleshy, big-boned, generously endowed. She had a large head with double chins, round pink cheeks, big brown eyes, a pouty mouth with brightly painted lips, and mounds of coarse bleached hair. Perfume and smoke preceded and followed her. From her full breasts and huge swaying hips she abruptly narrowed down to delicate feet pressed into narrow shoes with high spindle heels, in what seemed a precarious balance. A sophisticated lady from Virginia, at twenty-eight she was the bottom lady of Sweet Rudy, and an old hand in the life. "What does a man know about this work, honey? Now listen to me." ("Listen to Jacki, she's a very smart lady," said Prince. "I'd trust her with anything but my life.") Jacki had taught Robin many things: Turn down any trick you have a funny feeling about; always get your money up front; go twice for no one; save your body; stick to Swedish massages (by hand), or French (by mouth), and only go Spanish (between the breasts), Russian (between the thighs), American (a body roll), or Danish (inside) if it's worth the money. Never go longer than fifteen minutes for one trick. "The meter I use," said Jacki, sounding like Boots with a drawl, "is a cigarette. I light up when we get in the room, and when that cigarette burns down, that's it, I'm done. For special customers I light an extralong."

Now Robin was able to win the contempt match much of the time. Her island training served her well, confirming what Jacki said about the work: once you overcame the initial embarrassment and could tune out trick talk, it was just a job, better than free fucking or working for chump change, with plenty of drawbacks but with plusses too. "Where else," asked Jacki, "can a girl like me hope to land a job that pays fifty thou' a year working my own hours with no references?"

Jacki showed her the practical side of hooking. The first afternoon she dropped in on Robin, bringing with her a box of fried chicken and two large chocolate bars, it was a little after two. Robin had been up for about an hour and Prince was out. Jacki announced she had come over because her own TV was broken and she didn't want to miss her soaps; but privately

Robin wondered if Prince hadn't sent her over. True, Jacki did turn on the TV as soon as she arrived and pulled a table and chair up near the set, but the sound was off from the start. And as soon as Robin returned from the kitchen with beer, Jacki led right in talking.

"The things I've seen," she said, opening the box of chicken with her long red nails, then taking a bite of thigh. "Listen, nothing surprises me. Around here you see everything. Some of these tricks are so sick I feel sorry for their wives. One old fart, a big lawyer downtown, all he wants to do is to howl at me like a wolf—owooooo—and another one wants to hear me panting. They probably stepped out of the same wet dream. And a couple of my regulars want nothing else except to dress up in my clothes, especially my shoes and underwear. I charge them all extra and give them what they want. What do I care? I'll listen to them howl, I'll pant, I'll tell them how gorgeous they look in lace, I'll do anything they want as long as they're not diseased or dangerous and they pay. I'm building up my capital. Do you know how to check if they're clean?"

Robin shrugged and chewed on a mouthful of chicken breast.

"You don't need a doctor to tell you how to spot disease. It's easy. But I've still known hookers who've gotten so sick they've had to leave the life. I think that's the sickest, not taking care of yourself. Me, I've got too many big plans; no john's going to infect me! If you do what I say, you'll be safe, too, Button. You're young. You've got a dozen good working years ahead of you. You can build yourself a small fortune if you're smart."

A dozen years! Prince had promised her she'd be off the street by the end of summer.

"As soon as you get into the room with your trick," said Jacki, "you fill a basin with warm water and get it soapy. If Vego tries to cheat you on the soap, you just talk to Prince. At the Hotel Venus you're supposed to get clean towels and soap with every trick; only the key is extra. Anyway, once you've got that water good and soapy, you can start working on him. Use the washcloth first if you want, but then use your hands. If you're doing it right you'll be getting him hard while you're soaping him up. You'll be rubbing his prick and tickling his balls with your nails and talking real sweet to his cock. You'll tell him how you think his great big cock is your personal ticket to heaven. Then he probably won't even notice when you milk that prick like this"—she took Robin's hand and gently squeezed up and down on her thumb—"and watch carefully to see what comes out. If you get anything yellow or pus-y you give that john back his cake and send him on his way. I don't care what he's paid, believe me, whatever it is, give it back, it's not worth getting diseased. You'll be the only loser. But if you just can't afford to lose the bucks, or if you think he'll freak out on you, then you could give him a hand job or use a condom and wash yourself real good afterwards, and then go see the doctor. Some girls always use a condom and skip the examination, even if they're on the pill. You're on the pill, aren't you? Personally, I think they take too long coming with a condom, but it's up to you. With a condom it's not even messy."

Robin half agreed. Nurses and doctors had it messier, maids and masseurs. Robin herself had had messier jobs. When her mother was trying to kick, she vomited every time she swallowed water, and Robin was the one who cared for her. As she cared for her brothers the summer the Red Tide got the clams. Even cleaning fish for her father during mackerel season (and for a lousy eighty cents an hour he never bothered to pay her, talk about chump change!) was messier.

"But for myself," continued Jacki, "I wouldn't let a sick trick near my pussy or my mouth, even with a condom. I take care of myself, my body. You should too, Button. I give myself a vacation from the street for at least a month a year, just to clean out my system. Even if there isn't any heat I give my body a rest, maybe work a while as a stripper, get a change of scene. It's too easy to burn out in this life. I've got too big an investment down there, I've got too many plans, to take unnecessary risks."

"What kind of plans?"

"Didn't I tell you? I'm going into business. Very soon. I've got it all figured out. A beauty parlor with a mini-boutique in the front where I'll carry a small line of exclusive items. All class. Perfume, jewelry, maybe leather things, designer stockings, cosmetics—stuff like that. I'm going to do the whole place in white and glass and one color, maybe fuchsia. The ceiling will be fuchsia with recessed lighting and music and probably fuchsia chairs. I've got a collection of catalogs with all the kinds of equipment. Dryers, sprayers, shampoo chairs, and booths—you name it. You're welcome to come and see. Sweet Rudy says we've already got half the money saved up."

Robin was impressed. She had no plans. To find Boots or maybe a rich john; to be an actress or a stewardess and ride in planes and travel; to get to see Adam and Billy again. But her hopes were more a feeling than a plan. Prince was the one who made the plans.

"And another thing," said Jacki, picking the last crumbs out of the box, "watch out for pacemakers. Look them over for scars, on the chest of course, but sometimes on the legs too. It sounds unkind, but it's no joke when they croak on you. You don't want to be there, believe me, and the heat all over the hotel. It happened to me once, a trick died before I even got started. He just plops down on the bed and never gets up. There's this trickle of blood coming out of his nose, and I can't wake him up. Hey, I was scared. A bloody fuckin nose! I thought for sure they'd try to pin a murder on me. I didn't know what to do. I wasn't even sure he was dead."

"What did you do?"

"First I got him dressed. That's when I saw the scar on his chest. I knew what it was, cause other tricks had told me about theirs. Now I can recognize them half a block away."

"And then?"

"Then I split and phoned the desk clerk from a booth. They called the hospital to take him away. But he was already dead. It was too close for me. After that I worked as a stripper for a few weeks till I got my nerves back."

Nerves. Jacki said success on the job depended on your nerves. No matter what they said, you had to remember they were just johns and not let them get on your nerves.

That was the part Button hadn't yet mastered and maybe never would. She'd been at it for weeks now, but her nerves had got worse, not better. Prince was pushing her to do more specials, but she could still barely manage the regulars. There was always that moment with each new trick when her stomach dropped, her hands started sweating, and she wanted to run. She tried to dismiss her fears, remembering that, as she'd learned from the boys peeking into her tent, it was she who had the laugh on them; but the contempt she'd cultivated to use against shame was useless against fear.

But where else could she make that kind of cake? She hated the job but she loved the cake. Prince said that at a chump job (*if* she could get one) she'd be the boss's trick and have to work all day long for what she made off one twenty-minute trick of her own. In one night on the street she made a waitress's weekly wages. In a month she'd have enough to send for her brothers, get her nose fixed, trace Boots, buy two tickets to California, anything they liked. A little more time and Prince could buy new wheels, she could go back to school. . . . No, she couldn't think of quitting now, just when they were moving ahead.

The future was so long. Anything could happen later. She couldn't get into making plans like Jacki. Already she was a different person from the one she'd been a month before; when the summer was over and they were ready to move she'd be another one still, especially if she got a nose job. In a year she might be flying, in five years she could be married, and in ten years . . . But ten years was forever; in ten years she'd be twenty-six. Maybe she'd be rich and famous by then. Or maybe dead.

She was relieved when the scream finally stopped. At once she got the rhythm back again. After that, it was only seconds till the trick came. With the condom it wasn't even messy, just as Jacki said.

13

Owl lay curled up for the night in a recessed doorway across the street and three doors down from the Hotel Venus in clear view of her window and balcony. The kitten was tied by a ribbon to her waist; the Barbara and Susan bags were heaped as a makeshift pillow. Nostalgically she watched the window of her abandoned room, trying to remember the names of all the things she had stored upstairs that were now fair game for the looters. Her things! Her things! Soon now her legs would go too; without a bed there was no way to save them. Already the swelling had worsened, the blue veins pressed dangerously against the skin. Already she was plagued by painful cricks in her back and neck when she awoke in the mornings stiff, stooped, weighted down with fatigue.

But what else could she do? This was as close as she dared approach her now contaminated room. Up there the sick leer of the man she modestly chose to call the Flasher (though he might have been worse) hung in the doorway, awaiting her return. Owl could almost see it reflected in the luminous green of the neon sign flashing GIRLS, GIRLS, GIRLS, the teeth gleaming in rows like the bars of a cell rendering her room a dangerous trap. Each image of it, of him, made her shudder. Not even her bed, reduced by him to a dispensable luxury like love or meat, would entice her back, for what was a bed compared to freedom? A bed was the bribe they held out to get you in a hospital, a home, a shelter, a brothel. . . . No, she'd rather do without a bed than be trapped alone in a dangerous room or be locked up for life. Part of her had to be glad, even grateful to the Flasher for exposing that terrible baited trap of a room in time for her to escape!

The great thing was, she was still alive. She had cheated death and the Flasher for another week, and though she no longer had a room to offer Milly, at least her best bags were beside her or else safely locked in a locker. Perhaps one day soon she would feel safe enough to return to her room to rescue the few important things she wanted for Milly, since her rent was paid up for the rest of the month. If not, she would make do. She had survived on the street before. She knew several abandoned buildings and all-night offices where she could go in case of rain, and an alley where she could change her clothes unobserved. But as for sleeping, she preferred the safety of the crowded street where even in the deep of night she could hear the songs of sailors in port and the murmur of vice, and between naps she could keep an eye on Milly plying her trade across the street.

Owl closed her eyes to watch Milly out the kitchen window playing in the backyard. In and out of the garage she ran with that exuberant squeal, now fetching a rake for gathering leaves, now carrying tiny teacups, now playing hopscotch on the driveway or jumping red hot pepper through the rope, her yellow hair flying up and swinging down. The customers with their hot desires who stalked these girls up and down the block, then followed them into the Hotel Venus, reminded Owl of the neighborhood boys chasing the girls back into their own yards at dusk.

When Owl looked up she saw a soldier looking Milly over. Owl knew why. But couldn't he see she was just a child playing dress-up? She was teetering on those too-high heels, nervously twirling her handbag before her like a kid forgetting her lines in her school play—*couldn't he see*? But of course he saw; he didn't care. Just like a soldier. Thinking all he needed to take her away was that uniform and money.

Maybe nothing ever changed. She remembered her own unbidden passion for soldiers in uniform, that delicious long-

ing that never let up, that secret consolation of war. She remembered her first. She still carried his picture in the Ellen
bag—one of those pictures you took in a drugstore booth for a
quarter and that came preserved in a small metal frame. A
stranger on the way to the German front who offered to help
her find her way to the right platform, he had invited her to
have a drink with him. How could she resist the lure of that
uniform?

He cocked his head at a charming angle, rubbed his jaw,
tipped his soldier hat with a smart little bow, and took her
hand. Then, in the station bar, unwilling to release her hand
(for there was a war on and time was short), he persuaded her
to miss her train.

For half a second she hesitated, afraid to expose her inexperience; and weren't soldiers shipping out supposed to be
dangerous? But her eyes were drawn to his chevrons and medals,
she couldn't keep her hands off his khaki sleeve, and who was
there to stop them? There would be another train at midnight
and another the following day.

They took a room in the station hotel and were asked no
questions, for he was a soldier with a pass in wartime. Time ran
differently then, remembered Owl; you didn't have time for the
usual questions, you wouldn't suffer the usual inhibitions, you
seldom told each other your real names. Beyond the inescapable
fears—VD, pregnancy, fate, and hopeless love—there was
nothing to hold you back. Time was short—one night—and
weren't final nights of war reserved for love?

In that snapshot of the two of them, their sepia faces shone
with such eagerness that she deduced the picture had been
snapped before they'd gone to the hotel, though in truth she
no longer remembered. "For lovely Lilly from Alexander the
Great" was gallantly penned across the bottom—some private
joke, the meaning of which she had long since forgotten; for
her lover's name had certainly not been Alexander. Whatever

it was (Steven, maybe? Charles?), he had gone to Germany, she had had word of him once or perhaps twice, and then no more. Later, after she had enlisted herself, she heard he had probably been killed. She forgot the details (it was so long ago) except for a few. He had given her a box of Russell Stover chocolates and a red rose as he said goodbye (tipping his hat with a smart little bow), he drank rum and Coke, he smoked— Camels? But she forgot.

What she didn't forget—what she remembered with perfect clarity despite the years—was the disturbing way he got up to wash himself preceding and following each sexual touch; how he placed a towel over the sheets and then, when they were finally exhausted, how he slept in his underwear when she longed to feel him close against her.

At the time she accepted his fastidiousness as her due, even as thoughtfulness. Her inexperience kept her from knowing that men who so rigorously insist on the rites of cleanliness are either men who go with whores or men who have been impressed by the hair-raising hygiene lectures fed to GIs. Eventually she came to treasure the smell of sex (of love), the feel of a spent, sticky man against her, the dampness of his body and the sheets. Even then, she would have relished his lying on her with all his weight and sweat. But being shy and inexperienced, she said nothing. That he hardly touched her body with his hands or lips, as if she were somehow dirty from the start; that he ignored her inexperience (for she had confessed to knowing intimately only one man before him); that he leaped out of bed the moment he awoke in the morning, though she had been waiting half the night for him to wake up and renew their kisses; that he said nothing tender or reassuring to her afterwards, though earlier he had remarked on her eyebrows and lips, even tracing them with his fingertips, were details she would often remember over the years. His name was gone, but not his ways; and whenever she looked at the photograph she would compare him and his ways to men who had excited her less but loved her more, men who delighted in her body and gamed with her mind, men who loved and licked and treasured her. With the knowledge found in new experience and every passing year, she would judge him anew—sometimes more harshly, sometimes less. But that night she'd ignored his slights, attributing his habits to the mysterious ways of soldiers (he was her first), or to the fears instilled by war, or to her own vast ignorance. That night, carried away by the sheer thrill of sleeping with a soldier, she thought only how beautiful were the buttocks of a man and how fine it was to be able to rub against that lean body (underwear aside) all through the night while he slept without his pulling away. He came as a gift. He did not hold her in his sleep like a husband or fit himself against her like a spoon against a spoon; still, she was able to lay her head against his chest and throw her leg across his leg and twine her fingers in the curl of his hair without his drawing away, and over breakfast admire his magnificent uniform.

"You sure do go for this uniform, don't you?" he had asked, catching her eyeing him, embarrassing her beyond words. (For indeed, she did.) Was he insulted? "I wonder why?" he continued. "It's just a uniform. We all look alike in them, don't we? They're all the same."

She had demurred, feebly protesting, insisting to herself as well as to him that it was *he* she loved (Steven? Alexander? Charles?) and not the uniform at all. She had loved her soldier all the night; the feeling had been strong and new and pure; long after the war surely (she insisted) she would love him again.

But after the war he was gone, and what she remembered was not him but her own feelings—how exciting to be with him with his chevrons and medals and soldier hat perched cockily on his head (as in the picture), and how thrilled she was when he touched her and how confused when he washed her away.

There had been many others since, whose names she had also forgotten; she had learned to spot a soldier half a mile away, for a while she couldn't look at a civilian. She was sorry he hadn't come back, for she had wanted to get to know him better, get him to trust her enough to hold her naked through the night, feel that feeling again. Still, after that terrible war had ended (and a new one had begun), she knew she could always recapture the delicious secret of that wartime night simply by watching the springy walk of a dark-haired khaki-clad soldier; all it took was a photo, a uniform, a longing, a little imagination. What did the details matter? Or even his name? She could get the feeling now without the insult, she could have it any way she chose; for it had happened long ago and had lodged in her soul, she had loved an unknown soldier all night long, she could feel him inside her still when she closed her eyes, he was almost certainly dead now, and she was alive.

Robin had begun to consider herself one of the luckier hos on the stroll. She had been working six days a week for a month, turning more than half a dozen tricks a night, and had never once pulled a cop, a gorilla, or a freak. Not that she thought her life charmed; she still tensed when each new trick approached her. But unlike some of the sad hos in Sallee's Coffee Shop who recounted new tragedies every day, or the human wrecks who slept in doorways reminding them all of what could happen, after a month of steady work her worst fears seemed to be unfounded, and Robin felt more oppressed by the tedium, the squalor, and the dreary hours of her profession than by the well-known dangers.

Then one Tuesday night her luck changed.

The night had started out slower than usual. After standing for an hour in the same doorway as always in one of her better outfits, she was still waiting for her first trick. Hot and bored, she lit a cigarette and gazed up at the sometimes red, sometimes blue, but now green lighted tip of the Empire State Building, thinking how like a lighthouse it was, a beacon warning passing planes that this was New York City. When a sudden breeze blew up her skirt, making it billow out like the skirt of Marilyn Monroe in the poster in the window across the street, Robin imagined herself a flight attendant, walking hard against the stiff jet wind of her superliner, her hair blowing straight back as she climbs the stairs to the cockpit, just behind the pilot. Flying high, she looks down on the great lighted city and thrills to recognize below that landmark of light, the Empire State Building. The familiar green light signals to her that in another minute she will be flying directly over the scene of her own astonishing youthful triumphs. Down there, back then, when she was only sixteen, she'd held her own among the most accomplished and wicked women in the world. She, friend of jet-setters, confidante of the famous and rich, admired, widely traveled flight attendant, had even then managed to make hundreds of dollars in a single night by being extraordinarily desirable. Men sought her out among many and paid her large sums just to be alone with her. Some, unable to resist her, returned again and again; others tried desperately to lure her away. But she never succumbed. No; her love belonged to one to whom she would always be faithful, no matter who else might claim her. His love was her safety, her beacon, her protection, her green-tipped steady light.

While she gazed up, Robin became aware that someone was watching her. She pulled herself from her dream to see a trim man of medium height with clipped brown hair, a protruding chin, and intense eyes observing her from a short distance off. She quickly returned his look and strolled toward him with her most seductive walk, preparing her standard opening. But before she could get out the words he stepped forward and accused her sharply, "You're too young to be doing this."

Robin was puzzled. The man's neat appearance—fresh

blue shirt, well-creased trousers—was no guarantee that he would not harm her. Was he reproving her or coming on? The sentiment was one she'd heard often. Prince told her to call them Daddy and up the price when they went on about her youth, even if they seemed to disapprove. Prince explained how a trick's mind worked. "Look at it this way, baby. If you don't *know* a person, I mean know all about em, how their mind works, then you're gonna believe anythin you want to about em. Take you, for instance. A trick sees you, you could be anyone from a schoolgirl to a dropout, right? Now, that trick's got to believe somethin about you. What's it gonna be? What he wants to believe. That's why he's pickin you. Now, if you can open him up a little, see what he wants, you can play on his idea, whatever it is. Like, he thinks you're some poor little white gal, he's gonna want to save you. Then you let him know you're dyin to be saved, all you need is the cash. Another one thinks, only reason you're on the street is you love that dick, you're some kinda come-freak. You play it right, he's gonna make you one rich come-freak." Some tricks, he explained, tell themselves a young chick can't be a real hooker, she's just acting like one for the fun of it, not the cake; and some of them think if you're very young you're dumb enough to let yourself get taken. Without Prince to advise her about this one, Robin gave him her standard response. "Not too young to have some fun with you."

He searched her eyes, then quickly lowered his own to ask, "How much?"

"Depends on what you want to do." He was well dressed and soft-spoken; she went for the higher price. "Basically forty for the date and ten for the room."

He stepped up beside her, ready to follow. As she led him toward the Hotel Venus, she noticed that the clock in the window of the coffee shop showed exactly ten o'clock. They exchanged names: "David." "Button."

At the desk David asked Vego for a room key.

"Sorry," said Vego, signaling Robin with his eyes. "The only room left got no lock on the door."

"Never mind," said David and paid.

Robin took the towels and proceeded down the hall. Passing the marble stairs, she wondered if the garbage piled in the courtyard had actually increased overnight or if it only seemed that way. The dump on the island was bulldozed twice a year and picked over daily by the housewives and seagulls. But this dump was never emptied.

A young he-she named Alice seated on the bottom step looked up from examining his nails to whine at Robin, "Button, I broke a nail. Do you have a file I can use?"

"Later," said Robin, patting Alice's shoulder. The trick hurried them away. Robin might have been friends with Alice —they were the same age, both hookers, both from far away— if Prince didn't forbid it. ("I ever catch you messin with one a them filthy he-she hos again I got to charge you. My lady don't talk to funny folk!")

In the room Robin went straight to the basin to begin soaping the cloth.

"Never mind that, Button. You won't be needing it. I'm not going to do anything dirty. I just want you to pull down your panties," said David, making no move to undress himself.

Either an easy trick or a pros cop, thought Robin, remembering that New York City police were not allowed to remove their pants, not even to make an arrest. Jacki had explained that massage-parlor girls avoided arrest by insisting that every customer strip as soon as he walked in. But street hos had no house rules and weren't offering massages.

"Money first," said Robin.

"Sure." David took a wallet from his pocket and counted out three tens and two fives.

"What do you want me to do?" asked Robin, slipping the money into the zipper pocket of her skirt.

"Just pull down your panties."

When she saw him unbuckling his belt she felt safe again. She stepped out of her underpants. But when she looked back he was still dressed, his belt was in his hand, and his body was blocking the door.

"I want you to bend over, Button, because I've got to punish you now."

He crooned his words so softly, so respectfully, it sounded almost like a song. Robin's muscles tensed. Her father's voice softened too when he was about to punish her.

Always let the trick go into the room first, Jacki had warned. *Stay between him and the door till his pants are off.* But Robin hadn't listened.

"You don't really want to do that," she said.

"It's not because I want to," said David.

Her father's very line!

"I've got to. You've been a very bad girl. Now I've got to teach you a lesson. You've got to be punished."

She'd always known her punishment was coming.

He took a step toward her. Should she scream and bring Vego running? But what if her voice failed her? And who else might a scream bring?

"You don't understand," she said, stepping backwards. "Really, I hate doing this, but I'm always watched. They won't let me leave. They force me. Right now there's someone outside the door waiting for me, and if I scream—"

David slapped the belt against his thigh in several short strokes, like twitches. "But you're not going to scream, because I paid you." In the ill-lit room his eyes seemed to disappear into their sockets and his strange jaw was set hard. "Bend over, now."

Robin winced with pain as she felt the metal buckle of the belt against her thigh through her thin skirt. She knew from years of experience how to take a beating; she knew even better how to run. Surveying the room, she made her calculations and was amazed at how calmly she planned to lure the trick around the bed and then break for the door. Speaking fast, she said, "Okay, I'll bend over if that's what you want, but you'll have to pay me more. Spanking's a special service. I have to charge extra."

"Oh, you are a wicked one." He swatted at her again, but this time she jumped away in time.

"Oh, no," she said, running around the back of the bed. "You haven't paid me." With strength she didn't know she had, she shoved the bed toward him. "You can't do that unless you pay."

He looked indecisive. "How much?"

"Twenty-five more."

"Twenty-five? For the devil's work? I won't pay the devil. I don't have to pay you anything. I'm going to save you." He thrust his jaw forward belligerently and once more lashed at her with the belt, this time grazing the mattress with the buckle.

She winced at the thud. "If you pay up, I'll bend over for you. But I'm a working girl; I can't give you specials for nothing. Tell you what I'll do, though. I'm supposed to charge twenty-five, but I'll make it ten dollars for you cause I like you a lot. That's the best I can do." She held her hand out toward him, without budging, willing him around the bed.

He looked at her for a long moment, then began to respond. When his hand was in his pocket and he was advancing toward her, she scrambled across the bed and dashed for the door, practically flying down the hall and past the stairs, not stopping until she reached the street. The running music was screaming in her ears, filling her head. People were fighting down the block, and across the street the crazy old woman who slept in the doorway was shouting something. No one was safe.

When she got her wings she would fly far away. But now she had no place to fly or even to run. Except to Prince.

. . .

Owl saw Milly running toward her with terror in her eyes. Her heart clenched. Had the Flasher found Milly, too? She raised herself from the step and opened up her arms. "What is it, my baby? Tell me. What's the matter?"

If they wanted to make her suffer, this was the way: through her child. In all other ways she had made herself strong; but here she was weak. Bert had known it. Not enough they had hounded her out of her room into the street, now they were after Milly too.

"Milly! Stop!" she cried, stepping forward. But it was too late. Once they were grown there was no stopping them and once they were gone there was no way ever to get them back.

She watched Milly fly past without stopping, like a bird heading straight for the windshield.

Bursting through the door, ready to tell Prince everything that had happened, Robin was crushed to find the room empty, Prince out. With her chest still heaving for breath, she collapsed into a chair and tried to think. Now, Prince would have to let her quit. She'd take a straight job instead, anything, taking care of kids, selling, waitressing, even stripping if that was all she could get. But not hooking. If he knew how it felt to have that belt coming at her and no way out of the room, then he'd let her quit now . . . if he loved her. He'd even help her leave, the way her brother had helped her leave the island. Boots would understand. She rummaged through her bag till she found the old phone number, then dialed.

This time a woman answered.

"I'm trying to find Boots Fergusson," said Robin.

"Who is this?"

"A friend of hers from high school. She gave me this number to call if I ever got to New York. Well, I'm here."

"Well, she's not. She's gone to California."

"California?" said Robin, incredulous. That was as far away as you could get. "Did she leave an address?"

"No. I haven't heard from her since she left. But if you want to leave your number, I'll give her a message if she gets in touch. She said she would."

"No," said Robin, "I'll call back again. Just tell her Robin called."

She hung up in despair and lay down on the bed. Using her real name for the first time in weeks gave her a weird feeling. *Robin. California.* Both so far away.

When she opened her eyes again some time later, Prince was standing over her looking down with his hair falling over his brow and a strange smile on his lips and whiskey on his breath.

"What are you doin home at this hour? It's way past git-down time. Why aren't you down on the street?"

She threw her arms around his neck and quickly recounted what had happened.

But he shook her off, put his hands on his hips, and said, "I am really disgusted with you, Button. Totally disgusted. I thought you had guts. I thought you were comin up boss material, not just baby-pro. But if you lose your nerve and get ready to blow after your first little half-ass freak, then how'm I ever gonna trust you? Maybe Sweet Rudy is right about baby-pros. Maybe I need someone more mature, someone I can count on."

Robin stared at him. "How can you trust *me?* Is it *my* fault I pulled a freak?"

"You been out there a whole month and you pull one freak, maybe the only one you'll ever pull, and look at you. Do you call Vego, who's there to protect you? No, eleven o'clock you come runnin home. Shit, if all you want is safety, baby, you're no different from any square. You don't get nothin without takin a risk. You could step off a curb in front of a car.

You could go up in flames sleepin in your bed. You could be gunned down by a cracko or picked up by the cops for sitting on a bench in the park, or you could be tracked down by your dad or ripped up by lightnin. Are you gonna lay up in bed all day long worryin? No. These are the chances you got to take."

She listened silently, watching the muscle go in his jaw. She could hardly suggest quitting now.

"Now, Button, this time you know I got to correct you or else I ain't doin my job. I got to charge you for comin off early without my permission. I got to do this for your own good, cause how you ever gonna learn if I don't charge you now?"

Robin felt tears of outrage spring to her eyes. She could not believe she was to be punished for pulling a freak. Please don't let me cry, she prayed.

"Anyone else'd whip your ass for bein outa pocket, but all I'm gonna do is charge you this time. And you got to pay that charge, baby; you got to find me two more bills. You got to git right back down there until you make that trap and the charge besides."

Her father would have beaten her for sure. Some of the girls claimed that a man who didn't correct you didn't really love you. She hoped being charged meant he loved her. At least he was speaking calmly again.

"And if you do this tonight, if you git down and show me you're not just a scared, half-steppin ho, then Saturday we'll spend the whole day together." He raised her chin with his index finger and looked steadily into her eyes with his own bloodshot ones. "Understand, baby?"

For the first time, she pulled away from his touch. No, she did not understand. But she couldn't fight him.

He watched her steadily, saying nothing, until she finally pushed her feet back into her shoes and moved toward the door.

Back on the street, she lit a cigarette, searched the sky for a star, and tried to concentrate on Saturday.

14

Owl opened her eyes to a glistening morning and rejoiced. Birds chirped urgent messages somewhere overhead, though the block had no trees. Sunlight glinted off shop windows and shimmered above the pavement like footlights on the day. Even the rattling of the grates as a train passed under 42d Street sounded important, like a drum roll preceding momentous celebrations.

Owl stood up creakily, untied the kitten from around her waist, stretched, yawned. She felt it must be Saturday, for the summer air was thick with festivity. She accepted the cricks in her neck and back, the cramps in her legs, without complaint. A full-time street person now, she respected the elements. Her season of comfort was brief—without a room to sleep in, briefer still. Forced to wear, like a dog, her winter coat all year round (for it had a fur collar, deep satin-lined pockets, a pile lining which cold people understandably coveted; the embroidered label read "Pierre"; even if she had not been forced by circumstances to vacate her room, it was hardly a garment to leave unguarded anywhere, even in summer, in a climate of harsh winters), she appreciated all the more a day as sparkling as this. Her bladder and belly would have to be served (and soon!), but today she would serve them out of respect, not misgiving or fear, for her body was her safest dwelling.

Suddenly the meaning of the day was revealed to her. The drum roll announced her mission, as urgent as her full morning bladder pressing to be emptied. Today was the day she must win back Milly.

But first things first. She gathered up her bags (with the kitten curled inside Misc. Gloria) and searched for a place to pee. As she did each morning, she considered the toilet in the Hotel Venus lobby, then rejected it. Though she was well disguised from the Flasher in a brown curly wig, a hat with a feather, and an old green shawl, she saw no reason to risk recognition by the manager. He would be sure to ask insulting questions even though her rent was still paid up. She was through with furnished rooms in run-down hotels and their unjust managers, at least while the weather held. And the lobbies were as bad as the rooms. Screaming matches were always breaking out among the residents over nothing more important than which TV channel to watch, and if a fight got bad enough the manager started throwing his weight around, evicting innocent people on the spot. Just like Bert. The manager of the Midway, her last hotel, had evicted Owl for merely trying to heat her room. If they didn't want fires they should send up heat; it was the manager's own fault. Was a person supposed to freeze? She had warned him but he had ignored her. Worse, he had laughed when she told him that there were actually icicles forming inside her room, hanging like swords from the sill beneath the window she couldn't get closed.

(Naturally he laughed. His office had an electric heater, and in the lobby you could hear the pipes whistling with steam.)

"If you don't believe me, come up to my room and see," she'd challenged him.

"Gee, I'm scared to go into your room. I might get stabbed by one of the swords," he'd answered, mocking her.

So she had gone back upstairs and made a small fire fueled by useless summer clothes in the empty can she used for trash. We'll see if he comes up now, she raged, shooing the black smoke out the offending window.

He came up all right. Pronto.

That was a lucky day, too, her last day at the Midway. Even now she wasn't the least bit sorry, she was pleased, remembering the manager's face. He thought she would burn down his whole hotel, not just a few rags. His very face resembled a hot, red flame. After he kicked her out of the Midway, she banked her rent money for the next rainy day when her check failed to arrive, then she went to the Shelter, where the sisters were understanding. They served hot thick soups with chunks of meat and beans and asked no questions. They didn't force you to empty your bags or fill out forms or disinfect, like the city shelters; they prayed for you; they listened; they gave you advice when you wanted it and help with your papers; they told you your rights; they never laughed at you or mocked you; they allowed you to shower, do your wash, and use the toilet.

Now her bladder was too full, she knew, to make it to the Shelter in time, or even to the bus station. No matter—she would settle for a doorway. At the end of the block she squatted at the top of the stairs leading to the back entrance of a porn palace. Having dispensed with underwear for the summer, she could huddle inside the tent of her skirt and relieve herself without attracting attention. She watched the dark stain of urine trickle past her sneaker, down three iron stairs to a landing where it widened into a pool. In winter, she remembered, pee turned to steam as soon as it hit the pavement. That terrible winter before last when she had slept in the steam tunnels underground, she had learned what people would do for steam. Muggers and madmen lived in harmony for love of steam. The snows had come in torrents that year, but her room had so little heat that her very breath formed steam, hinting to God to send her heat. After leaving the Shelter she'd spent one night in the train station, one in the bus station, and then she was ready to face the dangers of the notorious steam tunnels under Grand Central Station.

Down under, hundreds of homeless men basked in the heat. Florida, she called it. Others called it Hell or the Waldorf, because you descended through a passage beside the Waldorf-

Astoria Hotel, where rooms were a hundred dollars a night. She was terrified below: you could lose your way among the turnings or be scalded on a pipe or be robbed or even raped. But one thing the tunnels had was plenty of heat. Certain pipes were so hot that people heated cans of soup on them for dinner. Earlier that week she had cut the sleeves off sweaters to wear as warmers on her legs, leaving seven layers of vests on her bosom; but the tunnels were so warm that instead of bundling up she gave sweaters away and folded up her coat to use as a pillow.

Heat, toilet, food: the body's necessities. Now that her bladder was empty, it was time to fill up. At the corner where she waited for a light she conjured up breakfast, wondering what Grace might have left for her. Inside Misc. Gloria the kitten was mewing. Soon she would have to return him to the alley, let him out of the bag, for he was growing large, straining at the leash. Love and lose—but not yet. If she provided for him, then Grace would provide for her, for there was order in the universe on such a day.

Behind the door at Sallee's she found her breakfast waiting in a white paper bag. It smelled of coffee, felt like donuts. Through the window she searched for Grace, hoping to wave her thanks, but she saw only unconscious people sitting on plastic stools at the red Formica counter, sipping coffee, huddled over newspapers, oblivious of the announced magic of this day, unaware of how quickly the past was slipping by, breaking old connections, one by one. She sighed for pity of them all.

Owl settled on her favorite bench in Bryant Park where she could imagine the library a palace and, ignoring the drunks sprawled on the stately rectangles of untended lawn, enjoy her memory of the small, once splendid park (hedges carefully pruned, borders planted with flowers, fountain dancing in the morning sunlight), now spoiled and gone to seed. Times had changed. She lifted the kitten from the bag, secured his leash under her foot, and placed before him a mound of cat food. Only then did she open her own meal. One large cardboard container of coffee (light and sugared—bless Grace!) and two cinnamon donuts. She teased her tongue with a lick of cinnamon, then carefully raised the coffee. The aroma was nutty and titillating, strong as magic. With coffee like this, she needed nothing more to start her day, though she wouldn't have minded an egg. Nothing matched the concentrated protein in the white of an egg. In the DP camps, where the rations consisted of potatoes and gravy, bread and butter, coffee and sugar, some people would have killed for an egg. If she'd still had a flatiron, she could have plugged it in and fried an egg on it whenever she pleased, even without cooking privileges. But her iron had long since been stolen, and even if she found another, she'd have no place to plug it in. Too bad. Cholesterol of eggs was said to be bad, but she did not believe in cholesterol. Man-made poisons, yes, but an egg—passage from bird to the world—was clearly God-made.

Not that she believed in God, but she did know there was something controlling the universe. She had lived long enough to see the pattern. It was something large, important, very strong. Fate, maybe; destiny; Nature—*it. It* was as good a word as any. *It.* Once, speaking of *it,* she'd said, Oh, what the hell? Why not call it God? And the name had stuck. She knew *it* wasn't, technically, God, but what difference did it make what you called it? Whatever it was, *it* had set aside today for settling things with Milly. She hoped she was ready.

She took a sip of coffee and a bite of donut and let them blend on her tongue. She pressed the donut to the roof of her mouth, and suddenly, there on her tongue, she felt something restorative, life-giving. Holding it against her palate, eating the gift of life, she felt a familiar rapture, a transformation approaching bliss.

Gently she returned the kitten to his bag to protect the

birds; then she reached into a plastic bag in a paper bag in the Gloria for a handful of bread, and with a large sweep of her arm that made the old flesh quake, she scattered it joyously to the wind.

There was a fine breeze blowing by the time Prince, springing on shiny cordovan shoes, tucked Robin's hand up under his arm in her favorite way and took her walking through Bryant Park. He bought them hot dogs and ice cream and talked, as she loved, about "plans."

At a little past noon, a slender young man in black pants, black slippers, and white shirt rode a unicycle past them. Old people feeding pigeons and drug dealers setting up all followed him to the center of the park.

"Come on," said Prince. "It's Fidelio. You gonna see somethin now."

From a black leather bag the young man Fidelio took a rope. He tied one end to the trunk of an elm, the other end to the pole of a lamp, pulled it taut, and tested it with all his weight. After tightening the slack, he flexed his muscles, donned a bowler hat, and began to juggle with impeccable style five yellow balls.

"Now you gonna see a real show." Prince danced on his toes and rubbed his hands together. "Wait."

While Fidelio juggled, the curious and knowledgeable continued to assemble. It was the usual Saturday crowd: students from the library breaking for lunch, tired shoppers, the unemployed. Some sipped soda, some licked ices, some stood around with their hands in their pockets watching Fidelio's work grow fancy as he altered his rhythm and added objects to his juggling act. When a sufficiently large crowd had gathered, Fidelio gestured them back and drew a large circle around him with a piece of yellow chalk. He raised his hand and held the spectators behind the line with a look, then he mounted his unicycle and rode it twice around the circle, establishing his inviolable space. He bowed to all sides until the audience was in his control and then began his beautiful, intricate juggling dance.

Prince stood behind Robin with his hands on her shoulders, watching Fidelio, enthralled. As far as Prince could tell, he used no shills, though he often drew the public into his act, giving them props to hold and roles to play. His investment was nothing but a few balls, some rope, four bowling pins, a riding wheel, and the resources of his splendid body. That was it; yet he could build a big audience, cast a spell over them, hold them, and keep them. They could be anyone—kids, businessmen, bums—it didn't matter; and in half an hour several hundred folks, including Prince himself, would be just begging to give him their cake. Damn! He'd be stuffing his hat with it! And afterwards, when he'd mounted that silly wheel and disappeared, instead of feeling they'd been had, folks would be dying to have him back again to give him more.

With respect, Prince calculated the preparation that had to go into this act. Fidelio's warm-up juggling and sleight of hand made three-card monte look like making Jell-O. He'd heard Fidelio had been busted more than a hundred times, but it didn't seem to bother him. Nothing ever tempted him to break his front. Nothing riled him, he just kept those balls circling in the air, adding his hat or shoe or a dog's stick, keeping them all dancing in the air at once. How did he do it? He was a little guy, slender, even slight. But he could discipline hecklers with a scowl, build confidence with a stare, control whoever got out of line by raising a finger or just an eyebrow. He used every part of the scene in his act. He mimicked passing dogs, babies, drunks who wandered into his space, converting each mistake to a challenge, incorporating every distraction. He was a master of con, comedy, and timing. The crowd was his. It was more than instructive, it was inspiring to watch so tight a game.

And the climax of the act was still coming. Like a boss player, Fidelio always waited until he had his marks right in his fist—like now—before giving them what they wanted: that rope.

Fidelio bowed, tested the rope again, removed his shoes, dipped four bowling pins in kerosene and tucked them under his arm, then started up the elm. He reminded Prince of the lithe Tahitian youths who walked straight up the sides of the coconut palms to pick the fruit when they were thirsty or who dived into the water to spear a fish when they were hungry. Now, with one arm raised like a plume behind him and the other spread like a wing to his side, two pins in each hand, slowly, cautiously, with unfaltering grace, Fidelio slid one foot onto the rope.

"Get ready," whispered Prince, leaning down to Robin's ear.

Ready? Oh, she was ready, she'd been holding her breath in anticipation from the start. She didn't need Prince to tell her. Fidelio was like a bird, Robin thought—a graceful heron gliding through the air, or a ruddy turnstone flitting from rock to rock, or like finches on branches, one step and another and another, while waves broke distantly below. Without wings he moved across the rope to the center, then stopped. She and the crowd sucked in a single breath, like a gust of wind across the shore. Spreading his arms for balance, he bowed his head to one side of the audience, then to the other, letting them know he took this risk for them. Fixing his gaze on one face in the crowd (On mine! prayed Robin, glad Prince was standing behind her and couldn't see), carefully he lowered himself till he was resting one knee on the rope.

The crowd and Robin returned their breath to the air.

His eyes, with the will of her father's, the charm of Prince's, held her up in the sky. Oh, to be part of such a man!

Kneeling midair, Fidelio took a lighter from his pocket and held it to the kerosene-soaked pins. One, two—the tips burst into flame. Now, a dip of the arms, a prayer, and the master kneeling on a tightrope juggled the torches toward the sky.

Could it be true? Had he looked at her? Seen her eyes? Felt what she felt? For such a man, thought Robin, was there anything she wouldn't do? She saw herself in a costume—a leotard, a mask—holding his hat, testing his rope, kissing his lips, lighting his pins, handing them up. The envy of all. Oh, her love would sustain him, and for this he would love her too. Even Prince at her elbow would have to bow to such a perfect love.

Without altering his rhythm, Fidelio reached out, plucked her heart, and tossed it up until it blended with the rest. And for a little while Robin, like him, stood free of gravity, a flame dancing in the windy air.

Ahead of her, through an opening in the trees, Owl thought she saw a man in the sky wearing a halo of flames, kneeling in a circle of fire. A flasher assaulting the sky? She thought not. But then, what could it mean? For she had seen in a vision that everything has meaning. Earth, breath, fire— since she had moved out of her room she knew that everything was part of the pattern that had been revealed to her; she felt herself in phase with the universe. Like the animals and plants, she was part of the whole. This park, the food she ate, the birds she fed, the infants she ogled in their carriages, this day that followed yesterday like a faithfully kept promise—all were part of the whole. Deeply she breathed the bright air of the day with its brew of bark and soot and flame, wafted to her nostrils by a slight breeze that marked this day as absolutely unique and unparalleled in the entire history of the universe.

Once, many years before, she had been taken to a private garden on a hill in Rome. The garden had a wall, the wall had a gate, the gate had a keyhole. And through the keyhole in that garden gate she had seen the splendor of Rome with its spires and cypruses and ancient ruins, the rubble of time and war, all spread out before her. And there, in the exact center of the keyhole view, was the dome of St. Peter's itself. A nobleman, it was said, had had the wall built; nevertheless, through that hole in one glance she had seen the pattern of part and whole, past and present, dome and spire, earth and fire, that held together the universe. And now—this breeze: part of this moment and also of all the breezes that ever sailed around the earth in all former moments and now connected the cloud blowing toward the noonday sun (she sneezed to look at it) with the halo of flame through the trees, image of the sun (she sneezed again).

He was tossing the flames around his head, and as the breezes passed through the branches the flames dipped and danced. The very breeze that now blew a kiss up her skirt and kissed her knees and neck fanned the flames. The breeze did not avoid old women. On her neck the skin responded with blushes and tiny knots; in the sky the flames leaped. As a wave of prickles flashed through her in one erotic shudder she was one with the flame, one with the quiver of leaves (green to silver to green again), one with the crumpled papers, wrappers of straws, and straws themselves that held the touch of lips and scooted across the ground, one with the universe.

She gathered up her bags and walked toward the man of flame. A yellow circle enclosed him and held her back. At the edge of the circle she stopped; and seeing all the eyes bound in the circle, she began to see the meaning of the flame. It was the dome of St. Peter's, the melody, even the scream which, once screamed, joined all the other gusts and hurricanes and cries to make a universal wind, flame, breath of life, voice of God. Of this she was quite certain, because there—there!—was Milly.

The magic held. She now knew what she must do.

Owl lifted the kitten out of the bag and held it close to her cheek one last time, letting him watch the fire.

At last Fidelio leaped to the ground. In one sweeping movement he smothered the flames of the pins in an asbestos cloth and bowed. The crowd applauded wildly. Fidelio placed his shoes back on his feet and his hat back on his head and with one upheld palm stayed the crowd.

No one moved. Robin blushed and held her breath, knowing he'd soon be coming near. She wondered, Will he remember me?

He tipped his bowler, crown over brim, down the steps of his lean body—nose, chest, elbow, wrist—into his hand. Then he stepped nimbly to the edge of the circle and began circulating with his hat outstretched.

"Now this is the best," said Prince, shifting his weight from one foot to the other. "With one hand he can keep the whole crowd from walkin off free. God damn! See them just dyin to throw him their cake?"

Prince took five silver dollars from his pocket and gave two of them to Robin.

She waited for her turn, wondering what she would say. With Prince beside her she could say nothing. She longed to toss her soul into Fidelio's hat, her body into his arms. But when he was finally beside her holding his hat to her, she could only drop her coins in the hat and look one last time into his eyes.

At that moment, as Fidelio moved on toward Prince, someone thrust a kitten into Robin's arms. It was an old woman with gnarled hands, a missing tooth, and a mad look on her face. "Take him, take him, there'll be more—," she said and moved quickly away.

Robin wanted to follow her, but now Fidelio was moving back into the center of the circle. He tossed the dancing balls in the air for one last act, a virtuoso play. Then quickly he untied his rope, packed up his pins and balls into his black bag, strapped the bag over his shoulder, steadied his unicycle, and bowed a final, appreciative bow. While the crowd continued to applaud, he gestured them to open up a path for him. He mounted his wheel, backed up to the edge of the circle, and with his hands folded behind his back rode across the circle, through the crowd, out of the park.

"What's that?" asked Prince when Fidelio was gone.

"A kitten. Isn't it the sweetest thing you ever saw?"

"Where'd you get it?"

"I don't know. Someone just handed it to me and disappeared."

"Handed it to you?"

Robin shrugged. "Too many kittens born, I guess. People must have a hard time getting rid of them. At home they leave them in boxes on the steps at school. Isn't it dear?"

Prince looked at it suspiciously.

"You'll let me keep it, won't you? Please? I love it." She saw his expression, calculating and cool, and vowed, remembering her father, If he says no, I'll run away.

Prince shrugged. "A cat, is it?"

"Please, Prince. Please."

He shrugged again. "Sure, baby, if you want it, keep it. If a cat makes you happy, keep it. I want to see you happy."

15

When the scream began Owl believed it was her own voice defending herself from the Flasher. Still? Again? She tried to wake up and protect herself, but she couldn't; instead she watched the dream change until the sound came from the infant Milly, crying for her four o'clock feeding. The stench of garbage from two full cans beside the doorway she slept in called forth dream memories of diaper smell; the high-pitched wail from the hotel across the street made her dry breasts yearn to help; the very hour of night (for ever since she'd nursed Milly in the rocker while Bert slept, her body knew the feel of four a.m.) tricked her back to that deceitful time when an infant at her breast made her feel the future a high, pink, cloudless sky.

Since she'd moved to the street, her dreams lasted only a moment. Now, in this one, when Milly cried, Owl leaped from the bed, dripping milk from her breasts, to suckle the child. But the basket she kept her baby in was filled with rags. Where was the baby? Frantically she began to search through the rags as her power leaked out through her nipples.

Between two worlds, Owl reached for the Susan bag and felt inside for her glasses. The night gave off its eerie green cast; Owl was cold, even under layers of wraps. She wondered if the wail from across the street was the same scream she'd loosed on the Flasher, become one now with the countless other voices in an unending fugue that played on, night after night. The cries of the wounded soldiers, the displaced persons, the infants bawling to be fed, all the patients in the hospital, the junkies, the cats, herself. Had the Flasher returned? She tried to sing an air, her part in the fugue, but her voice faltered.

A moment later she heard a thud, as if a large bag of garbage had struck the pavement, special delivery, bringing the song, the scream, to an end. Coda. Thud. End.

Now the street became deathly quiet. Owl huddled inside her coat under the green light and pulled her shawl close around her. She tried to sleep, but with the first hint of dawn she opened her eyes and remembered. A scream, a thud, something airmailed to the pavement, night people stepping around it in the eerie green light. A body? An egg fallen from the nest? An infant flung against a wall? Bad dreams? There was something on the pavement across the street.

She stretched out her swollen legs and laboriously picked herself up. She reset her wig on her head, covering her unwashed, matted hair, pulled up her stockings, and assembled her bags. A workman in cap and apron walking past the hotel detoured slightly around the heap. Another pile of clothing discarded in the glut? Owl thought of all the dead, discarded things she passed each day. She had to pee, but first she would investigate.

She made her way across the street. In the chilly gray Manhattan dawn, there on the pavement, partially hidden by trash, she saw the broken body of a child. A small adolescent child with a broken neck, face smashed on the pavement, arms akimbo, dirty nails, yellow hair, bloody head. Milly? Owl reached down and lifted away the hair covering what remained of the face. The child's mouth hung open and her eye stared out like the eye of a fish, the limbs were bent at an inhuman angle, as if they were floating in a smooth blue lake in which the water's surface bent the shapes beneath. The knees were skinned and bloody, like a roller skater's knees, and blood matted the yellow hair.

The time Milly fell out of the swing and split her scalp, the blood poured out; I thought her skull had cracked open, finished her. I picked up my baby, ran inside, wrapped her in a blanket, and desperately tried to reach Bert. Calling, calling, busy wire, dial again, finally through. But he wasn't at his office, the secretary didn't know where he was. And when I called him from the hospital emergency room he still wasn't there. I called him again and again but he was never there. He was never there, not once, when I really needed him.

Owl thought of the dead birds, the wasted lives. The boy, her firstborn, dead after three days; she never even got to take him home. She wanted to salvage this one, take her home—but she had no home. She would have to leave her here. Bert could bury her.

I should never have chosen a name for him so soon. That was tempting fate. There I lay on a long sterile table under a spotlight, legs in stirrups, waist distended while a medium in a white coat listened to my navel through a stethoscope. Was it my own wild heartbeat spilling over? No—definitely a separate pulse. Alive! Well, why not a name, then?

A mistake. In the fifth month I stained; when I smoked my gums bled. Then one September morning the pains came, a whole season too soon. I'd been expecting them anyway. The book said: to prevent contractions, pant. All the way to the hospital and onto the ward I panted like a sunstruck hound; they couldn't get me to stop. But the pains kept coming, weak but persistent, like the creature that followed them nine hours later, a perfect little miniature.

"Is it alive?" I asked.

"Yes," said Bert, sitting on my clean sheets looking down at me. "He's alive."

He!

They brought him to me for five minutes three times a day, straight from the incubator. We kept looking at each other. Beautiful huge trusting eyes.

Then one evening I asked, "Is he still . . . ?" And from the look on Bert's face I knew he was dead. Nothing left but the *footprint they took when he was born, and I never spoke his name again.*

Owl reached down and touched the cheek. It was cold. Too late, too late, too late. Her tears fell freely this time. She had waited too long, thinking there'd be time enough; but there was never time enough. For how many years had she and Milly been out of touch, except for a card at Christmas? She'd given her a kitten, but it hadn't helped; Bert bided his time, then took Milly away. This time too: A kitten and then . . . Gone. Everything repeated. She'd given her a kitten but it hadn't been enough. If she had given her cash, would it have saved her? But she'd been afraid to impose. Always afraid. And now? Too late. Now she would have to drop her suit. What would be the point with no one to carry on, no one to leave her treasures to?

She lifted her own brown wig from her matted hair and placed it over the bloody head. She would try to get a blond one from the Shelter, but for now the brown one would have to do. She took off her shawl and covered the body, though it was already quite cold. How many times would she bury Milly before she was through? Too many. Too late.

The bad vibes hit him the minute he walked into the Casanova Bar. The dim lights behind the bar seemed dimmer than usual. The TV was off, the jukebox was silent, and the airconditioner hummed eerily. The players had left their fancy threads behind and no one was laughing. The place was practically empty, just a few men huddled at the end of the long wooden bar with grim faces talking very soberly, very low, without a glimmer of their usual flash. No one selling bracelets or cameras or radios; no couples in the back; not even any johns. Sweet Rudy, who usually sported outrageous boots and covered his black balding head with a fancy hat, now wore only work shoes and a tweed workman's cap. Prince put his hands in his pockets and ambled down to the group at the end of the bar, taking a fast reading of his stomach on the way: bad news.

Sweet Rudy threw his arm over Prince's shoulder. "Let me buy you a drink, bro. I thought it was your people when I heard the news. Man, I'm glad it's not."

Prince checked the room in the long mirror behind the bar. Not one woman in the place. Something was wrong. Forget the stomach; he needed a drink right now.

"Thanks, Sweet Rudy. Run it down for me, will you?" He lit a cigarette and ordered a Scotch as the men gathered to tell the story.

It seemed a white ho, street name Vicki, was found dead on the pavement in front of the Hotel Venus. No one really knew what had happened, but under her brown wig Vicki was blond, blue-eyed, and not a day over fourteen. The cops were all over the stroll, and in another hour Father Glendon would be holding a press conference. Reporters and photographers would be down, camera crews would be swarming everywhere, politicians would get into it, before night a grand sweep would be on and it would be open season on pimps.

Prince felt his body stiffen. Whenever there was trouble with a ho it was open season on pimps. Just when he had a little money saved, just when he was getting ready to lift his game, something like this happened. Every time you moved up you got pushed back down. Before he even got born his father ran off, leaving him to learn about life the hard way. Watching his mother slave and suffer just to keep them alive sent him back to start. In the service, where he finally got some of the pussy and cash coming to him, his own stomach betrayed him. Goodbye, navy; goodbye, Tahiti. Even his wife turned against him when the cash was low, stealing his son, trying to stick him for alimony. Not one step up without two steps down. Running his best game laid him up in the joint.

Just as he settled back into the life, Sissy, that bitch, whom he thought he could trust, disappeared out of state. And now? He should have known the day he turned Button out that a sweep would be coming down.

He slammed his fist on the heavy bar so hard the pain shot up through his arm. "Shit, man. I'd like to kill the gorilla who's pollutin the game, drawin the heat down on everyone. Pimpin's a mind game, not a muscle game. Just once I'd like to see the dude that did this."

"Hold on," said Sweet Rudy, smoothing down his mustache. "You don't know she was pushed. Maybe she jumped. She was a kid, you know, maybe she was speedin. If she was a dog, maybe she checked out on her own. Mighta been an accident, you don't know."

"I was there when the heat came. I saw her," said Shorty, sipping a beer. He waited till everyone had turned to listen. "It was really weird. She was all twisted up, with everything broken, her neck and her legs and her arms, like someone really wanted to mess her up. Twisted like a pretzel, you know? With a curly brown wig setting on top a her head. Weird, man. But they found her covered up with some kinda blanket, or some kinda shawl, like someone wanted her to die comfortable and look neat. Like someone was sorry for what he did. Sounds loony, right? So now I figure who that gotta be? That gotta be some freaked-out crazy trick. Right?"

"Yeah, nine times outa ten it's a freaked-out trick," said Sweet Rudy. "A pimp can cut a bitch loose easier than droppin her out a window and bringin the heat down on everyone."

As Prince saw it, it didn't matter. Whether she fell or jumped or got pushed out the window, she was young and white and the heat was on. Tricks never got busted. Tricks were the lifeline of the life—no con without marks—but the man always played right past them. When one of them got violent, the man just clicked his tongue and called the trick crazy. But if a player turned up with a new set of wheels, the man was ready to lock him away. No one even knew who this Vicki was, much less how she checked out; but the man was out to get himself some pimps to burn anyway.

All the men were busy figuring where to move their operations or how to lay low till the sweep was over and the heat was off. They were taking their women to Miami and Atlantic City, Boston and Vegas, or over to Jersey City. Not Prince. Button was too young to take out of the state and too hot to work in the city, even in Queens. Bad risk. If they busted her now they'd do everything to make her finger him. He'd have to get into something fast or they'd be out of money in a week.

Sweet Rudy put his hand on Prince's arm. "We're all cuttin out tomorrow for Boston. I got somethin goin there, you know? I'll run it down for you and you can tell me if you want to come."

Prince shrugged. If the sweep went on for a couple of weeks he'd be right back where he started, with no cake, no one on the bricks, no work of his own, alone. "Crossin two state lines with Button? Can't do it, man." Maybe he'd never get past today, tomorrow, and one day more.

"Leave the young stuff here and bring yourself. Let Button visit her mother for a while. We'll be back in a few days, soon as it's safe," said Sweet Rudy.

Prince wondered if he dared leave Button now. Sometimes he dreamed of a different life—moving up into some legitimate game, living in a real house with a family, fruit trees, a yard to fix up, his lady so tight with him he could just relax backstage, instead of being onstage every minute. But he knew it was a dream. A *blow to the heart kills*, Sweet Rudy had told him, and Prince kept it in his own heart as a motto. A blow to the heart kills. Let that woman open you up and you were on your way down. She'd be tricking off you the next day, gaming on you that night, destroying your manhood, bringing you straight down. Let her strike a blow to your heart and you'd be just another trick, free fucking, used, wasted.

He wondered what Button had heard about the accident and if she knew the chick. He had to get back and calm her. If she wasn't too shaky, maybe he could go to Boston with his buddy. But he had to think out his plan.

"Thanks, Sweet Rudy. I'll let you know later. You planning to be at home?"

"If I'm not there leave a message for me here with Tony. I'll be by for my messages."

Prince felt his stomach starting up. He needed some milk. "Thanks," he said, clasping Sweet Rudy's hand. Then he left an extra large tip for Tony on the bar. For good luck. They'd all need it.

Who was Vicki?

All afternoon the whores sat in Sallee's Coffee Shop huddled together over coffee at a table in back, avoiding reporters, trying to piece together what had happened and figure out what was coming. Who was the dead girl? Even after carefully pooling their stories, they knew almost nothing about her.

Someone said she'd been on the stroll for nearly a year. Robin was shocked. A whole year here and no one knew her? No one knew Robin either, but she'd been there only a month. By the time a year went by she supposed she'd be living differently. She looked at the five other hookers at the table. The most she knew of any of them was their street names, their home states, their old men, and how long they'd been in the life—about as much as they knew about the dead girl. Her street name was Vicki, her man (though some said she didn't have one) had conveniently disappeared. She was a lot younger than she looked. She liked to wear little ruffled tops and tight skirts in shocking colors. Though she was reported in the papers to be a natural blonde, for some reason she wore a brown wig. (Funny.) No one had claimed the body yet, but a family had been traced and was supposedly on the way from somewhere out West. One paper said there were seventeen warrants out on her. Another paper said she was only twelve years old.

Quietly, Robin listened to the women talk. Lana (California) speculated wildly; Pearl and Sugar (New York) wept, wadding handfuls of tissues in their laps. Jacki (Virginia) was being practical ("Give me a quiet old geezer anytime. They're too weak to kill you"), and Cheryl (New Jersey) seemed to be speeding on the sheer excitement. "Of course, I'm really sorry about Vicki, it's a real tragedy; but as long as there's heat here, Bluejay is taking me to see my sister in Louisville. Boy, can I use the vacation!" Robin was subdued. Like Vicki, Robin was young, white, unknown. Like Vicki, she put her life in the hands of strangers. Like Vicki, she was a runaway, probably wanted by police at home. But for all the parallels, Robin could not mourn. Pearl, the large woman beside her with a pervasive smell of spice and soft, powdered cheeks, kept offering Robin tissues. She was one of the copious weepers whose tears made Robin feel acutely embarrassed for her own dry eyes.

All the buildings fronting Eighth Avenue flanking the Hotel Venus had been cordoned off, bringing to sudden scrutiny the cracked, shaded windows, the sagging sills, and the staring faces behind them. Now suddenly the neighborhood was flooded with uniformed police looking for suspects and private detectives looking for lost daughters. From every paper headlines announced that across the city sex was for sale. Newly noticed and newly deplored. The mayor had ordered a special task force to investigate youth; slum clearance projects were fished out of the files; little-known ordinances were invoked; photographers and cameramen stalked the streets; a sergeant was suspended, a lieutenant was promoted, a deputy commissioner was appointed; security tightened in the Port Authority; the Council committed emergency funds; and the dreaded Pimp

Squad was assigned three additional cars, ten in personnel, and an executive mandate. The whole neighborhood, usually so cocky, had been quietly subdued. The movie palaces on 42d Street conducted business-as-usual and the buses arrived and departed from the Port Authority more or less on schedule, but the normally tumultuous streets and bars seemed abnormally quiet. Now no hawkers hustled outside the Live Sex Paladium, only one silent ticket taker covered the door; the Casanova Bar and Grill was all but deserted; Rena Ray, the topless dancing star of the famous Riviera, was fired after calling in sick; the pimps and girls, big time and small time, were lying low. The Lighted Way, the religious bookstore, kept its doors open extra hours, but many other establishments were slowing down or closing up for a while as the sweep spread.

The big question still was, What had happened? Though someone was always popping into Sallee's with the latest reports, you couldn't believe what you read in the papers. Had Vicki fallen, leaped, or been pushed? No one knew. No note had been found, but who knew what she'd been on? The press was playing up the angle that she'd been shoved and reported all the usual rumors about violent quarrels with her pimp, about kidnapping, rape, detectives on her trail, about a furious father, about arrests, about attempts to escape; but no one really knew.

And what if one day I happen to "fall" from my window, thought Robin, who would care? She wondered if and how they'd be able to discover who she was. Would Prince, like Vicki's man, refuse her body? Yes, she knew he would refuse. He loved her now, but if she were dead, if they were after him, if there was a sweep, if the action was out of town, he'd have to split. For a moment she saw her mother with that grief-stricken face, tenderly clasping her broken body to her own; she saw her father, at last abject; she saw her brothers, ashamed, teased, and taunted in school (*Robin, Robin was a whore, / She's not fucking anymore*). She wasn't sorry for her father but she would have done anything to spare her brothers that humiliation. Like Vicki, she was only one fall from exposure. Vicki's family was coming from the West; her name was in all the papers; her hometown was probably celebrating with laughter and sneers. No one had heard of her yesterday, but now the women in Sallee's all spoke her name easily, as if they had always known her:

"She always had a smile, you know? A bright word to say to everyone, even though her man treated her like shit. God knows why she put up with it," said Pearl, dabbing at her red eyes.

"She should have left him ages ago. I would've," said Jacki, crossing her legs and lighting a cigarette.

(Oh, yes, thought Robin enviously, you would. You don't need anyone. But Prince says you're getting old, Jacki. You'll need someone, too, one of these days.)

"No you wouldn't," said Sugar, "not if you was just a little kid with no mama and nowheres else to go."

"Yeah, some folks, they be born a ho; some folks ain't never been treated nice one day in their life."

"She musta been stashin, holdin out on her man."

"You sure she wasn't shooting up?"

"She looked a lot older than twelve to me. Where'd they get twelve, anyhow?"

"From papers they found."

"By her teeth."

"From her mother, who's coming for the body."

"I remember," said Lana, "she never could stand still. Kept running back and forth, up and down Eighth Avenue. A funny kid. Last week she told me she thought she'd be going home for Christmas. Christmas! That's half a year off."

"Isn't she the kid who always had chewing gum? She used to offer me some when we were working, I think that was her. I liked her, you know?"

"Isn't she the one who took on Bruzer, that freak trick? Well, let me tell you about *him!*"

Which was worse? Robin suddenly wondered. To be exposed when you die, or to die unknown to anyone but a few whores who thought they saw you yesterday?

"Yesterday she was crying in the Casanova Bar."

"Yesterday she knocked off early, I wonder why?"

"She said she had a headache."

"I tried to warn her."

"I had a feeling."

"I just knew something like this would happen."

"Yesterday she was alive, but now she's dead," said Pearl, the tears still gushing from her eyes.

"You never know what's going to happen."

16

That night Prince brought Robin a gold S-chain bracelet. (Probably hot, but what did she care?) Since he was going away "for a few days," he let her get very stoned and took her out to a new disco in Queens.

The club, lined with billows of deep blue satin and thousands of tiny reflecting mirrors, was dotted with people from the life, including Prince's running partner, Sweet Rudy, and two of his ladies, Jacki and Lana. Prince was more openly affectionate than he'd been since their first days together. It seemed to Robin he held on to her hands nearly the entire night, across the table, dancing on the dance floor, even on their way back to the parking lot. She was proud to be with him there. She was proud of the way he danced, the special way he stood in his perfectly creased pants and black silk shirt with the red satin trim, his almond eyes, the mysterious tattoos under his skin, the muscles she could see and feel under his fitted clothes. He held her eyes with his while they danced and made her feel so proud and pretty that once, laughing, he taunted her with, "Hey, I wonder if you care about me or just wanna front me off?" All the way back to Manhattan she wanted to go on holding hands, it made her feel so safe. But he was a busy driver, forever adjusting the windows and vents, using the window washer, changing the music, weaving in and out of traffic like a skater.

It was after four when they got back to their apartment at the Royal Arms. The cat was asleep on their bed. Robin wanted to chase him off before Prince had the chance. Prince was funny about the cat. When he bothered to notice him, he often found him amusing. The first time they gave him a ball of catnip, for example, Prince was so impressed by the cat's performance—grabbing it in his teeth and shaking it, batting it wildly with his paws, rolling over and over with it on the floor, then leaping with it from wall to wall—that he invited Sweet Rudy and Jacki to come over and "see a kitten with a catnip Jones." For a week thereafter he gave the kitten a fresh dose of catnip every night and joked with Sweet Rudy about selling tickets to the show and raking in the bucks. But soon he got bored with the performance, turning his attention from catnip to coke, and ignored the animal except when he saw him violate his rules. Prince tried to be strict in the exercise of discipline, even with a cat. Sensing this, Robin tried to keep the two apart, though usually the cat disappeared on his own as soon as Prince appeared.

"I should pack tonight," said Prince, unbuttoning his shirt. "But shit, I'm too tired. I'll do it in the morning."

Robin was glad he was too tired to pack. All night she'd been thinking, if he's really going away then he has to make love to me tonight. If she kept him up late enough, then maybe in the morning he'd oversleep and decide not to go at all.

He lit up a joint and handed it to her while he stripped to his yellow underwear and carefully hung up his clothes, taking special pains with the creases in his pants. Long and deeply she drew on the reefer, wanting to be quickly stoned again, wanting not to think about his leaving her. She was glad not to have to go to the Hotel Venus for a while, but she was afraid to be left alone in this city with no one but a cat to talk to.

He helped her out of her dress, ran his fingers softly across her breasts, pausing over her nipples, and down her hips, sheathed in the lace-trimmed satin slip he had bought for her. "You're very sexy for a kid, you know? Go and wash yourself."

Obediently she went into the bathroom to wash and powder her body. She saw the glow of her own excitement on her face in the mirror. When she returned, Prince was sitting in his yellow underwear in the wooden chair with his feet up on the table, one hand holding the reefer, the other behind his head, his gaze off in some distant place. The radio was turned low.

She knelt on the floor beside him. She laid her head upon his smooth thigh and took four good hits of the joint. She let her mind go blank to everything but this man, this thigh against her cheek. Stoned, she ran her fingers slowly up and down the long, smooth limb in time to the music until all the feeling in her body was concentrated in her cheek leaning on that thigh.

Prince moved his fingers to the back of her neck and with small, slow, circular strokes caught her rhythm. His penis began to stir and rise beneath the yellow shorts, like a thick stalk of purple kelp swaying beneath the surface calm after the ebb tide. Moved, she pulled aside the yellow curtain of his fly and released him.

Deep inside, Robin felt herself stirring. She moved her fingers to his cock. If she could make him happy, would he stay with her? She had no other power. She ran her tongue along the back of his cock, feeling the heat of her own loving, and up over the mushroom's ridge. She slid her lips slowly down over it. When his fingers tensed on her neck in a sign, she began to move her mouth slowly up and down, like a buoy in calm waters, feeling the delicate skin of him against her tongue and throat.

After a while she glanced up. His head, thrown back against the chair, was perfectly still. His hands hung limp, his mouth fell slightly open, his eyes were closed. Was he giving or withholding? She wanted to see him respond, to know where he was, but he remained still. She felt in that moment's calm as if her own veins and nerves were melting together inside her, becoming one smooth flow. She pressed her pelvis against his hard leg as she sucked him, feeling a pleasure, a melting pleasure, she wanted to save. She willed the feeling never to stop.

After a long while Prince sat up, leaned over, and kissed

her full on the mouth. He ran his tongue inside her mouth and over her lips, sucking gently, softly pulling her breath into his mouth, then blowing it back again. Then he lifted her in his arms and carried her to the bed.

They dropped their clothes to the floor. Then he lay with his face buried in her thighs and began to kiss, then lick, her cunt. Though she had stopped coming since the night she pulled a freak and Prince had punished her, she moaned to let him know how she treasured this caress, this sign that he cared to please her. He stopped too soon and moved on top of her, abruptly ending her pleasure, but she cherished the gift no less, knowing that it was forbidden. According to the pimping code, as much as a woman desired that caress, that much must a player withhold it. To her a little was the same as a lot, since she could never have enough; she was always ready to begin again. It was for this reason that she allowed him to believe, as he pumped himself up toward his own explosion, that she was exploding too. The pleasure she felt with him was more than she'd ever known; she wouldn't endanger it with intimations of failure or even restraint.

At last he came. "That should tighten you up till I get back," he said, kissing her forehead and rolling away.

Sometimes, after Prince rolled away from her to the edge of the bed to sleep facing the wall, her mother would appear to her, drink in one hand, cigarette in the other, standing on the high deck, thin, delicate face staring far over the sea to the distant, ever-changing horizon, passion acknowledged, abandoned, unfulfilled.

"Prince? You asleep?"

"Can't be asleep if you're talkin now, can I?"

She feared to ask her question, but she had to. "Can't I go with you tomorrow?"

"No, baby, you can't. Too risky."

"Then, if you're worried about crossing out of state with me, can't I take a bus and meet you there?"

He lay still, with his back to her. "I told you. I don't want anythin messin us up now when there's so much heat. I'll be back. You rest yourself up here, read some books, take it easy till I get back." He reached over to the table beside the bed and lit a cigarette.

"But if you don't want me working, why can't I rest up in Boston with you? I just want to be with you."

The muscle in his jaw started to jump. "You're thinkin with your pussy instead of with your brains. You better leave the thinkin to me."

He got out of bed, crossed to the window, and stood there smoking, looking out. His face was lit by harsh neon light. He looked tired to Robin, tense, muscle weary, like the exhausted fishermen who chased the herring up and down the coast, laying and pulling their huge nets every night for weeks, until the fish escaped to deeper waters where the hunters could not pursue them.

"I'm afraid," she said from the bed.

He turned to her and, with the strained patience of a teacher who knows he must go through the lesson one more time, folded his arms and asked, "What's the trouble now?"

She knew she was out of bounds pestering him, but she couldn't help it. "I don't know. What if something happens while you're gone?"

"What if, what if. What if the city blows up?" he shouted. "Do I take care of us or don't I? I'm leavin you money, I'll phone you every night, nothin's gonna happen if you do like I say."

When the herring were running, her father turned mean. Six or more fishermen sat in their house playing poker and drinking whiskey and eating sandwiches that her mother fixed them all night long, waiting to hear where the fish had been spotted. Sometimes they waited a week or even two, talking about the big money to be made, while the tension of the hunt mounted. When the fish were sighted the men leaped into action, becoming one person, manning the boats, racing through treacherous seas to spread their giant nets for that once-a-year, multithousand-dollar haul. Sometimes they won, sometimes they lost. But the women fed the children and prayed, either way.

And if Prince copped another girl in Boston, an older one whom he liked better and was free to travel with—what would happen to her? He was taking his things; the rent was paid up; he had his wheels. "How do I know you'll come back?"

He returned to bed. "I'm gonna play right past your worries, baby. We ain't got time for jealousy. I'm leavin you here because I got to, it's the best thing for us, no other reason. Now, turn over, close your eyes, and let me hold you the way you like. Close your eyes and get some sleep and leave the worryin to me."

Owl sat in a side pew toward the back of St. Agatha's Church where she could pile her bags beside her without attracting attention and weep for Milly. She loved the slow, sure, ceremonial pomp of funerals, the way the light through the stained-glass windows spilled jewels on the stone floor, the church's deep respect for age, dignity, death. She took comfort in the knowledge that she and everyone gathered there were in communion. The rich organ music, now low and ominous, now high and serene, that caused the pews to vibrate as it filled the church and the glass to tinkle as it soared to sonorous crescendos stirred her deeply. She remembered her grandmother's parlor in winter with Aunt Rose at the piano and all her aunts singing in harmony, and then that other time when red-nosed weepy aunts and angry uncles reeking of alcohol clasped Lilly to their bosoms, squeezing and wailing, placing wet, boozy kisses on her cheeks, and Aunt Rose played the organ at the funeral.

Even as the mourners, the neighborhood regulars, the religious, and the old gathered in the church, spreading themselves on the hard wooden benches like birds on branches, Owl gave herself up without shame to her most extravagant feelings, the pure contemplation of life and death.

How easily the tears flowed now. In her youth she had witnessed terrible acts without feeling or understanding: a burning house, beggars in the streets, humiliated children, bombed cities. But now, the slightest thing could move her. One golden leaf still clinging to the branch, its color heightened by decay, one alley cat licking another's ears, one dead fledgling in the gutter, a broken teacup in the trash that reminded her of something gone, and her tears would well up and overflow her lids. She cried for kindness, for sadness, for no reason; she cried for memory and loss, for Milly and the boy, for life and death. Sometimes she wondered if she didn't suffer some physical defect to produce so many tears. Her mother had cried whenever she read aloud. Whatever the book, at a certain point she would have to stop and blot her tears in order to see the next words on the page. Scrupulously she explained away her tears so Lilly would know it wasn't sadness or even the story that made her cry but some peculiar connection between voice and ducts. Then she had died.

Father Glendon in his black robes walked solemnly to the pulpit. Now the service would begin. Owl raised her black veil and looked around for Bert. He hadn't come. Well, hadn't she known he wouldn't? Had he ever been where he said he'd be? Or where she needed him? All the more comforting was Father Glendon's tall, lean presence, his gaunt features, his velvet voice. He, at least, would do his duty; he was not a man to wait until you had made yourself over and then, with a fanfare of lies, disappear.

But she was growing confused. Hadn't all this happened before? The music was music she'd known before, the incense, the candles, were comfortingly familiar. They opened their books to page 267 and sang a hymn that merged with other hymns; among the pews people wept tears that flowed into rivers of other tears. And now he spoke of "holy unity."

Owl sank herself deep into unity and remembered her grandmother's house in Buffalo the night her mother died. One moment the house was throbbing like Christmas, with all her aunts and uncles talking at once; the next moment her grandmother was flinging herself onto the high-backed velvet sofa, and there were screeches and moans and grief.

They tucked Lilly into a strange bed in the attic of her grandmother's house. A clock ticked loudly on the bureau, the rocker in the corner where she laid her clothes threw frightening shadows on the wall. Aunt Rose had told her her mother's heart had stopped because someone had put her to sleep while her brother was being born but had forgotten how to wake her up. *Forgotten how?* Lilly was afraid that if she slept, the clock would stop and with it her own heart and she would never wake up.

After a while she heard her papa's voice downstairs. She stole down the attic stairs and sat on the familiar landing from which she could watch the others in the parlor below. Papa sat on a chair with his head in his hands. He looked so unhappy, she wanted to run down and comfort him and make him laugh. But they were talking about her, so she sat on the stairs and listened.

"Who will take Lilly?"

"Rose says she's willing."

"But does Rose honestly have the patience for a ten-year-old? Hilda is farther, but at least Hilda has the space."

"Why don't we see what Mama thinks?"

"Mama? No, she's too upset, we can settle this ourselves. Don't ask Mama! There's no tragedy in life worse than burying a child before her time."

Later, after Lilly had returned to the attic, Aunt Hilda slipped into bed beside her. Her aunt's tears wet the pillow, her sobs pierced the night. All through the house where people slept, sounds of mourning broke in on the steady tick of the clock. Lilly thought that if she closed her eyes not only she but all of them might die in their sleep. Bravely she sat vigil, watching the clock's big green hand drag the little one slowly behind it, moving minute by minute across the night, until at last the black sky began to lighten through the window of that small attic room. The rocker became a chair once more, the birds began chattering on the grass as if nothing tragic had happened, gradually the clatter of hoofs and wheels and horns from the tradesmen's carts and cars began to fill the street as they did each day. Aunt Hilda, waking, took Lilly in her arms and told her she would have to go home and put on her best clothes for the funeral. It was then Owl first observed that though everything had changed, nothing had changed.

Now, Father Glendon delivered his eulogy. His voice rose like a flame, curled against the high arches, leaped from the walls causing Owl to suffer once more that worst of tragedies, burying a child before her time. The name of the departed was not Milly, but what difference did it make what he called her? Owl had been born Lillian, had taken her husbands' names, was now known as Owl, yet she was the same. She had called Milly many names herself. The dead were one. (Holy unity.)

The organ was playing softly, sadly, as the mourners filed out of the church past Father Glendon, who stood nodding gravely just outside the door. Owl collected her bags and followed. When she reached the door she welcomed the feel of his strong hand resting comfortingly on her shoulder as she passed from the cool dark church into the hot midday city.

"Goodbye. God bless you," said Father Glendon in his funereal voice.

"Goodbye, Lilly," said Papa, as he climbed onto the train and waved goodbye.

Goodbye, Milly.

17

Prince had gone away, leaving Robin money and instructions. For the first time since she'd arrived in New York, she was on her own. For several nights she had barely slept. He had promised to come back, but what if he didn't? Jacki, Lana, Sweet Rudy—they had all gone away; she might never see any of them again. The only way she knew how to keep Prince was to be the best little hooker on the stroll; but while the sweep was on hooking was out. He had deprived her of everything else by making her see the mean hypocrisy of the square world. She thought now she would never be able to return to it except to game. As her father would say, once a whore always a whore. She finally understood why. Once you knew what you knew, how could you ever return?

Now, Saturday, at the start of a stifling heat wave, Robin lay in bed brooding. He had left her—and in the middle of a sweep! She would never forgive him. At the same time, she rejoiced at being free of work and the hassles of the Hotel Venus. Suddenly she could go anywhere she wanted, keep her own hours, talk to anyone she pleased, and the hell with Prince.

She walked to the window and looked out over the city. The endless march of buildings—from the shabby four-story houses across the street with their crumbling stoops and their tattered shades, to the high cliffs and grids of endless offices blocking the horizon as they invaded the blue sky, to the massive green glass towers standing like mute glittering guards high above the honking cars and shops and scurrying pedestrians—made her feel like a visitor to a strange land. The very air—heavy and humid, carrying the city dust of a world of people and cars, without a trace of breeze or scent of grass or fresh sting of salt—was suddenly strangely new to her. The day was coming up a scorcher, and what should she do without Prince? Go to an air-conditioned movie? The beach? The zoo? Maybe with Prince's big sure hand resting gently on the back of her neck, steering her now to the ice-cream vendor, now to the monkey house or the lion's cage, the zoo would be a treat. But the thought of going alone to watch the poor dumb animals lying bored in their pens, or to see boys tease the polar bears, or to hear the gaudily feathered birds screech in cages strewn with rotting fruit depressed her.

One minute she contemplated revenge, imagining all the ways to defy him. She could pick up a guy for the fun of it, or call one of her johns and stash the cake she made, or pal around with Alice and his friends, or just go down to Bryant Park, score some reefer, and get stoned. That would teach him to leave her! But the next minute she realized she'd be better off using her unexpected freedom to track down Boots, or look for another man to save her, or just to enjoy herself.

She was glad she didn't have to decide yet. It was hard enough deciding what to wear or eat without Prince to guide her. She fed the kitten, showered, put on her sexiest sundress and highest-heeled sandals, and made up her face, carefully disguising her naked skin with three separate products. But even looking her best, she felt the panic rise as soon as she hit the street. Two grim policemen emerged from the corner deli as if they'd been expecting her. The sex shop down the block was closed, and among the shoppers and secretaries crossing the busy intersection she thought she saw a host of reporters. The minute the traffic signal flashed WALK, she dashed across the street, flagged down a taxi, rushed inside, and told the driver to move.

"Where to?"

"Oh, I don't care. I want to see the sights."

He turned around. "The Village? World Trade Center? Rockefeller Center?"

"Rockefeller Center, I guess," she said, relishing the millionaire sound of it. She would have liked to find a millionaire of her very own, a rich john who wanted to marry her. In her purse she had a pack of business cards from johns who'd offered to save her or buy her outright from her pimp. Prince said blackmail was the only thing the cards were good for, but there were two or three numbers she wanted to try, steady customers she almost trusted. Why not? That would be the life: go off with a rich john and the hell with love. Prince could visit her when her man was out of town; she'd pick him up in her Eldorado and take him out to her estate.

The driver dropped her at the tour office in Rockefeller Center. Even standing on line for a ticket she felt out of place. If only she hadn't been alone. When she and Boots had sparechanged tourists, she had never seen a tourist alone. Following along behind the pretty uniformed tour guide through fancy airline offices, TV studios, and expensive shops, walking among the cozy families of tourists—impatient mothers and trick fathers and frisky, freckled children asking what's that and why about everything—she'd felt that everyone looking at her could tell what she was. It was crazy, she knew. Still, she was glad when the tour ended in a souvenir shop in the bowels of Radio City, where the group spread out to buy presents for relatives until it was showtime at the Music Hall.

The cases and racks were filled mostly with the same souvenirs she saw on 42d Street. Halfheartedly Robin looked for something for Prince. But seeing the youngsters on the tour pressing their noses to the cases begging to buy, she decided on an impulse to buy presents for her family instead. For Adam she bought a NY Mets mitt; for Billy, who was only ten, she bought a small brass replica of the Empire State Building; and for her mother she bought a Rockefeller Center ashtray and a coffee mug decorated with a large red apple. She knew she wouldn't dare send the gifts. It was too risky; Prince would be furious if he found out. But she gave herself the pleasure of buying them. Like the others on the tour, she had them gift wrapped and wrapped for mailing, and she carried them in a large shopping bag into the Music Hall.

She had never imagined such a theater—the gigantic stage, the vast space, the ornate swirls of gilded decoration. Watching the chorus line of famous high-kicking Rockettes, tapping her own now bare feet (for the shoes she chose had been wrong for sightseeing), she imagined herself dancing in the spotlight, or guiding a tour in a smart-looking uniform, or presenting her presents to her family. They would be so happy to see her that she would buy them first-class airline tickets and fly them out of Maine—all of them except one.

It was midafternoon when she left the theater. Her feet were hurting again and she had a bulky package to carry, so she took another taxi, this time downtown, where Prince had never taken her.

"This is the Village," said the driver, letting her off on a busy corner with bars on either side of the street. She was hot and thirsty, but it was too early for dinner. She flipped a coin to see which of the two bars to go into. The winner was heads, McGraths, but perversely, Robin chose the Blue Lion, the loser. Not that she preferred one to the other; but at so little a price she would do what she could to evade her destiny.

Cool air soothed her as she stood inside the door in the blue TV light. The two men nearest the door at the bar were already eyeing her. She wondered if they had recognized her or could read her past by looking. She walked quietly to the far end of the bar and turned her back to them.

Before she could order, the bartender slid a beer down the bar. It stopped in front of her. Seconds later a tall young man with unkempt auburn hair, a large nose, thick glasses that made his eyes look too close together, and shy full lips inched down the bar until his beer was next to hers. "May I?" he said.

She smiled and looked steadily into his eyes, as Boots had

taught her, and cocked her head, like Jacki, listening. "Sure," she said, trying to become the receptacle he wanted.

"I bet you don't remember me, do you?"

She widened her eyes.

"Here, a couple of days ago, during the last scorcher. So—let me guess—you live around here, right? And you came out to cool off cause you don't have air conditioning. And you're a sophomore at—maybe NYU—and you're working for the summer. Am I right?"

She a college girl? She smiled. She was surprised he took her for a student, though finally, as Prince had taught her, tricks took you for the person they wanted.

He said his name was Clarence and without waiting for her to answer launched right into an explanation of his own reasons for being there. He was a student at Columbia, but he liked to spend time in the Village. Depending on which day you asked him, he said, he was a student of philosophy, physics, or computers; he kept switching his major. His parents wanted him to be a lawyer, but he thought he should put off deciding until he was absolutely sure what he wanted to do. "I'm good at lots of things. I get A's in everything. Sometimes I think my life isn't *real* because everything comes so easily for me, know what I mean?"

"Oh, yes," she said, nodding earnestly, "I think I follow you." Tricks had often made pitches for pity, gratitude, sympathy, but not for admiration. She smiled a certain way to let him know she was impressed. He ordered another round of beers.

He said he was thinking of taking a year off if he could convince his parents to let him. "To travel, figure things out. My parents have more money than they know what to do with. Why shouldn't they let me?"

Could he be the one to save her? It wouldn't take much to save her, she thought. He had a slight stammer that reminded her of her brother Billy when he was afraid; she found it touching. She was sorry she hadn't gone home to wash, drop off her package, and put on perfume.

"You're a little shy, aren't you?" he asked finally, looking at her closely for the first time. He pushed her hair off her cheek as if to get a better look. "Tell me about yourself," he said.

She said her name was Sue, that she was a student in Maine, but that she was working for a New York family for the summer taking care of their kids. Two sweet boys, Billy and Adam, for whom she had just bought some presents. Today, though, she had the day off.

Clarence clapped her on the shoulder. "That's great. I have the day off too. I should be working on a paper at the library right now, but who can work in heat like this? Besides, it's Saturday." He paid for their drinks and said, "Let's go celebrate. Tell me what kind of food you like."

"Celebrate what?"

"I don't know. Saturday. Summer. Meeting here. Do we have to have something special? I just want to celebrate with you. I know what we'll do. Let's go down to the pier and cool off—would you like that?—and then we'll have a good dinner. I know a place. And I'll tell you the story of my life."

Picking at pancakes that had been served them aflame and now lay limp in a pool of sweet brandy sauce, Clarence sat across from her at a candlelit table for two, talking. For hours he had been explaining the running down of the universe and the state of his soul, stopping only to search her face for a response. Prince talked game, Jacki talked plans, tricks talked sex; but Clarence talked of invisible particles invading space, of brains split in two, of the end of the world. "I intend to design a computer that will have two hemispheres in its brain just like ours. One will be a memory of everything that ever happened. And the other will be pure projection."

She had let herself get giddy on the wine and stopped listening. Eventually, Clarence paid for their dinner with a credit card and led her back outside into the heat.

On the sidewalk, his stammer returned. "What would you like to do now? Do you want to go hear some music?"

"I don't care. Sure."

"You know, we could go back uptown to my place. I have a pretty good exhaust fan in my room. We're not allowed to put in air conditioning because of the wiring, but the fan works and I have excellent music to play you, and wine. Okay?"

She had no reason to say no. If she went home now she might get depressed. Besides, she thought, Prince is probably chipping in Boston this very minute, so why shouldn't I? Why shouldn't I do anything I want to do?

"You don't have to be afraid of me," said Clarence. "I promise I'll take you home the minute you say."

"I'm not afraid of you," said Robin, laughing her mother's laugh.

He grabbed her by the shoulders, almost lifted her off the ground, and kissed her. "Great! Great!" he rejoiced.

He hailed a taxi. Inside he held her hand and watched traffic, silent at last. The driver, gunning his way uptown, missed every light. Robin thought about how Prince would rather get killed than miss a light.

The heat was heavy and thick. Robin thought she saw it emanating in waves from the pavement whenever they stopped for a light. In Maine at this hour the sun would be a red ball coloring up the sky, and mosquito hour, as Billy called it, would be beginning: everyone take cover! Mosquito rush hour, she thought. She thought of the swallows at twilight against the tinted clouds passing through the blue cove like sails through the ocean and did not even notice when the taxi crossed 42d Street.

She had expected at least the satisfaction of revenge for her night of free fucking, but she hadn't got it. If anything, she felt slightly ashamed. Watching Clarence go on and on trying to impress her before finally taking her to bed, she kept thinking of her father putting on his charm act for the ladies. At one moment Clarence reminded her of the Wonderful One Man Band she'd gone to see with Boots and two men in a roadhouse south of Portland. He had worn a big polka-dot tie, white shoes, a red blazer, and navy pants, and his Wonderful Band included a pedal-operated drum, harmonica on a stand, squeezable horns, and ukulele, guitar, trumpet, and sax, alternately played by him. That was the awful night she had gone to the ladies' room and, glancing into the small barroom on her way back to the table, had seen her father sitting at the bar with his arm around a girl. She'd been so terrified she had just run straight outside and hidden in the shed next to the parking lot until she saw her father leave. Clarence played music, recited poetry, told jokes and stories, talked and talked. When he finally got her into bed he was so excited he came before he even got inside her. Poor Clarence. She felt sorry for him, but Prince would only laugh if he ever found out.

Late that night she'd taken a taxi back to her own place and slept for hours. She might have stayed in bed all the next day if the kitten hadn't woken her up. He rubbed against her again and again until she thought of the waves lapping the shore and the sandpipers running behind the waves; and after she got up and fed the kitten she took paper from the table drawer to write a letter home.

Dear Adam and Billy, she began. She thought she would

send it to them care of Billy's best friend and hope it wouldn't get back to her dad.

I bet you're surprised to hear from me. I wanted to write before but I didn't get a chance. Anyway, I can't tell you where I am, but I just want Mom to know I'm okay and you don't have to worry. I miss you both a lot. One of these days I hope maybe I'll get to see you. If I sent you some airplane tickets, would you be able to come away?

She crossed out the last sentence about the tickets. Where would they think she ever got money like that? Then she continued:

I bought you some presents yesterday. But guess what, I don't know where to send them. I guess I'll just hold on to them for a while.

She crossed out the paragraph about the presents, it seemed so futile.

Seen any porpoises or whales? Are the apples ripe yet? I think about you whenever I have a piece of pie, but it's never as good as ours. When it's pie time, please tell Mom

Here she broke off and reread the letter from the beginning. It said nothing; anyway, nothing worth taking a risk for. She wanted to tell them she was okay and that she missed them and that they shouldn't worry about her; she wanted to ask how they were doing and if they were lonely without her and what about their mom? But thinking about her mom made her want to cry, and how could she ever write what she felt?

It suddenly seemed to her very sad that she couldn't even write a letter to her family without getting everyone in trouble. She tore the letter in pieces and took it to the bathroom to flush down the toilet, so neither Prince nor her father would ever know. Then she went back to the bed and sobbed.

An hour later she set out for Bryant Park to score some reefer. On 42d Street she paused to watch a grizzled old black man in a pin-striped suit dancing furiously on high white platform shoes. Slight, gray, and very old, with shriveled skin hanging loosely from his neck, his legs flying and his head lolling, he looked like a marionette. His head was dwarfed by the large blaring radio he held in his arms. Robin watched him work himself up to a frenzy. So old, and still dancing. And for what? Not for money; there was no hat for coins. How many years had he been there, dancing alone? His face was creased and wrinkled behind the rigid smile whose neat square teeth made Robin think of death. Suddenly revolted, she hurried away from the dancer, afraid.

The other hos never seemed to be afraid. They liked to act tough, strong, even mean. Sometimes in Sallee's, where they sat drinking coffee at a big back table near the noisy air-conditioner, Robin heard them brag to each other about their dangerous escapades: their mean men, their freak tricks, their narrow escapes, their fights, their reckless risks. Proudly they flaunted their scars: broken jaws, false teeth, bald spots under their wigs, slashed wrists. Robin wondered if she would still be there when the summer was up, if Prince would ever come back.

Clarence expected her to call him on her next "day off." Maybe, she thought, she would tell him she'd lost her job and ask him to let her stay with him.

In the park a group of kids was making good music with sticks, empty soda cans, and other improvised drums. When she had scored, she lay down near them on the grass, kicked off her shoes, and proceeded to get stoned.

18

Owl was astonished to see a girl who looked like Milly lying in the grass. Had she not one week before seen her dead on the pavement like a fallen bird? Yes, she had covered her face with a green shawl and even mourned at her funeral, she was sure of it. Yet here she was, back again, alive.

Or was she? Owl felt the same confusion she had felt after losing her fingertip—was it gone or wasn't it?—for the feeling remained. How confusing: she had always taken her fingers for granted, and then a driver had slammed a car door on her finger and begun driving away, and by the time her screams had stopped him, part of her third finger was no longer attached to her body. She'd felt no pain—only a kind of detached curiosity that gradually turned to nausea. She'd felt as detached from the accident as her fingertip from her hand. Even as she'd wrapped her shirttail around her bleeding stump and retrieved the severed joint from the car door, she'd felt nothing in her hand; not for many minutes did she feel anything at all, and then only a dull throbbing. And even when pain began pulsing through her and panic mounted in her throat, she felt more ghoulish than violated as she ran through the streets in search of a doctor, carrying her severed fingertip in her good hand.

At the hospital they praised her for her foresight in bringing in the severed part. But the graft did not take and in fact resulted in several gruesome days of torment and painful weeks of infection. Eventually, the stump healed, leaving no feeling at all when she touched it, only when she didn't. And in the following years, whenever she thought of that particular accident, it was not the pain she remembered or the embarrassment or even the physical shock, but that numb detachment, that odd feeling of uncertainty as to how to regard the severed part of her: the place it held in her body, the place of her body in her life, the place of her life in the world.

Just so, she now regarded Milly. Had she not accepted her loss as one of a steadily expanding series of losses the last of which would be life itself? But now that Milly appeared to be back again, Owl was confused. Were losses like Milly reversible, like the loss of her voice? And what should she do? Declare herself? Forget her? Try to reattach her in her heart like a severed joint to a finger, going through all the pain of healing perhaps only to lose her again?

She walked toward Milly for a closer look. Somewhere in one of the bags she had a packet of clippings about the dead girl. Raped in a ravine. Mugged in the hallway. Trapped in a burning bed. Pushed from a window like a bird from a nest. Owl took an envelope from the Barbara bag and searched quickly through it. Pushed, or maybe jumped. If Owl had been locked in a room she might have jumped too. Out of pride, if not revenge. Some things were simply not to be tolerated. Being forced to answer foolish questions, to eat vile food, to speak of certain things, to beg, to be locked up, shunted aside, humiliated. Not only by the welfare people or the manager, but by your own husband, your child, your flesh and blood . . . Now, though, she was ready to chuck her pride if this was really Milly. Not since her last round with welfare had she so longed to seem reasonable.

She put back the clippings and approached the girl. "Excuse me. I thought I had my cigarettes in here somewhere, but they've vanished. Do you have a cigarette?"

"Sure. Here."

She pronounced *sure* "*shu-ah*" and *here* "*he-ah*," noted Owl, taking a cigarette. Who could she be? Maybe it didn't really matter who. Might not Owl explain herself as easily to a neutral party who had never heard Bert's lies? This one seemed sweet enough, offering to share her cigarettes. She might just be the one. "I have something for you, too," promised Owl.

"Forget it," said the girl, lighting Owl's cigarette first, then her own.

Now how fiercely Owl regretted that her effects were scattered among lockers around the city or forever lost, instead of neatly ordered in some presentable form to prove how, though she had been maligned and abused, she had fought back. Since the Flasher's attack, everything in her life was in a shambles, rendering her need for an heir all the more urgent.

"My name's Owl. What's yours?" she asked, as if she were one of the Shelter's nuns doing outreach. She smiled at her own mastery of the social forms. No doubt she would still be able to ride a bicycle too, and perhaps do a presentable tango, but for the swelling of her legs. She was a mother still, and here was a child. If the answer to her question was not "Milly," she would accept it anyway; she was quite prepared to compromise in exchange for acceptance. This would not be the first time Owl had accepted a stand-in; she was used to substitutes. The park for a yard, the street for a home, a bag for a drawer, a doorway for a room. Her mother had died leaving her an aunt instead. She took what jobs were offered her. When it was marriage time she accepted the one who most wanted her. And even pleasure—she remembered a certain Venetian doctor who had offered her the rare opportunity to sample cocaine, extolled as an aphrodisiac. The war had ended, leaving him in possession of a small supply which he'd been saving for the right occasion; when she came along he offered it to her with himself, as a package. She remembered him: short, sagging, middle-aged, with gray skin and jumping eyebrows and a little gray beard and a bald spot in the center of his head. Hardly the man she would have singled out for a lover at that time, but if she wanted cocaine, that was the deal. She remembered her calculations:

if the cocaine possessed those vaunted properties, what difference would it make who her partner was? That extraordinary feeling—she wanted it, no matter with whom. (The drug had done its work, the feeling had come, though she had been disappointed. Like the time she had allowed herself to be hypnotized. Or had she? Never mind . . .)

And now, too—this Milly had a different face, Owl admitted it, and she was a generation too young; but the other one was dead or vanished and she needed someone to press her suit; otherwise her case would be lost, the years wasted.

"I'm called Button. Don't I know you?"

Owl cocked her head, alert. "Maybe you do. I'm a woman with a past."

"Aren't you the person who gave me my kitten?"

Owl snapped to attention. Recognized. Admit nothing. She took a last puff on her cigarette, coughed smoke until her breath came in spasms, and flicked the butt away. Then, as the meaning of the girl's question took shape in her mind, she realized her luck. The kitten! Then it was Milly after all!

"Yes, I am," she said. "The manager of my building won't allow pets. He'd rather drown them than turn them loose. He's the same way with people—a very evil man. Like certain others I won't mention. . . ." She looked off and sighed. "Oh, you can tell a lot about folks by the way they are with animals, let me tell you. A lot. I remember one story I heard from a man who used to live in my building; he wasn't even ashamed. Imagine! He told me that when he was a boy they used to catch the stray dogs in his town and bury them up to their necks. Barked and howled all night, he said. I said to him, 'Well, I should think so! And when you let them out, what did they do to you?' 'Out?' he says, like *I* was the crazy one. 'We didn't let them out.' 'What happened to them then?' I asked. 'Oh,' he says, 'they stopped barking after a while.'"

. . .

The way the cat lady puffed on her cigarette with her dry, wrinkled lips, holding the butt between stumpy yellowed fingers, then flicking it carelessly off into the grass while she told weird stories of the past, reminded Robin of the weathered old-timers on the island who sat around Jacob's Spa in the afternoons sniffing the salt air to predict the weather and entertaining whoever might be waiting for the ferry. They told of record storms that changed the shorelines or turned nubbles into islands; of the submarine sightings during World War II and the Coast Guard occupation; of the deadly Red Tide that came in as suddenly as a nor'easter to poison the shellfish, then disappeared as quickly, leaving a wake of corpses all over the East; of the oil spills that killed the birds; of the mysterious five-year disappearance of the mussels; of the deer that swam over from Stimpson's Isle; of the incredible spring tides; of heroic rescues; of the sailboat-racing scandals; of the enormous ten-pound lobsters that were no more; of fortunes made and lost in fish; of schooners and Russian trawlers; of brave widows and daring boys. Some of them had grandchildren and great-grandchildren with their own names; the island belonged to them.

This cat lady was weird, like some of them, but she was someone to talk to. "Remember the kitten's white paws?"

"Of course I remember. I remember all my cats, every one."

"I named him Boots."

"Boots? That's a good name for him, though his paws weren't *all* white."

"Actually, my best friend's name is Boots, and the kitten's sort of wild like her. I love them both. Prince—he's my man—went to a pet shop and got everything they sell for cats. A basket to sleep in, with plaid pillows, a carrying case, and a neat rhinestone collar so we could take him out for walks. I hate to see animals on leashes, but in the city, what else can you do?

Two little dishes—for food and for water—and this package of catnip. Well, you should see that kitten with the catnip. He really turns on. He rolls over on his back and squirms around on the floor, just like a person freaking out."

"He *is* a person," said Owl.

"In fact," continued Robin, "when Boots is high I have to keep the window closed, or else I'm afraid he'll jump out, like they say some people do on acid."

"I know, I know," said Owl, remembering the child on the pavement, the green shawl. Her eyes filled up as she remembered all that could go wrong. Not just windows. They fell out of swings and cracked their skulls, even out of highchairs with the tray in place, slipping out through the bottom. They could go through the ice and drown. They could also drown at the beach, sometimes even in swimming pools. They used to die of polio, you had to keep them away from the water all through August. Now it was brain tumors or leukemia and there was nothing you could do. Some of them went in car wrecks—it was hard to believe how many. That's why, thought Owl, it's safer in the city, whatever they say. Or if they survive the wrecks they wind up as vegetables. She knew of many. The woman across the hall at the Hotel Midway had had a grandson in college, University of Pennsylvania, a vegetable now. Many vegetables. But Milly was too young to understand. "And of course," said Owl, sharing her knowledge, "the war gets them, especially the boys. And love gets the girls."

"Love?"

Owl nodded regretfully. "Love or worse. It happened to me when I was young. It'll happen to you. People just don't learn, and when they do, it's too late. Young people think they know everything." She remembered that she too had once thought she'd be home free if Milly just got past puberty. But in fact, it got worse the longer she lived. "You lose them eventually, one way or another, you'll see. My mother died in childbirth. My father left. Three days isn't long enough to live but that's what happened to my boy."

Milly puffed on a cigarette and stared at her. What you need, thought Owl, is money, not youth, not love. She raised a gnarled finger toward the sky and said, "Take care. When you're young, you're trusting; then people betray you. You care what people think. It takes years to learn the truth. Fortunately, I'm through with people." She lowered her hand and sat staring off into the past like a passenger facing the back of a train.

"When I get married, though, it's going to be different," said Milly.

Owl smiled. When I do it, it's going to be different. Everyone thinks that. Me too, I thought that. I traveled all over Europe thinking, when I do it, it's going to be different. Then I did it and it was the same. "Not if you have kids," she said smugly. "Once you have kids, he'll have you. I was married, I can tell you. . . . Right here in this bag there are papers I could show you. . . ." *Not now*, she cautioned herself. Not now.

Robin saw the old woman's face change before her like a werewolf on a horror show. The dull eyes suddenly glistened. Owl's bosom heaved and her nostrils flared. Her mouth, long frozen in a harmless grin, trembled, tightened, then drooped like a mustache. The voice rose abruptly. Even stoned, Robin knew the warnings. Time to grab her sleeping bag, leave the house, and take cover before the explosion. Recognizing that look was instinct now, as familiar as the path to the outhouse. Her father maddened, her mother damned, tricks too weird or furious to risk taking on. (Not for nothing had she learned the hard way.) She rose abruptly.

"Well, so long," she called back after her and headed across the grass, carrying her shoes.

"Wait! Don't you want to help me feed the birds?"

"Tomorrow," called Robin from the pavement.

"Wait!" called Owl again. "I'm coming too." But Owl's left leg had fallen asleep, and when she tried to stand it collapsed beneath her. "Damn!" she cursed, trying to break her fall with her hand. "Damn! Damn!"

Robin went to a phone booth and dialed Boots's number again, hoping the woman would have heard from her by now. But this time no one answered at all.

19

Crime and punishment resumed in other parts of town, freeing the midtown girls to stroll again. Prince returned a new man. He had a new blue suit, a silk shirt the color of the sky, a pair of pointed white leather shoes, a new swagger, and new advice. Did he also have a new woman? Robin didn't know, but he looked so good she was suspicious. The first night she kept touching his clothes, his hands, his hair until git-down time, when he sent her back to the stroll. It hurt her when he said, "Don't you think you had enough vacation?" though she hadn't seen him in a week; and by the time she'd turned her first trick, she was already wondering why she hadn't run away while she'd had her chance. But now she was hooked again, her vacation was over, and nothing had changed.

It was deep summer now, the air was heavy with dust and heat, stirred only by an occasional breeze from the west. Business was brisk; the streets were full. Johns in shirt sleeves or with their ties undone stopped by the stroll for a quickie before going home. They undressed faster and came more quickly in the heat; and taking up the slack, Prince raised her trap again. Was it Prince she hated or herself or them for the weakness that made them pay her to do something they could do to themselves for free (or for the price of a vibrator, said Jacki)?

As she stood in her doorway brooding, a green car moved slowly downtown. It looked familiar, part of a scene she felt she had seen before. More than the car made her think so: music coming from the Sea Breeze Tavern; the smell of the air; the old stooped panhandler across the street working the night people; the young ho to the south of her with the street name of

Chicago though she came from the South. She had felt them in just this pattern before. Out of the side of her eye she slowly became aware of a large, darkly clad man lumbering toward her among the pedestrians. Her eye picked up the heavy walk —where had she seen it?

Once Boots had said that the feeling of déjà vu might be a memory from a former life. Was it Peter Delawney walking toward her, or had she lived before? Living now, seeing the man approach, she had two violent and opposite impulses: curiosity and terror. The thought of Peter always summoned up shame; but this sudden specter of his finding her here on the stroll, of his taking both her worlds into that single leering eye, took her beyond shame. She knew him; she knew if he could he would use his knowledge of her weakness to lead her again to the sand—

Quickly, before he could see her, she bent to fix her shoe, averting her face from the street. Her pulse raced as she felt him drawing closer. That lumbering walk—she was afraid to look at him. She imagined taking him for thirty dollars into a room in the Hotel Venus, removing his pants, getting the washcloth, the condom; but suddenly the image changed. Instead of working him over in the time it took a cigarette to turn to ash, she let him lead her to the bed of shifting sand, remove her clothes, cover her throat and mouth with kisses. . . .

Desire was treacherous, disarming. Sensing the man directly before her, she pressed herself back into the shadow and peeked up.

He was not Peter, was nothing like him. Peter had a beard, a paunch, a leer, while this man, slimmer and smooth shaven, had a look that was solemn, even grave—an entirely different face. She wanted to laugh with relief, but that remembered passion kept her pressed in the shadow of the doorway, stooped over her shoe. She no longer needed Jacki to tell her to trust her premonitions.

She felt him peer, then pass. That was the great advantage,

Jacki had said, of working the street, rather than out of a house or massage parlor. On the street you were free to turn down anyone you wanted on the slightest whim. If you worked inside, said Jacki, the tricks did the choosing, but on the street you could choose and you could run.

When the danger had passed she felt suddenly cocky for having the power to choose, until she saw the man—her reject —grab Chicago's arm and tug at her.

Her instinct had been right, then! Chicago! Poor Chicago! Maybe he was a bondage freak? Had two rejections been too much for him? Peter would have struggled too if she had turned him down. Run, Chicago!

For one moment it seemed Chicago would get away, but no, he had her, and twisting her arm behind her back was forcing her toward the green car now idling at the curb. Like a small, fierce dog clinging by its teeth to a treasured stick, Chicago pulled back; and like a small dog fighting a man, she was subdued. She let out a fierce, wild scream, but it was too late.

Now Robin remembered. The car—old, unmarked, without chrome or frills, two men inside—it was one of the cars of the pussy posse that Prince had told her about. He had shown her the red one parked at the curb in front of a topless bar they'd been trying to close down (was it the man she took for Peter who got out at the curb?) and had warned her of the green one.

"You can always spot their wheels by the way there's not one thing special about em. What real man would drive around in wheels like that? Even tricks have more pride!"

Suddenly everything made sense. The man forcing Chicago into the back of the car was a pros cop who'd been busting her. At that very moment Chicago was on her way to jail. Her man might be sleeping or running around, but Chicago would be staying put.

Robin was stunned. But for the memory of green or the

accident of a funny walk, she would have been the one. She looked at her hands; they were trembling. Her whole body was trembling. This time, somehow she'd known. But next time?

Once when they found her taking a bit of food from the school kitchen after she'd run away from home, she was dragged off to Mr. Hayes, the principal. She remembered watching his secretary send someone for her father while she sat on the bench outside his office, waiting. When her father saw her sitting there he had bowed his head and wept for the disgrace. It was the first time she'd seen him cry. She was humiliated but also proud that she had moved him to tears. And when he got her home and punished her she was amazed to see him cry again.

Now she thought of him coming to jail for her, finding his daughter arrested as a common whore, fingerprinted, photographed, thrown into a cell, put on trial, convicted, sentenced. . . .

She held one hand with the other, but she could not stop them from shaking. She needed another trick before she had enough money to go home. Home? She had thought herself protected by Prince, but if she'd been arrested instead of Chicago (perhaps at that very moment being shoved into a cell), Prince, her great protector, wouldn't even be aware of it! The things he had done to reassure her meant nothing. The ID he'd bought her from her first week's earnings might save him from a minors charge but it couldn't help her. If they didn't pick her up as a juvenile they'd get her as a prostitute, but unless she talked he was clean.

She crossed the street and turned a corner, not caring where she was going. Tricks trying to lure her from the street offered her more safety than Prince. If she stayed on the street she'd be arrested; it was inevitable, merely a matter of time.

She walked to the bus terminal, open all night, sat down at the counter in Walgreen's, and ordered a milkshake. She had a hundred and seventy dollars and change, one night's take: a lot more than she'd arrived with. If she took off now she'd be ahead. But all her things, her clothes, the presents Prince had given her, Boots waiting to be fed—she hated to leave them for his next lady.

A bald man sat down at the counter a few seats away. Without looking up, Robin felt him eyeing her. Hunched over his menu he looked like an ordinary traveler between buses. Prince had told her that the Runaway Squad patrolled the station in pairs, a plainclothes cop and a social worker. She didn't see a woman with him; still . . . it would be dumb to be picked up here the moment she'd decided to quit! She stole a look at him and met his eyes. Her hands began shaking again. Why was he watching her? This was not the night to hang around and see. She sucked deeply on the straw of her barely touched milkshake, left a dollar on the counter, and walked briskly toward the waiting room where she could hide in the head. When she looked back, she saw the bald man following her. She ducked quickly into the ladies' room. She had to pee but nothing came. Too scared—worse than on the day she'd arrived knowing nothing. She sat and figured.

Even if Prince allowed her to quit, he'd take her money first and charge her for the missing thirty and her clothes, of course, and maybe her food too. That was how it worked. Some pimps charged their women every time they looked at a man; some of them charged for breathing, according to the girls in Sallee's. And without money, where would she go? Down the toilet and out to sea. At last. She flushed.

Back in the waiting room the bald man was sitting in a chair, pretending to be reading a magazine. She walked swiftly to the concourse, then without looking behind her broke into her fastest sprint. She knew it was dangerous to run, but now it was more dangerous to walk. Besides, running was a reflex;

she was not in control of her legs. Plunging back into the familiar streets she headed for Jacki's building, half a block away.

Another scream had pierced the night, joining all the other voices in the universal fugue. Was it one of the other whores, or Milly, or had she only dreamed it? If she strained her ears she could probably still hear it now, but then she'd always had special powers of hearing.

Sitting in the WC in that small hotel in Paris where she'd stayed with Jay while they both recovered from dysentery, she had heard a familiar air on the violin, high, sweet, melodious, coming in through the courtyard window. It was a melody she'd loved as a child, something her uncle had often played for them before he had gone to war; she even remembered the name, the "Air for G-String." How sweet to hear it there in Paris after so many years, to have it sweeten her sick days all over again. Food was scarce, the war had wrecked so much; still there were some enchanting things.

Was a neighborhood virtuoso practicing or a recital in progress in the quarter? She listened to the notes as she climbed the stairs and followed the corridor back to their room, heard them still as she opened the door.

"Love—listen," she said excitedly, "this is the music my uncle used to play for us on his violin."

Jay looked at her quizzically. "Music? What music?"

"Don't you hear it? The violin. Listen."

He shook his head.

"Really? You don't hear it?"

But he simply went on shaking his head.

"Come to the window, then," she said and began to hum, for she heard every note perfectly.

But their window gave onto the street, from which rose

only traffic sounds and the voices of children. (Across the street Madame was moving large crates of vegetables while a truck too big for the ancient street drove up over the curb, scattering children, vendors, pedestrians. She covered his hand with hers resting against the sill as together they looked out on the ancient cobbles and listened. Even recovering from dysentery, she was happy.)

"There's no music I can hear, Lil," said Jay gently.

As the "Air for G-String" had a life of its own, playing on and on forever once it was loose in the world, maybe the screams too would stop only when they reached their natural ends.

Prince flicked off the TV and reached for his hat. Button usually came home by two, never after three, and now it was three-fifteen. The pang in his stomach told him she'd probably been picked up. If so, he'd have to wait till morning to bail her out because he was low on cash. But he saw no harm in walking past her spot on the stroll, in case his stomach was wrong. The odds were against him: she couldn't expect to stay clean forever.

He walked into the street and headed for the Casanova Bar. He considered it beneath him to watch his woman working. That was for popcorns who couldn't keep their bitches in line any other way. But checking on news at the bar was different; staying informed was part of his job. If he happened to see Button working, maybe he'd tell her she could knock off and he'd take her out for a meal before tuning her down. If he didn't see her, he'd assume the worst and have a double Scotch to fix him for the drive downtown. Because if she'd been busted, he'd need all his skill to keep her from blowing as soon as she got out. She was still fresh and did not love her work.

It crossed his mind that she could have blown already, though he doubted it. He knew his women, and Button was straight as any bitch. If anything, she was too straight, unwilling to roll or creep on the johns, no heart for specials. Not even a pro like Jacki had got Button thinking like a ho. Most girls in the life had larceny in their hearts before they took on their first trick; you had to stay five moves ahead of them or they'd be tricking off you. That was why pimping was a mind game. But Button was different.

He walked toward the Hotel Venus with his eyes alert. No trace of her, only the he-shes clogging the entrance to the Hotel Venus, gossiping and giggling like a flock of hens. Prince had seen queers in the navy and a few in jail, but none so disgusting as these fags who dressed up like women. They put on wigs and heels and wagged their asses when they walked and sucked the cocks of other men. They were sick, gross. What kind of animals could be born men and act like women? Where was their self-respect? He understood how the system turned men into tricks. But into fags? They were worse than the crackos wandering loose or the repulsive bag lady sprawled in the doorway across the street sleeping in her own filth. He cursed and spat as he passed them to register his disgust.

He'd once heard Bluejay explain that it was the mothers who turned people queer, treating their sons like girls, killing the precious manhood in them. Either that or they trained them to be tricks, perfect little gentlemen putting the female first, letting her have the upper hand. That was why a boy needed a father. When he worried about his son, his one great fear was that he'd grow up into a fag. He swore if he ever learned his son was one of them he'd kill him. And his ex-wife too. If his own mother could raise him fine without a man, letting him be the boss as soon as he was old enough to shave, then so could his ex-wife. She'd better, he thought, if she wanted to live.

He pushed through the door into the bar. Almost no one there; getting near closing time. Suddenly he thought about the bail. His stomach contracted in a painful spasm. He'd have to pay the bond in cash. He hoped Button had been picked up late enough to have made most of her trap; otherwise, he might have to borrow the cash from Sweet Rudy for a day or two. And after that there'd be the fine. Too bad he still had only one shaky woman working for him. "Double Scotch, Johnny Walker Red," he said to a new man behind the bar. For one moment he allowed himself to hope that maybe she hadn't been busted at all, that she'd just been rented for the night by a loaded trick. And flashing his roll as if his fate were not in the hands of a thirty-dollar ho, he peeled off a deuce, straightened his hat in the mirror, and imagined himself with a stable of beautiful, adoring women.

"Of course you're scared, baby," drawled Jacki, stroking her. "Chicago's got unbelievable lungs. She could scare a corpse out of a coffin when she starts screaming. I'd be scared myself if I didn't know from experience." She moved her strong fingers slowly down Robin's back with long rhythmic strokes, pressing away the tension. With her large head and ever-confident voice, Jacki always seemed to know what to do. Already Robin felt better.

"But Chicago will be all right, believe me. She'll call her man from the station. They always let you use the phone. He'll get his lawyer down there, he'll post her bond, and by tomorrow she'll be out. You'll see—she'll be working tomorrow night as if nothing ever happened. And you know what, Button? Nothing did happen, really. Because her man will pay the fine and that's that. You just have to know Chicago. She makes a lot of noise, she likes the attention, but believe me, she won't lose a day." She kneaded Robin's shoulders with her fingertips, sometimes digging into the skin with her long red nails.

Robin sank deeper into the couch. "I'm scared."

"Nothing to be scared about, sugar. Long as the government gets its cut, nothing's going to happen to Chicago."

"Cut? How's that?"

"I'm telling you, the biggest racket of all is the government. Why do you think there are laws against hooking? What's so special about hooking? I'll tell you why. They want to take their cut. Because think about it: doctors and nurses do some of the same kind of work we do, and nobody wants to lock them up. Really. We perform a similar service. Ever hear of sex therapists?"

She waited a moment for her point to sink in. "Or take dancers and actresses and strippers. What's the difference between our work and theirs? Not much, I can tell you, except that ours pays better and we're our own bosses. But the work itself? I started out dancing in a strip joint before I met Sweet Rudy. The place I worked, there was a dance floor called the Pit, surrounded by private booths. When the johns put a quarter in a slot, a curtain would go up and they got to watch us dance nude for about three minutes. They could stick their hands through the window, and if you danced up close to them and let them touch your parts, they tipped you. A dollar a part to touch, more to kiss. Meanwhile, they're jerking themselves off in there, see, and there's no law against that. So what's the big difference? Just who touches their dick? Well, what about wives and girl friends, then? You think they don't do it for the money? But can you see them busting their own wives?"

All Robin could see was their busting her.

"No, the whole thing is just one big setup so the cops and the government can take their cut. Talk about pimping—the government is the biggest pimp of all, busting us, fining us, then sending us back out to work. That's why they're after our pimps, they're their competition. Well, it stinks. The whole fucking system stinks. And it's probably unconstitutional, too. But you don't have to worry about Chicago getting busted, because it's just routine."

Robin was not comforted. "Maybe for you or Chicago it's

just routine, but not for me. If they ever get hold of me I know they'll call my dad. You don't know him. He'll kill me, he really will."

Jacki put her hands on her wide hips, tossed her head till her chins shook, and pouted her painted lips. "Now, Button, really, how can they call your old man? Be realistic. They don't know anything about you. They don't know who you are or where you're from, so how can they find your old man? The only way they can find out is if you tell them. You have ID, you know where to reach me and Prince. If they ever pick you up—and I don't see why they would, but that's a different question— you just call up Prince and he'll come right down and get you out. Or I will."

"But what if I don't reach Prince?"

"Baby, if you're not home when you're supposed to be, Prince will start looking for you. He's probably looking for you right now."

She shot up suddenly, terrified.

"Don't worry," said Jacki, easing her back down on the couch and rubbing her shoulders. "I'll stop by and tell Prince you got sick and came to my place for the night. Then he won't worry."

Jacki continued to massage her with words and fingers until the fears began to loosen and Robin succumbed to a dreamy lethargy. Perhaps she would be safe for a while. She was worn out. Her bones and muscles ached.

"I know, I know," said Jacki. "Sometimes a girl gets scared, sometimes a girl gets tired, sometimes a girl just don't know what to do. I understand, sugar, I do. But you see, honey, you're still just a little thing. How're you gonna manage all by yourself with no one taking care of you?" Jacki's fingers and words were soothing, like the sun and breeze on her back at the beach. "Now you just relax, baby, and let me massage you, forget those silly ideas about running away. I'll forget them too,

I'll forget you ever mentioned them. Just work on getting your-self together before Prince sees you. He doesn't have to know about this scare at all. I won't say a word if you don't. He has enough on his mind. He really trusts you, Button, you know that? He'd be very upset to think he'd made a mistake with you. If you want, I'll lend you the money you're short and we'll just forget all about what you've said. Why don't you get yourself some sleep now? I'm going to work."

She covered Robin with a sheet, tucking it under her feet, and kissed her lightly on the cheek with her rosy lips.

Robin felt grateful for the kiss. The tall woman with bulging breasts and maternal eyes seemed to dissolve her cares. If Jacki were in charge of her instead of Prince, she thought wistfully, closing her eyes, maybe she wouldn't have to run at all. But of course Prince would never allow it, and Jacki belonged to someone else.

When sleep came, it was fitful, startled by bad dreams. In one she and Boots were in a green truck, being taken against their wills across a long makeshift bridge of vines, something like a hammock, too flimsy and narrow to hold them. Below was a deep drop, but when she moved to see it through the window, the truck veered dangerously. In another she was hid-ing in a cove with her brother Billy, waiting for the tide to recede. Billy was crying and it was her fault. In another she was being held down by two nurses while someone forced a mask over her face. She couldn't breathe, but at the same time she knew if she did manage to breathe they would have her. In panic she forced herself awake, just in time, and when she opened her eyes she saw daylight.

The city was already at work. She heard the trucks bellow-ing below and remembered Chicago's scream. Sweating, she kicked off the sheet and considered hopping the first bus headed out. She checked her shoe; the money was still there. But she was afraid of what Prince might do to the kitten. If only she could explain to Prince, make him understand; but she was afraid if she saw him he'd sweet talk her right back down on the street and take her will away.

On Jacki's coffee table, beside ashtrays, papers, and magazines, Robin saw a framed picture of a family. A seated mother who looked vaguely like Jacki smiling in the shadow of a wide-brimmed picture hat, a father beside her looking straight into the camera, and two little girls, maybe seven or eight, with their arms around their mother's neck from either side. Robin wondered which one was Jacki, and what had happened to her since the click of the camera. One never knew what might happen. . . . She decided to sleep until afternoon, when Prince would be out. Then she'd call him to make sure he was gone and go quickly over to pack.

The kitten rubbed against her leg as if he knew Robin was leaving. She filled his dish with food, then went to the closet for his carrying case. Before her hung the wardrobe Prince had bought for her. She had come to the city with a few tops and jeans, and now she had a closetful of pretty clothes. Here were the skirt and tops he'd brought as his first present, the red dress he loved her in, the satin pajamas he said made her look sexy, the ruby shoes she'd admired in a window that made her feel like the Wicked Witch of the East. But she had no suitcase to pack them all in, only the backpack she'd brought stuffed full from Maine.

She took her money from her shoe, put it in the satin case, and secreted the case deep in the bedroll. She left out the red dress, his favorite, to wear, and began packing whatever would fit; the rest she would have to abandon. Hastily stuffing the backpack, she worked herself into a sweat, then had to take the time to wash herself. Noticing the towel they reserved for sex on the back of the bathroom door she began to waver: she had grown used to a bath every morning and a man beside her; it would be hard to do without.

She slipped into the red dress Prince loved and examined herself before the mirror. It was made of jersey, with a scooped neck and little sleeves. Seeing herself as he had made her, she almost hoped he would return and stop her. Maybe if they ran away together she could grow pot like Lana's sister and he could sell it.

Without warning she heard the door open.

"Going somewhere?" asked Prince.

In the mirror she watched him, very small, with ice in his almond eyes.

"I—I don't know."

"You don't *know*?" He walked toward her.

She shrank back, feeling trapped, until all her fear suddenly turned to rage. She blurted out, "I'm not hooking anymore, Prince. You can't make me!"

He looked at her with icy eyes and said nothing.

"I mean," she retreated, "can't we do something else? We have some money saved, don't we? And—"

"*We* have money? *We*? It'll take you months, maybe years, to pay back what you owe me."

He threw his hat on the bed and strode toward her with long strides like her father's. She thought he would hit her and veered aside, shielding her head with her arm. But he moved past her to the kitchen.

A moment later she heard dishes, ice. Maybe he was getting a drink? She clutched at the thought: he must be fixing them both drinks, getting ready for a serious talk. For a second she had a wild fantasy of them as a couple in some TV movie, he pouring drinks, ice cubes tinkling, she in a beautiful red dress.

He came back in carrying a large pan. He walked directly to her and dumped the entire basin full of ice and water over her head, letting the basin clatter to the floor. "Bitch!" he said, mouth set in contempt.

Icy water dripped from her hair, her face, her dress, her shoes. Robin sank to the floor, covering her face with her hands. Everything was ruined: her love, her dress, her shoes, her hopes, her plans, her life—ruined, ruined, in a pool of ice.

Prince emptied first her purse, then her backpack, onto the wet floor with one shake each and kicked through the pile of clothes. Then he tore open the bedroll till he found the money. She watched him extract the bills from the satin bag and drop the remains on the wet heap. He counted the money quickly.

"This all you brought me?"

"Yes." Slowly she pulled off the soaked and ruined ruby shoes and let the tide wash over her.

"You're a mess," he spat at her. "You're no better than a junkie. You disgust me. Any other man would toss you out a window, cut your lyin face. You're lucky you're with me, cause I'm gonna give you one more chance before I whip your ass." He looked at his watch. "You got fifteen minutes to fix yourself up and git down on the street and show me you're not just a weak, spineless, worthless, half-steppin ho. Half-steppin hos are lower than tricks."

He kicked the pile of clothes into the pool of ice and water, then walked to the door. "I'm comin back in fifteen minutes and you better be outa here. I don't want to see your face again unless you're really *choosin*. From now on you don't walk in here without three hundred, to show you mean it. Plus I'm chargin you one bill to cover this mess and another to teach you a lesson. Now *move!*"

Even after the door slammed she did not look up but sat with her face buried in her arms, sobbing, her shoulders heaving, her tears feeding the pool of melting ice in which she sat shivering with rage and sorrow.

Three

20

Owl had a precious picture of her mother that she had kept all through her childhood wrapped in pink tissue in a small satin-lined cedar box under whatever bed she slept in. Somehow it had mattered less to her where she slept knowing that the box, which had once belonged to her mother, slept with her. Now the box was gone, but the picture continued to console Owl for every unwelcome change.

After her mother's funeral, Lilly had been sent to live with one aunt after another while her father, that handsome, whiskey-voiced gambling man who alone in the world was permitted to view her mother's picture, "married" one woman after another. Each time he changed wives, Lilly's relatives always expected him to take Lilly away. But Lilly knew he wouldn't. Not that she doubted his love; she and Papa had a strong secret bond shared by no one else, not even her baby brother, who lived with yet another aunt. Still, what wife would want to share him?

At first Papa came to see her every several months. Usually he arrived unannounced, just pulled up the drive in his latest car—a black Ford with rumble seat, a white Plymouth coupe with black running boards—whistled his special whistle, climbed the stairs, and scooped her up in his arms. For these visits she waited, she lived, storing up trophies to share with him, dreaming up stories to tell him. He would pick her up, twirl her in the air, set her down and inspect her, then take her out with him—sometimes to the Gardenia Tavern, a fancy bar-and-grill where he was known; sometimes to the races, where he allowed Lilly to pick their horses; sometimes just for a drive in the country to see the cows; or, when he brought his newest wife along, for ice cream and half an hour alone in her room, just Lilly and Papa, while the wife stayed downstairs with the family.

"Got anything to show me, Lilly?" he would say when she had seated him on her bed. It didn't matter whether he had just arrived or it was the drooping end of a full day; she would pull the little cedar box out from under her bed, unwrap the picture of her mother, hold it silently between them for a little while as they looked together into those serene sepia eyes, then wrap it carefully up again and place it in its corner of the box. Then, under the spell, she would show him her most recently acquired treasures. First the cards and presents he had sent her himself, then the trophies of her adventures: a feather from a blue jay she had rescued, a special marble she had won, the trinkets from a certain restaurant mostly stamped "Made in Japan."

But gradually her papa's visits tapered off. First he sent cards of apology, then he stopped mentioning visits at all, and finally the cards began arriving from greater distances and with longer intervals between them until they stopped altogether. Though she had once known better, now, secretly, she fixed on the hope that one day he would arrive unannounced, pull into the drive in his latest car, whistle for her up the stairs, and carry her off with him. Such fantasies flourished in direct proportion to her aunts' complaints that Papa no longer sent any money, that he'd fallen in with bad company, that the crash had ruined him.

When she was twelve, Lilly's uncle, long out of work, landed a job in a china factory in a town fifty miles away. They packed hastily and moved in a day. Lilly was in a panic because she had dreamed Papa was on his way to see her from New York City, and now he would drive up to an empty house. "We'll write to him, don't worry," promised Aunt Hilda. But Lilly knew Papa would not come again. At her new school, where naturally kids avoided walking with the new girl (an orphan who lived in the old Stokes house on the hill with her aunt and uncle) and on the playground withdrew to tell their secrets, Lilly stood proud. No ordinary orphan, she let it be known that she was the child of a handsome soldier, a great hero who was off fighting battles and just might be returning any moment. Around her neck she proudly displayed the necklace of shark's teeth he had sent her from as far away as Alaska, and under her arm she sometimes carried her cedar box. She carted it through the halls, peered into it during recess, examined its contents between classes, fondled the rabbit's foot, the seed containing a dozen carved ivory animals, and the precious oblong object wrapped in pink tissue paper which, however, she never opened except in the perfect privacy of her room.

Now, seeing Milly in Sallee's with her backpack on as if she was being forced to move, her nose red and eyes swollen from crying, Owl longed to comfort the child. She would have taken her home if she could, but as she no longer had a home to offer, she decided on second best: she would try to give her a photograph of Owl herself.

As Robin sat in Sallee's Coffee Shop drinking the Coke Grace had kindly served her free of charge, all she could think of was the poor kitten. When she'd looked for him to take with her, he had disappeared. She had called to him and searched the room—under the bed, in the closet, everywhere—until there were only moments left until her deadline. She'd had no choice but to shove a few wet clothes into her pack, roll up the wet sleeping bag, and leave the Royal Arms without him. Now she worried about what would become of him up there alone with Prince and tried not to worry about herself.

When Lana came in on a break, Robin asked to borrow a few dimes.

"Trouble with your man?" asked Lana sympathetically.

Robin nodded and went straight to the pay phone. First, on a long shot, she called Boots; no word yet. Then she tried a couple of the tricks who had given her cards with offers of salvation. The first one played dumb and the second hung up angry. Finally, she called Clarence.

"Clarence? It's me. Sue."

"Sue? . . . Sue! God, you can't imagine how lucky it is you called this minute. I was already out the door—I've got a date to play tennis at Columbia in fifteen minutes—and I came back for some new balls. And then you called. Can you beat that? I would've missed you. How are you, anyway?"

"I called to ask you a favor, Clarence. See, I just lost my job—it's a long story, I'll explain the whole thing later—but the thing is, right now I don't have any place to stay and I wondered . . . I mean, I wondered if I could crash with you for a little while. I could cook for you and—"

"You mean, stay here? Of course you can. Look, I'll just run down and cancel the tennis and you can come right over. I'll meet you at the door. This is great, great!"

On her way uptown she made up a story to tell him, but she didn't have to use it. He was too excited to ask her anything. Again, he put on music and poured them wine, but this time he went on talking for only an hour or so before turning off the lights and taking her to bed. This time when he fucked her he managed to stay inside her a full minute before coming. "Oh, I love you, I love you," he said in rapturous gratitude. The next morning, however, when he tried again, he came on the bed as soon as Robin touched his penis. "God, I'm sorry," he said, covering the wet spot with a pillow and turning away.

"Please don't say that," said Robin. "It's okay. Really. Don't worry."

"You shouldn't have touched me, though. I was too excited. You get me much too excited."

After coffee they left the apartment together, going

straight, as he suggested, to the employment agency on Broadway, where he left her on his way to class.

Inside, a receptionist handed her several short and long forms to fill out. Name, address, age, telephone, Social Security number, education (high school, college, other), skills (typing, shorthand, data processing), experience (most recent position first), past three salaries, and references (employment and character). She stared at the forms for a while, first the white ones, then the pink, blue, and green, hoping for inspiration. Soon it became clear to her that there was not a single item on any of the forms that she could answer truthfully. She wondered what to say to the confident, efficient personnel women at their cluttered desks. Finally, she told the receptionist she was going to the ladies' room, left the forms on the table as if she planned to return, and walked quietly out the door.

Clarence had said he'd be back in his apartment at noon, after his class; it was only ten-thirty when she left the agency. She walked down to Riverside Park. The air was already heating up but there was a cool breeze off the river. She lay on the grass wondering what to do next, what to tell Clarence when he got back. The old people in ragged clothes dozing on benches depressed her. She wanted some reefer, but she didn't have the money for a single joint.

Beneath her the grasses were teeming with insect life. She watched the ants dragging morsels of food several times their size across the dry, uneven turf. How, she wondered, did they know where to go? Even in the heart of a huge city, they knew exactly what they were doing. Compared to them, people made no sense. Seeing the joggers running back and forth, she thought: If I were a runner I wouldn't go round in circles. I'd start running and go straight on and just keep going until I was far away and maybe I'd never stop.

. . .

The rain struck him in a blast, like sirens in a raid. Prince pulled down his hat and made a dash for the street. Just getting into his car, Prince's pants lost their creases and his shoes their shine. The sky was black. Glancing into the rearview mirror while starting the motor, he could see nothing through the window but a sheet of water; trying to adjust the mirror, he could still see nothing but his own face. My face looks like my stomach feels, thought Prince, pulling out from the curb. He could coat his stomach with milk to sweeten it up, but his face felt raw and sour. If only he could do some coke or swallow a happy pill and feel calm again.

Only a few days ago, walking with his woman, pocket full of money, he'd thought the life a beautiful thing, a game of skill and style. But now that he was hurting again he could see it was just another hustle, everyone gaming off everyone. Now he was driving to Brooklyn to rent out his wheels, and in a couple of hours he'd be returning to Manhattan in the subway, on his belly. After the wheels he could pawn his ring. And after that? He'd be out of gas until he caught himself a woman.

As sheets of rain assaulted his windshield, Prince imagined Tahiti, where the rain on the water was as gentle as seltzer. At night the sky over Tahiti glistened with stars and the air was perfumed with jasmine. His ship had put in for only a fortnight, but it was long enough to let him see. There, strange, smiling women had thronged the ship, five or more to a man. Not for sale like all the rest, they had only wanted to please. They wore gardenias behind their ears or hibiscus in their hair. Long bare arms, bare feet, broad smiling faces, soft brown skin—in Tahiti women still followed nature, treating every man like a king. You didn't have to train them to keep their mouths shut, consider your desires, light your cigarettes; they had natural breeding. That was the life: everything you could ever want, right there at your fingertips. Loving women, fresh fish, breadfruit and bananas growing on trees, and if you got thirsty, cool coconut milk.

On Tahiti
Life is easy
No one needy
No one greedy

Not like here. Driving south, Prince saw tricks everywhere, even in the rain. Jacki said rain made men horny. He flicked on the radio and turned the dial until he found a Spanish station. On Tahiti French was the language of love, but for now, Spanish would do. He remembered the outrigger canoes on the black sand beaches, and small boats rippling through the harbors as you watched from the café.

At a yellow light he gunned the engine, hoping to make it through the thirties without stopping. The lights were fixed at twenty-five, but you couldn't always make them, you still had to play the odds. Someone could slow down on yellow or stop for a turn, some old bag could chug along not caring and you'd be stuck behind. Still, whatever happened, you had to keep trying.

He reviewed his position. There was a square broad named Paula he'd been opening up, but he still had a way to go to catch her. She worked as a waitress in a Ninth Avenue diner where he showed up every afternoon. Now she brought him his coffee without his asking and was definitely giving up rhythm with her sassy questions. But as soon as he tried to pin her down to a time and place she came up square, first giggling, then pouting out her plump red lip. Not easy and sweet, like the women of Tahiti.

There were the bus station bitches, but they were proud and pushy. Hard to catch, harder to control.

There were the turned-out hos on the stroll, all that used-up pussy. When he was new to the life he'd liked to crack on them just for the sport. But now their voices grated and their games depressed him. Except for the few free-lancers, who wouldn't want him, all the hos he knew were either working for someone else already and out of line talking to Prince, or else they'd been cut loose by their man for good reason. (No pimp in his right mind fired a ho without good reason.) Which meant that if he took one of them on, he'd be dealing with someone else's shit.

A light caught him. He skidded to a stop. On the radio someone was singing "Siboney" in a high-pitched falsetto, accompanied by guitar and castanets. Listening to the music of another world, he remembered the hermits of Tahiti he and two buddies had tracked down on the back side of the island. Everyone on his ship had heard of them. Each lived alone behind high walls of piled-up shells in a palm-thatched hut, speaking to no one, not even the other hermits. They raised vegetables and a few chickens, wore loincloths and long beards. Walking up the path to the hermit hut, he half expected to be chased away, but those strange men were eager to talk to anyone willing to listen to them. Alone for as many as thirty-five years, they were bitter and lonely and old. Even the new ones were bitter. They spent all their time denouncing the cost of cigarettes, the French, women, the other hermits.

If they couldn't make it alone even in Paradise, then how would Button manage?

She had no money and no friends but him, he'd been strict about that. A player's first duty with a fresh ho was to cut her loose from all her old ties. With Button it had been easy: she'd cut the ties herself. If she'd gone back to Maine he'd know where to find her, but she would never go back with her father there. Maybe she'd finally found her friend Boots. But if she'd really gone for good, why had she left her cat behind? He'd been feeding it every day, certain she'd be back to claim it; now, though, he was no longer sure. Maybe she was too scared to come back, even to get her cat.

Sweet Rudy said it was his own fault she'd blown. "Just

like a popcorn," he said. After her big scare he should have consoled her instead of scaring her more, said Sweet Rudy. That was the part that hurt, knowing Sweet Rudy was right. Prince had studied the pimping code and knew it was always the man who blew the ho. If a woman acted out of weakness she wasn't to blame. She was weak and fickle by nature: it was his job to control her. He had to get the upper hand and keep it. If Adam had kept the upper hand with Eve, instead of letting her trick him into eating that apple, maybe the world wouldn't be made of tricks and hos. A player had to remember, a woman was only as good as her man. And he hadn't been good enough.

Maybe he'd never been good enough. He'd blown his wife and child too. He had wanted to be a good father. He considered the day his son was born the first day of his real life. He named the boy after himself and passed out real Cuban cigars, the most expensive he could buy, to everyone on his ship. He wanted to give his son everything his own daddy had deprived him of, everything money or love could buy. The love he felt for his wife and boy in those first few months was the purest feeling he'd ever felt. For the first time in his life, at twenty-one, he felt like a real man.

But at the end of his hitch when he got back home to DC, things began to go sour. The two of them, his wife and son, made him feel like a stranger. They were always together, needing things he couldn't give. He needed a few things too, but his needs didn't count. When he wanted to dance, his wife had to feed the baby; when he wanted to make love, she wanted to sleep; and when he just wanted to talk, it seemed, that was when she had to get the baby off to sleep.

She didn't understand that he too needed a little understanding and a little rest. Money was what she said they needed to be a real family; money, not rest. She tried to run his life. She blamed him for his jobs, those he couldn't land and those he could. Instead of treating him like a man, she treated him like a meal ticket, a trick: always, *do this and do that* when he wasn't working and *why not more?* when he was. For the family, she said.

When they began to fight, she used their son against him. If he spoke his mind she accused him of not caring about his son. When he raised his voice in protest, she said his protests proved it.

He not care about his son? He cared about nothing else! If not for his son, he would never have put up with the things that woman said! One day, after a raging fight, he grabbed up his son and took him away. First he went to his mother's house, but when his wife came looking for him there, crying and screaming at the door, it upset the boy; so he moved him to an old girl friend's place instead, where his wife would never find him.

When he figured he'd finally proved how much he cared, he took the boy back home. But his wife would not speak to him. She clutched the baby to her and cooed and sobbed, but had not one word for her man. As soon as he left the house, she bolted the door against him; she locked him out of his own house and put his clothes out the door and never spoke another word to him except through her lawyer. Oh, she was righteous as a schoolmarm, sitting there holding the one thing in the world he cared for.

If he couldn't have his son she wasn't going to get a penny off him. All the money he could spare he sent to his mother, but not one penny for that righteous wife. When she took him to court, he had to leave DC; and after that he never saw his wife or son again.

When the light turned green he decided to take the Brooklyn Bridge. Another bridge would take him closer to Bed-Stuy, but he loved the Brooklyn Bridge. Each tower was a hand pulling a thousand strings to put one over on gravity. Why save minutes when this was his last drive till he got something new going? The feel of the wheel in his hands was like bills in his pocket; he might as well enjoy it. He took the outside lane, where you could see down the river, the harbor, the great city.

Then he saw a young black beauty in a white Impala trying to pass him in the slow lane. She wore a wide hat at a smart angle and smoked a cigarillo. He stepped on the gas and shot ahead. When she failed to pursue, he fell back abreast of her, tipping his hat for introduction. (Take an application from anyone you can find, advised Sweet Rudy. Rich, poor, young, old, hip, square, what do you care, if the money's right.) Once he gave up his wheels he'd have a hard time copping, but he still had a few more miles in which to press his advantage.

She kept her eye on the road, looking distressed.

Being friendly, Prince honked his horn and buzzed her, flashing his widest grin. But she locked her doors and clutched her wheel, falling behind. He looked in the mirror, watching her, planning his strategy, until, readjusting the mirror, he caught sight once more of his face. Sour, sour, he thought, no wonder, and skidded on the wet bridge.

The Impala fell farther and farther behind, leaving Prince alone in the slippery outside lane. When he left the bridge he gunned the engine and turned abruptly toward the expressway.

21

Owl was sitting in the waiting room of the bus station waiting out the thunderstorm when she saw Red Mary from the Shelter's Monday coffee hours coming toward her. Owl did not feel like talking. Red Mary was wet and her wig was askew; her features were contorted from the strain of waging an endless battle in her head.

"Sister Theresa's been looking for you," said Red Mary. "Where the hell have you been? She says she has some mail for you at the Shelter."

Mail? Owl tensed. "Where'd she get it? How long has she had it?"

Red Mary, with hands on hips and chin thrust belligerently forward, said, "Now how the hell should I know?" and marched off in a rage.

A long clap of thunder, loud and ominous, interrupted Owl's calculations. She hadn't been to the Shelter for several weeks. After moving to the street she had asked Sister Theresa to pick up her welfare check from the Hotel Venus because she couldn't bring herself to speak to the manager. But was it check time yet? She wasn't sure.

Quickly Owl crossed the concourse toward the lockers, feeling for her key. Check or letter, she wanted it now, though for years all news had been bad news. From deep inside a locker she withdrew a large bag and extracted her galoshes. It was a brand-new Brentano's bag, not yet named, for her inventory was still in flux. For safety's sake she planned to keep switching her possessions among several lockers the way the military kept switching the deadly missiles from one silo to another to confuse the Russians. Unless the Russians got enough warheads to bomb them all, they were safe; unless the muggers were staking out the station, so was she. But even if she were watched, the most the muggers could get off her now at a single clip was a third of what they could have got before. Using several lockers was like keeping your money in several different banks in case of another depression.

She pulled on her galoshes, retrieved her umbrella (whose major flaw was a missing handle), and deftly rearranged her possessions so that she'd have only one rainproof bag of necessities to carry. Then she relocked her locker and set off in the rain for the Shelter, trying to guess at what treasure awaited her.

What was more romantic than a letter? Love poems from a young poet who had flourished and died, poems she'd sold for fifty dollars to a collector, had come in the mail. In her time, years before, when the mail had been delivered twice a day except on Sundays, and each sealed envelope promised unguessable news, the mailbox had been the focus of her hopes. From all over the world love and desire had flowed to her—from the picture postcards her father had sent when she was a child, to the chatty letters from her Aunt Hilda, to the V-mail from soldiers, love letters from Jay, and birthday cards from Milly, down to the lying letters from Bert.

Bert. What a nasty trick he'd pulled, reading all her mail out of jealousy until she no longer wrote to anyone, then leaving tattered letters of his own where she could piece together his betrayals. No, she wouldn't forget his betrayals just because time had gone by. The more time that passed, the longer she'd have to dwell on them. When the wind was right her mind could glide agilely across entire decades and land like a bird squarely on a single word. One word, like: *sorry*. He dared to write: *I'm sorry*. After he moved her to the suburbs and cut her off from the world, after he drove her near to madness replacing sleep with rage, after he hurt and betrayed her, he dared to write: "I'm sorry, Lilly. I just can't take any more. I don't want to spend my life like this." She stood in her hospital gown with his letter fluttering between her fingers, tears streaming down her cheeks, crying, You bastard! You dirty shit! and tore the letter into hundreds of ugly little pieces.

The first time he'd left her at least she'd had Milly. But later, when he sent her to the hospital and he was outside free, he left her nothing. After she got out, every letter brought bad news. A divorce in Spanish tied in ribbons. Doctor bills and lawyers' bills. Evictions. And after she got herself on welfare, along with checks came forms, threats, and accusations.

As she moved crosstown, the wind whipped trash against her legs and hurled it against her umbrella. Pressing on, she remembered how once, during a terrible rainstorm in Salzburg, the colonel had insisted to her that if you were walking toward the raindrops you got wetter than if you were walking away. She had thought he was joking, but after they stopped in a café for shelter he began drawing diagrams on the tablecloth to prove his point. She could never tell with him whether he was pulling her leg or telling the truth, but at that moment she was quite certain he was making fun of her. For how could two people walking on the same street not get equally wet? It was ridiculous! Did he think she would believe him over common sense? In that moment she hated him.

But after she had married Bert and seen how easily two people living the same life could be so differently drenched by circumstance, she was no longer sure the colonel had been teasing her with his story of the wetness of rain. For when the storm of her marriage was over, Bert, moving in one direction (up!) had a house, car, job, wife, and child, while she, moving steadily down, had nothing.

By the time she entered the last block on her route, the rain had stopped. Like a miracle, she saw the Shelter standing in a haze—a gray, rickety, tilted house, surrounded by rubble and parking lots, that alone in the block had escaped the wrecker's ball. In one of the lots boys were already playing stick-ball, and on the sidewalk girls in dirty cotton skirts with scabbed-over knees jumped rope, though the pavement was still wet.

> "My sister's name is Anna
> Her husband's name is Albert
> They come from Alabama
> And they pick apples."

Owl listened to the rope chants she'd heard more than fifty years before near the railroad tracks in Buffalo and again in Milly's youth on the sidewalks of Connecticut. The rope slapping the ground marked the endless tick of time going all the way back and on; and as the sun came back, throwing the light of knowledge briefly through the thin scrim of reality, again Owl saw the unity of All. The rope endlessly turning, the songs endlessly sung, the street children, her own, herself.

Owl mounted the five steps of the Shelter's stoop, lifting her bag high above the stairs, and rang the bell. She would try to take a bath while she was here. How long, she wondered, had it been since she had bathed? She remembered washing up for the funeral, but not since. Living on the street, days and weeks flashed by like minutes. The Shelter was the only place she knew where you could drop in any time and use the bath, no questions asked. You couldn't drink, of course, or start a fight or fire, or stay longer than two nights; but otherwise there seemed to be no rules. And though the sisters were always blessing you and saying prayers, you were not obliged to believe in God, not even to pretend. Even the blasphemous like Red Mary were welcome to Thanksgiving and Christmas dinners, coffee hours on Mondays, bingo on Wednesdays, and evening prayers as long as they controlled themselves. In fact, the only problems Owl ever had at the Shelter were certain other women, whose hostile attacks or pathetic conditions too often reminded her how tenuous was her own existence, and how high a price one paid for freedom. Usually after a visit to the Shelter Owl found herself consulting her running list of lucky women who were fifty-five or older, famous, and alive.

The door opened at last. A young woman in jeans, shirt, and sandals smiled at Owl. "Can I help you?"

"I'm looking for Sister Theresa."

"She's up in the chapel now. But come in. I'm sure she'll be down soon. I'm Sister Elizabeth. Is there anything I can do for you?"

Owl hesitated. She didn't like to reveal herself to strangers, even sisters of the Shelter, or be pinned down. "I'd like to take a bath," she said, letting on nothing about mail.

"Okay. Just let me make sure the bathroom's empty," said the sister, leading Owl into a large, fluorescent-lit room, the downstairs lounge. With a wave of her arm she offered Owl all the comforts of folding chairs, an old wooden table painted white, and on the floor checkered, worn linoleum, yellowed with age but shiny with care. "What's your name? I'll tell Sister Theresa."

"Owl," she said after a moment, remembering that nuns too renamed themselves when they took their vows.

As soon as Sister Elizabeth had gone, Owl went into the storeroom across from the lounge where the clean clothes were kept on racks and tables for anyone who wanted them. It was comforting to know they were there. She ran her hands across the rows of coats and dresses, preparing to select her clean, après-le-bain costume, and remembered the last real letter she'd received, square, oversized, addressed by hand in light blue ink to Mrs. Lillian Fox. The handwriting was like her own, but like Bert's letters, the envelope had no return address.

The desk clerk at the Midway (before she'd moved to the Hotel Venus) had watched with a smirk as she lifted out a card with flowers and a border on the front, HAPPY BIRTHDAY printed inside. Across the bottom was scrawled, "Hope your winter was better than ours. We'll be moving next month if Harry's job comes through. Happy birthday. Love, Milly." "A birthday card?" asked the desk clerk. "How old are you?" But she had hidden the card and walked away. After that she had been evicted and received no more letters.

Most of the dresses were wrong—too small, too hot for summer, too light or loud. Not that she permitted herself to care about how she looked, not anymore. She remembered buying a new flowered dress the last time she saw Milly. She'd spent everything she had on that visit, including new hat, presents for everyone, and the ticket out west.

I vowed not to say one word about Bert, not let old wounds open up. But then I heard you fighting upstairs—every night from the very first night, while I tried to sleep on the sofa in your living room—and it all came back. Harry's voice, like a badly muffled engine, and yours, frightened and shrill—they sounded so familiar. When I thought of the children listening I wanted to march upstairs and defend you, but of course that would have made it worse. I was a guest; so naturally I had to pretend not to hear. But I knew what you were fighting about. Me.

Why was it that all conversation stopped dead every time I walked into a room? Even on my best behavior. Silence. Shame. The children were in on it too. Young as they were, they ran off whenever they saw me and squirmed away if I tried to kiss them. As if I were an enemy who had taken over their living room. What had you told them to make them so ashamed?

I suppose I should have turned around and left as soon as I heard you fighting. Foolish to think I could win you back after all Bert's poison. I should have known you were ashamed by the way you hid me away from the neighbors, even from the children's friends, the way they looked at each other when I spoke. I should have thanked you and gone away. But it was my first visit and I'd spent everything to get there. Instead of leaving I tried to make myself useful. Cleaning the kitchen, straightening up the living room, looking for clothes to mend. But it didn't help. "Please, Mother," you would say coldly, "stop. I've got everything under control. Really. I don't need your help. Go in the other room and sit."

Sit! How could I just sit, doing nothing, and Harry always watching me with his look of hate?

Then one night I accidentally dropped the salad bowl and broke it while I was cleaning up after dinner. Little Bobby ran into the kitchen and out again, shouting, "See? Now she's started. Grandma's breaking the dishes!"—as if I were some kind of crazy person and you'd all been waiting for this.

Then you came in. "God, Mother, I told you not to fuss in here. Now see what you've done. Everyone's all upset. Why must you interfere?"

"I was just trying to help. I'm really sorry, honey. I—"

"Sorry! But I told you not to! My green salad bowl! Why can't you leave anything alone? Why do you always manage to wreck everything?"

All the others were standing at the door watching us. "Why is everyone in this family against me?" I cried. "It's because of Bert, isn't it?"

Sister Theresa came into the room and hugged Owl. Owl pulled away. She hadn't bathed and knew she smelled. She was not used to being touched.

"Red Mary said you have something for me. Some mail. Do you think it's a check?"

"I don't know," said Sister Theresa, handing her an envelope.

No light blue ink, no familiar hand, only an official-looking envelope. She should never have come out in the rain for another welfare communiqué.

"It's not a check, is it?"

"Why don't you open it, Owl, and see?"

Owl turned the letter over in her hands. She took her glasses out of the bag and balanced them on her nose. Then with her stubs of fingers she broke the letter's seal and quickly read it through.

Disaster. She had missed her face-to-face interview with her social worker and therefore her case was closed. No more checks. Termination.

She stared at the letter. She had never even been notified of her appointment, so of course she had missed it. Or had the manager written to welfare denouncing her? She wouldn't put it past him. She'd have only her savings to live on now, enough for a month or two, and then nothing. Nothing for cigarettes or coffee or food, nothing for the cats or the lockers, unless she could get back on the rolls. And how would she persuade them to let her back? She knew the procedure: once you were terminated you had to start again from scratch. Go down there day after day, stand on endless lines—Application; Employment; Medical; Housing—through all the obstacles.

Even if she could stomach the social worker's insults ("That sweater seems awfully nice for someone who's been on public assistance; what are you trying to tell me?"); even if she could produce the necessary documents to establish her identity (her divorce in Spanish in lieu of a birth certificate or her ancient passport with the picture of the smiling woman Jay had loved whom they always failed to recognize); even if she could once again answer the impossible questions in the twelve-page application form and go downtown to Employment every two weeks to wait half a day to be told that there were no jobs for her; and report to Housing, and return to Application, and request assistance—even if she could travel up and down on the

subway to all the different sections and manage to keep all of
the sometimes overlapping appointments, still she would face
impossible impediments.

First, to establish residency she was required to submit a
current rent receipt, which she could no longer produce. They
would tell her to return to Application Section with such a
receipt in five days or her case would be closed. (Closed? How
could they close it if it was closed already?) She thought the
room was still hers for a few more days, but no one would believe her. Without a room they would send her to the city
Women's Shelter where she'd have to be deloused and surrender her bags. Then they'd try to place her in a home, which
was worse.

Her second problem was the Medical. Her legs were badly
swollen now, with ugly open sores. She couldn't deny it to
them though she managed all right to herself. When they saw
her legs and certain other things they would try to get her to a
hospital, that was how they worked, and once they got her in
they might never let her out. More people died in hospitals
than anyplace else. If she had only a limited time left to live,
she certainly wasn't going to spend it locked up in a home or
a hospital! (If they sent you up as a mental, they took away
your child and gave you three years to prove you could provide
a "stable environment" before they gave your child away forever.)

Her third problem was money, the noose they held you by.
Since she had a little saved up in a bank she was bound to fail
the means test. That she'd saved up the money from her welfare by living in the tunnels and making other extreme econ-
omies meant nothing at all; they would put her through the
computer until they found her out and then they would con-
fiscate her savings and destroy her bags and close her case.

"Don't worry, dear, we'll help you reapply," said Sister
Theresa, always encouraging. But Owl only shook her head.
Not even the sisters could fight City Hall. Until she was flat

broke and had a room she could not qualify. Until her legs improved she wasn't safe. And even then the odds would still be slim.

"Acutally, I was hoping it would be a birthday card," Owl confided.

"A birthday card? Oh, Owl, is it your birthday? When?"

"Every year," she said, tucking the letter into her bag to protect it from the rain. "Every year."

Sister Elizabeth poked her head into the room. "Here you are. You can take a bath now if you want to, Owl. The bathroom's empty. I just hope there's enough hot water left."

"Your legs, Owl!" said Sister Theresa as Owl moved toward the door. "You poor dear! Don't they hurt you? We'll have to get you to a doctor."

Owl hurried from the room.

Robin leaned against the door, dripping, and closed the umbrella. She rested the heavy bag of groceries on her hip and waited in the locked foyer for Clarence to buzz her in. Examining the once handsome mosaic tile floor, now cracked and stained, she thought how much easier it would be for both of them if he'd give her a key. But he never offered. He wouldn't permit her to answer the telephone, either, though maybe that was different. He said he had to stay on good terms with his parents, or they'd cut off his funds. Not that they disapproved of girls in his room, he said, but he didn't want them asking questions.

She didn't care about the telephone—she had no one but Clarence to talk to; but without a key, she could come and go only when Clarence was home. Without a key, she didn't really live there, though it was five days since she'd left Prince. Without a key she was a prisoner. She decided to make a special effort to be ingratiating and then ask for a key.

The bag grew heavy. She was afraid Clarence was asleep.

She rang the bell again. When the clock-radio had awakened them that morning, Clarence, handing her a ten from the wallet he kept beside the bed, had sent her out for the *Times* and some croissants; then he had turned down the volume and gone back to sleep.

Instead of buying croissants, Robin had gone to the supermarket and bought the makings for a real breakfast—bacon, eggs, pancake mix, syrup—and ingredients for an apple pie. Her mother said the smell of bacon mellowed her dad, and the pies they made from the wild green apples that grew on the nubble softened up everyone. This was part of a larger plan Robin had conceived to make herself useful to Clarence, starting from her first day with him. When he was at the library she had walked around the apartment emptying ashtrays, throwing out empty beer bottles, and generally tidying up; after that, each day she'd tried to be helpful in another way. One time she polished Clarence's shoes and bought him a plant. Another day she cooked a chicken she found in the freezer when she was cleaning the refrigerator. And once she tried to collect all his magazines and newspapers into neat piles: all the *Ouis* in one, the *New Yorkers* in another, and old *New York Times*es in a third, stacked neatly on the floor. She thought he would be pleased when he got back from the library, but instead he told her icily never to touch his papers, not any of them; he said he'd put them all exactly where they were for a reason. Instead of coming to need her, as she'd hoped, he seemed to be getting more distant. For the last two days he had not even tried to make love.

At last the buzzer rang. Robin pushed open the door and walked through the dark lobby to the elevator at the back. When the elevator arrived she pushed four.

Of course, today's pie would be made of store apples instead of the wild apples of the nubble, but she had no choice. At home the apples would be just about ripe for picking.

Rising toward Clarence, Robin thought how she and Adam had always climbed up among the scratchy branches and out on the shaky limbs to get at the best, largest apples, while Billy stayed below to catch them. Then they would all sit far out on the rocks with paring knives and plastic buckets, preparing the apples for pie, watching the seagulls dive, tossing the peels and cores into the sea. Though the apples were tiny, misshapen, and far too bitter to nibble raw, they always produced the best apple pie she'd ever tasted. She and her mother would roll out the dough and the boys would mix in the spices and fill the shells. When the fragrance of apples and nutmeg and cinnamon filled the house no one entered or left without some comment. There was a family joke that her father stayed calm at pie time.

The elevator arrived on four. Walking down the hall, Robin planned to ask Clarence for the key as soon as he tasted her pie.

When he saw the bulging bag of groceries, Clarence clapped his hands against his head and cried out, "For God's sake, Sue, what's all that? All I asked you to get me was the *Times* and some croissants."

"Don't worry," said Robin as her stomach sank. "I'm going to cook you a real breakfast. And then I'm going to bake an apple pie."

"A what? A *pie*?" Clarence leaped from the bed and thrust on his glasses. Clasping and unclasping his hands, he began pacing nervously back and forth. Finally, he looked at her and said, "In this heat you want to bake a pie in the oven? You're nuts."

On the island there were always breezes crossing through the house as soon as they opened the windows. But here inside the air never seemed to stir, not even on a rainy day. "I guess it's a dumb idea. I'm sorry." She put the bag down on the table. "We can just eat the apples plain then."

"Jesus," said Clarence, shaking his head and raising his

brows into an anguished V that made his eyes look even closer together than usual. "I've got to memorize the whole damned LISP manual this afternoon and you want to bake a *pie*. A pie! Jee-sus!"

He said it in the same tone he assumed when his cock slipped out of her and he couldn't get it back in again, as if his troubles were all her fault. In such moments she was afraid even to speak, for anything she said was likely to anger him. He was as unpredictable as her mother when she was drinking. He was so strange, with his weird talk and his mess of auburn hair that he ruffled and mussed till it stood straight up and his thick brooding lips—one moment frantically trying to impress her, the next moment seeming to resent her very presence—that she always tried to play it safe.

"I'm really sorry, Clarence. I thought you'd like it. Well, anyway, I can still make you breakfast."

Clarence swiveled around and looked at her ruefully. "No. It's okay, Sue. *I'm* sorry. You didn't mean anything, I know. But, look—" He came to a stop in front of her. "Look, I don't know how to say this." He cracked his knuckles one at a time and took a deep breath. "Shit, you've been here a week already, and have you even tried to get a job?"

She looked down at her sandals. They were soaking wet.

Clarence scratched his head, relenting. "I'm going to try to help you out. I know of one lead. A partner in my brother's firm is looking for someone to watch his kids. I don't know what the deal is or even if they're still looking. You can check it out and see. But if it doesn't work out, Sue"—he started cracking his knuckles all over again—"then I can't help you. I mean, you really can't stay here anymore."

22

She was not afraid to climb the highest rocks at the back of the nubble or ride the ferry in a bad storm. But looking out the window in this twentieth-floor apartment as she waited to meet her new employer rocked her balance. Too high. She was high above the tops of the tallest trees; the cars below looked like snails; straight ahead of her the horizon was blocked by a blank window in another twenty-story building. To feel safe she would have to steal back through the kitchen, the hall, the foyer; she would have to buzz for the elevator, sink twenty floors under the operator's stare; she would have to cross the high-ceilinged lobby and walk past the doorman before she could touch her feet to the ground and run.

"Sue?"

She turned around to see a slender lady, beautiful as a movie star, in a soft peach-colored dress, smiling at her. She had pink cheeks and full breasts, and as she walked toward her she smelled of roses.

"Yes, ma'am."

"Oh, no, Sue, please don't call me ma'am. Just call me Ruth, okay?"

"Okay." Robin thought Ruth's voice too was like roses: like the petals of the wild roses that grew on the nubble, gentle, velvet.

"Come into the living room, dear, where we can talk." Ruth led her down a hall to a living room, large and elegant, the sort of room Robin imagined in a palace. Three white plush sofas were arranged around a square glass table, shiny draperies hung at the tall windows across the room, and in the center lay a soft, thick, rose-patterned carpet like a giant powder puff. Between the windows stood a dainty white desk, against one wall stood a piano, and here and there tall lamps rested on dark wood tables.

With a touch of a finger to a switch Ruth turned on the spotlights poised above the paintings that hung in heavy gold frames on every wall.

"Come," said Ruth, "sit down." But Robin couldn't move. Potted plants the size of trees and cut roses perfuming the air seemed less out of place than she. She thought she would never be able to cross the polished floors to reach the island of rug in the center where Ruth, kicking off her shoes and dropping onto a sofa, called to her.

Ruth opened a box on the glass table. Finding it empty, she crossed to another table and took a cigarette from a silver box. Dazzled, Robin watched Ruth's gold-tipped bangs fall across her eyes as she leaned down for a lighter. Her hair haloed her face with soft waves; when she stood up to touch the flame to the tip of a cigarette poised between her glossy lips, the gesture fixed itself in Robin's mind: a beautiful lady in stockinged feet bending her head to a tiny flame, a silver lighter in her hand, a vase of tall, dark roses on a glass table perfuming the room.

"Sit down with me, Sue. First we'll talk a little and then I'll show you around."

Gingerly Robin approached the white sofa and sat on the edge.

"I hear you've had some experience with children."

Robin watched Ruth exhale slowly and nodded. She wanted a cigarette but couldn't ask.

"You really look like a child yourself. How old are you, Sue?"

"Seventeen," she lied.

"Seventeen? You don't look that old. I like the closeness

in age. I think it makes for good rapport, don't you? Seventeen. Then you just graduated from high school?"

"No. I'm taking a year off," said Robin, aping Clarence's phrase.

"How old were the children you took care of before?"

Robin thought of her brothers. "They're ten and thirteen now, but I took care of them when they were younger."

"Perfect!" said Ruth, clapping her hands. Each nail was long and carefully manicured. "Let me tell you a little about us, now. Our children are five and seven, a wonderful age. Allison is five and Jeffrey is seven. They're both in a summer play group at the school half the day, but we need someone to take care of them afterwards and stay with them in the evenings. My husband travels a lot and I have to be out quite a bit, too, so we really need someone who can live in. Does that suit you?"

"Fine."

"We were thinking of room and board and, say, thirty dollars a week?" She paused. Robin didn't answer. "And your parents," continued Ruth, raising her arched eyebrows slightly. "Where are they?" She tucked her small stockinged feet up beside her on the white sofa and held one of them in her hand.

Robin didn't know what to say. Her mouth was dry, her voice weak. "In Maine," she finally confessed.

Ruth nodded, waiting for more, but nothing more came. She rescued Robin by conducting the rest of the interview by herself, answering her own questions. "Well then," she concluded, "I think you may be just the person we've been looking for. I'm so glad Ned's brother told us about you. I hope you can find what you're looking for here with us, too." She slipped her feet back into her shoes. "Come and let me show you your room."

Robin followed her down a hall past the kitchen into a small room.

"God knows what they had in mind when they built these

old apartments, the maid's quarters are so small," apologized Ruth, "but you do have a bit of a river view." She pulled back a shade to reveal a window giving onto a court.

At first Robin saw only other brick walls forming an air shaft outside; but after a moment she saw a narrow slit formed by two walls through which she caught a glimpse of water in the distance. True, the room was small, but Robin thought it looked like a picture in a magazine. Her bed was covered with a fitted red spread and pillows to make it look like a couch. There was a chest of drawers, a bookshelf, a framed print of a sea-scape, a reading lamp with a fringed shade. Her own room. She had never had a private room before.

"And here," said Ruth proudly, leading Robin back to-ward the kitchen, "is your bathroom."

The tub was short, as if it had been built for a child. Three large dresses were hanging on the shower curtain rod.

"Amanda, the wonderful woman who's been coming to clean for us for years, changes her clothes here on the days she comes. But otherwise, this is yours. I hope it suits you. We're very lucky, I know, to have this space, with real estate the way it's gone in the city."

After a few minutes, Ruth withdrew, leaving a faint smell of perfume behind her. As Robin hung up her few clothes, she remembered the Douglas house, her second foster home. The Douglases were an old couple who had lost a son in the war and whose other children had grown up and gone away, leaving empty rooms in their old house. Mrs. Douglas, who took in sewing as well as people, was kind enough, allowing Robin to hand her pins when she was doing hems and to eat only what she liked. But she spoke incessantly of her dead son; she had a pinched-up face like a pincushion, scaly red hands, and a hollow breast. "That's one way to do, but this is how we always do," she would say to Robin of everything from washing dishes to tying her shoes, until Robin became so homesick for the beach

and her family and her own sleeping bag that one morning
after breakfast she ran away and never returned. At her first
foster home, a potato farm on the mainland, at first she was not
homesick at all. Though there were endless chores to do, there
were four other children, many animals, open fields, and she
even got to ride the tractor once. But after she'd been there
several weeks, one day she discovered her foster mother, Mr.
Henderson's pretty second wife, weeping behind the outhouse.
After that, she often came upon her in tears. Mrs. Henderson
began to disturb Robin deeply, making her think of her own
mother, now gone away (but where?). Though she dreaded
speaking to the weeping Mrs. Henderson, she began to spend
more and more time stalking her, hoping to read in her hunched
shoulders and anguished face the cause of her unhappiness. But
she was able to read nothing; and gradually she came to hate
the sight of the doomed Mrs. Henderson until she wanted nothing but to be elsewhere, anywhere, away from the constant
image of unhappiness.

It would be different here in a rich family twenty floors up,
she thought, as she stashed her backpack at the back of the
closet. She repeated the name *Ruth*, feeling a great desire to
please the beautiful rich woman who was like no foster mother
she'd ever known.

Owl knew it was all over with her room when she saw the
manager fling open the doors and step out onto her balcony
with his nose and mouth curled up into one of his ugliest
puglike scowls, as if the very air outside were contaminated.
Treachery! Her rent was still paid up. Nevertheless, the manager
had demolished her barricades and probably thrown out all her
things. Next would come the fumigators to obliterate the last
trace of her.

"Good riddance!" she cried, shaking her fist at him and

bidding her home farewell. There was nothing in this world she couldn't get along without. Even the precious parts of her she had lost through the years she had learned to manage without. Her teeth, her womb, the feeling in her thumb, the missing fingertip, the color in her cheeks and hair—to each of these losses she had learned to adjust until she barely thought about them anymore. Now she would try to adjust to the loss of her room. Some people got along without eyes or hands or feet. A dachshund in the neighborhood had wheels rigged up in place of both back legs. Some people lived locked up in cells. The knowledge that you could somehow manage without necessities even brought a certain relief, like the freedom that went with no longer bothering to hold in your stomach or your farts. She had the lockers for storage and had learned to change her clothes discreetly in the street. Now that Milly was gone, what need had she of that terrible room? The whole block had turned ugly. Several days after she'd found Milly's broken body, a large rat had turned up dead on the pavement exactly opposite the spot where Milly had fallen. The flattened body with its matted gray fur, brown tail, one glasslike eye, and four tiny pink paws like little hands had been a sign. What would turn up next? Maybe she'd be next. No point waiting around to see. With a farewell string of curses out of her long and varied past, she registered her departure, then moved the operation west.

"Watch me," called Allison, climbing cautiously up the smooth black boulder in Central Park, slowly moving, inch by inch, first hands, then feet.

From below, Robin saw instead the huge surf-pocked rocks at the back of the nubble where she and her brothers had played away their summer days in endless games of hide-and-seek. Wilder than these tame city rocks, some of the nubble rocks were craggy and steep, some smooth as marbles, some veined with sparkling quartz or shiny mica, some pocked with deep irregular pits, like giant footprints left behind by a thousand years of stomping seas. There among the craggy peaks she had always known how to hide from Adam's searching eyes before barefoot Billy ran in free.

"Sue!" called Allison impatiently from her temporary perch a quarter of the way from the top. "You aren't watching me!"

"Yes I am. You're doing great," lied Robin.

She had wanted to recreate with Allison and Jeffrey the mystic world she and her brothers had named, founded, and ruled on their nubble. But these city kids with their bikes and books inhabited a land already named and ruled. In it, she was not their big sister or even their companion; she was their audience, their subject, their serving girl. They wanted not to hide or seek but to be seen.

Jeffrey let his bicycle and bat crash to the ground and ran to the base of the rock to begin his own ascent. "Don't watch her. Watch *me!*"

"I'm watching you both," called Robin. She walked over to retrieve Jeff's equipment which she dragged to the base of the rock. "See? Here I am."

Robin was amazed that these kids, who were never alone for a single waking moment, wanted so much to be watched. Did they think they would disappear if there were no eyes holding them up? Though their father was seldom home and their mother was usually busy, all day long they were observed by appraising eyes of adults. Besides their play group they had swimming lessons, pottery classes, music lessons, eurythmics (whatever that was), even acting lessons if you counted the children's theater group they went to on Saturdays in winter. Ruth wanted them to "stretch their minds and bodies" and enlisted Robin's help, even steering Robin toward lessons of her own. "I know you can't go back to school until fall, but there are plenty of classes you could take now if you wanted. Mime, for instance. Or yoga. They'd be wonderful for you. You might even find a class that would count toward your diploma."

Robin wanted to stretch herself for Ruth. During her first days on the job she had hurried home as soon as she'd delivered the children to play group, hoping to be with Ruth. But often Ruth had already gone out, leaving Robin to walk like a stranger through the lavish rooms. She peered into closets hung with expensive clothes, opened boxes and drawers, touched the kitchen appliances, tried out the furniture, smelled Ruth's perfumes, ran her fingers over the piano keys, and sometimes sat on the white sofa with her feet tucked under her as Ruth sat. When Ruth stayed home and talked to her, Robin clung to her words. She loved nestling beneath the soft maternal wing to hear Ruth improvise a sparkling future for her. "What nonsense! There are all kinds of schools and special programs for young people like you. Why, my friend Karen told me about a school downtown, or maybe in Brooklyn, where you can design your own courses. Anything you want to learn. When we lived in California I worked in a school like that. The Spivak School. It was marvelous. If you wanted to be an actress, say, you could go to work in a theater and get school credit. Isn't that the best way to learn? I know there are schools like that here. I'll see what I can find out for you."

But as the days passed, Robin got less talk from Ruth and more orders. Usually when she returned home from dropping the children off at play group, Ruth would be waiting with a smile and a list of chores. "Do me a favor, Sue dear," she would begin. And then it would be run out to the store, or drop some things at the cleaners', or take a package to the post office, renew a prescription, return some books to the library. And after the outside chores, there would be laundry to do or groceries to put away or lunch to make. Sometimes it seemed she barely had time to manage lunch before it was time to pick up the children; and then it would be their turn for her services. She took them to the swimming pool or the playground, got Jeff to his music lesson, settled a quarrel for Allison, fixed their skates. Back at home she saw that they practiced, fixed them their dinners, wrestled with each of them, nagged them into their baths, limited their TV, told them bedtime stories; and when they were at last both in bed, she got the dishes done, the playroom straightened up, the laundry sorted. Despite the running water—and an automatic dishwasher!—plus a maid to clean and a doorman to deliver, there seemed to be even more chores to do here than in Maine. And though she was supposed to have her mornings to herself once she had dropped the children off, as much time as she managed to save, that much did Ruth appropriate. Yet, like someone hypnotized, she could not refuse Ruth anything, could not even resent her asking.

Jeffrey was scrambling toward the top of the boulder, letting off one victory whoop as he moved past Allison and another as he planted his sneakered feet at the top. For a moment Robin was afraid he would shove Allison off the rock; but instead he seemed to inspire her to attempt the peak. Everything one of them did, the other had to try. If one got to choose a story, the other chose another; if one wheedled from Robin a piggyback ride, so must the other; if one didn't have to eat the vegetable, neither would the other; if one stayed up late to kiss their mother good night when she came home, then both must stay up, even if one was already nodding off. There was no one to stop them or even slow them down, for their father took no interest and their mother seemed to say nothing but yes.

At the top at last, Allison, waving her arms to assert her momentary reign, cried triumphantly, "See me now?" Instantly,

Jeffrey started down. Robin thought of herself as a small child, standing on the highest rock of the nubble, frantically waving to her father below. He was piling the boys into his boat for the greatest treat they knew: to go along while he hauled his lobster pots. "Wait for me! Wait for me!" Robin shouted. She didn't believe they would leave without her. She jumped, she shouted, she flailed the air wildly with her arms to get her father's attention; but he failed, or refused, to notice her. He lifted Billy into the boat. She wanted to fly down to the beach, climb into the boat, and squeeze in beside Adam. She was the oldest; she deserved to sit beside their father. But she knew she wouldn't reach the boat in time unless she caught her father's eye. And now they were all ready to go. Her father was bending over the edge in his yellow mack, untying the boat from its mooring, starting up the motor, pushing off to sea. Without her. She saw it still: the high rock, the gulls, the small boat starting off to sea without her.

Later, when Robin was in her teens and even her most private thoughts seemed open to her father's ceaseless scrutiny, even then she felt left behind by him. Now, too, she had to admit. Here in a city hundreds of miles from home, in a life her father could not imagine, she never walked a block without half expecting him to grab her at the corner and slam her against a wall; and when he failed to appear, part of her felt left behind.

Allison, concentrating hard on her feet, was slowly descending the smooth, steep boulder, braking with her hands, heels, and seat. Jeffrey ran to Robin and pulled at her hand. "Come on, Sue," he said mischievously, "let's leave before Allison gets down."

Robin was dismayed. "We can't do that, Jeff."

"Why not? Come on," he said, tugging harder.

Robin had an urge to grab Jeffrey and shake him to his senses. After they'd been sent to separate foster homes, she and her brothers had made an unspoken pact to stick together, no matter what. Her greatest regret over running away was to have left Adam and Billy behind to deal with their parents alone. She still hoped to make it up to them by somehow slipping them off the island too. Jeffrey should be helping Allison, not making life worse for her. "No," she said emphatically. "We're going to wait right here for Allison. God, Jeffrey, she's your sister. How come you're so mean to her?"

He cocked his head at her and stuck out his lower lip. "How come you talk so funny?" he retorted. "You don't talk like us."

"I don't talk funny. Where I come from everybody talks like me. I think you talk funny."

"My daddy says it's cause you're a maid. All maids talk funny." He took her hand again.

She didn't know whether or not to believe Jeffrey. The two times she'd met their father, who was usually out of town, he didn't treat her like a maid. Right there in front of Ruth he had insisted that she call him Phillip and followed her around with his eyes. The way he watched her from the start made her wonder if maybe Clarence had told him something, or if he'd known her in the life and had recognized her. She was relieved that Ruth didn't seem to notice, because at one point he had actually patted her behind in the kitchen the way her father did, with a slap and a short, hard laugh. She knew then he'd be trouble. If she'd met him on the street she'd have known how to handle him; but with Ruth hovering near, Robin could only try to avoid all contact.

Allison, back on the ground, ran up to Robin and began tugging at her other hand. "Did you see me?" she cried. "Did you? I was at the top."

"Yeah, but I got there first," taunted Jeffrey.

Robin remembered how Billy had warned her about the police in the principal's office and had stolen money from the drawer and sneaked her backpack out of the house to help her get away.

"Okay, get your stuff together now. We have to get to your lesson."

In the distance they heard the ice-cream cart music. "Can we have ice cream first? Please?" begged Allison.

"Ice cream! Ice cream!" chimed in Jeffrey, jumping up and handing Robin his bat.

Robin looked at her watch. "I don't think we have time for ice cream."

"Then I'm not going," said Allison.

"My mommy lets us have ice cream whenever we want it," said Jeffrey.

If they were late for the lesson someone might complain to Ruth; but with the rest of the day and evening to spend with the children, Robin didn't feel like saying no to them. She wanted to be their ally, not their enemy.

"Okay, we'll get some ice cream first. But if we're late for your lesson, remember, it wasn't my fault." She gave Jeffrey a dollar of Ruth's money and the two children bounded ahead.

Robin walked the bike and carried the bat, wondering if her father would be waiting for her at the ice-cream cart. And when she reached the corner without finding him, part of her could not forgive him.

Hearing the way the children raced down the hall toward the door, Robin knew that their father had returned.

"Wait a minute. Just a minute there," she heard him say. "Let me put down my papers and hang up my jacket first, okay?"

Never before had he come home this early. It was Tuesday, Ruth's night for her group. Trouble. Robin dried her hands on a dish towel and walked slowly toward the foyer. Down the hall she saw Phillip, tall, athletic, even handsome in his straight, craggy way, with sharp features and thick, wavy hair—attractive enough for Ruth. As she watched him lay his briefcase on the table, throw his jacket on the chair, pull off his tie, and squat to greet his children, it occurred to Robin that since she'd been working there she had only seen Phillip and Ruth together once.

"Okay," he said, opening his arms, "who's got a great big kiss for Daddy?"

Both children leaped on his neck like puppies, jumping for kisses, vying for first.

"Ah, that's just what I've needed all day," he said, picking up Jeffrey and hugging him tightly. He returned him to the floor and lifted Allison. "Were you a good girl while Daddy was away?" She giggled her delight. He tousled her hair and with a jovial growl said, "But look at you two. Why aren't you ready for bed? It's almost eight o'clock. What's been going on here? Is your baby-sitter spoiling you? Where is she, anyway?"

"Sue! Sue!" called Allison. "Daddy's home!"

"Ah, there you are." Phillip handed Robin his jacket and placed a friendly kiss on her cheek, as if she were another of his children.

She pulled away and busied herself with the jacket. "I told them they could stay up for the Special tonight," she said. "Ruth said it was okay."

"I don't know. They look pretty tired to me," said Phillip, reaching down to tickle Allison. "Okay, kids. Run along and whip into your pajamas. If you're ready for bed by the time I finish my drink, I'll have a surprise for each of you."

"What kind of surprise?" asked Jeffrey.

"Something you'll like."

"Something to eat?" asked Allison.

"Never mind. You'll find out if you get at it. But if you stand here asking me questions, you'll use up your time and never find out."

The two children raced off together, squealing under the spell of their father's attention, which had already shifted to Robin.

She was starting off after them when he touched her arm. "Not so fast, Sue. I'd like to have a talk with you. We've never really had a chance to chat. I'm going to shower and make myself a drink now. And then I'll be watching the news while you get the kids off to sleep. Try to speed them up, okay? I'll be in the living room waiting." He winked a broad friendly wink and handed Robin two silver dollars, their surprises. "Give them these to hurry them along." He released her arm, kissed the air in her direction, and headed toward the kitchen, whistling.

Phillip was already a little drunk by the time Robin joined him in the living room. He was sitting on one of the sofas with his legs crossed under his robe and his arms spread out along the back pillows, a high color in his cheeks. She sat down opposite him. He offered her a drink, but she refused, settling for a cigarette. She was terrified Ruth might come home early and find her sitting on her white sofa, smoking her cigarettes, talking to her handsome husband clad in nothing but a robe.

"It's really nice having you with us, Sue. The kids seem to have taken quite a shine to you. Ruth says you're terrific with them. You look pretty good to me, too." He leaned forward, smiling across the table at her. As Robin smiled back uncomfortably, she searched her memory to discover what she might have done to give him ideas. The way she walked? Her father had often criticized the way she walked, as Prince had admired it. Her clothes, maybe? Her easy way with the kids? As Phillip talked on, she sat unmoving in the center of her sofa with a frozen smile on her face, wondering how to set him straight without offense.

After a few minutes, Phillip got up to freshen his drink. When he sat back down, it was next to her.

She didn't know what to do. Staying seated beside him could be dangerous, but she was afraid to get up and reveal her suspicions. She remained uncomfortably in place, smiling stiffly, looking for some escape. When he rested his arm on the back of the sofa behind her shoulders, she had a bad moment; but then he went on talking in his easy fashion and moved no closer.

"My wife loves the coast. But to me, there are only two good reasons to be in San Francisco. The salmon and the crab."

Sitting in this living room twenty floors up, she could barely remember her time on the stroll. Only a few weeks had passed, but already it was slipping away like a dream. Sometimes when she passed a pair of prosses on Broadway, or when she walked past a certain bar on the way to pick up the kids, she was astonished to remember that she had been one of them. It seemed easier to imagine herself waking up one day without any memory of the life at all than to accept it as part of her. But though she had forgotten, the way Phillip looked at her made her think he knew something. Maybe that was the meaning of *once a whore, always a whore*: something would always show through.

When the grandfather clock chimed ten, Robin stood up and excused herself, saying she had to get up early in the morning.

"Too bad," said Phillip. "I was just beginning to enjoy myself. If the kids are wearing you out, Sue," he said, swirling his ice, "we'll have to see what we can do." He laughed his big jovial laugh.

Robin picked up the ashtray and started toward the kitchen.

"Well, another time then," he said, following behind her with his glass.

When she had rinsed out the ashtray and the glass, suddenly he pulled her to him and pressed his lips hard against hers. His beard was rough, his grip firm. His chin scratched her chin as she tried to back off.

"What's a matter? Just a kiss good night," he said in a hurt voice. "Christ, is there anything the matter with that?"

"No, no," she said smiling, hoping to undo whatever insult she had given. "I'm just really pooped now, that's all." As quickly as she could, she turned toward her room. But before she was out of the kitchen, Phillip managed to swat her once more on her behind and left her with a short, loud, familiar laugh.

23

Prince emerged from the shower to find Boots sitting peacefully on his newly cleaned navy blue pants depositing white hairs all over them. In that instant he resolved to get rid of him.

The thought was not a new one. Every time he caught the cat sharpening his claws on the most comfortable chair in the room, Prince considered it. It was not that he disliked the cat. Actually, though he wouldn't readily admit it, during his weeks alone with the animal Prince had developed if not a fondness then a respect for him that sometimes amounted to admiration. For one thing, Boots seemed to Prince admirably clean, even vain. Unlike most humans, who let themselves go, the cat could be seen systematically washing himself half a dozen times a day, including before naps and after meals. His recent attacks on the furniture were simply part of his grooming habits. For another thing, Boots was proud. Unlike dogs and people who came sniveling up to you wagging their tails or whining for attention, Boots eyed you suspiciously from a distance, approached with caution, and at the least affront stalked off with a dignity Prince could only describe as manly. His lean body was swift, his movements deliberate and graceful. When he looked down from the window on the world below, he seemed detached, like a useful friend; even when he sunned himself with his eyes closed, he seemed alert and watchful.

But the amount of affection for a dumb animal Prince would permit himself to indulge depended exclusively on the price, and recently the price had shot up. A week earlier, Prince had noticed a powerful, sickening smell in his room when he walked through the door. Though it was stronger and sweeter than the ordinary urine smell Boots left in the litter box, Prince immediately changed the cat's litter (a job he had grudgingly taken over after Button left), washing the box with detergent. But the sickening smell persisted. In response, Prince began locking Boots in the bathroom whenever he went out.

Still the smell hung in the air. Several days later Prince returned home to find that a fresh dose had been applied to the room. When Jacki and Sweet Rudy stopped by for a beer, Prince apologized for the awful smell. "You know, it'll never come out," warned Jacki, shaking her head. "That's the smell of a tomcat staking out his territory. You should have had him fixed before he matured. Now it's probably too late. He'll probably spray up your whole place." Jacki sniffed the air and searched the rooms until she located the offending odor near the bath mat. "Nothing much you can do except throw out the mat and hope he stops," she said. "Do you feed him vitamins?"

Prince put the bath mat in the trash and got another. Secretly he wondered if the cat wasn't retaliating for being locked up in the bathroom at night; and though he couldn't blame the cat, he felt challenged to reassert his power. The one thing a player could never afford to compromise, not even for a minute, was his position of power. If, for instance, a man let a woman begin to dominate him, his manhood would soon be threatened; he had to regain the upper hand quickly or else, according to the pimping code, the woman would take over and make a trick out of him. At bottom, the art of pimping was the art of control.

Not that he believed a cat could actually feel what humans felt. Still, sometimes he was convinced that Boots had locked eyes with him in an effort to stare him down. Prince knew he alone had the power to win those matches if he chose; but the idea of a small, dumb animal having the balls to challenge his master appealed to him so much that he sometimes rewarded the cat with catnip or a short session of petting when their contest was over. At such times, the sensation of the silky fur coat against his hand, the sight of the sleek handsome animal with his eyes half closed, lips drawn back, lithe body rising to meet the master's hand, meow reduced to a long vibrating purr, gave Prince an unexpected pleasure. And though Boots, like a true player, would protect the soft secret fur of his underside with a warning swat at Prince's approaching hand and a lunge with his unsheathed claws when the hand struck home, Prince was tempted to consider their feelings as affection. Why else would Boots leap purring into his master's lap and rub himself against his legs whenever Prince permitted?

It was thus with a mixture of triumph and regret that Prince, finding Boot's destructive raids extending beyond the air and furniture to his personal clothing, added up the pros and cons and decided to dump the cat. "That's it," he said, after a futile attempt to brush the navy pants clean. He took the cat's carrying case down from the closet shelf and opened it up on the floor, inviting Boots to enter. When, after several investigatory sniffs, Boots obligingly leaped inside and waited for Prince to latch down the top, Prince accepted that he might even miss the animal. More than once since Button had taken off he had delighted the girls in Sallee's by showing up with Boots on a leash. Watching the cat get high on catnip was always good for a few laughs. And one of the current stories he most liked to tell in the Casanova Bar was about the time Boots, catching sight of the life-sized picture of a cat on a large bag of cat chow, went into his macho act, arching his back, puffing out his fur, doubling the thickness of his tail, and hissing at the cupboard. At first Prince thought Boots had smelled a mouse or rat; but after examining the cupboard and experimenting with the bag—turning the picture to the wall and back again—he had no doubt that it was the picture Boots tried to attack. The cat seemed to see nothing at all when he faced his own reflection in a mirror; yet somehow he responded to the image of his rival pictured on the cat food bag.

Prince picked up the case and carried it down the stairs, planning to unload the cat in the Casanova Bar. Not that he was reluctant simply to turn the animal loose in the street. He was getting big now, more tomcat than kitten, and could probably survive. Besides, Prince believed that if there was a crime at all it was taking a proud, healthy animal off the street in the first place and making him into a helpless domestic creature. He felt it was as much against the nature of an animal to be cooped up in a room or tied on a leash and forced to beg for his food as it was against the nature of a man to be kept on a leash by a woman and forced to beg for pussy. If you interfered with their nature you turned men into tricks or fags. As surely as men were born to control women, cats were born to roam free. Still, Prince saw no reason to waste an opportunity to score with one of the girls who just might appreciate receiving a beautiful pet like Boots.

It was still early evening when he got to the bar, well before git-down time. At one of the tables in the back Bluejay and Cheryl were drinking beer. "Hey, Prince," called Bluejay, "come on over here."

Prince put the cat's case on the floor and pulled out a chair.

"What you sellin, buddy? What's in the box?" Today Bluejay's eye patch was red satin to match the band on his latest hat.

"A pretty little tomcat, lookin for a home."

"No shit," laughed Bluejay, slapping his thigh. "A cat?"

"For real?" asked Cheryl, opening wide her round green eyes and tossing her frizzy curls, "Oh, let me see! Maybe I'll take him home if I like him." Daintily she pushed back her chair and started up to investigate, but Bluejay pulled her back down.

"Wait, bitch. Did you ask me first if you could have a cat? Did I even say you could get up?"

Cheryl jerked her shoulder away from him, crossed her arms over her breasts, and sat back down sulkily with her back toward Bluejay. "Then you show him to me, Prince," she said.

"You tryin to disrespect me, bitch?" shouted Bluejay, lowering his head like a bull. His medium-length Afro that grew low on his brow and merged with a trim, pointed beard gave him a fierce look when he frowned, despite the bright red patch.

Prince looked from one of them to the other. It was his duty to back up Bluejay, but he wanted to get rid of the cat. He hated to get pulled into family quarrels. Cheryl was a handsome, headstrong woman who tested her man every chance she got, and Bluejay was always struggling to keep her in line. Prince had seen Cheryl disrespect Bluejay so blatantly that Bluejay had had to rough her up right in the bar just to protect his manhood. Even when they were silent you could hear the struggle going on between them.

Sitting with Cheryl and Bluejay made Prince appreciate again Button's beautiful childlike docility. Never once in the weeks he'd had her had she shown a moment's disrespect. He couldn't remember a single time she'd interrupted him or openly disagreed with him or tried to trick him or defy him. Even when she'd blown, in a way she'd been following his orders. He'd blown her. Sweet Rudy had tried to console him with good advice. "Forget the bitch. Ain't a bitch alive worth moanin over. Cop and blow is the name of the game. Now it's coppin time." But down to the bottom of his roll Prince felt his loss. Weeks had passed since he'd last got paid. Lonely weeks.

As Cheryl and Bluejay went at it, the cat began to meow. By this time the others at the bar were watching too, laughing and making predictable cracks about pussy. As the center of attention, Cheryl and Bluejay both felt pressed to defend their positions, until finally a reluctant Bluejay was on his feet ready to strike her, and the cat was howling to be let out.

Prince picked up the case in disgust and walked toward the door past the men at the bar, wishing the cat would shut up, deciding the hell with the girls. Outside, he started toward Bryant Park, where the cat had come from, but with every step, Boots's howl grew more insistent. Prince shook the case, embarrassed and annoyed, but the cat ignored him. Enough! he decided, nearing the end of the first block. Who was in charge here, anyway? He took the case to the curb and opened it.

At first Boots sat inside the box looking intently at Prince, as if he knew better than to leave. But after a few moments, the cat stepped out, sniffed the ground in a small circle, and scooted under a parked car.

At that moment Prince felt a small twinge of regret. He felt it in his stomach, his weakest spot. He had let Button go and she hadn't returned. Now Boots slipped off without a backward glance. True, he had cut them loose himself; still, his stomach sent him messages of pain.

He kicked the carrying case off the curb and turned quickly back toward the bar.

Robin had already fallen asleep and was dreaming of love when Phillip knocked on her door and entered the room.

"You're not asleep, are you? It's only ten-thirty." Gently he shook her shoulder. "Come on, honey. Wake up."

The voice reached her from a distance and blended with the voice of someone in a dream that began to fade as she woke. She wanted to go on dreaming, or at least hold the dream for a moment more and learn its message, but Phillip's chatter chased it away. She opened her eyes.

"Where's Ruth?" she asked, suddenly sitting up.

"Now, where do you think? She's out, of course. It's Tuesday. Really, honey, credit me with a little brains."

Tuesday night, Ruth's night for her group. Robin was relieved but she could hardly relax. All week she had tried to believe Phillip had forgotten about her; but now that he was sitting on her bed in his robe calling her honey again, she gave up hope. Her smile had misled him and now he was here to collect.

"Sorry I woke you up, but I'm home so damn little I didn't want to miss the chance to talk to you again."

Robin scrambled out of bed and walked to the window. She had wanted to leave her past below, at least not drag it up to the twentieth floor of her new life; but somehow Phillip had got hold of it, and now he was shaking it at her, and she didn't know how to get away. Through the window she saw the narrow crack in the wall behind which she knew flowed the river.

"Come here," he said. "I won't hurt you." He took her hand and pulled her toward him.

She had never been one to voice her protests. In moments of stress her voice deserted her. She held her protest inside, like breath for the long plunge under, then used it to propel herself quickly away.

He held her tightly and once again pressed his lips to hers. "There, now. What's the harm in that? It feels good, doesn't it? No one knows. There's no harm, honey. Don't pull away."

Was this to happen every Tuesday, then? Robin had constructed a long chain of chores, like a rocky reef, to stand between herself and Ruth's betrayal: the children's baths, teeth, TV, bedtime stories. But Phillip had sailed over it by coming to her room after she'd gone to sleep.

He took her hand and pressed her fingers to his penis. "Feel that, Sue? See? That's how much I want you."

All Robin could see was Ruth, coming home any moment. . . . For an instant she considered bolting. But how could she get past the doorman without making a scene that Ruth would hear about? She tried one feeble protest. "Do you think we should be doing this here? Ruth might come home early."

Phillip smiled wryly. "Yeah? You want to know something,

honey? If Ruth walked in right now she probably wouldn't even notice." He shook his head. "You don't have to worry, believe me. It's Tuesday. She won't be home for hours."

He eased her down to the bed. Robin wondered if she ought to submit quickly, in case Ruth decided suddenly to come back home.

"Kiss me, honey, please, kiss me," he said, letting his robe fall open and guiding her head to his lap.

Robin slung her pack to the floor and slid into a side seat of the downtown local. She hated the subway, but she was almost broke. If she'd finished out the week and collected her thirty dollars pay, she could have taken a taxi, but she'd rather have died than have faced Ruth again. Instead, she had taken the kids to school and then split.

She avoided the eyes of the other passengers. Every day lately headlines spread news of victims being pushed onto the tracks, of madmen holding entire trains, of women dragged into tunnels and raped, of sleeping derelicts set on fire by teenaged gangs. At home in the winter people drank too much and sometimes murdered; but here perfect strangers could get you. She couldn't walk down the stairs into a station without wondering if she was being followed, and once inside the train she was afraid to let her eyes meet someone else's for fear of being pulled into a trap.

Somewhere in the city she knew runaway kids lived together in happy gangs, but she hadn't been able to find them and no longer cared to try. She was getting out, taking off. For California, where it was always summer and she could live on the beach on mussels and oranges and fish, and maybe team up again with Boots, who was probably having herself a wild old time.

In the Times Square station she pushed her way out of the

train with relief. Clutching her sleeping bag to her, she let herself be swept up the stairs and hurried through the tunnel toward the bus station. The summer was almost gone; thousands of dollars had slipped through her hands since she'd left home, probably more than her whole family spent in a year; yet here she was back in the Port Authority, too broke to take a bus, too scared to hitchhike (where was a highway, anyway? She'd never seen one in the city), ready to spare-change tourists till she had the bus fare to the coast.

In the station she spent precious cash on a candy bar to allay the hunger that grew with every step, then dropped two coins into the slot that opened a locker and pushed her pack inside. City life sucked up cash like barnacles sucking in plankton. Everything cost. At fifty cents a day for a locker and dollars a day for food, even if she slept in the park her money would run out in a couple of days.

Walking toward the ticket window to check out the fares, she searched the faces for Prince. Arming herself against him, she kept vigilantly before her eyes the image of his special walk, that lean body, those eggplant-colored eyes, the silky black hair, the sweet-talking lips, and neglected to notice the woman observing her.

She seldom noticed women—except the pretty ones her own age. Even when the woman approached her, saying, "Excuse me. Mind if I ask you a couple of questions?" Robin was not particularly suspicious. The woman was middle-aged and had a flat, kindly face; in her undistinguished suit and sensible shoes she looked to Robin like a traveler wanting directions, or perhaps one of the bus station's survey takers. Not until her hand was gripping Robin's arm and she had asked for her name and age did Robin recognize danger.

"Why do you want to know?"

"We're with the Juvenile Division. This is our job. You look young to us," said the woman. The man who had suddenly appeared beside her flashed a badge and displayed two sets of indisputably authentic ID.

Robin felt her knees weaken and the world spin. Finally, the Runaway Squad. The Muzak was playing a familiar tune she couldn't place and a baby was bawling. She had to concentrate all her attention on remaining upright and could not think of a name.

"Don't be afraid. We're just doing a routine check," said the man. "But if you can't tell us who you are and establish your age, you'll have to come into the station."

The station was probably filled with descriptions, photos, and criminal records of all wanted persons. "Why? I haven't done anything," she cried.

"We never said you did. We just want to make sure you're supposed to be here. We don't want your parents worrying about you."

"But I'm eighteen!"

"Well, I'm glad to hear it," said the man. "I'm sure you can show me something to prove it. A driver's license? School pass? Library card? Anything that has your name and age."

"Where you from, honey?" asked the woman.

"California."

"What year were you born in?" barked the man. He snapped his fingers in her face. "Quick!"

"I don't have to answer you."

"I'm afraid you do," said the woman sweetly, "unless you can prove your age."

"That's right," said the man. "It's the law."

"Well, I am eighteen, I just don't have any ID on me."

"Too bad. But there are other ways to prove it. We're not unreasonable. We can go into the station and call your parents. Check out your age with them and make sure they know where you are. It's for your own protection, honey, believe me. Are you hungry? After we call we'll get you something to eat."

"But they don't have a phone. We never had a phone."

Her captors looked at each other. "That's all right," said the woman. "We can call someone else—a neighbor, a relative —and leave word for your parents to get in touch with us. We've got lots of time. What time is it now in California, anyway?"

They had her now alright, and they were leading her by the arm. She was flunking every question they asked her. How familiar it all felt: being led toward a small office where a stranger—the principal, a social worker, a trooper—would ask questions, make phone calls, decide her fate, maybe send her away. She knew just what the room would look like inside: a dark oak desk with three drawers on each side and one in the center, a swivel chair, fluorescent lights, a row of wooden arm chairs along the light green walls, maybe one small window. There'd be two black phones and a big glass ashtray with maybe a cold cigar. The smell of stale coffee. A secretary with a bouffant hairdo and high heels or else glasses on a cord around her neck, file cabinets to the ceiling. It was always the same. If this pair found out who she really was they could send her to jail for leaving school, running away, stealing, hooking, maybe for more.

"You can't make me tell you anything."

"True. But after a few days or weeks you'll probably decide to talk to us on your own," said the man. "We can wait."

They were only steps from the station now—that room Prince had warned her of on the day she arrived. In another moment she'd be theirs to lock away just as her pack was stashed in her locker. . . . Her pack! That was it. She turned to the woman and said, "Okay. You win. My ID is in my pack if you want to see it. I checked it in a locker." She took her locker key out of her pocket and held it up.

Her captors looked at each other. "Where's the locker?" asked the man skeptically.

"Right back there. Don't you believe me? It's number"—
she looked at the key—"ten sixty-eight."

"Okay, come on then," said the woman. "We'll go and
get it." She turned to her partner. "Why don't you get us some
coffee and meet us back in the office?"

Robin and the woman doubled back alone. Quickly Robin
estimated her chances of shaking one guard in a tight skirt. Her
heart thumped so loudly she was afraid it would give away her
plan as they retraced their path back past Walgreen's, past the
newsstand, past the escalator. Near the ticket window the baby
was still bawling. A few yards ahead three religious women
were distributing leaflets and selling gospels from a table they
had set up at the top of a flight of stairs. When they reached
that point on their route, Robin decided, she would make her
break. She had nothing to lose. She would plunge down the
stairs like a porpoise diving under, letting the crowd close behind her, and not resurface for air until she reached the park
and freedom.

How to stay free? Owl counted out her money one last
time before leaving the bank, then tucked it deep in a secret
place. It came to just under one month's welfare, including all
the interest. One month's worth of freedom. Since she had received her termination notice she had repeated the word so
often that it no longer had a meaning. *Free?*

The old ways were gone now—the bustling jobs, private
home, relatives; probably out of the question now. And the
newer ways she had adopted were disappearing too, one by
one. The Hotel Midway was boarded up; the Venus was
closed to her. With all the renovations going on there were
hardly any rooms left to rent in the neighborhood, even for
those on welfare. Her luck had changed. The Flasher had
pulled the drain on her luck; now it was seeping away; now she

had only a trickle of choices left. Round and round she went, reciting the remaining possibilities until they were nothing but small black images with names attached, distant birds circling in the air, crows, starlings, rising out of sight. Locked doors, barricaded balcony, green bankbook, breakfast waiting behind a door, lockers, coffee, food—going, going, gone. Winter would soon be back with dark, cold afternoons, frostbitten fingertips, steam tunnels, raging legs. She'd been sure that Milly would save her, but Milly was gone again—angry, sullen, indifferent, dead. Not even the Shelter offered comfort anymore with Sister Theresa bugging her about her legs whenever she saw her.

The wail of a siren made her quake. She would have to spend her money fast and try to become eligible for welfare before winter came. Better to spend now than be carried off on a stretcher to a place where she'd be forced to surrender everything. Better to go south for the winter, hire a lawyer to press her suit, fly to Rome for a week in a nice hotel—anything but let her money fall into the wrong hands. For they would trace it in a bank, she would lose it in a locker, they would mug her if she carried cash. They were after her now. Her luck was gone. She was afraid.

Robin lay on the grass beneath the calm trees and cloudless sky listening to the beat of wings, letting her weight sink into the earth. In the exhaustion that follows fear, she thought she would sleep in the park forever in the safe darkness behind her eyelids. As the hot sun beat down on her, she drifted back to the nubble, to the water's edge, where at low tide three rocks rested together in such a way as to form a cool, dark passage. Inside at the center a secret chamber formed a perfect hiding place for a small squatting child. Sometimes when the fog was so thick outside you could barely see the tips of your fingers, inside you could see clearly the dribble castles on the chamber floor and the barnacles clinging to the walls. In her first years on the island Robin hid from her father there.

But you cannot hide forever, and now she sees herself run up the beach through the fog to hear Billy announce, "Boy, Robin, are you gonna get it. They've been looking all over for you. You better hide."

She wants to ask why; but her father always gets madder if you try to defend yourself. Too late now; Adam has spotted her too. And there at the top of the nubble is her mother, walking distractedly through the brush wringing her hands, crying out "Robin! Robin!" but softly, as if it were no use.

Her father appears through the fog. She wants to rush to her mother, disappear behind her skirt, but that no longer works; if he wants her, he can get her there too.

"At last!" he cries with joy. Like a fisherman hauling in a great hunted prize.

If she could disappear like a mole, hide in the brush, fly— but her muscles, her knees go limp. His immense feet come toward her in three giant strides. He seizes her, yanks her up by the arm, drags her toward the steps, to give her what she deserves.

She remembers.

"This . . . will . . . teach . . . you . . . to hide. . . ." Locked against his knee, her buttocks received one blow with each assaultive word. "This . . . will . . . teach . . ." Impaled on his knee, squeezed breathless against his rigid thigh, she heard each word as a separate statement. Like the numbers in bingo, building to . . . what? She did not understand. Sighting down his shin through a fog of pain and fear she saw a rosebush crushed under one huge paint-splattered shoe.

". . . a . . . lesson." This will teach you a lesson. But somehow she always learned the wrong lesson. He wanted to teach her not to hide, but from the moment she saw his savage face, red, nostrils distended, eyes electrified, she wanted only to run and hide forever.

"Why didn't you answer?"

"I didn't hear you."

"Do you think I'll believe a story like that?"

"We looked and looked," said her mother. "Where were you?"

"Answer me!"

She could not. If she tried to answer he would accuse her of lying. His rages were all the same. He would force her to cry, then beat her for crying, making her cry the more. He would force her to run, then punish her for running. He would scare away her words, then punish her silence, or he would force her to speak and slap her for insolence. There was no way to appease him. She had been playing in the rocks as she did every day. It was the fog that had hidden her. She wanted to hide in the fog again. To disappear. To close her eyes and vanish.

Owl tossed the bread high in the air, watched the birds circle down, and suddenly saw Milly sleeping on the grass like a baby.

After the initial exhilarating shock she was not surprised. Had she not lost and found her many times in her brief life? And not only recently. She remembered starting when she miscarried in her second month; then when her milk dried up and Milly left her for a bottle; when she watched her march to school up the hill in a pink pinafore; when Milly announced at ten, "You're not my mommy anymore." And later, when Bert stole her and taught her to lie to her mother and be ashamed, hadn't she mourned her then? Yet she'd always returned. And was this not the very spot they were to have met and fed the pigeons? Only the timing was off.

Carefully, Owl studied the girl's body. The birds, too,

hovered around the spot, as if awaiting some important event. Sweat on the brow, eyelids flutering, pink flush on her parted lips and dirty cheeks: it was Milly alive, sixteen as the day Bert had stolen her away, transported and preserved outside of time like the Sleeping Beauty for the sake of this moment. Not yet married or buried; not yet ashamed.

Owl knew there were discrepancies between this child and the one she had raised. A sadder mouth even in sleep than the other's, a sturdier nose, higher, bumpy bridge—Owl didn't care. Beneath the veil all discrepancies disappeared. This she had seen in a vision along with many things that were hidden to most. Birdlings in gutters, treasures in trash, vanished buildings of her youth which still stood before her where they belonged, exactly as they had been before the wrecker's blasts, as vivid as sensations from her missing finger joint. Celebrities leaving the vanished Hotel Astor, bargains on the tables of defunct department stores, cheesecakes piled high with fruit and towers of whipped cream in the window of Hector's now stacked with dirty books. Beneath the veil, where All was One, past was present, time an illusion, this child was her own. Any moment she would open her eyes and speak.

24

The bobbing bodies of feeding birds made her think of sandpipers at dusk until she saw the green trees overhead, the roof of the library, and the face of the old woman smiling at her through her missing tooth. It was the cat lady, Owl.

"You came back," said Owl. "I knew you wouldn't let me down. And just in time for dinner, too. Watching the birds eat makes me hungry. I'm ready to eat, aren't you?"

Indeed she was. She'd had nothing to eat all day but a candy bar. But she didn't have the money for a meal. She could eat in a diner and slip out without paying or hustle a meal from a man and shake him after dessert, but not with the old woman there. "I'm broke," she said simply.

Owl wanted to give her the money now, but not here. "I know where there's plenty of food. We can have a picnic. If it were Thursday, we could get wine and cheese at the college there at seven. But we'll make do. Pot luck. What time is it?"

Robin looked to the sky. Seeing nothing she recognized, she looked at her watch. "Quarter to six."

"Come on, then. Let's go shopping before everything closes. The bakery closes at six, and we want to get you a cookie." She pushed off the ground clumsily, wincing with pain from her swollen legs.

Robin leaped up to help her. A few hours ago she'd thought everything was over. And now she was going on a picnic.

"This is Milly, my little girl," said Owl, beaming at the baker. "She's going to help me feed the birds. Have you got something special today?"

The baker winked at Robin. "I do have something special. A star loaf with sesame seeds. Pretty, isn't it? But Sicilian loaves stale fast. By tomorrow it'll crumb when you break it. Take it." He winked again.

Robin wasn't sure who the joke was on.

Owl shook out a fresh shopping bag with WALL STREET SAVINGS printed on the side. "Here, this will be for the groceries," she said, slipping the bread inside and handing it to Milly. She thanked the baker reluctantly, remembering how in the past the baker had always had a cookie for Milly, even close to dinnertime. In those days Owl disapproved of filling up on cookies. She limited candy, pushed milk, promoted protein. Now she wouldn't have cared how many cookies he'd given her. "If you were little again," she said aloud, "I think I'd let you eat anything you wanted. Because you never know what's going to happen. Look at me. I have very little protein, I eat too many starches, I smoke, I don't get my proper sleep, but I'm still kicking."

"Then do you mind if I take a piece of bread now?"

"Eat," said Owl. "Eat."

When they reached the long row of vegetable stalls, Owl told Robin what to do. "Look everything over first and see what's good. I mean bad. Well, turning. Fruit is the best buy. Bananas go fast and tomatoes. Look for cukes going soft, burst-open peppers, and in this weather when the greens go limp they throw out the outside leaves of the lettuce, the part with all the vitamins. Watch for the box at the side where they toss what they don't want. There, see that brown carton? Now watch."

She put down her bags and searched through the brown box. After a bit she raised aloft a large but shriveled green pepper with a brown spot on one side. The grocer's assistant nodded and waved her on. "Thanks," she said, depositing the pepper in Robin's bag. "You see?" she explained. "I like to spread out my purchases so no one ever feels slighted. You don't want them to think you're piggy. One piece at a time and no one objects. Some of them are even glad you came by. It makes them feel good if it doesn't cost them anything."

Had she been alone, Owl would have stopped after the bread, the pepper, a lemon, and one nice ripe tomato. She was no longer very hungry, having that afternoon lunched lavishly on the pulp of oranges squeezed dry and discarded at a fresh juice stand, the abandoned heel of a ham-and-cheese, part of the second donut from day-before-yesterday's coffee hour, two fresh pizza crusts from the stand in the bus station, and the discarded portions of several cans of soda and diet soda she'd salvaged in the outer lobbies of Broadway theaters just after intermission. But with Milly to feed and instruct she went all out, soliciting from the dozen rival grocers on the vegetable strip donations ranging from a black avocado for appetizers to spotted sugar plums for dessert.

"When I had a kitchen I ate like a queen. Without an icebox it's harder, of course. At first I missed the hot meals too. They don't allow you burners anymore because people turn them on to heat their rooms and then the sprinklers go off and flood the lower floors. But in summer everyone prefers fresh fruits and vegetables anyway. Don't you?"

If Owl was a witch, Robin decided, watching her slice and mix and stir, she was the kind who turned straw into gold or mice into coachmen. In plastic containers retrieved from the trash she had made a rich salad dressed with lemon juice; she had cut the star loaf in slices and spread them with jam she carried in individual packets in one of her bags; and from similar packets of sugar dissolved in lemon juice and water from the fountain, she had produced perfect lemonade. "I always stock up when I go for coffee," Owl explained, displaying an impressive collection of individually packaged portions of condiments and jams.

Robin thought of the tea parties she'd made at the beach

as a little girl, using seashells and rosehips and sand. And of the summer days when she and Boots rowed the dinghy out to one of the small deserted islets to pick berries where they would make themselves banquets of whatever they could find. They steamed periwinkles and blue mussels over a driftwood fire, ate salad of freshly picked sweet pea pods and the plentiful green called mare's shank that grew wild near the shore, and all the berries they could gather. Except for the berries, such foods were scorned by the islanders—a difference that created a special bond between Robin and Boots. And here too: in this city where love and loyalty were for sale, where the best of everything, according to Jacki and Prince, was the most expensive, here was Owl living on nothing. She decided on an impulse to confide in her.

As Milly explained that someone was probably watching her locker, waiting to get her pack, Owl grew increasingly alarmed. "But the police guard those lockers, don't they? I always thought they were safe! Half my treasures are in there," said Owl, clutching her own locker keys.

"You don't understand," said Milly, shaking her head. "It's the police I'm afraid of. If they find me they'll send me back to my dad."

"To him?" cried Owl, dismayed, trying to rise. "Oh, no! You can't let them do that!"

"All my clothes, my sleeping bag, my ID, everything I own except the stuff in this shoulder bag is in that locker."

Owl spoke with great agitation; her eyes were gleaming coals. "Now, listen to me. First of all, you don't need a sleeping bag in summer. And I can get you some clothes, don't worry. And if it's documents you want"—she held up a bag— "I've got plenty of documents. Only don't go near those lockers. Stay with me. I won't let them send you back to him. Come—I'll hide you so well he'll never find you again. Don't worry. Just stay with me. Stay with me and you'll inherit everything."

The sun was a red ball falling fast, reminding them each, as they silently walked west toward the river, of other sunsets over other rivers, oceans. Owl led them to a block of condemned buildings where city officials marked white X's on those destined for destruction.

At a jagged hole in a boarded-up door, Owl stopped. "Scoot inside, dear, and see what you can find for us. Be careful, though. Someone may be in there. Holler if you need me. I'll wait right here." For herself, since the Flasher's attack Owl preferred sleeping on the street or even in a very large carton to sleeping trapped behind a door. But Milly needed to hide, and for your children you made compromises you would never make for yourself.

Milly popped her head through an empty window frame. "This is great!" she called down excitedly. "Come on up. The place is empty, I think. I'm in the first room on the right after you get up to the first landing." Then she disappeared.

Owl entered gingerly. For years after the war, forgotten mines exploded in the rubble. In the hall behind the stairs she made out a half-burnt mattress and some scattered trash. But except for the graffiti of a gang of kids, the upstairs room was empty. "Ah," said Owl, pleased, "this will do just fine." She stood with Milly at the window. To the east lights began to appear as the city prepared for night, but to the west the river still remembered the kiss of the sun. Recalling the refugees in the DP camp—Germans, Latvians, Slovenians, Estonians, Lithuanians, Poles, Ukrainians—left homeless by the war, Owl rejoiced in her luck. Some of the refugees stayed in the camps for years awaiting word from a loved one; but she and hers were reconciled. "You'll be safe here," Owl reassured Milly. "Not even your father will find us here."

While she spread a few rags on the floor and arranged her bags to improvise beds and pillows, she stole a glance at Milly, gazing out the window toward the river. Soon, Owl vowed, if all went well, she would execute her will, with Milly as her witness. She dug a candle out of the Misc. Gloria bag and held it up. "When it's dark we'll light the candle and tell each other stories. I've got a million of them."

When Lana reported seeing someone who looked like Button picking through trash in Paddy's Market, Prince was puzzled. Why would Button pick trash when she carried a gold mine between her legs? Knowing how many skinny little blond chicks were in the neighborhood, he dismissed it. But when Bluejay said he'd seen her too, hanging around Bryant Park, Prince got ready to act. Fast. Now.

He held his foot firmly on the brass shoe form as the shoeshine's cloth flew back and forth across his shoe in time to the disco blasting from the box at his feet. Unless Button was working for someone else, Prince figured he'd catch her sure. Because if she wasn't ready to go to work, why had she turned up in this part of town? Even if there was a man in the picture, he'd still try to catch her. He knew his woman. He'd been her first, he'd trained her, he'd have her again.

While the shoeshine applied the brush, Prince went over his plan. He'd left word with his friends at the Hotel Venus, the Casanova Bar, even Sallee's Coffee Shop, to alert him the minute she showed up; then he'd pawned his ring for working capital and paid the porter at the Royal Arms to take messages for him as if he were still a regular resident instead of a weekly tenant at the rundown Moon. (As soon as Button came up with choosing money he'd move back into the Royal Arms; then he'd get back his ring, pick up his wheels, and score again. All he had to do was give up a little dick at the right time to the right woman. . . .)

He whistled along with the music as the shoeshine pushed down the polished shoe and lifted his other foot onto the form.

The difference between those two shoes—both quality, though one was dull and drab, the other gleaming and rich—was the difference between his life yesterday and his life tomorrow. With Button back on the bricks, maybe they'd go south for the winter, maybe Miami or Acapulco, and if they played it right, by spring he might even manage the down payment on a white Jag with mauve suede seats like one he'd seen in Boston —who could tell?

Owl brushed off the ripped baby carriage set out on the street for collection and gave it a try. The brake was shot and the carriage looked as if it had been used for bayonet practice. But the wheels worked, that was what mattered.

She searched around until she found a sturdy cardboard box to fit on the chassis. Then she placed her traveling bags in the carriage like a proud mother and wheeled it into the street. She would call it Carrie, she decided. Rolling Carrie toward the station, she remembered how cars slowed down and people made way for mothers with carriages.

One by one she emptied her lockers, loading their contents onto the carriage until the carton-seat was piled high with bags. Her umbrella, protruding from the box, was hung with bags; the broom she had lately carried to sweep off her step at night sported several bags on its handle. The pile-lined winter coat she had kept folded at the back of a locker was jammed between two bags.

Surveying her load, she was astonished to see how her holdings had grown. Although she had been forced to abandon most of her things when she'd left the Hotel Venus, she had immediately begun to build up a stock again, filling locker after locker. Sometimes she'd even forgiven the Flasher, since his cutting her off from her reserves had freed her to collect again.

Owl wheeled the carriage out into the street. The bags

sitting upright in the box seemed to Owl to be enjoying their
ride quite as much as she, locker lady no more. Of course,
there would be a price to pay for the carriage. Accompanied by
so many bags, Owl would now be an easy target. No more
would she be permitted to rest undisturbed in the lobbies of
hotels or banks, use the rest rooms of department stores, nap
in museums. She suspected that even the waiting room in the
bus station might prove inhospitable to one so laden. Yet it was
worth it to have the scattered parts of her together again in a
single place, so convenient for presenting her life to Milly.

At last he saw her, crossing 45th Street. Though he saw
only a flash of face, Prince recognized Button from the way she
moved her hips—like a little girl, but not exactly. He waited
till she was across the street, then stepped off the curb to tail
her. Horns honked and traffic shot ahead. From behind the
wheel he hated all pedestrians; but now he cursed the drivers
and scanned the speeding stream of cars for a break in traffic
before the small, diminishing figure disappeared again. The
traffic light turning red on him was like his luck.

At last the light turned green. He sprinted ahead. Button
turned a corner going south, then west again. At a distance he
followed her. They were getting farther and farther from the
stroll. He tailed her to a burnt-out block near the river. From
the corner he watched her walk halfway down the block and
disappear into a building. After a couple of minutes, Prince
crossed to the other side of the street and walked slowly down
the block, puzzled to find that the building Button had entered
sported large white X's in the few remaining windows.

He looked up and down the block. No clues, no men
lurking, only condemned buildings, tenements, parking lots.
She must be free-lancing, he speculated, turning daytime
tricks in an empty room and keeping the extra ten. Or maybe

she was posing for pictures. A ragged cat slithered past the building and darted out of sight. Prince backed into a doorway to wait. If a man came out alone, he would know.

He lit a cigarette. It angered him to think of all the cake she might be raking in up there, cake she was probably splitting with someone else, cake he needed, cake she owed him, cake she'd never have managed to get if it hadn't been for him. He'd turned her out, trained her, taught her everything she knew. And then she'd cut out.

It seemed to him then that all his life women had been cheating him of what belonged to him, from the high school girls who tried to say no at the last minute, to his very own wife who cheated him of his son, to all the lying women he'd ever taken care of who had tried to steal his manhood by stashing or gaming off him or running away. Standing in that dirty doorway in his shiny shoes, he could not think of a single woman he had ever been able to trust, not even his mother, who, though he loved her more than any, had always wished him different than he was.

He looked at his watch and took a last puff on his cigarette before flicking it into the street. No one had gone inside or come out since Button. He'd give her twenty minutes and if no one came out by then, he'd arm himself with a bottle and go in.

Robin was shocked to find Owl, dirty and disheveled, muttering over a packet of papers in a downstairs hall behind the stairs. Beside her was a battered baby carriage piled high with stuffed shopping bags.

"Finally! I was afraid they'd kidnapped you," said Owl. She grinned happily through her missing tooth. "Just wait till you see what I have for you here."

Robin stared at the carriage. Bags of rags and boxes of

junk, all wedged into a seatless carriage. For a moment, seeing the old woman grinning on the floor, her horror returned, her shame. (Her mother drunk, her father in a rage . . .) How had she picked a crazy to confide in? Owl had told her astonishing stories of a daring life, but suddenly Robin doubted them. "My God, Owl, what's all this?"

"You'll see in a minute, dear." Owl beamed. "Hold your horses. I'm going to show you everything."

Creakily she unloaded the carriage and placed the bags one by one in a rough circle around her on the floor. "If anything happens to me now, this will all be yours," she said with a sweep of her arm. "Of course, Bert will try to grab what he can for himself if he finds out where we are, especially these"— she held up an envelope of papers. "But you can tell him they all belong to you. Everything will be spelled out in my will, but I want you to know what's here now, so you can fight him."

Robin watched Owl raise the curtain on a monumental show-and-tell. Squatting at the edge of a burnt-out mattress, drawing sundry objects from her bags as if they were precious treasures, Owl reminded Robin of a magician who pulled incredible objects out of hats and sleeves, each with a strange story. Any minute she expected a live rabbit or a warty toad to leap from one of the mysterious shopping bags; any minute she half-expected Owl to open one of her broken umbrellas and float out through the open door.

She had opened an envelope of old photos. Robin peered over Owl's shoulder at a picture of a young woman with a soldier, both smiling, maybe in love. Owl's daughter? But the style was from long ago. Then it hit her. "Is that you, Owl?"

"Yes. Cute, wasn't I? Him too. That was during the war." She shook her head and sighed.

Robin was jolted by the picture of Owl, a pretty young woman in love. "Funny hat on him. What kind of uniform is that?"

"US Army, Second World War. Probably ancient history

to you. You were less than a twinkle in your father's eye." She gazed fondly at the photo. "You can see what we had in mind, can't you? Talk of twinkles in the eye."

Robin stared at her. The glasses Owl had perched on her nose didn't match the earpiece, which was held to the rest of the frame by a safety pin inserted through the hinge. Her eyes watered, her jowls drooped. Robin took the picture in her hands.

"Is this your husband?" she asked, pointing to the soldier.

"Bert? Heavens, no! It's just a soldier, I don't remember his name. I remember the night, though, like yesterday." She rolled her eyes. "He was my first good lay. But after that night I never saw him again. Probably killed in the war." She sighed again. "What a waste."

Good lay? Robin was suddenly filled with pity for the old woman, too old to turn a trick, too nuts to stay on welfare. She tried to picture herself an old woman but could not. Instead, her mother popped into her mind, now pale and gaunt, then young and beautiful, and herself as a little girl filling her mother's evening bag with magical objects.

She was relieved when Owl returned the bags of documents to the carriage and moved on to the bags of old clothes. Now came a parade of tops: T-shirts, blouses, sweaters: the kind of things, said Owl, that never went out of style. Like a sales clerk, she held up each one, showing first the front, then the back; then carefully folding it up again, returned it to its bag. "Go on. See if any of them fit you. Take anything you like before I put them away."

Of course she wouldn't be caught dead wearing most of the clothes in Owl's bags, but as she had nothing of her own at the moment other than what she had on, and didn't want to offend the old woman, she inspected them carefully and deposited two T-shirts in her shoulder bag. "Thanks," she said, and spotting a purple feather boa, picked it up and draped it around her neck. "What do you think? How does it look? Do you think it'll go in California?"

"California?" Owl blinked her eyes, alarmed.

"That's my next stop."

"You're going to California? Why?"

"It's as far away as you can get. My best friend is out there already. My dad'll never find me there." She suddenly lowered her voice. "They're after me here. There, maybe I'll be free."

Owl put her hands to her temples and closed her eyes. If she were young, she'd do the same. In her time she'd gone farther than California to stay free.

"When are you planning on going?"

"As soon as I can get up the fare."

Should she give her the money now? Owl didn't want to lose her so soon. But even less did she want Bert to get her.

Well, that was youth, wasn't it? Always restless, always on the move. She'd spent her own youth reeling across continents, knocking around Europe, never in one place for more than a few months at a time. Wild, the colonel had called her, saying as he made her his mistress, "Lil, you take terrible risks." But like Milly, she'd only wanted to be free. After her discharge, she'd slept in fields, haylofts, churches, cellars, so she wouldn't have to register with the police. Not because of the money; in those days she could easily have paid for any room. But the police demanded your passport whenever you went to a new hotel, kept it till you left. That very passport, her old ticket to freedom, was still in the Barbara bag. Lillian Fredericks, hair brown, eyes blue, height 5'6", weight 119. Extremely valuable document, in those days worth more than love. One night she'd slipped her precious American passport to a group of GIs, perfect strangers who happened to be sitting in uniform at a nearby table in a Naples café, because her Italian lover had threatened to take her passport to keep her from leaving him. "Excuse me. I'm an American. I need your help." (*Too many movies*, said the colonel.) "I have reason to believe" (*reason to believe!*) "that some Italians I'm involved with may have designs on my passport. I'd feel safer if you'd hold on to it for me, there's no one else I can trust. You're the only guys I know who appreciate how valuable a document this is." That was the riskiest act of all, according to the colonel. But she didn't think so. Sure, the soldiers could have sold her passport for a pile or even blackmailed her, but uniforms had honor then. They might have turned her in, too, that was the real risk; but she'd been trusting. "Listen, I can't explain it now. I have to get back to my table before my friends do. Here—take it. Please." (Drawing it from her bosom.) "My name's Lil, it's all written down inside. I'll meet you back here on Saturday at about nine, okay? Bring it with you then." Of course they were flattered, intrigued. She squeezed the nearest hands. "Thanks a lot, boys. Thanks." She'd had looks and a bit of money then, plus the colonel looking out for her. But then too—even then!—she'd cared most of all about freedom.

Milly was posing in the boa like a little actress, looking Harlow-like over her feathered shoulder. Her delight gave Owl the kind of lift she felt seeing the skinny cats eagerly lap up the food she set out for them, a mother's joy that made the tears start under her lids. She thought of all the birthdays she'd had to miss; she thought of how easily she might have overlooked that boa in the box of remnants set out for collection. It was short, after all, only half a boa; but she'd fancied the lavender feathers, gaudy as a bird's, and now she was vindicated. She fluffed the feathers around Milly's neck, then tentatively touched her hair. Silky as a fledgling's down. Sniffing loudly, she ran the back of her hand beneath her nose, fighting tears. She delved into a secret place and pulled out an old beaded purse, stuffed with cash. "Here, darling. Take this. It should get you safely out of here."

"What is it?"

"Money."

"But—?"

Owl laid her hand on Milly's arm and shook her head. "No buts. I want you to have it. It's no good to me anyway. But you can get to California with it. Not as far as I went, of course, but then you're still young."

"I'll pay you back, Owl," she said, taking a handful of bills from the purse as if she didn't believe they were real.

"No, it's yours," said Owl firmly. "What's mine is yours." She retrieved her passport from the Barbara bag and dropped it into Milly's shoulder bag. "And this too. And the fish knife."

Milly stammered thank-yous like a birthday child, till Owl's grin turned into a grimace as she felt the tears slip down her nose. Damn! Quickly she brushed them away, then took one step forward, opening her arms to Milly. When Milly didn't recoil, Owl wrapped her gently in her arms. "This is all I wanted, you know? To give you something to remember me by."

"I'll pay it back. You might need it."

"You don't have to worry about me. I'm tough."

Feeling the feathers against her cheek, Owl suddenly remembered the birdling Milly had found as a child and the boy who had never taken wing. Both too fragile to live. But Milly was tough like her. With luck she could survive.

"Well, now. A kiss goodbye and you'll be gone. Remember me."

Prince walked through the doorway carefully so as not to dirty his pants, but looking through the steps to the hallway beyond he felt his gorge rise in disgust. There she was, the low-down ho, with purple feathers around her neck, holding a fistful of bills, hugging and kissing one of those creepy old hags with stockings rolled to her ankles and holes in her shoes —and getting paid!

Prince raised up the bottle he'd carried inside and hurled it crashing against a wall. "Rotten skinny-ass mutha-fuckin bitch!" he thundered. "Cunt!"

In terror Robin clung to Owl. The man silhouetted in the empty doorway, face shaded in backlight, half hidden by the stairs, was blocking the only exit. No fog to hide in and nowhere to run.

So! thought Owl, slipping out of Milly's embrace and backing slowly away. So! The Flasher had followed them. He must have been watching them all along, waiting for her to get all her treasures out of her lockers and show her money at last. He must have planned it from the start. She should have known. She should never have let herself be lured inside. Now he had them both.

Through the stairs she could almost see the awful leer spread across his shaded face as she stood blocking the doorway and the light. He had dyed his hair, but that didn't fool her. Feeling her heart thud against her chest, she knew she ought to scream; but what if he went for Milly? That was her weakness; he knew it, of course. Headlines gave it away: "Infant Plucked From Breast, Hurled Against Wall." "Child Ravished While Helpless Mother Looks On." He was coming toward them now, looking at Milly with a horrid leer. Oh, where had she hidden her knife?

The man strode into the recess behind the stairs where she stood cowering with Owl. Prince! He stood there in his cream-colored pants and shirt, chest puffed out, hands thrust into pockets, asking with a nasty nod toward Owl, "That your new man, baby?"

Speechless, Robin stepped back.

"You know, baby, I been thinkin about you, bout helpin you out. I heard you weren't doin so good lately. But I don't know." He turned toward Owl. "With granny here, looks like maybe you don't need no help from me."

What did he mean by help? Throwing bottles at her?

Suddenly Prince softened his eyes, lowered his voice to a croon, and ran his fingers along the curve of Robin's waist till his hand rested on her hip. "Thought you could do okay without me, did you?" he purred. "I knew you'd be back. We had too good a thing goin for you to stay away. Like I told you, no one else is ever gonna treat you good as me. It's okay, baby, it's okay. I'm glad you got a chance to see what's out there, who your friends are." He pushed the boa gently to the floor and kissed her neck. "Bet you'd like a nice bath now, wouldn't you? You went and got yourself dirty. And a decent meal, hmm?" He took her face between his hands and kissed her mouth. "And some lovin," he whispered.

He was calm now, sugaring Milly up. Come to take her away. Clever man. He'd waited till she'd given Milly the money, then came in time to outbid her. He'd looked right past Owl, trying to erase her by pretending she wasn't there, as he'd done when he'd sent her away. But that only proved who he was. Bert in disguise, afraid to look at her. Now was the time to serve him with the papers, let him know his bribes were stolen property. Time to strike back. From somewhere in the carriage she extracted the envelope of papers pertaining to her suit; then she searched for her knife.

. . .

Robin turned her head to one side, avoiding Prince's eyes, and asked, "Aren't you still mad at me?" Those uncertain rivals, terror and trust, crouched together at the starting line, waiting for a signal.

"No, baby, I ain't mad, not if you're really choosin. I'm ready to forget about what's past and just look ahead, if your choosin money's right. Let's see what you got there." He held out his hand.

Robin hid her hands behind her back and shook her head. "I can't, Prince," she said.

"Can't, Button?" Prince laughed. "Still singin that old song, can't? C'mon, now, baby. Cut the crap. You know you're gonna. You just want me to coax you, don't you?" He began to tug at her elbow. "Okay, then, if that's what you want."

"Please, Prince," she whined, transferring the money from one hand to the other behind her back.

His breath was hot on her face, his eggplant eyes, staring into hers, finally showed what he really wanted.

"Please, please, please," he repeated. "I know what you want, baby." He bent over her arched body, reaching for the hand behind her back, and whispered into her neck, "I know what you want. Only one way you're gonna get it, though."

She dipped to the side and jerking her arm free slid out from under him, throwing him off-balance. While he righted himself and brushed off his pants, she darted past Owl toward the door.

"Run, honey!" cried Owl, rolling the carriage across the narrow passageway and crouching behind it. Let him kill her; better her than Milly. She raised her knife, trying to be ferocious, as if she were still a WAC who had never gotten old.

"Outa my way," said Prince, trying to push the carriage aside.

But Owl had jammed the wheels against the mattress. Her chest was heaving with exertion and rage. She had to hold him off till Milly got away.

"I know who you are. You don't fool me, Flasher. This is my house. How dare you come barging into my house, throwing things, trying to take my little girl? I can throw things too, you know, things you don't want to see. See this, Bert?" she cried, tossing a handful of papers at him with her free hand. "And this? And this? I have papers here that will put you away for life!"

Papers and rags fluttered to the floor as she reached exultantly into bag after bag and threw their contents through the hall, shouting, "Rat! Snake! Thief! Impostor! Monster!"

The old hag was cracko, throwing handfuls of trash in the air, calling him names, and waving a knife. All he had to do was grab her wrist to twist the knife out of her hand, but the carriage and her body were in his way, both too filthy to touch. He didn't want to mess up his copping clothes or get close enough to smell her.

With two hands and a foot he shoved the carriage over, knocking the woman down, burying her under a load of junk. She let out a short cry that ceased abruptly. "That should shut you up," muttered Prince, picking his way around the mess to the spot where the knife had fallen from her hand. From still, glassy eyes the old bag stared up at him like a dead rat, filling him with disgust. She didn't move; nevertheless, he prudently picked up the knife and tossed it across the hall.

He lit a cigarette to quiet his nerves. His stomach had started up. Through the doorway ahead, he glimpsed the moon in twilight and remembered calm, moonlit nights at sea, soothing coconut milk, women who knew by nature how to love. Not like the shaky bitches of the stroll. Against the pimping code he'd given Button kisses without getting paid, and she'd tried to make a chump of him. He'd blown it again. Next time she'd have to come crawling on her knees before he'd give her the time of day.

Holding the cigarette between his lips, he picked up the purple feather boa and with it polished the new scuff marks off his shoe. No point feeling sorry. Here the game was cop and blow, and in half an hour a bus was due in from Chicago, then two more coming down from Boston. He brushed off his hands, tucked in his shirt, and prepared his face for the world.

At the doorway, Prince paused and looked out. Behind him nothing stirred. He took a last puff of his cigarette, flicked back the butt, and walked out into the street.

25

Owl smelled smoke and felt something heavy weighing down her legs. An air raid? Buried in debris? She strained to see and hear. No roar of engines or whine of bombs, only traffic sounds and Latin music in the distance. But she did smell fire and could not move her legs.

She patted the floor beside her to locate her glasses, but her hands encountered only rubble—metal, paper, cloth. The bombed-out guts of Stuttgart? The ruins of Rome? Ed Malone, the colonel's friend, had laughed at her for being unable to distinguish the precious ruins of the past from the fresh wreckage of war. "That happened a thousand years ago," he said when she gasped at the sight of the Roman Forum. She had blushed with shame at her ignorance, but now, remembering, she no longer saw why. The length of yesterday meant little. What died aeons ago and yesterday were all the same; the vanished, like the living, were one. Either way, she salvaged what she could.

With a great effort she pushed the debris from her legs and chest and raised herself on an elbow. A hot, sharp pain shot through her left hip. She looked around. In a puff of black smoke a small flame flickered near her feet, revealing the cluttered hallway, the stairs, the derangement of her bags. Gradually she remembered: she had held off Bert the Flasher, bombarding him with the past, while Milly got away. Then, once again, he had grabbed everything she had and turned it against her, like the dirty fighter he was.

A rag smoldered; a paper flared up and went out. Danger-ous. Somewhere in the heap lay her mother's picture, the footprint of the boy. . . . If she could smother the fire before it spread. . . . But when she tried to stand, the pain from her hip shot across her like a bolt holding her down. She collapsed on the floor.

This time, though, the money was safe. Milly had taken it and gone; Bert had been too late. Owl's life, which for years had seemed like a large check that couldn't be cashed, had finally been redeemed. Milly had listened to her story, seen the tracings of her life, accepted her gifts of food and money and love, and flown away free. What more could a mother want? She had beaten Bert at last. Owl smiled, remembering her splendid barricade.

Suddenly the flame shot up, leaping like a dancer in the air. Owl turned to see the Belle ignite. "Belle!" she cried, "Belle!" with horror she watched the top of the bag crackle and curl, like Christmas wrappings in a fire. One, two, gone. The picture of her mother, which she had kept with her for more than fifty years, was melting to ash. Fifty years, then—gone.

And Misc. Gloria too, now (or was that someone else?): gone. Up they rose to join all the other precious objects, stolen or lost long ago, that lived only in her mind. Half a century of reminders, gone now, like the trains to Erie that once whistled every evening, calling her away, but ran no more. Gone like the lace-trimmed handkerchiefs embroidered with the days of the week. Gone like her aunts with their marvelous hats with plumes and streamers and veils. Gone like the autographs of the stars. Gone like the valiant soldiers, slain in war. Gone like Finland, Poland, Norway, Belgium, France, fallen to the enemy.

She watched, remembering them all, until at last the flame licked her feet, then kissed her stockings and ignited her skirt all at once with a whoosh and flash.

Pain like frostbite threatened to numb her brain, but just in time the houselights dimmed, the footlights glowed, and in that instant Owl saw the curtains part one more time.

Reality, which till then she had glimpsed only for moments through a veil, stood poised before her. As the veil perished in the fire, truth leaped about her, a golden flame. In the dazzling light, she saw her brief life, which she had spent apart, merge and spread till she knew she was one with her mother and father, her daughter, her son, all the cats and soldiers she had loved, the fallen birds, all who had ever lived. In the brilliant flame all differences dissolved. Truth, light, flame, love—these too she saw were one. Though nothing had changed, everything had changed. With rapture, Owl gazed on the golden light. This time the curtain would not close.

Robin was surprised to find more than a hundred dollars left over after she paid for her ticket. Where had Owl picked up that kind of money? She wished she could take it right back to her, but the bus was leaving in half an hour and she didn't dare leave the station. This time she had a ticket in her pocket to protect her from the Runaway Squad; still, she hardly even dared walk past the lockers to the waiting room.

In the ladies' room she began washing off the grime. She wondered, looking into the mirror above the sink, how much longer she'd last without a bath. She was hardly even blond today. In seventy-two hours she'd be in LA. Then she'd bathe herself clean in the ocean, dry herself in the sun, and spend the leftover cash on a brand-new set of clothes. Meanwhile, before the matron could catch her, she stripped off Prince's dirty top and slipped into one of the T-shirts Owl had given her. Then she went to the phone booth to try to reach Boots one last time.

Searching in her shoulder bag for a dime, she came upon Owl's old passport. She dialed, and while the number rang she studied the dated document. For one moment she thought she recognized the wonderful, mad Owl in the face of the pretty woman with long, curly hair, startled eyes, open smile, and a full set of even teeth. But the more she considered the picture, the more the resemblance eluded her until, in the end, she thought it might be a picture of anyone.

At last someone answered the phone. The woman. For a second time, Robin gave her real name. (It didn't matter anymore; she was on her way.) The woman said she'd finally had a postcard from Boots, but no address. "If I were you I'd check out Hollywood. The kid has big ideas," she said. "And good luck. If you find her, give her a big hug for me."

On her way down to the platform where her bus would be boarding, Robin bought gum, three packs of cigarettes for the trip, a ten-cent stamp, and a picture postcard of Times Square. The picture, taken at night, showed traffic jammed in gridlock and all the billboards lit up. The caption read, *42d Street & Broadway, "crossroads of world," looking west into the bustling Midtown area.* Robin smiled. *One of these days,* she wrote, *I'm going to send you each a Greyhound ticket. You haven't lived till you've seen New York. There's something for everyone on Forty-Deuce.* Boldly she addressed the card to her brothers at the house on the nubble. Let her father chase her to New York; by the time he got here she'd be gone.

Acknowledgments

The generosity of many people has enabled me to write this book. To the MacDowell Colony and the Millay Colony for the Arts I am grateful for a private place in which to work. I thank my dear friend Ann Snitow and my editor Robert A. Gottlieb for their tireless support. Of the many people who ungrudgingly shared with me their resources, knowledge, and time, I would particularly like to thank Carl Weisbrod and Mary Bleiberg of the Midtown Enforcement Project, Lt. José A. Elíque of the Port Authority Police Youth Services Division, Dr. Vernon Boggs of the West 42d Street Project, and most especially Stephanie Golden and the women of the Dwelling Place. Although I am also deeply indebted to the many scholars and writers whose researches helped illuminate for me the dark doorways into which my fiction led me, all the characters and events in this novel are drawn solely from my imagination, and any resemblance to real persons or events is unintentional.

The phrases *a blow to the heart kills* and *born a ho* are taken from Christina and Richard Milner, *Black Players*, Michael Joseph Ltd, London, 1973.

A Note on the Type

The text of this book was set in Electra, a type face designed
by William Addison Dwiggins for the Mergenthaler
Linotype Company and first made available in 1935. Electra
cannot be classified as either "modern" or "old-style." It is
not based on any historical model, and, hence, does not echo
any particular period or style of type design. It avoids the
extreme contrast between thick and thin elements that
marks most modern faces and is without eccentricities that
catch the eye and interfere with reading. In general, Electra
is simple, readable typeface that attempts to give a feeling of
fluidity, power, and speed.

W. A. Dwiggins (1880–1956) began an association with
the Mergenthaler Linotype Company in 1929 and over the
next twenty-seven years designed a number of book types,
including the Metro, Electra, Caledonia,
Eldorado, and Falcon.

Composed by Maryland Linotype Composition
Company, Inc., Baltimore, Maryland.
Printed and bound by
The Haddon Craftsmen, Inc., Scranton, Pennsylvania.

Designed by Albert Chiang.